COME AND BE KILLED

COME AND BE KILLED

Sally Spedding

Severn House Large Print
London & New York

This first large print edition published in Great Britain 2007 by
SEVERN HOUSE LARGE PRINT BOOKS LTD of
9-15 High Street, Sutton, Surrey, SM1 1DF.
First world regular print edition published 2007 by
Severn House Publishers, London and New York.
This first large print edition published in the USA 2007 by
SEVERN HOUSE PUBLISHERS INC., of
595 Madison Avenue, New York, NY 10022.

British Library Cataloguing in Publication Data

Spedding, Sally
  Come and be killed. - Large print ed.
  1. Detective and mystery stories 2. Large type books
  I. Title
  823.9'2[F]

  ISBN-13: 978-0-7278-7646-1

Printed and bound in Great Britain by
MPG Books Ltd, Bodmin, Cornwall.

For Adrian

Prologue

A fortnight's rain has bloated the bowels of North Hill. Filled each of its ancient crevices to capacity, spilling the glut of water past those few houses which cling to the westerly side, facing the grey smear of Welsh hills.

This overflow silvers the tarmac encircling its girth. Turns the land below soft and spongy underfoot – quite treacherous in parts – the worst possible conditions for cycling or running. Or, more importantly, grave-digging. Yet the young man, sodden though he is, must satisfy his curiosity and follow where the lean female jogger takes him. Her Lycra-clad body glitters like a magnet, pulling him still further away. He pushes himself and his bike through ranks of giant late-flowering cow parsley whose umbelliferous heads bend low, weighted by moisture. Past hawthorn hedges where the Heritage Trail begins; where his target has suddenly vanished, leaving deep distinctive footprints which lead him to an iron shack, so old and rusted that the slightest gust of wind would surely topple its frayed and flimsy sides.

His nostrils take in the whiff of sewage and lanolin from the creeping sheep in the fields beyond, but once he's eased the skewed door open, there's a different smell altogether.

Of meat. Raw meat. The kind that clings to every butcher's shop he's ever been in.

But this is no commercial butcher's. And nobody's buying. Least of all him, for when he discovers what lies half-hidden in the gloomiest corner, it's as if he's wandered into hell, and from now on, there will be no way out.

One

'Name?'

'Holt. Frances Ann. 358 Dartmoor Road, Openshaw.'

She was a quick learner if nothing else. Surname first, then the rest. A month of trekking back and forth to the Benefits Office had seen to that. The faster she got it off pat, the sooner the dough was in her hand.

This time the woman the other side of the security grille wasn't quite playing ball. She was being less than automatic on this occasion, and she was fat. Really fat. In fact, the fattest person Frankie had ever seen in her life, and that was saying something. Heavily ringed fingers checked through a file containing sheets of headed notepaper; all too easy to read upside down. Boots, Woolies, Iceland, which to the other scrubbers in 5G who'd all bunked off the last two weeks of term represented a kind of Nirvana. But not her. Frankie. No way. She knew what was coming next.

'Did you try for the sanitary-wear assistant's job?'

Her excuse was off pat too.

'Can't be doing with all that stuff, sorry. Periods, babies. Having them, getting rid of them...' Here she stopped herself as her adversary tutted. Found the next sheet.

'Pick 'n' Mix helper. What was wrong with that?'

I don't pick and I don't fucking mix, Frankie nearly replied. She just wanted her dole. No questions asked. It was the least she was entitled to. Considering.

'I'm not very clever round kids,' she said at last. 'If you must know, they do my head in.'

The official looked up at her, the whites of her eyes a yolky yellow in the corners.

'OK, Miss Holt. No interviews, no benefits. Simple as that.' The file was closed. Thick red lips also pursed together.

'Nursing's cool. Anything doing there?' Frankie found herself asking. Washing and dressing her baby Lila was the best thing ever. Even better than boys or clubbing, which her stepsister Shannon – well ... stepsister wasn't the correct term, but it seemed right to Frankie – did every weekend while she'd stop in her bedroom either rereading her collection of library sale books – Peake, Tolkien, Shakespeare – or brushing and re-brushing those glossy blonde curls to perfection...

'You willing to train?' The voice interrupted her memories and Frankie became aware of the room behind her filling up. The drumming of heels on the linoleum. Impatient sighs.

'Yeah, I might be. Where? How?'

'Your sixth form possibly.'

'I've had it up to here with that dump.'

'The Tech near you's starting GNVQs in

10

Caring.'

'Caring? I said nursing.'

The official leaned forwards.

'By 2010, Miss Holt, over sixty per cent of our population will be elderly.'

Frankie hoped she couldn't read her thoughts.

'What's the pay like?

'It's not so much the pay, but satisfaction.' That last word sounded like the woman was licking honey off a jar lid. Frankie stared at her, mind churning, visualizing her baby daughter suddenly grown old. Her plump cheeks withered, like the old tarts in the Railway where she bought her fags. Her feet spoilt by crusty yellow toenails...

'I don't know. Mopping up after them. Washing their willies, wiping their bums.'

'It's all about giving them dignity, Miss Holt. Giving them hope.'

'OK. I'll sort it.' Probably the most reckless words she'd ever spoken. Within five minutes she had the dole safe in her purse and an appointment to see a Mrs Beavis at Openshaw Tech.

The college's corridors were empty save for the odd old fogey trudging behind their whirring floor cleaners which puffed out dust as they went. No one seemed to notice her. It was as if she was invisible, which of course in a way she was. That's what being adopted did to you. Whoever had produced her, hadn't wanted her. Bottom line. Why she was here, wasn't it? And it would do until her next move, wherever that

11

might lead.

'Lookin' for someone, pet?' A man's voice from behind. She spun round to see a cleaner come out of the WCs carrying a mop and bucket. The smell of its contents made her catch her breath.

I'm not your fucking pet...

'Health Studies. Mrs Beavis.'

'Room thirty-two. Next stairs up, then third on your left. Last official day for staff today. Lucky you'll be catching 'er.'

As Frankie reached the door, she smoothed down her denim skirt which Beryl – because no way was she calling her Mum – always said was too short. 'Pussy pelmet' were her exact words. Only jealous. Got to be. A daughter who runs rings round her and hitched to John Arthur. Gone from a posh house in Fallowfield to a semi the wrong side of town, after he fiddled the books at work and was sacked. He was now drawing the dole too and had no right to preach at her. Fucking cheek...

Mrs Beavis, dressed in a red tent with matching beads draped over her freckled cleavage, asked if she'd like a cup of tea. Frankie blinked. No one at Elm Park Comp would ever have done that. She watched in awe as the tutor busied herself around an electric kettle.

'Two sugars, then,' Frankie shouted after her, just in case. Apart from Shannon, she disliked unsweetened tea the most. 'Cheers.'

'Mrs Watabe has just phoned me from the Benefits Office,' said Mrs Beavis, now placing a full mug in front of Frankie.

'Checking up, was she?'

'No. She thought you'd be ideal. That you looked the part.'

'For what? Goneril?' To her mind, by far the best character in *King Lear*.

Mrs Beavis looked surprised.

'For caring. Now then...' She withdrew a shiny college brochure bearing a colour photo of a building Frankie didn't recognize. If this was the Tech she was in, where was the grime or the graffiti? 'Page forty,' added Mrs Beavis, swivelling the double-page spread towards her. Underneath its title, 'LET'S MAKE A DIFFERENCE', lay an arty montage of old and young faces. Too close together for her liking, but then she was fussy.

'Nice, that,' she lied, eyeing up the photo of a young guy pushing a crust in a wheelchair. 'One of your students?' she asked, thinking if he wasn't then he was probably moonlighting from catalogue modelling.

'No, but he epitomizes perfectly how carers enjoy their work.' Mrs Beavis put down her mug. 'You see, serving people, especially those in need, is the noblest occupation. Look, Frances...' she began as if she'd a secret to share.

'It's Frankie.'

'Frankie, as I was saying, the more qualified you become, the more pay you'll receive. Whether from social services or private sources.'

'Private? I thought all them homes you see were subbed by the government.'

'Not true. There are other agencies, other providers. Not everyone wants to go into local-

13

authority care. Or be visited for just a few rushed minutes by some busy council employee.' She pointed a finger at the fossil in the wheelchair. 'Take Homely Helpers, for example.'

'Never heard of them.'

'You could earn over five hundred pounds a week helping people stay in their own homes.'

'A *week*?' Frankie gripped both sides of her vinyl chair. 'You're kidding. Who on earth can afford that?'

'Let me assure you, there are some very well-off clients around who've worked hard all their lives and don't see why they should be institutionalized.'

'Quite right too.' That quoted sum of money burrowed into her brain like a maggot. 'So, when can I start?'

'Formalities first.' Mrs Beavis reclaimed the brochure and, with her head lowered to read the small print at the back, Frankie noticed deep bags protrude beneath her eyes. Age spots on both hands and wrinkles at the base of her throat. Give her another ten to fifteen years, she thought, and then, for one brief scary moment, her mind fast-forwarded to herself struggling with a stupid walking frame. Wetting herself. Shouting rude words at no one in particular. 'And remember, Frankie –' Mrs Beavis looked up at her – 'the police will need to run a check, so that means keeping out of trouble.'

'I always do.'

'Your parents will have to sign this application form and send it back to me here by the fourth of July. After that, I'm on holiday.'

All right for some, Frankie thought bitterly.

Through the single bare window she spotted a vast orange crane swaying against the sky. Part monster, part normal. Just like us, she thought. Then in her mind's eye, saw Dartmoor Road again.

'Beryl and John Holt aren't my real parents,' she volunteered. 'They adopted me when I was six weeks old. I didn't know what the fuck was going on. They don't tell me anything about where I came from.'

The woman appraised her with frank green eyes.

'Well, if you do decide to join our Level Three group in mid-September, I can guarantee a warm welcome.' She extracted a stapler from her desk drawer and began punching sheets together. The noise was like gunfire Frankie had heard on TV. It had always unsettled her.

When the rules and regulations were in her hands she saw they included book lists, a First Year syllabus. How to Swot and Why It Was Illegal To Plagiarize. A word she'd never seen before.

'I'm going to hunt for my real mum and dad soon as I'm eighteen,' she announced.

'D'you think that's a good idea?'

'Definitely.'

'Well, you are entitled,' she conceded. 'I'm just thinking if you were my adopted daughter...'

'I'm not. OK?'

Mrs Beavis looked uncomfortable. Frankie saw the crane move out of sight leaving a blank oblong of blue sky. 'Will it be all girls in Sep-

15

tember?' she quizzed. The answer was important.

'No, as usual there'll be a handful of boys.'

'Good.' They were less sly. Less likely to stroke your arm then stab you in the back. She thought of Justin Rosser whom she'd met last summer at a barbie in St Mark's cemetery. He'd seemed keen and even given her a love bite on her neck, now faded altogether. Keen that is, until her stepsister Shannon had rolled her big grey eyes at him. Wiggled her tits – 38D to be precise – while Frankie's own body was morphing daily into something totally different to hers and those of John and Beryl Holt. Growing bigger as their income got smaller. She was thinning in every way, even her hair, which clogged up her funky metallic hairbrush. It was most likely diet, or lack of it. She'd forgotten what an orange tasted like.

'During your first year here' – the woman's voice invaded her reverie – 'you'll have one day a week work experience at Pear Tree Residential Home, who kindly offered to participate in our programme. It's all goodwill, you know. That and kindness.'

'What'll I be doing?'

'They'll decide. Not me.'

'Not cooking. I'm shite at that.'

Mrs Beavis's eyebrows rose in surprise.

'It won't be cooking.'

The tutor began tidying her desk, and brushed stray pencil rubbings to the floor. 'Remember July fourth, Frankie.'

'Independence Day.'

16

'Good Lord, I'd forgotten.' She stood up and extended a hand, which the girl declined. She didn't like strangers touching her. In any way. Private stuff, she told herself, seeing a frown on the woman's forehead.

'So, how long till I'm making big bucks?'

'I wouldn't put it exactly like that, but Level Three takes two years. After that, the world's your oyster.'

Frankie liked the word oyster. It sounded sexy, mysterious.

She almost skipped out of the door and back along that dreary passageway to the exit sign. And then, the sunlit street, the noise, the litter, the horny creeps eyeing her up and down outside an amusement arcade. But none of this mattered. Only the college start date. 15 September 1997. As far as she was concerned, the sooner the better.

Two

While Frankie Ann Holt, some two hundred and fifty miles away in Manchester, was placing Lila, her newly washed and fed baby, between the worn winceyette sheets in readiness for bedtime, an equally youthful eighteen-year-old Martin Webb in Buckingham Avenue, Blackheath, had just completed his application to join the Metropolitan Police.

17

His parents rarely fought with words. Silence was their chief weapon, and now its chill – yes, to his mind silence has a temperature – reached his sanctuary and snaked around his tracksuited body as he signed and dated the final page: *Martin Donald Webb. 30/6/97*

Done. He licked down the envelope flap and kissed it seven times for luck.

That same chill accompanied him downstairs to his escape via the back door of the new granite-topped kitchen.

'Wait there, son, if you don't mind.' His father appeared from the far side of the fridge freezer, a half-empty tumbler of whisky in his hand. Martin's watch showed 8.30 a.m. Just enough time to catch the post office's first collection.

With his free hand, Donald Webb reached out for the offending A4 envelope, but his son was quicker.

'I don't need your bloody consent.' He tried edging past him, but years of sitting in cockpits for days on end had given Webb Senior a padded bulk which now blocked his exit. 'I am eighteen.'

'D'you want to mix with a bunch of total thickos? To *die* in some back street, aged eighteen? That it?' he snapped.

Christ, thought Martin, he could be almost poetic at times. The smell of spirits reached him as his dad's mouth hung open long after the question.

'It's good pay. Good prospects and I don't have to waste my time at university. You and Mum did what you wanted. Something that

18

interested you both.' He nearly added what had a First in Economics and an MA ever done for her? Twenty years at the kitchen sink. Well, OK, so it did have gold taps, but it was still a sink.

'Besides, you won't have to sub me,' he went on regardless. 'I can give *you* rent...'

'What does Ria say?'

'She's easy.'

'Apart from that.'

He could have kicked his dad in the nuts. Ria Lewis, like his best mate Chris, had made the sixth form bearable. Had been there for him.

His push against his father became a shove. He managed to open the back door.

'You can't stop me.'

Martin spotted his mother hovering by the garden shed, shears in hand. He couldn't quite tell if she'd been crying or not.

'Martin? Please...' She advanced, blades at the ready. For what, he wasn't sure. 'Let's talk, for God's sake.'

'You've had a whole hour for that, Mum.' Aware of his father's fist closing around his lower arm like a nutcracker. 'And whenever I do want to discuss anything with either of you, you're always out or about to go out.'

'Who's paying for the roof over your head, eh?'

'I didn't ask to be bloody born.'

His mother gasped and retreated outside, while his father released his grip and downed the rest of his drink. Martin thought in a flash about the plane he'd soon be piloting from Stansted to Strasburg. Two hours in fact.

19

'OK,' the big man faced him. Speech notice-ably slurred. 'How about this for a reminder? August last year? The fourteenth to be precise.'

'Donald. *Must* you? It's all in the past.' Louisa Webb's forehead bubbled with sweat, her watery eyes with hate. This was a Domestic about to happen, Martin told himself. He could see it now...

'Well, I don't think our friends in the Force would be chuffed knowing they'd got a coke-head in their ranks.'

It was the smile which hurt the most.

Martin shoved his way through the small gap like a fly-half, knocking the empty tumbler to the floor as he went, then kicking the back door wide open before bolting round the side of the house where his car lay dwarfed by the two Passats. His and Hers in blue and silver, like two whales beached on the weedless gravel.

'Come back, son!' his mother called. 'He didn't mean it.'

But he did.

Last summer had been his best mate's birthday in an empty house near the Vale. Parents away. Neighbours out of earshot. Someone had brought in crack off a guy in Acre Lane. Someone got loose-mouthed. End of story. The stuff hadn't made him feel like he was sitting on the world. More like, under it. Leaving him with a migraine for a week.

Only now was the stored heat in his car lessening, and the breeze from both open win-dows snatched his light brown hair, pulling it this way and that, so that when he finally pulled up near the station he knew he looked like a startled chicken. Once his envelope was safely posted with a minute to spare, he made for Waves, the unisex hairdressers.

Forty minutes later, with his scalp bare to the sun, and the roar of roadworks hitting his brain, he wandered over to a letting agency whose front window was stickered with possibilities. Him and Ria in a studio in Hemel Road? The longer he stared, the more potent that dream became.

'You DSS?' enquired the suit once his client had reached his desk. So much for the skinhead look, thought Martin.

'Do us a favour.'

'Age?'

'Eighteen. Last March.' He dug out his driving licence and a tattered copy of his birth certificate, specially kept for the more picky pubs and clubs Ria liked to go to. Mother – student. Father – commercial pilot.

He handed the thing over. If he looked his age, there'd be no hassle. But then he never had. 'Goldilocks' had been his nickname at his bullying prep school. Another reason why, as a copper, he wanted to see justice done.

'Top limit per week?'

His mental arithmetic went into overdrive. He'd been promised more work at the local pool. Sundays no problem. Double time, in fact.

'Two hundred.'

'Hmm.' The David Ginola lookalike swivelled round to the nearest filing cabinet and pulled out three well-thumbed postcards. 'Any particular area?'

'Nope. Need space for my car. That's all.'

'Leaves just one, then.' The man handed over the lone card. 18a Belling Grove. No photo. Room measurements minute. More Lewisham than Blackheath, judging by the postcode.

'This a flat or a kennel?'

'Come on, sir. You're in London not Barnsley.'

'OK. I'll take a look. Now, if possible.'

The guy whose label read Ian Timms checked his Rolex then stared Martin in the face.

'Sir, get the deal. You got wheels here?'

Martin nodded, then wished he hadn't.

'You run me there and back, OK? Car's out of commission till four o'clock. Ignition problem.'

The fragile dream of independence was already turning sour like an old photo browning round the edges. Fuck it. His dad would be on the road by now, heading north. And after France would come Greece, followed by Germany. A month's flying at least, and time for himself to sort something else out.

'Cheers,' was all he said, reclaimed his documents and walked away.

Buckingham Avenue wasn't an option just then, but Ria was. She'd probably have her head stuck in some anatomy book, Alanis Morissette on her CD player. Clever, sane Ria. Destined for a PhD and the rest. He'd read what private consultants earn. Nothing wrong in not being the main breadwinner, he mused, unlocking his car door. Yes, he'd often pictured life ten years on. A new detached in Billericay. Cream-leather sofa and prints of bullfights, topped by a Sunday visit from ... well, at least his mother.

Suddenly the sound of an emergency siren grew louder. Police or ambulance he couldn't yet tell, until the familiar yet thrilling sight of a blue-and-yellow-chequered Mondeo sped by. The driver, he noticed, was not much older than himself.

He stared at how it cut a swathe through the busy village, like Jesus parting the waves in a picture kept from Sunday school all those years ago. As the traffic lights changed to green, he thought of his application form on its way and, in that instant, realized the certainty of his decision. To sort stuff out. Like he'd done that time last month when a kid had gone under in the pool's deep end and had taken too long to reappear...

Kelly was her name. And he'd still got the soft toy she'd sent him in gratitude, propped up on his bed. Proof he was good at something. But even that wasn't enough for Donald Webb. Well, sod him, he thought, turning into Mansion Mews, having negotiated more roadworks and an animal-rights march near the park. Ria was into all that. Had gone veggie after Christmas when her family had been laid low with a turkey bug. She'd gone from a size fourteen to eight. He smiled as he recalled what his mate Chris had said. 'A thin woman always makes your cock seem bigger.' He couldn't argue with that, and just thinking about it made him reckless. He had to see her. Now. Having found a residents' only parking space, he took a chance on its legal

23

occupant not returning for a while. Just then, he didn't care.

'Is she in?' he asked the moment Mrs Lewis came to the door. The smell of home baking wafted out past her ample figure, making him more than hungry.

'Who on earth are you?'

'Martin, of course.' Then he realized. 'I've had a haircut.'

But her relief soon changed to hesitation. Nothing obvious. Just the shift of her eyes, the imperceptible closing of the door. 'Sorry, but Ria's gone into town with Michelle. You know, her friend from gym club. Wanted to catch some sale. I'll tell her you've called, mind.'

'Thanks.' His disappointment obvious.

It somehow didn't feel right and back in the car he dialled Michelle's number.

'Yes?'

'Martin here. Martin Webb. Is Ria with you?'

A pause filled with din.

'Reckon you got the wrong number,' she shouted, and he felt as if an ice cube had settled in his stomach. That was bollocks. She was covering up for her. He spotted a traffic warden in the middle distance, checking windscreens. It was 9.23 a.m. Should he risk staying put and try Ria's number? The warden decided him and once he'd reached the leafy confines of Buckingham Avenue he saw that his father's car had gone. However, any joy at that was soon eroded by his mother, standing like a lost child by the window, staring out.

Three

June 30th, 1997. Her sixtieth birthday, filled by rain rather than any sense of celebration. Not the gently falling variety either, favoured by the Romantic poets, but violent, constant, scouring the patio free of moss. Nudging the empty flower tubs nearer the house. Raising the new graveyard's water table where yet again the early Scott family graves had been defaced by graffiti. Her husband Samuel Colby lay impervious to this mischief in his thick oak coffin.

She wondered how long it would take his solid body built on three square meals a day and, over the course of sixty-eight years, at least ten vats of red wine, to be reduced to a goo of fat and tissue. How long before he merged with his less well-fed neighbour on his left, and infiltrated the plot on his right, saved for her?

As if to expunge these foul thoughts, Evelyn Scott went over to her Edwardian rosewood desk and wiped her late husband's framed photograph with the cuff of her navy suit. A typically spontaneous action resulting in a dusty residue embedded in the material's expensive fibres. Her best suit, in fact, specially chosen for the latest shareholders' meeting in one hour's time. And maybe this flaw was symbolic, she argued to herself. Because since Labour's recent landslide victory, her belief in Scott's Rifles' continued expansion had taken a few knocks. This political party wouldn't be on her side like the Tories had been. Oh, no. She'd heard whispers already over paternity leave. And yet more red tape fresh from Brussels.

She sighed to herself as she laid the picture back in its exact place where Samuel could meet her eye to eye while she worked. Yes, time will tell ... And, thinking of time, she glanced at her Cartier watch, wondering how long her journey would take, given the weather.

Sean Brownlow, her production manager, had offered to take her there, but as always, she'd politely refused. Damn it, she still felt more twenty years old than sixty. More than able-bodied *and* alert to boot. Despite the blow of losing Samuel to a massive stroke last November, it had been Business As Usual, the words designated for her white marble headstone when her time came. An order for ten thousand stalking rifles had arrived from North Carolina on the day of the funeral. And this would be just the start. New Labour or not.

Evelyn walked from the lounge into the hallway, hearing the deluge punish the glass porch stuffed with her favourite indoor plants. For the first time since Samuel had died, she felt truly alone. She shivered under her clothes. Not because of any noticeable drop in temperature, but because just then, and despite the many sympathy cards which still adorned every shelf, the sense of isolation was overpowering.

She immediately felt ashamed of such feebleness and thought of Merle, her one and older sister less than five miles away in the village of Colwall. She'd lived on her own since their parents' deaths, growing more forgetful every day. Wearing unmatched shoes, pouring cooking oil into the bath and wondering why she smelt odd afterwards.

It was a good job, Evelyn thought, that given these trials her sister hadn't wanted anything to do with the business. Instead, she'd been content to breed her King Charles spaniels, and very successful she'd been too. Enough, with a little help, to stay on at Teme House in comfortable retirement.

Better ring her, she thought. Just in case. The desk phone with its fax machine was nearest, and Merle took longer than usual to answer.

'How's my big sister doing in all this rain?' Evelyn began, first off the block as always.

'Sister?'

Evelyn's insides took a sudden dive.

'Yes. *Evelyn*. The only one you've got. Remember?' Merle had never queried *that* before. 'I'm at the Gables. West Malvern. Just round the hill from you.'

'Of course. I'm sorry. It's those bad dreams again. They make me forget things.'

Evelyn frowned. Some things never go away.

'Write them down,' she said briskly. 'That's best. By the way' – she saw the seconds ticking away – 'is there anything you need while I'm in town?'

'A notebook. Because I'll do what you

27

suggest. Oh, and some Dolly Mixtures.'

'Fine. I'll be with you around four o'clock.'

It was time to go, but she never liked ending calls to Merle. 'By the way,' she added, 'do you know what day it is today?'

'My birthday.'

Evelyn started. Alarm bells clanging even louder in her head.

'I'll get you something nice, then.' All the while, thinking the unthinkable. That Merle, who in the old days completed the *Telegraph* crossword in record time, was losing it. Thinking too, of the front bedroom here, with its valley views and own en-suite bathroom. Then, realizing with a heart made more of base metal than anything else, that having her sister at home with her would be impossible. Irresponsible to both of them.

There'd already been a toaster fire in Merle's kitchen. Nothing serious, but alarming nevertheless. And only last week she'd put a costly dry-clean jacket in for a hot wash. No, Evelyn thought, eyeing the umbrellas in the hall stand and wondering which would best preserve her new hairstyle until she reached her Jaguar, the reality was that Merle needed full-time surveillance.

She picked out her black-belted mac then the newer of Samuel's golfing umbrellas and, without thinking, clicked it open. Her dead mother's warning about this bringing bad luck made her quickly close it. She then picked up her ready-packed briefcase and set the alarm. Once outside, the umbrella was swept from her grasp. She reached down to retrieve it but twisted on the slippery step. Something Samuel had long complained about. She fell hard. Her cry of pain unheard. She saw blood erupt from her ankle, thinning out like a cheap rosé wine on to the sloping drive. Then came the strangest sensation – as if she was surveying herself from above – a black heap reduced to a sodden scrap. Moments later, nothing.

Four

'What's got into you, then?' Beryl quizzed Frankie as she poured baked beans on to four pieces of white toast. 'I heard you've not stopped singing since you got back from the Benefits Office.'

'Who says?'

'Shannon.'

'Typical.' Frankie sat down on her usual chair, whose tapestry seat depicting a brown otter building a dam was now so worn it was scarcely visible. She crammed the food into her mouth then got up just as Beryl sat down.

'Aren't you going to tell us, then?' The woman loaded her fork then looked up at her.

'No. Anyway, it's nothing to do with my dole. It's a job.'

'All right, let's guess.'

'Guess all you like. It's secret. What I want to do.'

'And what about that doll of yours? You be taking her into work with you an' all?'

'Might be. Is that a problem? Besides' – she glowered at her – 'she's *not* a doll.'

'Could 'ave fooled me.'

Frankie wanted to hit the smirk off her face. She saw Shannon and her father leaving the lounge and tried to exit via the kitchen door but was too late. Sniffed a mix of Poison and BO as they both pushed past her.

'Anyway,' she added with a half smile, 'I'm going to be quids in one day. You'll see.'

'Quids in, eh?' John Arthur's eyes rested briefly on her crotch.

'Yeah. So make a note of the date.'

With that, she made her way upstairs, to her sanctuary, where Lila was propped up against the bed's headboard, waiting for her with that same angelic expression she'd had since day one. No questions. No crap judgements. Just unconditional love.

It was a hot windy night, delivering diesel and curry smells through her half-open sash window. She couldn't sleep, not with thinking about college. Imagining what the first day would be like.

Suddenly, a floorboard creaked outside her door, but before she could investigate, the thin yellow line beneath it began to widen; the door handle twitch from left to right under someone's hand.

John Arthur. She could smell him before she saw him. Larger it seemed than any man should be. A silhouette moving towards her. No use screaming ... Beryl was out at some Union do, and Shannon...? God knew where she was.

He was too big for her to fight. Ten times her size it seemed.

She leapt out of bed to lock the door like she usually did, but he was already in the room, pushing it shut behind him. Keeping his back to it, flicking on the light switch. His blue shell suit straining to contain him, especially down there.

'Going to lock me out, were you?' he growled. 'That's not very friendly, Frankie.'

'I don't want to do it. OK?' The last time had been like lying under a bus. And he'd hit her for not doing what he wanted.

She saw his left hand reach behind him. Heard the key grumble in the lock. He slipped it into a side pocket out of reach. She glanced at the window. It was a possibility.

'I know what you're thinking,' he said. 'Can read you like a book. And right now I'm ready for chapter two...'

'Chapter two? I don't get it.'

'You will. But first things first.'

He made for her bag slung over the back of her dressing table's chair. Tore it open, just like he'd done with her last week. Then he pulled out the forty pounds from her purse.

'Quids in, eh? Just like you said.'

She charged at him, trying to beat him off, but she was little more than a bamboo stick next to a boulder. Her few precious tenners stayed in his

31

grasp, just out of reach.

'I'll tell the pigs. They're *mine*.'

'How much d'you want them back, then?' he taunted. 'Come on.' Already he was pulling down his shell-suit pants to lie like a wrinkled pool about his knees. She saw the familiar white flesh, the trickle of black body hair spread to a forest and from that forest grew not a tree trunk exactly, but something pretty close. The only way she could deal with this was to make up a fairy story. Make the sight in front of her something it wasn't. No happy endings, though. At least not so far...

'Kiss it.'

That was a new one.

'I said, kiss it.'

She thought of her money. And the application form he had to sign on her behalf. If she shut her eyes and pretended it was a dog's nose or even Lila's cheek, then it might be OK. But before she could get her mindset ready, his hands were forcing her down to its level. Forcing her on to it. Choking, gagging until he climaxed and she passed out.

'I heard you, you slut,' Shannon muttered to Frankie next morning as she rammed two slices of thick white into the toaster. 'He's my dad. I mean, how low can you go?'

Not much lower.

Frankie's stomach rumbled as the smell of warm bread met her nose, but no way could she eat anything. Not for a long while. And where was her forty quid? No sign of it so far.

She'd woken up to a pitch-black bedroom, her mouth seeming full of sea water. Her tongue rough and sore.

Bastard.

But who else could she tell? Who'd believe her?

She thought of Mrs Beavis warning her to keep out of trouble. Instinct told her that if she was ever to earn that magical sum per week for caring, that's exactly what she had to do.

'Cat got your tongue, then?' Shannon sat at the table, her lipgloss now overlaid by margarine oozing from her toast. Her mouth crammed so full she couldn't scream when Frankie reached down and took a studded ear lobe between thumb and forefinger and pinched.

'You bitch. I'll tell Mum.' Her stepsister's eyes began to fill up. She looked pathetic.

'I wouldn't if I was you. Not if you want to keep your looks.'

'Threats are all you can do, isn't it, pie-face?'

Frankie bit her lower lip till it hurt. No one had called her that for years. Look, she told herself, in seventy-six days' time she'd be walking through the glass doors of Openshaw Tech. That's all she could think of. The rest wasn't worth it.

She'd delivered her application form by hand as neither Beryl nor John Arthur had cooperated with its signing until the last minute. Beryl had insisted that she find evening shift work to keep some money coming in, while he made her promise that when care was needed at 358 Dartmoor Road, she'd provide it.

33

Frankie had licked down the envelope's flap and run all the way to the college's front entrance, with no intention of fulfilling either of their selfish demands. She'd need her evenings for study, not putting toys into cereal boxes or packing toiletries for Christmas.

After this stressful and nail-biting interlude, a kind of lull descended upon the soot-covered semi during the next fortnight, in which Beryl Holt worked longer hours at the school and John Arthur spent more time hanging round Manchester's Piccadilly Gardens and the pubs there. Then he'd keep out of everyone's way, sitting in front of the TV in the front room until the small hours.

The whites of his eyes were pinker. His BO was worse too, from wearing collarless nylon shirts for weeks on end, until Beryl ordered him to bundle them into the machine. He obeyed her, since it was her monthly cheque which kept him in beer. But now they slept apart, with him in the box room next to the toilet. And he still owed Frankie forty pounds. As if she would ever forget.

Frankie agreed to spend the rest of the summer holiday at Mellor's, a liquorice factory in Oldham Road, then going straight on to work a late shift as a potato sorter for six quid an hour, ruining her hands in the process.

But what about Shannon, the White Goddess of Dartmoor Road, whose photos since birth lay dotted around the house? Shannon had ignored her, except to rub her nose in it that she'd got all

As in her A-levels, a photo in the *Manchester Evening News* and was going to university to read geography.

How do you 'read' geography, mused Frankie, who thought it the most boring subject. Who needed to know Bolivia's annual rainfall? Or the biggest producer of alfalfa in the southern hemisphere? After three years, Shannon would know everything there was to know about the world, yet that still wouldn't stop her from plucking the cruellest little arrows from her sling and firing them where they hurt the most. Worse was the fact that Beryl intended to make up any shortfall in her expenses from her Woolwich savings account.

That Sunday morning, Frankie had sneaked a look in her handbag. The total in the little navy book was £8,520.25.

Beryl's gesture of favouritism represented the chasm between her and her stepsister, as deep and dark as the River Irwell itself. So *Shannon* was worth it. But not her.

She heard Shannon slam the front door and watched her stride towards the bus stop. Her jeans snug around her arse. White ankle boots clicking on the tarmac. Her hair like a sheet of silk against her back, lifting up at the corners as she walked.

Frankie pressed her lips to the window and mouthed the foulest words she knew. All from Elm Park Comp. Suddenly, without warning, Shannon paused, glanced back as if she knew she was being cursed. A frown spoilt her perfect face. Frankie ducked down. Heard the WC flushing and Beryl using air freshener.

'What are you doing?' Beryl asked from the bedroom doorway, bringing a hint of Floral Glade and something else in with her.

'Nothing. Just mucking about.' Her blush was the giveaway.

'I thought your liquorice shift starts at ten on Sundays.'

'I've packed it in, OK?'

Beryl Holt came closer. Prodded her finger into Frankie's back.

'Perhaps you've not understood me, but in this household we all have to pull our weight.'

Frankie couldn't look at her. Nor bear to see those granite-coloured eyes, that floury skin, and to mention John Arthur just then would have risked her head being shoved down the bog bowl. Like the last time she'd stood up for herself.

'Mellor's not good enough for you. That it, eh?' Beryl began tidying up without so much as a by your leave. First her precious books, lying topsy-turvy on her shelves, then the worn Dralon armchair full of T-shirts and underwear. Next, her bed with its furrowed candlewick bedspread and then...

'No. Please leave her alone!'

'It's only a bleeding doll, you.'

'She's Lila, and she's mine.' Frankie edged towards her. The bitch was holding her aloft, by her hair. Her just-brushed hair...

'How old are you, Frances? Just remind me.'

Frankie didn't reply. Instead she head-butted Beryl off the scene but not quickly enough to

36

stop her flinging Lila high into the air to hit the landing light and tumble down the stairs. With each bump came a cry. But more than that. A gross distortion of such a familiar and comforting sound; high and wild, nothing like those times when she'd gently pat her back to bring up wind after a feed or brush imagined snags out of her hair. No, Lila was hurting, dying, and Frankie knew, as she scooped her broken body off the bottom step, something inside her too, had died.

Seconds later came Beryl's hateful voice behind her like a spike through her heart.

'Honest to God, Frances, I wish we'd never taken you on. You've brought us nothing but bad luck.'

'I never asked you to, did I?' Frankie retaliated, running to the front door.

Frankie saw the bus arrive and Shannon step on to it with all the confidence under the sun, leaving for the briefest moment a white bootee glinting, an elbow jutting out. For a split second she wanted to catch her, but Beryl's shadow was touching hers and Mrs Tilley from next door was lingering by the low dividing wall, pretending to fiddle with her flower pots.

Beryl tapped her watch. Her lips puckered like a dog's arse.

'You've got ten minutes to get to Mellor's or else. I don't want you back here till your shift's finished. Got it?'

Lila felt cold to the touch. Her big blue eyes half covered by their eyelids as her left leg suddenly came away in Frankie's hand. A piece of

37

twisted elastic still attached to its joint.

'And *I* don't want Mr Holt making me suck his cock any more. So there.'

The neighbour let out a gasp of astonishment and scuttled indoors. Frankie didn't hang around either.

Five

Martin sat at the edge of Blackheath Leisure Centre's pool, letting his bare feet dangle in its warm chlorinated water. It was too early for the yobs and poolside pimps to be polluting the place. Instead the city's workers were sluicing away another hot, humid week alongside parents with kids.

So far he'd heard nothing from the Metropolitan Police or Ria and he didn't know which was worse. A slightly embarrassed Mrs Lewis had fobbed him off with the news her daughter had gone to Bali. Whenever he'd called her number there'd been no answer and keeping her house under surveillance might land him in trouble when he least needed it.

Donald Webb was still away after six weeks, ferrying tourists back and forth across the Balearics and the Mediterranean. Places he himself had no desire to visit. He preferred the green, green grass of home. He thought of his best mate Chris Mears, cooped up as a trainee call-centre manager in a seventh-floor office in the Tottenham Court Road. His dream was to travel the world on a black Suzuki. Fat chance now, he mused. Yes, Chris was out there in a suit, getting his first foot on the ladder. Him and Martin, the only two from their year not to have applied to uni.

'Penny for them, baldy.' Liz Stirling touched his shoulder with her toe as she walked behind him. But he wasn't interested in this other so-called lifesaver, though she carried herself a certain way. She wasn't Ria. Never would be.

'What time d'you finish here?' she asked.

'Twelve.' They'd cut his normal hours by three for filter repairs so he'd put in for extra tomorrow. 'Why?'

'Ditto. Fancy a drink afterwards?'

His hesitation let him down. Gave her the chance she needed.

'See you at the George, then.'

Ria's favourite watering hole.

But before he could come up with an alternative, she was out of reach at the far end of the pool near the diving boards and there was a mum near the 2.5m marker with an asthma attack. He could spot the signs a mile off. He got up and dived in.

Two other swimmers helped him haul her out of the water and stayed with her while he fetched a nebulizer from the first-aid store. He could see Liz staring, motionless at the far end. She'd done this before with Kelly. Left him to deal with the kid, but he'd never shafted her.

Was this how it would be in the police? he

39

asked himself, trying to calm the woman and keep her warm. Everyone sticking together, watching their backs? If so, this might be the one factor to make him change his mind.

He gestured for Liz to come over and instead of responding by running, she took all the time in the world. Time in which a small crowd had gathered and a dark-skinned man in his forties arrived on the scene. Ricard. His boss.

'Have you called an ambulance?' he asked in a strong French accent.

'Yeah. Just now.' And in minutes, a siren wail snaked closer through the neighbouring streets.

Liz pulled back the woman's hair none too gently. When she saw Martin looking, she held her hand.

'You could have bloody got here,' Martin hissed at her.

'Someone had to be up the deep end,' she replied. 'Supposing I'd had an incident there?'

Jesus, she was smart and confident. Teflon-coated, more like. And Ricard hadn't noticed anything, so how on earth could he, Martin, be the turncoat? He couldn't.

The struggling, wheezing woman was stretchered away to the ambulance and, after the form-filling in Ricard's office, Martin showered before jogging out of the centre towards his car. He heard a voice behind him.

'Look, I know you're pissed off with me, but are you still up for a drink?'

The sun was on her face, her hair sleeked back. The kind of smile he'd missed.

'OK. Jump in.'

40

'Thanks. Look, Martin,' as she chucked her holdall on the back seat and climbed in next to him, 'there's something I've not told you. Nor anyone else, for that matter.'

He started the engine and hit first gear. Remembered he needed fuel.

'Go on.'

She looked straight ahead as he drove along Berwick Avenue.

'The reason I held back there, and it's been twice now, is because...'

'Because what?'

'I can't swim, can I?'

He crashed top gear. Slowed up to look at her. All her confidence was slipping away.

'I hate the water. Always have. I'm sorry.'

'But how the hell did you get the job? I mean, I had to do three lengths plus a frigging interview.'

'I lied and said it was that time of the month, you know. Then I showed him my sister's swimming certificates. Took me ages changing Emma's name to mine.'

'And lifesaving?'

'Emma's certificate again. She's like a fish.'

What could he say? He wasn't a copper yet, but people's lives were at risk. He wondered if Ricard had noticed. He was the one who dealt with complaints.

'Look, it was the only job I could get. My mum's off work since Dad started seeing this other woman. I swear to God it was that one with the asthma just now. I've never seen her in the flesh, but she was the spit of a photo I found in

41

his trouser pocket. And she had two sprogs.'

'How old's Emma?'

'Thirteen.'

He saw the George set well back from the kerb, fronted by clusters of benches and flower tubs still full of colour. A more welcome sight he couldn't imagine and so involved was he in her story that he forgot all about the possibility of meeting Ria there.

'What will you do now?' she asked, retrieving her holdall once he'd found a parking slot behind the pub. 'Tell Ricard?'

He shook his head, knowing he had to tread carefully, for if any of this came to light and he was found to have kept quiet, what then? His Met application was already being processed. His future just beginning.

'I'm going to order you a double of whatever you'd like.'

They sat with their drinks and a packet of crisps apiece, within range of the wall-mounted TV screen not because there was anything worth watching but seats were scarce, and as an antiques programme finished, a slightly strained silence fell between them. Normally Martin would have freely admitted to his plans to join the police, but not now, and when, as if mind-reading, she asked if he was planning a career at the leisure centre, he immediately said no.

'My dad thinks I should train to be a commercial pilot like him. But it's a helluva life. Here, there, bloody everywhere. And – ' He recalled his mother standing like a lost soul at the window – 'it's tough on those left behind.'

'Well paid, though.'

'God, yes.' Then he realized that wasn't the most sensitive thing to have said. 'But then, money's not everything.'

'Well, *we* could do with a bit more. Christ knows what'll happen if Dad decides to up sticks. Maybe I should go and finish that woman off. Take off that nebulizer and watch her breathe her last.' She finished her vodka and lime, unaware of Martin's surprise at her sudden, alarming change of tone.

Just as he was thinking that despite Webb Senior's antics, he was considerably luckier than her, something caught his eye. A girl he half recognized. The gloom made further scrutiny impossible so he excused himself, stood up and was just about to check her out when, for an instant, she turned his way.

Ria.

'What is it?' Liz's voice sounded miles away.

'Nothing. It's OK.'

But it wasn't. His beautiful dark-haired girl-friend was with another guy. A suit, with longer hair than his had ever been, curling over his collar. And worse was how he leant forwards, staring straight at her as if he intended to eat her face. Anger and a profound sense of loss welled up inside, swiftly followed by the thought that she'd deliberately brought the guy here to rub his nose in it. After all, this had been *their* regular haunt. Where all the intricacies of her life and family had become bound with his. Where after a few drinks on the eighth of March

43

last year, a week after his eighteenth birthday, they'd gone back to her house and, while her parents had gone out to a film, made love for the first time.

She was coming into focus now. Tanned from somewhere. A scoop-necked top and black trousers. She looked stunning. Doing well without him, obviously. If she'd seemed miserable he might have backed off.

'What's going on?' He stood over their table. 'Who's this creep you're with?'

'For God's sake, Martin. I'm not your bloody wife.' She'd had a few to drink, he could tell. Their table resembled a spritzer graveyard.

'I'd better go, yeah?' The other guy made a move and Martin was about to clamp a hand on his shoulder when he realized where he'd seen him before. The letting agency. This was Ian Timms.

He was aware of people staring. Of conversations petering out as the one o'clock news began to roll on the TV. For a moment he was unsure as to his next move. Ria wasn't even looking at him, but rummaging in her bag. That same bag in which she'd kept his letters and emails...

Something on the TV screen caught his eye. A face which made him grip the back of Timms's chair. Made him freeze.

His dad.

There'd been an accident on a runway somewhere in Spain. The newscaster's words about the pilot possibly being under the influence of drink sent him flying through the bar and out into the sunshine, unable to later recall his journey home.

'Mum?'

His broken voice carried up the stairwell of 10 Buckingham Avenue. 'You there?' Only silence replied. A silence he was used to, from those after-school days when he'd let himself in and headed straight for the fridge and the cake tin. But this time he felt no hunger or thirst. Something worse than fear.

He could switch on the radio and TV in the kitchen but what he'd already heard in the pub was swilling around every part of him. He didn't need any more.

'Under the influence ... Under the influence...'

'Mum?' Her crocodile-skin bag sat in its usual place. Her jacket and mac still hung from the free-standing coat rack, rubbing up against his dad's few things. An Aquascutum waterproof and a beige windcheater he used for golf...

The house was silent. The garden ominously empty. She lived outdoors, did Louisa Webb. Gardening her one consolation. What was wrong?

Next the stairs, one by one, soundless on the thick blue pile, past framed aerial views of faraway seas and beaches lined by palm trees. Up to the landing where he had a choice.

Suddenly his legs felt like leaden traitors, his throat dry as he crept towards their bedroom, only to be met by an awesome stillness. The kind he associated with the Chapel of Rest in Eastbourne where he'd once kissed his grandmother's waxy cheek and stroked her stiff ringless fingers.

Lastly the 'family' bathroom whose door rewarded his impatience with a thwack to his forehead. He called out, 'Mum? It's me, Martin. You in there? Hell, why don't you just open up? Say something? Come on, eh? For God's sake. It'll be OK. We'll all stick together on this.'

What utter fucking drivel, as his father would have said. We'll all stick together? Really? His application for the Met was already on someone's desk.

And then, just as a hammering of fists began on the front door, he spotted something which made his blood run cold. A wine-dark trickle appeared from beneath the door, gathering momentum, spreading on the shiny oak floor to reach the toes of his trainers.

Six

The day after her fall, Evelyn found herself staring out at the view from the private clinic's first-floor window. She felt a mix of wonderment and frustration.

'Osteoporosis,' Dr Khan had announced only an hour ago, after so many tests she didn't want to see another needle for as long as she lived. 'However, we are mystified as to what exactly has been attacking your bones.'

'Attacking?' The word seemed grotesque. Surely a mistake?

'Targeting your receptor molecules on the surface of your bone cells. There's real damage here. And –' he'd peered at her over his glasses with some embarrassment – 'I venture to suggest that one culprit might be cannabis.'

She'd needed a minute to recover, before threatening to protest to the clinic's director about such an assumption. After this Dr Khan trod more warily, offering other possibilities such as age, heredity and too many G and Ts.

'Why them, for goodness' sake?' Her favourite tipple at the end of the day.

'Sparkling tonic water uses up too much calcium.'

He'd then recommended that once back home at the Gables, she increase her calcium supplements and take life more easily.

'More *easily*?' she'd challenged. 'I'd die if I did that. Look at my husband, Doctor. He's taking things easily. I'm only sixty, damn it.'

'Madam, you are paying for my professional advice. Another fall like the one you've just sustained would mean—'

'What? Go on, tell me. I'm not some fragile old biddy!'

'But that's it, precisely. You *are* fragile, and the next trauma could see you permanently disabled.'

'You mean a wheelchair?'

He'd nodded then left her to her own whirring thoughts as her sister Merle had entered her room bearing a concerned expression and gifts

47

she'd clearly given much thought to, except that she, Evelyn, wasn't a dog.

Her older sibling had proudly set out the various chew bars and dried pigs' ears on the bed, but after a kiss of thanks, Evelyn promptly bundled them into her bedside cupboard. It wouldn't do for any medical professional to see how Merle was already treading enough of a fine line between coping and being a liability.

She knew and, for the moment, that was enough.

Now those hidden offerings were beginning to smell, and when the ward cleaner next appeared with her mop and rubbish bag, Evelyn asked her to please remove them.

'Who got you these, then?' the woman enquired, a puzzled frown on her face.

'I really have no idea.'

'Odd that. I'd better check these cupboards more often or heads might roll. Mind if I give them to our Pippin? Though he's only a Yorkie, he's like a bottomless pit.'

'I'd be glad if you did.' Once she'd gone, Evelyn lay back on her pillow thinking not only of Merle still driving around, clinging on to that last precious bastion of independence, but herself. Her mortality writ large on the doctor's record sheet.

Khan had also used the word hereditary, but both her parents had met their sudden deaths with bones and brains intact while on business in South Africa. Maybe this weakness of hers stemmed from a previous generation. Once she was up and running the show again in her normal way, there'd be no time to indulge herself in that kind of research. She was only interested in where the next big outlet could be established and whether their many shareholders were happy.

Suddenly she heard a man's familiar voice outside the door to her room. Sean Brownlow, her production manager, was chatting up her nurse with his typical charm. The fifty-two-year-old bachelor certainly knew how to woo people to his cause, but had overstepped the mark when he'd suggested a meal with her at Rizio's, a smart new restaurant on Belle Vue Terrace, while Samuel was still warm in his grave. Her refusal had been too swift, his reaction less so.

Instinctively, she reached for her medical file and hid it under the blanket. Those details were private and she knew his motto was Knowledge is Power. His stride was purposeful, his smile partially obscured by a spray of half-opened white lilies.

'These'll cheer you up.'

But he was wrong. They were identical to those she'd chosen to adorn her husband's coffin and their smell brought back such vivid memories that for a moment she closed her eyes as if to shut it all out.

'How's our patient, then?' he asked drawing out a chair for himself and sitting down. 'Nasty shock for all of us, I must say.'

'You mean, *you*.' She gestured at him to pass her the flowers. Any thanks already dead in her throat.

He seemed to let her first remark pass, clearly

49

used to them by now. Her innermost thoughts slipping out like those annoying little bursts of urine whenever she laughed or sneezed.

She watched him acting as if he owned the place. Which of course he would, given half the chance. And why was it, whenever she was in his company, she felt the need to call into her solicitors' and write her will?

While Samuel had duly written his in her favour on his fiftieth birthday, her own remained the one neglected aspect of her busy life. Soon all his stocks and shares, his rents from various properties in the town would be trickling into her account. Whereas her own assets, including the spacious Victorian house and its twelve acres, would go where? Where, you stupid woman? she berated herself. She realized that unless Merle had made secret provision of her assets, she too would die intestate.

'Now then, Evelyn,' he began, having seated himself once more and moved his chair to face her. Eyes like a fox. 'What does your doctor say? What's the prognosis?'

'I'm fine, really. It's just my left knee, that's all. I must have twisted it when I fell. Damned step.'

He stared at the pronounced lump under the open-weave blanket in such a way she felt moved to further defend herself. To watch her back.

'It'll be bandaged up like this for a few days. Nothing major. Certainly nothing to keep me away from the job.'

Brownlow leaned closer, poised to place his hand on hers, until she withdrew it.

'Excellent news.' His smile returned. 'Just what the board and everyone wants to hear. They all send you their warmest wishes for a swift recovery.'

'Thank you. That's very comforting.'

She tried to raise herself to a more upright position. He didn't help her. Just watched her manoeuvre first with one painful elbow then the other.

'Incidentally, Davidson wants me to do that USA trip with him.'

A knot of panic in Evelyn's stomach seemed to unravel and spread throughout her whole body.

'Instead of me?'

'We were just being practical, Evelyn. Life has to go on.'

Life? What does he mean? I'm not in the ground yet.

She was regretting buying the plot next to Samuel. It was as if it was beckoning her, led by this man's firm hand...

'No, please. I'll be fine. Do I look ill?'

'Of course not, but you know how much Health and Safety means to him.'

Evelyn nodded numbly.

'We may not be able to guarantee you, how shall I say, the right facilities.'

'You mean *disabled* facilities?'

He nodded, colouring lightly.

'I'm only thinking of you.'

'I'll be there, Sean. I'm not finished yet.'

'Quite.' He stood up, tweaked out the creases

51

in his trousers and pulled a slim-line Filofax from his jacket pocket. 'We'll be leaving the office for Heathrow at seven a.m. on that Tuesday. Would you like me to pick you up?'

'I'll manage perfectly well, thank you.'

Was she imagining that smile of his faded just a little before he turned to leave? That walk to the door slightly quicker than when he'd arrived? She wasn't sure, but what she did know was that with no wife or dependants to worry about, he'd soon be ensconced on her shooting range in the solitary pursuit of perfection.

Six weeks later, with new orders firmed up in Washington and Philadelphia and strong interest from Texas and Wyoming, Evelyn decided to spend the weekend with Merle. The American trip had proved gruelling and not solely because of her physical limitations. On more than one occasion she had to remind Brownlow and Davidson that it was *her* forebears' ingenuity which had started the company, and *her* money now financing its latest research. And competitors from London and Birmingham were nipping at their heels with new guns for a younger, less affluent shooter.

But it wasn't only the men's excluding tactics during the four-day tour which had unsettled her, but the fact that yet again Sean had asked her to dine with him. Why? she wondered. What was he hoping to learn? And more to the point, what did he know already?

Her instincts for the business had proved right so far and, she reminded herself as she redressed the bandage on her knee, she was the boss. However, thinking about Dr Khan was less comforting. Having just prescribed the latest serms – selective estrogen receptor modulators – and biphosphonate medication, he'd suggested she keep a pain diary.

'Absolutely not,' she'd muttered after her latest check-up. It had been a painful enough experience shelling out what her private medical insurance hadn't covered. The hire of a wheelchair for bad days. Taxis to and from work. At this rate, she'd have to consider trading in her assets for some kind of annuity. Given that the Grim Reaper had so startlingly imposed himself in the doorway of her life...

At least now she was mobile again and the crippling ache in her left knee and both elbows was bearable. Nevertheless, it made getting herself ready each day a much greater chore, especially to her exacting standards. In Washington, she'd been mortified one morning at a breakfast meeting when Sean had mentioned a conspicuous ladder in her stocking.

Already she'd taken forty minutes longer than usual to dress, but she would never have anyone in the Gables to assist her. Nor let herself become dependent upon someone else, least of all a stranger. She'd heard horror stories about these so-called home helps and hadn't worked hard all her life for some whippersnapper to take over.

And what about Merle? Was this the only solution for her, short of going into a home? Evelyn shuddered to think of it. It was time to

53

talk to her sister. To assess her financial situation and help her make the right decision.

Evelyn pulled up her thirty-denier end-of-summer stocking over the bandage and secured its top to her suspender belt. Then, having checked the contents of her weekend case, she dragged it step by step behind her down the staircase. She glanced outside and saw a lone figure in dark green waterproofs, bearing a rifle in each hand, move towards the rifle range, discreetly painted in camouflage colours. Sean Brownlow would probably still be there when she arrived back on Sunday evening. Such was his dedication. Perhaps if he'd married and had a family, things might be different, but, just as for her, his life had taken some unexpected turns.

As she drove away from the Gables, giving Brownlow the merest wave, she scolded herself for her previous negativity. She was still the torch-bearer for Scott's Rifles, not only in a cut-throat global market but closer to home for her family of employees with their dependants and ever-increasing mortgage interest rates. This realization might have alarmed others but never her. In fact it never failed to deliver a frisson of energy, even joy – if that was the right word.

As she reached the double gates of Teme House, with pain in her knees and ankles, she caught the end of a news bulletin about some drunken pilot who'd rammed another holiday plane at Gerona airport. However, the sight which greeted her made her pull up sharply and stall the engine. For there, with a watering can in her hand, wearing only her caramel-coloured brassiere and knickers, stood seventy-three-year-old Merle, grinning from ear to ear.

Seven

The three years since Lila's murder had seen a sea change in life at 358 Dartmoor Road. Frankie had not only been awarded Student of the Year at Openshaw Tech that summer, but also gained her GNVQ Level Three with Distinction. Mrs Beavis and the other teaching staff had filled the embarrassing gap left by Mr and Mrs Holt at the presentation. Frankie had been referred to as 'a dedicated perfectionist and a huge asset to any future employer'.

At least Mr Vikram Patel had believed it and Frankie was now in her eleventh full-time week at Briarfield Care Home in Windrush Street. A large Victorian building, newly cleaned of a century's soot, whose red-bricked walls were criss-crossed by pipes of varying thicknesses. Mostly due to the many bathrooms and toilets – the first thing she'd noticed about the place at her interview.

It was now more like a home to her too, and its smells of dinner, polish and stale incontinence pads never failed to invoke a powerful sense of belonging each time she admitted herself by special swipe card.

She'd also become the family's main bread-winner, what with John Arthur having bunked off to an Aberdeen oil rig in May, keeping his pay to himself, and Beryl being on a permanent sickie from her school office with an ever-depleting savings account and a drink problem. She'd grown more reserved towards her these days, thought Frankie. Doubtless worrying whether she might still spill the beans about John Arthur's assaults. And a good job too. Even the sponging Shannon Holt, BSc, hadn't forgotten the threat about her face and kept a low profile.

Another significant event was the arrival of Ellie, her new baby. Having buried Lila in a nice spot in the back-garden flower bed between clumps of what later turned out to be Michael-mas daisies, Frankie had ordered her replace-ment from Newborn Ltd, a firm based in Swindon. Their full-page advertisement in the *TV Times* had proved irresistible. After three years of grieving and uncertainty as to who should replace the golden-haired Lila, it wasn't until six days ago that the postman had asked for her signature upon receipt of a pale pink box adorned with tiny white silk rosebuds.

Ellie would never be Lila but she was special in her own way. The sheer newness of her. That super-soft skin making every tiny wrinkle in her clenched fists seem so lifelike. Every tiny pucker around her mouth so expressive. But it was the pink plastic hospital bracelet which had made Ellie worth all of the eighty-five pounds she'd cost.

Ellie Scott. D.o.b. 10. 11. 2000.

A Scorpio destined to be her best mate for life, whatever happened. Never to grow old, unlike the wrecks at Briarfield. But why Scott? you may ask. Surely Holt would have been more logical? Having reached her eighteenth birthday last February, marked by a few drinks down the pub with some of her health-studies group, Frankie now had rights. The main one being she was able to start her search. Her first port of call, once she was back in Dartmoor Road that evening, had been Beryl, slumped in the kitchen in her dirty dressing gown with her third vodka and lime in front of her.

Frankie had threatened to withhold her weekly household contribution until the boozer had weakened and confessed what her mother's surname had been.

'Scott? Are you sure?' she'd said afterwards.

'I ought to be.'

This took some getting used to. She thought of Scott of the Antarctic, of Peter, a famous painter/birdwatcher, and Walter the author of *Ivanhoe*. Yes. It was an OK sort of name. Better than Holt, anyway...

'Is that all you can tell me?'

'Yes.'

'Where was I born, then?'

'Can't remember.'

'I earn two hundred and eighty-eight pounds a week. Up to me if you see any of it.'

'Worcestershire.'

'That's nice. Sauce country. Where exactly?'

57

'I've forgotten, haven't I?'

Frankie persevered.

'So what about my real mum? You must have known her first name. How old she was. Where she and my dad lived...'

'Your dad?' Beryl turned to look at her. 'Whoever said you had one of them?'

Frankie blinked in disbelief. Four Red Bulls and the rest weren't doing her brain much good.

'I never saw no dad. And that's God's truth,' her mother said. 'And the stuck-up bitch never said where she lived.'

'Stuck-up bitch? What d'you mean by that?' Beryl topped up her glass from the Smirnoff bottle.

'Nothing. I was thinking about summat else.'

'You liar.' Frankie loomed over her, her blood heating up. This was a clue. A fucking clue. But that was clearly all she was getting, short of holding a knife to Beryl's throat.

Once Frankie had settled into the care home's routine, she was swiftly promoted to events manager, thus giving her Wednesday afternoons off to source affordable artists, magicians, comics – anyone who could alleviate the tedium of daily life at Briarfield and provide its residents with 'a little sparkle'. She had her own agenda and the regular visits to the library's Internet-access PCs had shown her that the search for her mother was going to be a long haul. Scott was the tenth most common surname in the UK. However, nothing daunted her, she just had to milk more information from the

58

pissed incumbent of Dartmoor Road before her hunt could begin in earnest.

Christmas Eve 2000 featured a dirty grey fog blocking the view of houses opposite from her new bedroom window. New, because Beryl had conceded it to her, despite Shannon's protests, for an extra tenner a week. But the real bonus was the double bed even though the left side still smelt of John Arthur from before his move to the box room. She and Ellie had that much more luxury. More space. The curtains boasted tie-backs, unlike the cheap ones in her old room, and there was also a walnut-veneer dressing table where she now sat by the triple mirror brushing her hair and spraying it into place until it shone like her black vinyl Entertainments folder.

Thicker now, with those bare patches growing over since she'd bought in her own shopping. She could also afford more expensive colorants and keep up with the trends in Primark. But on £6 an hour and then tax, no way could she even think of renting somewhere on her own.

The Shannon problem, although lessened, was still ongoing. She'd returned from a summer fortnight in Ibiza with skin the colour of a pumpkin and cheap gold not just on all her fingers but looped round her neck as well. She'd bragged on that she'd met a bar owner called Chuck and it looked like her MA plans were on hold. An MA paid by Beryl, of course, whose savings were now down to £5,245 with the rent set to rise again next year.

Frankie made sure that Ellie was safe and snug before switching off the light and locking the door behind her. Down in the Formica-coated kitchen, under the shrinking balloons which she'd tied to the main light, she lit up one of Beryl's Marlboros and was just about to add hot water to the instant coffee in her Scooby-Doo mug when she heard footsteps on the stairs. Furtive steps, not those of someone simply going from A to B, and for a brief, awful moment Frankie was reminded of John Arthur's nocturnal visits.

Every smallest noise carried in that 1950s semi. Each WC flush sounded like Niagara Falls. Even Mrs Tilley's movements next door could be logged if you had the inclination for that sort of thing. Whenever she switched on *Women's Hour*. When *Corrie* hit her screen.

Shannon was dressed from head to toe in white, like the bloody Snow Queen, thought Frankie. Her boat-necked top revealed the extent of her topped-up tan, her jeans the unmistakeable cleft of her sex between her thighs.

'You got any dough?' she asked, helping her-self to a cigarette from the open packet on the draining board. Frankie let it go. Season of goodwill and all that. Besides, she had her future to consider and from now on, just like the college principal had said at the prize-giving, Perfectionist was going to be her middle name.

'How much you after?'

Shannon shrugged. Lit up and channelled her first exhalation towards the balloons.

60

'Thirty?'

'Why?' She'd a right to ask, after all.

'Clubbing.'

'Now?'

'Yep. Down at Gee's.'

The hottest spot in town, with a dance floor suspended over the river. Where just to step over the threshold would set you back twenty. To leave your belongings in their guarded cloakroom, more again.

'Tell me something, then.'

'What?' Eyeing her bag like a dog hooked on a promised bone. Clearly wondering how long this was going to take. 'About where you came from? All that stuff? Excuse me while I yawn.'

Frankie killed her dimp in the glass ashtray and unzipped her bag. Heard Beryl stirring in her old room above.

'Ask *her*, for fuck's sake.' Shannon's made-up eyes scrolled to the ceiling. 'She was the one who fixed it all up.'

'What d'you mean?'

'They took some four year old in for a few months, then a nine year old after that. Disasters both of them.'

'Both girls?' Frankie asked hopefully, to cover up her disappointment.

'One of each. Don't think they knew what they wanted. Then I overheard Mum say they'd try for a newborn. I'm surprised the powers-that-be let her have a third bite of the apple.'

Frankie thought of Ellie. Her newborn. She'd already shown her off to the home's residents so there was no need to make her endure tonight's festivities. But the fact that Beryl Holt hadn't necessarily wanted a girl or picked her out sent a distinctly unfestive chill to her heart.

Shannon finished her cigarette and checked her watch – another cheap import – as a flush of frustration crept up her neck. Frankie made her wait some more by opening up her wallet and letting her fingers play amongst its folds. Teasing the graduate into thinking the payout was imminent. Everyone she knew had photos in theirs. Family, pets et cetera. She always made a point of looking at these at checkout tills. But her wallet stayed strictly functional. At least, for now.

'Beryl says my mother was a stuck-up bitch,' she said, bringing a fiver half out of its slot. 'Did *you* ever see her?'

'Once.'

'Once?' Frankie almost shouted, letting the wallet drop. 'For Christ's sake, tell me what she looked like...'

'Thirty quid,' Shannon reminded her, opening her white vinyl bag in anticipation.

With shaking fingers, Frankie found the rest. Another fiver and a twenty. Worn and thin between her fingers as she passed them over.

'So?' But no sooner were the notes in Shannon's hand than she'd lunged for the back door and legged it down the passageway.

Frankie boarded the 219 bus into town, two stops from the home, so that by the time she and her bag were thrown together on to the nearest of its smelly velour seats she was not only freezing but knackered.

'Busy night, eh?' the black driver had quipped as she'd paid her fare. 'Hope this fog'll clear before tomorrow.' He kept his eye on her for most of the journey. There was no hiding place unless she crouched down out of sight between the seats, but why should she do that? She'd paid full whack, ninety-eight pence, after all. Perhaps it was her outfit that was exciting his interest. A zebra-striped top with the shortest, tightest skirt she possessed. Her hair trained last-minute into twenty short aggressive spikes. All because of Shannon.

The old folks and those few family members who'd bothered to visit them for the evening had clapped and cheered as she'd been pronounced the karaoke winner then duetted 'My Way' with Robbie Day-Glo, a local balladeer in his fifties, who'd been cheap to hire. Her heart hadn't been in it, of course, but she was learning to put on a good show. To be what people wanted her to be.

At the end of all the fun, with all the Hi Life diluted orange juice and ham sandwiches gone, the oldest resident, Walter Perkins, handed over a set of war medals embedded in a silk-lined box. He'd explained with tearful eyes how he'd no living relatives and that she, Frankie, was the next best thing. At least she'd appreciate them, not like some junk shop.

'Course I will, Wally. No worries. Thanks ever so much.' She'd kissed his whiskery head then held his hand for a moment, amazed that such valuables hadn't already been nicked from his room during escorted toilet visits. She also idly wondered about his will.

Frankie stared out at the dismal scene beyond the bus window, where sky and buildings blurred as one and bright lights were rendered faint smudges in the gloom. The remaining seats soon filled up with revellers – some pissed already, the rest halfway there. She prayed to a God she'd never believed in that no one would recognize her.

'Everybody out,' shouted the driver when the bus finally came to a halt. 'No one's kipping in 'ere tonight, if you don't mind.'

'You must be fucking joking,' said a chav in a Man U baseball cap.

Everyone disembarked to be lost in the city's smog. She resisted pushing her way through the wall of bodies exiting for fear of attracting attention to herself, so she was the last to leave.

'Off somewhere nice?' The driver leant towards her.

'No,' she muttered, lugging the heavy bag behind her. 'Just meeting my dad.'

'Lucky Dad,' he said, gathering up his things as she stepped out on to the teeming pavement. She'd only been to London once, on a Year 10 school trip to Madame Tussauds, paid for by the governors. By the time the party had glimpsed Winston Churchill and the Chamber of Horrors – which didn't scare her in the least – it was time to leave. She'd never seen so much heaving humanity seemingly going nowhere.

Now was different and she was swept along in a fog of smoke and liquor while carols from a passing Father Christmas motorcade filled her ears. She felt dizzy, losing her purpose. At last, she spotted a Ladies and took herself down into its strangely scented depths.

'Twenty pence, please.' A scraggy old crust held out her hand. 'And no tampons down the pan. More than me job's worth.'

Frankie passed her the right coin, trying to avoid making contact with either her eyes or her fingers. This was a disaster. The crone would surely recognize her later, but what else could she do? To turn and go would be even more obvious. Once inside the cubicle, and careful not to let anything touch the floor, she changed. She overheard the same woman in an argument with a group of foreign students. This gave her the chance she needed to slip away unnoticed and make her way against the human tide towards the river.

Gee's was throbbing with Duran Duran and testosterone. There were blokes everywhere and for one unnerving moment she wondered if it was a gay night. That her target had got it wrong. The uniformed bouncer outside the entrance to the converted warehouse eyed her up and down then, with a practised touch, frisked her bag. She held her breath for fear he'd focus on the old boy's medals, which might well take some explaining.

'On your own?' he asked, finally zipping it up again.

'Meeting some mates.' She smiled.

'ID?'

'What?'

She blushed. Her fucking name was on every-thing...

'Look,' he said, grinning, 'you don't look like no pusher. Least, not to me. Have a good time, eh?'

'Thanks.' Frankie winked at him, showing her best profile. 'I will.' She wasn't going to let him see how relieved she was.

Beyond the foyer, a curve of shallow marble steps led to a galleried landing full of drinking, braying bodies. As far as she could see, there was no one dressed in white. No one with the Snow Queen's hair.

Give it time, she thought, offering up her widest grin for the reception girls then handing over her bag. Her grin wasn't reciprocated. One stupid cow was eyeballing her as if she had nits.

'Cheers,' she said after the back of her left hand had been stamped with a number. 358. A bloody weird coincidence, she thought, setting off for the stairs.

Cher's 'I Believe' was blasting from all corners. Frankie mouthed the words, which, although not exactly mirroring her experience, nevertheless empowered her as she climbed upwards. They gave her heartbeat a stronger rhythm, the courage to press her way through to a vast dark room swimming with ribbons of coloured lights. It seemed like Heaven and Hell all rolled into one. Or an aquarium where verti-cal fish were moving close together, wide-eyed, striped blue, pink, purple.

Frankie shook her head at the words of the song. Except for Justin Rosser she'd never been truly madly deeply in love, and most pop songs were therefore irrelevant. After Shannon's victory, she'd tuned into the cool angst of Morissette and Coldplay. Just thinking about the tall, hunky football-mad Rosser refocused her mind. Partly why she was here.

She spotted the illuminated sign for the Ladies and slipped behind the crowded tables into its lighted doorway. Anxious to avoid being seen by those preening themselves in front of the wall-length mirror, she entered the first cubicle and locked herself in. Just as she was about to retrieve a pair of latex gloves from her jeans pocket and encourage them over her fingers as she would before applying hair colour, she heard the outer door bang shut and two voices, one of which she recognized.

'That's why there's nothing doing with my MA. If that lazy cow had a better job, Mum could afford the fees. As it is, what does my dear adopted sister decide to do for a living?'

'You tell me.' The voice had a strong Brummie twang.

'Caring. In some old folks' home. I ask you.'

'Hardly bringing home the bacon, then?' The girl chuckled before the sound of running water took over. 'Didn't think anyone in those places had an IQ of more than five.'

'Too right. Why it's probably about her level. You should see the state of her. Hair like a tart's beaver after a rough night. And that face! God was having a day off when that one came up for him to sort.'

'Bitch Face.' The tap turned off now, and the

67

hand drier activated, masking the worst of the Brummie's cruel laughter.

'*Stingy* Bitch Face.'

Frankie's stomach tightened. She forgot to breathe as the chat went on, accompanied now by 'Silent Night'.

'And guess what, Jess, she's got this doll, right? Like it was a real kid or something. Gives me the creeps. You should see it. I'm surprised it didn't arrive with placenta all over it.'

'Ugh. Please.'

'Exactly. Whoever's made that has got to be sick.'

Frankie slipped on each glove in turn, flexed her fingers ... Hold on, she told herself. Wait. And she did, until the pair had clacked their way back towards the door and let it shut behind them.

'*Ding dong merrily on high, in Heav'n the bells are ringing...*' sang the metallic choir and the girls, still ranged by the mirror, were singing along to it, too blitzed to notice her leave. Her hurt still stung like a wound and both hands felt hot, constricted inside the gloves, as she re-entered the disco. No way could she risk them catching the light, so she couldn't be chatted up or even order a drink.

Christ, she could do with a fag. Fifty, in fact. Before she got on with it.

She hunted for that all-too-familiar white hair with its devil's horns. Not a sign. Far as the eye could see.

'Fancy a jive?' A midget in a denim suit looked up at her from under his dark fringe. He'd appeared from nowhere like something out of *The Hobbit*. Another potential witness.

'Sorry. Waiting for me mate. Thanks all the same.' She smiled, before checking her watch in the spinning lights. She felt dizzy, hungry as nothing on offer at the care home had whetted her appetite.

It was 11 p.m. The last bus back was at 11.23. Forget it.

All at once, a peal of laughter hit her. Hers, without a doubt. Frankie followed it, hands in pockets, towards a pair of glass doors which lay open to the night.

Fog and river mist embraced both the smooching couples and those cokeheads who danced alone on the black-painted decking, absorbed only in themselves and their fucked-up world. It seemed to hover untainted by the colours from within. Paler where the floor heaters pulsed out their acrid warmth. Thicker when added to by human breath.

She was still laughing when Frankie moved through the glass doors and pretended to sway, head down like the others. The river below gave off the same smell as the insides of her trainers.

The Snow Queen faced the water, greeting someone or something unseen, pressed up against the trendy silver pipework which formed the safety barrier. Her jeans still right up her arse.

Seagulls, that was it. Hovering, squealing as if in reply. She was bombed, no question. Stank of neat vodka...

Frankie withdrew her hands from her pockets

and while the Black Star track was at its loudest, clamped them round that gargling chain-draped neck. She thought of Lila, of Beryl and the days and nights in Dartmoor Road.

Eleven weeks at the home had strengthened her muscles, tightened her grip – the best preparation for what she did next. Never mind the war medals, she had a lot to thank them for. Especially as Shannon had suddenly grown limp, just like Lila.

Frankie glanced round at her spaced-out companions, none seemingly aware of her at all as she then hefted the geography graduate upwards, limb by limb, over the waist-high barrier. Suddenly, without warning, that hated face turned to her with a shot of recognition, almost putting Frankie off her stroke. The scream just like a gull's as she fell was drowned by the dull plop of water which followed. Frankie waited for that soft gurgle from her filling lungs, and watched as she sank without trace.

'Had a good night, then?' asked one of the green-haired girls retrieving her bag from the cloakroom.

'Cool, yeah. Cheers.' She beamed, thinking of Shannon's last look and her bag which would never be claimed. 'Be back in the New Year sometime.' She left a one-pound tip.

'Ta. Hope Father Christmas brings what you asked him for.'

'He has. I got it early.'

Eight

The Verne   Portland. Jan 19th. 2002

Dear son,

I know you probably won't read this, but that doesn't stop me from writing to you. I'm allowed to pen one letter a week and who else have I got to send one to? Your uncle Malcolm and aunt Sheila haven't been near me since I arrived, nor have they written or called. So, you see, I have no one.

Once I'm out of here, believe me, I'll make it up to you.

Am still being pushed for damages and if I lose, I'll be bankrupt. It's gutting to know that the house – my hard-earned buffer for my old age, and, don't forget, *your* ultimate inheritance – should be lost in such a way. I get flak for being a poshy, as they say here. I didn't realize there was so much envy around. Like a plague of locusts.

That's all for now, and remember, a visit would buck me up no end.
Dad

Me, me, me ... Fuck him, thought Martin as he screwed the lined sheet of notepaper and its envelope into a ball and kicked it down the nearest drain outside his Vauxhall flat. Not just because the s in son wasn't a capital letter, but why should he even read a line of it, with his mother now rotting in a grave some fifteen miles away.

The past four and a half years of life had been marked without even the smallest achievement. And the careers-choice questionnaire he'd filled in during his first term of the sixth form was no more than a sick, tantalizing joke. He'd walked the Boulevard of Broken Dreams all right. All the bloody way, starting with the Met. He'd not even made it over the doorstep. The polite rejection had arrived the day after his mother's funeral. When the newspapers were still dredging up still more eyewitness accounts of the runway crash. Still braying for tighter controls on pilots' lifestyles.

Martin dismounted from his Raleigh Tourer and pushed it over the Silver Street traffic lights. If he'd wanted a sudden death, he could have toyed with the buses and taxis tearing towards Charing Cross Road but no. Covent Garden at this time was not the best place to be. He was late for work. A job he'd only been in since before Christmas; every evening he'd emerge from Thom's Turf Accountants reeking of fags. A world away from leafy, comfortable Blackheath with Ria just around the corner. The girl who'd dashed everyone's dreams, including, he suspected, her own. Now she was Mrs Timms with a toddler and another on the way. And as for Liz Stirling from the pool, he'd never clapped eyes on her again.

Still, Thom's was at least a job, giving him just enough wages over to run to a few beers with Chris twice a week, and a film if he was careful. But hell, he missed his old car. Probably crushed into a cube by now after its engine had finally failed on the South Circular. The year he'd lost everything else too, and gained a mysterious four inches in height, so that none of his clothes now fitted him. Perhaps it was down to grief. As if his body, like some church spire, was trying to connect with that other world he'd never once considered before his mother's suicide.

The usual punters were already huddled outside the premises as he secured his bike to a nearby cycle rack. He gave a brief wave to Jack, the news vendor whose main story about a missing Manchester graduate hardly stopped him in his tracks as he recognized the regulars, Ralph, Parker and Titmuss stamping their cold feet in turn.

'Get a move on, squire,' Ralph said, adding to the pressure to be in the relative warmth of the betting office. The stink of beer and fags surrounded him as, with freezing fingers, he fumbled for the keys and stepped over a pool of urine to unlock the front door.

'Hang on a sec,' he muttered, making for the alarm box and punching in the code, ensuring that no one could see the sequence of numbers which Ed, his boss, changed every fortnight. Friday morning opening-up was his responsibility as Ed was with his accountant. It was also his job at varying times during the afternoon to deliver the week's takings to the bank round the corner. He felt vulnerable. Let down. There'd been a break-in at the end of November and only last week a shop assistant had been mugged outside.

'Hurry up there, son. We ain't got all day,' shouted Titmuss. But they had. That was the trouble. He knew as sure as the sun comes up in the morning that these regulars would still be there at closing time with Ed showing them the door, jingling keys in hand. There was no online betting here. You either had to be in the place or phone up to lose your money. And lose they did, while Den Tanner, his Motown-loving co-worker, called out the current odds and possible betting combinations in his distinctive high-pitched voice.

Martin turned the door's sign to OPEN, flicked on the lights and was about to lift up the counter's hinged middle section to access the TV controls when an odd sound made him pause. It wasn't those same punters' shoe-shuffle following him across the floor, but the tap tap tap of steel on wood.

He frowned, feeling his mouth go dry. His pulse in overdrive. He turned to see an unshaven man aged somewhere between forty and the pension, buried in a black overcoat several sizes too big. Now that white cane was pointing at him, those previously closed eyes half-open, narrowing. Martin saw the door to the street was empty save for rush-hour traffic coursing by.

'Move to the till,' ordered the man, jerking his stick towards the counter.

Jesus.

The weekly staff drill took place every Monday morning before opening time, when Ed would remind them yet again of all the likely criminal scenarios, especially those surrounding the till. There were two. A convincing dummy and the real McCoy tucked out of sight below the counter.

'Show 'em the dummy,' he'd say. 'Let them see for themselves it's as empty as Den's brain on a Friday night.'

Now Martin was doing just that, trying to keep fear from his voice.

'Sorry, mate,' he said. 'All the money was banked last night. Look.' He pressed in the four code letters and pulled open the drawer. Its compartments contained nothing other than a couple of screwed-up betting slips.

'Liar.' The stranger's left hand slid inside his coat. His smell reached Martin's nose. He remembered the evening shifts at the pool when the pushers and pimps came off the streets and into the water, leaving a musky, sour drift in their wake. 'You think I'm stupid?'

Just then, he'd even have been pleased to see Titmuss, anyone in fact. Where were Den, Charlene or Nicci for God's sake? But no way was he staying to find out. With a leap not attempted since his schooldays, he skimmed over the counter and ran into the kitchen area, beyond which lay the fire exit. The only escape. As he did so, a shot no more than a whisper slewed

75

past his right ear.

He kicked the kitchen door shut with such force it rattled against the frame then slid the one stubborn bolt across. The meshed metal fire door was locked, of course. Its key the smallest on his key ring, hiding between the two gold Yales. Sod's law, he thought, hearing the dummy till being manhandled, its drawer banged shut in contempt. Next, the real one, full of ten grand at least, in coins, notes and cheques, and locked like a safe with its combination code of PONY 101. His fingers shook as they separated each key in turn.

No key.

This was crazy. Each of the team had one for emergencies. That was the law, Ed had said. There was no time to wonder where it might be or who had nicked it, because he could see the man's dark form through the frosted glass then his mouth pressed up tight against it like an open wound, beginning to move.

'Open that other safe, you. Stop pissing me off. You got five seconds to come out of there. One, two...'

Martin grabbed a pair of scissors and table knife from the drawer under the single draining board.

Ed didn't allow anything sharper on the premises.

Ed ... Was there time to call him at the accountants? he wondered. No. Because that same squashed mouth had been replaced by something entirely different. Something small, black and round, and the muffled blast which followed sent him hurtling for cover, his head pounding, sensing death.

'I know the code,' came the voice as a black arm reached through the ragged hole made by the bullet. 'And I know you're there. So, just give me the key, eh?'

Martin saw leather-gloved fingers probing for the bolt and without waiting for them to reach their target, he crept closer, gripping the scissors' handle in his fist.

He heard steel on bone then the man's scream as he lurched away. Then voices he recognized. Ed's for a start, then others he assumed were cops, urging him to drop his weapon. Then came another shot, barely audible, like the rest. Another dark shape – taller less bulky – at the kitchen door.

'Mr Webb?' came a different man's voice. 'Are you OK? Can you let us in?'

Webb. The name like a curse which he'd kept meaning to change.

'Who are you?'

'Sergeant Dunn.'

'Any ID?' Keeping his eye on the hole to the right above his head. Careful to keep his knees away from the glass fragments strewn across the linoleum.

'Good man. That's exactly what we tell people to ask us.'

Martin paused, aware of his pulse still on its marathon trip. Why didn't he pull back the bolt? Why not rejoin the real world? Because a certain instinct which his mother had passed on to him, her only child, kept him where he was.

The next few moments weren't meant for any memory, but later, in a different time and place, they'd sneak up and devour his mind. Turn him off course away from those he loved most and make him a stranger, even to himself...

'We're coming in. Lie down.'

He did, still clutching the blood-tipped scissors. The floor smelt of the street.

The door caved in with surprising ease, and so did he, being kicked where it hurt most as his key ring was snatched away. One of the two intruders, both men, both masked, then took his feet and dragged him over the broken door, under the counter and the gaping till and didn't let go until they'd reached the pavement outside where a black Mercedes C-class lay purring by the kerb. Of the so-called sergeant there was no sign. After the sirens came blackness, then the heat of tea and Charlene leaning over him on the leatherette settee near the toilets.

''Ere, drink this. You passed out.'

'Where's Ed?'

'Don't ask. He was one of them. I'd swear to God he was...' She pushed back his hair from his forehead and wiped it with a travel wipe. It felt cool and clean. At least he was alive.

'Insurance scam,' said Den looking pale, letting the cops in. 'And did any of us think to ask why he'd never mentioned a panic button? Well, I bloody didn't for starters.'

'Nor me,' said Nicci from the kitchen, reboiling the kettle. 'Hey, what a bastard.'

'What'll happen to us, now?' Den picked up the so-called blind man's stick. 'Only permanent job I've ever had is here, and they don't exactly grow on trees. No disrespect to you chicks, but you can go off to have a kid and collect no end of benefits. What about me?'

Martin heard their various protests, the uncertain futures rolling off their tongues, and it only served to strengthen his resolve. He wanted out. As far from this and his old man as he could go. And as a real constable began to quiz him, he saw his mother's face smiling at him before he passed out for the second time.

The ambulance delivered him and his bike back to 39A Juniper Road before darkness fell. His room and cupboard kitchen felt like the inside of his almost empty fridge. Apart from the need to go and see his mother's grave before dark, there also lurked the possibility that Ed, wherever he was now, knew where he lived. He and Charlene had both recognized him. He should give her a call, just to be on the safe side.

He mounted his bike and headed towards Greenwich, all the while, keeping a wary eye open for Ed's Merc. It was the kind of saloon which could creep up behind you unheard; straight out of those black-and-white films he and Ria had often watched.

Every girl who walked in a certain way could be her as she used to be. Every girl with a cap of shiny dark hair and a smile to light up the night. He felt more than just a deepening sense of loss. More the feeling he was being followed.

LOUISA HARRIET WEBB
(née Porter)
LOVING WIFE OF DONALD
Greatly missed
11.3.1948 – 15.8.1997

His father had chosen the headstone from his cell and it seemed to have taken for ever to install. Granite it was, with rough-cut edges which, Webb Senior argued, reflected her love of nature.

Bollocks. It was the cheapest of the range and looked it. Half-finished, almost – just like her life – a dull matt surface not like the other glossier markers on that miserable January evening. And why no mention of her as a devoted mother? That omission had hurt too.

Martin stared at those gilt-inlaid words. All lies, of course. He slipped the temporary marker, which had been in place for six months, into his bike saddlebag. He couldn't help but wonder what she looked like now. If her hair had grown, if her face so pale and peaceful in death was still recognizable. If worms had started work...

The purple chrysanthemums he'd bought last time were reduced to a few dark-brown stems. He was just about to gather them up when his phone rang from inside his jacket pocket. His headache, almost dispelled during the cycle ride, returned with a vengeance.

'Yes?' Ria had once told him never to give his name. Old habits die hard, he thought. 'Who is it?'

'Just letting you know I can see you.'

'So?'

Martin scoured the graveyard. Close-up and far away to the line of traffic along Shooter's Hill. The trampled grass giving off the smell of dog piss as drizzle began to fall.

'How about a last goodbye to Mom, while you've got the chance...'

Mom?

Now he knew who this was. Someone who'd worked a few months in the USA and fallen for its way of life. He crammed the phone back into his pocket and grabbed his bike, but the handlebars were wet and slippery. The front wheel skewered to the ground, taking him with it. He lost his balance, felt the rough edge of his mother's stone hit his ribs. He saw not just one all-too-familiar shape but two. Black and motionless against the deepening dusk, while beyond the graveyard's entrance the faint silver smear of a car whose headlights cast its eerie beams on to the land of the dead.

'Better say your prayers, man.'

Den. He was sure of that. But why? How?

An ominous click, a sudden scream from behind him, with torchlight trained on the two fleeing figures as Charlene ran towards him and flung her damp arms round his neck.

Nine

Friday April 12th 2002. Brownlow is everywhere, like the air that I breathe, except that unlike the scents of spring which go some way to lift my spirits, he suffocates me with his attentiveness which I now know isn't in my best interests. What makes things so difficult for me is that he is expert in his job – with never a day off work and highly respected within the company. It is, as I've felt many times before, because he knows me too well and is biding his time until...

Enough. He has taken my car, my one true friend, to his home in Upton, prior to selling it. He says it could lure thieves to the Gables. He's also pressing for an inordinate commission on the sale, but what can I do? I am in his clutches, unable to extricate myself.

However, I want Dr Khan to have my fears in writing. After all, like my poor weak bones, this is yet another pain...

Evelyn laid down her pen. The effort of writing even those few lines taxed her wrist to such an extent that letters to Merle were now a thing of the past. Sean had suggested that she install a computer, to enjoy the convenience of emails and the Internet. However, like his other offers, this too had been declined. She'd preferred to deal with clients, shareholders and employees directly – to look in their eyes, to judge their body language and inflections of speech. Now, more than ever, she was having to trust her instincts which so far, had served her well in keeping a happy ship and making sound appointments.

She locked the pain diary's little clasp and, as usual, hid the key in her purse. Then she picked up the phone from her desk and dialled Merle's number. The Rubicon had been crossed two years ago when her sister had refused to be admitted to a home in Leigh Sinton. What alternative had there been then but to make that call to Homely Helpers in Tonbridge to see if they had a suitable full-time carer who could start immediately?

Evelyn recalled the conversation with the company's personnel manager as if it was yesterday. Her making light of Merle's odd ways, even injecting humour into her brief references to the worst mishaps at Teme House. And now, six 'carers' later, with a new girl from Sydney started yesterday, it was time to check if all was well.

'Who's that?' barked a girl's voice at the other end. 'I'm in one helluva rush.'

'Is that Kylie Watts?'

'Yeah. So?'

Charming, thought Evelyn, restraining herself from ticking her off for her telephone manner.

'It's Miss Scott's sister speaking. If I could just

83

have a quick word with her.'

As the girl's footsteps faded along the tiled hallway, she stared out through the arched window beyond her desk where a soft wispy mist was rising up from the valley below. Her increased dose of painkillers from Dr Khan seemed to be dulling her responses to even these beautiful sights. Almost blinding her to the constantly changing nuances of what lay beyond her four walls.

Her familiar world for as long as she could remember, but no longer a safe one...

She heard Merle's flip-flopping feet coming closer. The girl's sharp instructions.

'Hold the phone *this* way, Merle, for God's sake...' followed by an impatient sigh. Evelyn felt her stomach tighten under her dressing gown. If she complained, the girl might take it out on her sister even more, until a replacement could be found. And that would be sooner rather than later, she decided.

'Merle, it's me,' she said. 'Evelyn.'

'I'm going to a party. My dress is all ready and my shoes. Do you remember what I wore to the Hunt Ball, when I was nineteen? Well, that's the one.'

Her voice faded as did Evelyn's sudden vision of that pale-blue velvet whose skirt was embellished with silk roses. The dress she'd always coveted instead of her own. The receiver dropped against the hall table there, filling her ears with a bang.

'She's just doing her usual, I'm afraid,' the girl informed her, as if she'd known Merle for ever.

'Kylie, listen to me,' Evelyn lowered her voice. Saying the girl's common name might help. Even though it seemed to stick in her throat.

'Yeah, I am.'

'See that she has enough Fortisips for the next month and if her feet need attention, please get the chiropodist round.'

'I have already. Miss Scott's toenails are like some old donkey's I saw in Crete last year.'

'Really?' Merle being compared to such a creature was bad enough, but she also wondered what the last carer had been doing. 'And are you keeping her notes up to date? It is important, you know. Especially for the next Homely Helper who comes in.'

'Next one?' came the indignant reply. 'When's that, then?'

'I'll have to review things at the end of next week.'

'But I'm booked here till August. Mr Brownlow said.'

Evelyn paused, waiting for panic to subside. A pause which the girl quickly filled.

'Who's paying me? That's what I want to know. The old girl can't even write her name.'

Evelyn winced. The term 'old girl' could equally apply to her.

'I'll see it's with you on Saturday morning. Of course you will be declaring your income for tax purposes, won't you?'

There was another silence.

Evelyn made a promise she knew she couldn't keep. 'I'll call in first thing tomorrow.'

'Fine. I've told her she's having a bath then. Could do with it, mind. I don't think the last one you were coughing up for here ever got a flannel near her fanny.'

Evelyn was just about to protest when the girl suddenly added, 'And she keeps going on about someone called Jenny. Weird that, 'cos that's my middle name. Kylie Jennifer. Nice, innit? After my mum.'

Evelyn started. Why did the study seem to grow cold? She tried to keep the panic from her voice.

'It's just another of her little games. Take no notice.'

Ten

If there was one thing Frankie Holt couldn't abide, it was sneakiness. The kind which causes that rush of cold sweat, the thumping pulse. Just when you thought everything had died down and life could go on as normal. Life for some, at least...

Two years had passed since the Snow Queen had gone for her late-night dip in the River Irwell, and the pigs' questions at the time, especially about her own whereabouts that evening, had even strayed into her dreaming sleep. Questions which she'd answered to perfection, aided by the stupidity of the staff at Gee's, so that by May 2001 with the white clutch bag intact but no body yet recovered, suspicion had fallen on John Arthur. All because of a few tatty photographs he'd taken of Shannon in the bath as a kid. 'Inappropriate' had been the word quoted by a Kodak processor, which had started the whole affair in the first place. Him fiddling the books back in 1988 hadn't helped nor Frankie chipping in with details of what he'd made her do. That had been the icing on the cake. Enough for his name to be added to the sex offenders' register and him to be taken to a secure unit in Urmston for treatment.

Two weeks later, the man who'd never returned to Dartmoor Road, hanged himself with his pyjama cord in the unit's boiler room. *I want to be reunited with my beloved daughter. The only one who understood me.* So said his scribbled note left with a fellow inmate.

Even Beryl, who'd been fast asleep when she'd returned home from Gee's at one a.m. on Christmas Day, admitted it proved his guilt. Beryl who had snacked on fries to a dress size twenty-six while her savings had gone in the opposite direction, leaving £934.70 exactly. There wasn't much Frankie didn't know, except what the Snow Queen might look like now. And that question bothered her more than she thought it might. Even the youngish WPC Avril Pilkington, who'd just joined the Force, had seemed to side with her grief, regaling her with tales of her own crap background.

But Frankie hadn't quite trusted her caring

smile, her unexpected presence at the crematorium for John Arthur's funeral, and had been careful what she'd revealed in return. Especially about her ongoing hunt for a middle-aged woman named Scott. So far she was getting nowhere. Directory Enquiries had quoted three hundred and sixty-five Scotts in Worcestershire.

'It's all coming back to me, what Gary said,' eighty-six-year-old Daphne Cope announced while Frankie piled cooked spinach on to her bent spoon. 'He was at that club the night your sister died.'

The loaded spoon quivered in Frankie's hand as Glen Miller's 'In the Mood' came from the two wall-mounted speakers. Sweat erupted everywhere under her nylon overall but she had to keep the sneaky old crust talking.

'Your grandson, right?' She'd found a naff postcard from him in the old girl's bedside table.

'Yes. All I got left.'

The smell of undercooked mince brought a surge of bile from her stomach as the wizened little widow opened her dry mouth to receive the spinach. But the synchronicity was all wrong and in that mismatched second the helping ended up like a blob of silage on her best Sunday blouse. Frankie swiftly cleared up the mess and spat on the stain. Mrs Beavis had once said that saliva contains powerful enzymes which break down food particles...? She wished it could demolish the old woman as well. It seemed this little incident hadn't stopped her flow one bit. On the contrary, she picked up where she left off.

'As I was saying, Gary was there. He saw something which he said he should have told the police ages ago ... Then, Frankie – ' she stared up at her with watery eyes – 'your poor dad might still be alive today.'

She felt her insides contract to deliver an all-too-familiar ache. Her monthly curse was earlier than usual, making her wipe that busy mouth more roughly than the rulebook recommended. She then reloaded the spoon.

'But they interviewed everyone who mattered. Why didn't Gary speak out then?'

'He was frightened, wasn't he?'

'Frightened?'

Frankie laid down the spoon in the middle of leftover mash. The first course was over. Punishment for spoiling her day.

'For you.'

'I don't get it. What d'you mean?' She was aware Tammy Small-Tits, another carer, was eyeballing her.

'He knows how close you two sisters were 'cos I kept telling him. And from what was in the papers. If you knew what *really* happened to that poor girl it might, you know, turn you funny. Might mean you wouldn't work here no more. Then where'd I be?' Her eyes began to flood again. Frankie patted the nearest bony knitted shoulder.

'You can tell me, Daphne. Me and my mum only want to know the truth. She's not gone out of the house since it happened. Seems to think Shannon's still alive. That one day she'll just let herself in with her key.'

89

Mrs Cope eyed her plate, then prodded the mashed potato with her forefinger and popped it in her mouth.

'Around half eleven, he saw her with another girl. Right close up, you know, as if...' She took another scoop of potato. Normally Frankie would have removed the plate but nothing must interrupt her efforts at recollection.

'Not strangers, then?'

'Oh, no. Like close friends. "*Very* close friends," he said. This other girl was taller. He noticed her hair. Auburn it was, spiked like a hedgehog ... And then, when he looked again, the shorter girl in white had vanished and the other one was walking away. I told him to put it all down on paper. Tell the police.'

Frankie forgot to breathe while she relived those last seconds on the dance floor. Tried to recall who exactly had been there, gyrating on their own, maybe just *pretending* to be spaced out.

'What does your Gary look like?'

'Why do you need to know that?' Daphne looked surprised.

Frankie fiddled with the woman's bib and pulled a strand of white hair from inside her collar. Daphne liked attention, however minimal, and answered the question herself.

'If you must know, he takes after his father. My Kenneth. Tall he was, with nice wavy hair, like James Stewart. And he's a good boy. Always was. Lives up in Scotland now and works in a fish farm out in the wilds. Couldn't afford Manchester no more. The pity is, he won't come all that way just to see me now, will he?'

'You never know,' she said absently with a frown on her face.

'But I do.'

She was right of course. Frankie knew the visitors' book off by heart. Knew that no one in Daphne's family had seen her since she'd been admitted to Briarfield after her daughter and son-in-law had been killed on a railway crossing in Suffolk. So that made two less for her to worry about. But who else was their only kid likely to have told about that evening? A reckless thought entered her head.

'I can fetch him for you, if you like. Tell him you're poorly...'

Daphne blinked. An expectant smile already on her lips.

'His address is in there.' She indicated her black bag hanging off the arm of her wheelchair, its zip harbouring a mix of crumbs and dandruff. Frankie soon found a piece of folded blue paper inside the main compartment, bearing a short letter almost obscured by stains.

Loch Cottage, Kilfargan. Argyll. Scotland. 10/01/02

Gran, this is where I am. No photos yet but there will be soon.

Love from Gary xxx

Frankie slipped the note into her pocket, knowing that the old girl was unlikely to notice. Then she swiftly cleared away the dinner things and fetched a pot of apricot yogurt.

'You just tuck in, Mrs C,' she said, peeling back its foil top and dipping a teaspoon in the creamy mixture. 'I'll be back in a mo.' While the diner stared at the carton with alarming concentration, she made her way to the main office and the sagging bookshelf by Mr Patel's desk. Like the visitors' book, she knew its contents from left to right and back again.

Feeding the Elderly, Employment Laws 1873–2000, and in between a set of volumes on disability needs and an Oxford dictionary stood a dog-eared AA road map of Britain. Its spine read 1988. It would do. She snatched the book and secreted it between her overall's lapels.

Outside, the coast was clear except for Vera Lloyd, who spent her days trundling around the linoleum corridors, dressed in a faded pink trackie and carrying a framed photo of her daughter for all to see. Today was no different, except that a bright yellow daffodil was pinned lopsidedly to her chest. Frankie caught a whiff of its pungent smell, wondering if her own mother, wherever she was, was showing such devotion.

Her period pain kicked in again. Damn it. She wouldn't want to be shackled with that where she was going. Vera was looking her way.

'Hiya.' Frankie smiled at her. 'How's things?'

The ninety-year-old held out the already familiar face. Her nails around the black frame looked like claws.

'Saw you coming out of the office,' she smiled a black smile. 'Naughty Frankie.'

Frankie gulped. Vera wasn't dubbed 'Snitch' for nothing. Her party piece was greeting visitors to the home with the fire-drill and no-smoking policy and, if they stopped long enough, the terms and conditions of residency.

'I needed a pen, that's all.'

'Let's see it, then.'

Frankie groped in her overall pocket, praying her blue Lottery pen was still there. But no. She'd removed it for yesterday's laundry.

'Couldn't find one. Only pencils.'

Why was she having to explain herself to this old bat? She increased the distance between them both but Vera didn't wear trainers for nothing and her dinner breath was soon on Frankie's neck. The stink from that daffodil overpowering.

'I'll tell Mr Patel. Only *senior* staff's allowed in there.' The way she said 'senior' was a bloody cheek. She'd been at Briarfield more years than the nutritionist and nurse put together.

Suddenly without warning, the AA book began its downward slide against her nylon overall, too quickly for Frankie to stop it hitting the floor.

Vera pounced first with her free hand, lifting the book off the ground.

'You nicked this, then?' she asked.

'Course not. It's mine.'

Mrs Beavis's warning about keeping a clean record hit her brain.

'Where you off to, then? You leaving us?'

'I could never do that.' Even though the words choked in her throat.

'You might have to, once I get talking.' Frankie felt her fingers begin to itch just like they'd done when she'd watched Shannon pressed up against that silver pipework at the club.

A skinny finger separated the cover from the first page.

'But it's got Mr Patel's name at the front. Clear as day. J.S.V. Patel. There we go.'

Frankie backed away and headed for the dining room with Vera's voice still in her ears. There were implications looming, she realized, as she rejoined Daphne Cope who was struggling to get out of her chair.

'I'll see to her,' she informed Tammy who'd stopped sponging the plastic tablecloths, trying to beat her to it. 'She's mine, remember?'

'And I'm hers.' The old girl gripped Frankie's hand with fearsome strength. 'Till death us do part.'

Five minutes later, with Daphne installed by the TV in the Rose Lounge, Frankie had already made up her mind. OK, so her long-term planning had been brought forward, but the end goal was still clearly in sight. It was therefore important to keep cool, because Mr Patel was now summoning her from the depths of his swivel chair in his office. On the desk besides his pile of record sheets lay the AA book. Frankie's period pain dug into her gut. Yes, she'd been here too long. Become part of its dreary fabric, its unique smells.

'Mrs Lloyd says you've been impolite to her.' His bony fingers began flicking through the record sheets. 'I'm more than disturbed to hear this, Frances.'

He'd never used the name she preferred. It

94

would have given her too much.

'Impolite? Me? Mr Patel, I love her to bits. Wasn't I the only one who'd take her out for a kebab whenever she wanted? The only one who offered to clean her up after her "accident" last week?'

His turbaned head nodded. Whether in agreement or not, she couldn't tell.

'And how about that time she fell in the toilets? Who did first aid and got an ambulance? Who?'

'We must take all complaints very seriously, Frances. I know you have endured a sincerely troubling time these past two years, but I have a home to run and word soon gets round.'

Frankie's gaze drifted to a photo of the now-dead Walter, blu-tacked to a nearby notice-board. *He* wouldn't have landed her in any trouble. In any case, he'd passed away last summer, while sleeping in a deckchair outside the store room. A copy of her GNVQ certificate too, lay half-hidden by thank-you letters from ignorant relatives and others.

'Mrs Lloyd also claims you've been stealing.' Her boss's right palm rested on the book's cover. 'Who am I to believe? My employee or my client?'

Client? That was a joke. He loved saying the word; how cool it had sounded in Mrs Beavis's office before the reality of Briarfield had kicked in.

All at once the dull pain below her belt became a gnawing, ravenous torturer. Frankie reached out to grip the door-handle; inwardly counted to ten.

'I've got to get the medications ready. Carly's waiting,' she said finally. Two o'clock was the time for the after-dinner pills and she was the double-checker for this particular nurse. Another task to enhance her record. Until all this...

Suddenly, he spoke again, his brown eyes resting on her breasts.

'Just a warning, then, Frances. On this occasion, I'm prepared to give you the benefit of the doubt.'

'Thank you, Mr Patel. I'm sorry if I've given Mrs Lloyd any offence. I honestly didn't mean to...'

He nodded again, in full control. His twig-like fingers tapping on the AA book's cover. Fingers which held the purse string.

'Sorry is the easiest word in the universe.'

'You're a cow,' Frankie whispered, adding three more soluble Lipitrax tablets and a dash of tap water to the tiny glass she now held at Vera's lips. Carly Wilde was busy dosing the other residents, red-faced and in a hurry because her daughter was waiting to be sent home ill from Sunday school. But Vera kept her lips pursed, her hands clamped around the arms of her wheelchair as if for grim death.

'Open up, you.' Frankie tilted the milky liquid forward, and the chill of it made those obstinate lips part just enough to allow the rest into her gullet. 'Well done,' she said, beaming. She patted her arm, knowing that within an hour there would be breathing difficulties, hallucinations

96

and who knew what else. Nothing untoward for someone who'd been around on this planet too long.

'Can you finish the rest for me and enter the info in the book?' the stressed nurse pleaded, lifting her white cap from her head and stuffing it in her pocket. 'I can't leave my Sophie a moment longer.'

'No probs. I hope she'll be OK.' Frankie followed her for a few paces, tapped the exit code into the outer door and held it open for the nurse to pass through. In twenty minutes she herself would be out of there and on her way to where an important and necessary adventure beckoned.

'What name are you looking for, madam?' asked the man. It was the third call Frankie had made to Directory Enquiries.

'Cope. Gary Cope. He's at Loch Cottage, Kilfargan, Argyll.' She waited. 'Look, this has cost a quid so far. Can't you hurry up?'

'I'm afraid there's no number listed.'

'None at all?'

'No. Sorry.'

Frankie slapped the receiver back into its cradle in the phone booth, wondering how any-one could manage to survive in some remote place without a phone. Perhaps he had to lie low for some reason. Maybe like her he had some-thing to hide. Whatever, there was no time to lose. Two days had passed already since she'd left Briarfield, having checked Daphne Cope had no other cards or letters from him. Two days in which she'd tried everything to prove he was at least around. No point in going all that way if he wasn't. However, despite the cost and the risk, it was a chance she had to take.

Eleven

Finding his dying mother marooned in a sea of blood had been the worst day of his life, but it was a different fear which made Martin push his bike harder than necessary into the Worcester train at Paddington that Monday lunchtime in early June. Fear of Ed Thom and Den Tanner on his trail, wanting to silence him for ever. If they were caught, who'd be a key witness? Him.

So far, the case seemed to have gone cold with no recent sightings of the unlikely pair. Certainly there'd been nothing in the news during that grim month when he'd shacked up in Titmuss's dive in Bethnal Green. He prayed no news was good news.

He'd planned to head west anyway, but just seeing those small stations' names on the train departure board had spurred him into this rash decision. After all, where else could he go?

''Ere you,' growled a male voice from inside the next compartment as a baseball-capped head peered round at him. 'I'll have you know that machine of mine cost me a week's wages.'

'Sorry, OK?' And, having locked his Raleigh

Tourer's front wheel, Martin stalled. Should he risk more grief from the stranger or try the further compartment, which heaved with a scout party?

'In a hurry, then?' the man asked as Martin manoeuvred himself down the aisle between mostly full seats. The blast of voices on mobile phones almost drowned out the stranger's chitchat. 'Don't blame you, mind. Getting out of London, I mean. Where you off to?'

Another hesitation. Ed and Den were still on the loose. Still larger than life in his head. It was far too early to trust anyone.

'Barnfield. Small place near Worcester.' His once best mate Chris's parents used to live there, but they'd split up and he was now in Australia, working in IT. Another reason why the city had lost its charm. He'd been hard-up, lonely and in danger.

'Posh there,' the man opined. 'A house price hotspot.'

'Yeah, I know.'

'You bought summat, then?'

'A year ago. Small pad for weekends and holidays.' The lie sounded good and the man seemed satisfied, staring out of the murky window at the passing houses. To Martin, their back gardens were the real giveaways. Just like people, he thought, squeezing himself next to a teen reading a sci-fi magazine with an illustration of an empty coffin with its lid raised accompanying a short story called 'Afterlife'.

He thought of his mother and her untended grave. He'd not been back there since that

March evening. How could he? And each jobless day that had passed increased his guilt at this negligence. But if there really *was* an afterlife, perhaps she'd understand his predicament. As for his father, his presence was neither missed nor desired. However, a parole date had been set for the 1st of September. Something to look forward to, then.

The teen eyeballed him, closed the mag and then as if in spite, extracted a cheese-and-pickle sandwich from its wrapper. The smell made Martin's stomach lift from its moorings. He got up and searched for another empty seat and, as Slough came and went, placed himself alongside the guy with the fold-up bike.

'What's yer job, then?' the other asked, letting an oily forefinger probe both his nostrils without success. 'Let me see.' His wrinkled eyes looked him up and down. 'A plainclothes copper? Yeah. A rookie, I'd say.'

A blush hit the base of his neck. Part pride, part embarrassment. Was his deepest desire actually *visible*?

'I'm still looking, OK?'

'Fair enough. You got a mortgage?'

'Yup. Fixed interest for two years.' He didn't know why he was lying, but London life had taught him to be all things to all people. That way he was left alone. Except for what had happened on the 20th of January.

'Greedy bastards. And there's a fucking great penalty for paying it off early.'

'Too right.'

Once he'd started at Thom's he'd looked into

buying a studio in Hackney, but even with regular overtime and Sundays, the repayments would have crippled him. Never mind finding the deposit.

'I'm Rio Docherty, by the way,' his companion told him. 'Named after the Rio Grande for some reason.' He glanced at Martin as if expecting a similar revelation.

'Dave,' he lied, on the spur of the moment. 'Dave Webster.'

'OK, Dave. You want to make good money? Own your place outright quicker than you think?'

Crack was Martin's first thought. People-smuggling a close second. The news was full of it. Crime seemed to pay.

'Tell me more.' As Oxford's dreary outskirts came into view.

'Monroe's my boss. Developments all over the south and west. Wherever they can start digging.'

'Yeah. I've heard of them. For professional singles.'

'It's the future, my son.'

Those last two words sent a further pang of exclusion through his system and he was glad for the diversion of the ticket collector doggedly nudging his way down the aisle towards them. So far, no one had been caught out, at least until now.

'Couldn't miss this bloody train, mate,' Docherty explained to the man, still with no ticket or pass in evidence, but whipping out his wallet instead. Martin noticed it bulging with old notes. 'Got a job starting at four. Time's money for me. Never done this before, mind. Honest.'

Martin doubted if that was true, aware of all eyes on them doubtless hoping for some drama. Just when he wanted to be anonymous, one of the crowd. Docherty was handing over the price of his fare and telling the official to keep the change. However, his relief once the uniform had gone, was obvious.

'First time for everything,' his companion smiled, but it was clearly an effort. 'Anyway, as I was saying, Monroe's big and getting bigger. How would a grand a fortnight suit you?'

Martin gulped.

'Gross?'

'Net.'

'I mean it. No kidding. I'm a foreman with them. I should know.'

'What's the deal?'

'Cloud-hopping. Roofing, to you.'

Docherty pulled out a small card from inside his tracksuit pocket and passed it over to Martin. Sure enough, he was who he'd said, plus there were two groups of letters after his name and an HQ address in Worcester.

'Give 'em a call. Why don't you?'

'I've never been up a ladder in my life.'

'Ever heard of training?'

The man gathered his few things together, signalled that Charlbury was his stop then stood up, leaving a stale odour in his wake as he went to retrieve his bike.

'Might see you around,' he called back. 'And good luck.'

102

'Cheers.'

Martin watched him disappear through the station's exit door.

At Worcester's Forgate Street station, Martin made his way to the empty waiting room and punched in the number on his mobile. The receptionist who answered, confirmed that yes, a Mr Docherty was foreman on a site near Evesham and yes, there were vacancies for roofers in Malvern. She also needed an address.

'I'll have one pretty soon, if that's OK. Just left London.'

'It's my job to ask for one, Mr Webster, that's all. No problem.'

'I'll get back to you. Thanks.'

He decided that the city centre's Travel Lodge would do the trick at least until the end of the week, and when the brief exchange ended he prayed they'd have a vacancy. He needed some luck coming his way. His father, bankrupted by a damages claim from one of the injured in the Gerona crash, had lost the house in Buckingham Avenue. Lost everything. It was important, or so he'd said in his latest letter from the Verne, that his son understand how he felt.

More bollocks. He'd no wish to see him ever again.

He cycled west down the Butts towards the River Severn and followed signs for hotels. Once he was ensconced in a plain but comfortable room, he made himself an instant coffee in one of the tiny plastic cups on offer and stood at the window looking up at the summer sky

103

imagining he was up there already. Closer to heaven and Louisa Webb than he'd ever been before.

The letter, franked with the Monroe crest, arrived at the Travel Lodge next morning and contained a single-sided application from to be handed in before his interview at 3 p.m. He'd also need his birth certificate and driving licence as proof of age and domicile.

He dug around in his backpack for the birth certificate. Seeing his parents' names again, scripted in such vivid black ink, gave him a jolt and he quickly folded them out of sight. Next came a note from Charlene which had arrived at Juniper Road only three days before. She had got herself another job in a travel agent's. She ended with the news that Ed and Den had been sighted in Kennington. The reason she'd started dating Constable Dunn. For protection.

He returned the silvery card to its place, aware his fingers were trembling. Kennington wasn't so far away. However far he might remove himself from the Big Smoke, its greedy tentacles still managed to reach him.

David Webster, he wrote in the application form's first box, suddenly aware of the mismatch with his birth certificate.

Damn.

Just this once he'd have to abandon this new name and be what he'd been for the first eighteen years of his life. But could it really be called a life? It seemed like one of those self-assessment tick-box sheets his former Head of

Year at the college made everyone fill out. And those crosses which meant 'No, I haven't achieved this' far outweighed any ticks.

The sun lay behind him this time as he cycled along Deansway towards the cathedral, where defunct offices were being converted into lifestyle apartments. He could smell the wet cement, feel the layer of sand under his wheels and realized, almost as if by Divine intervention, that to actually help *make* something might give him a whole new take on life. OK, the construction industry would never have figured on either of his parents' wish-list for him but, in a perverse way, that made the idea more appealing. It made him pedal all the harder towards Monroe's white, glistening edifice.

The same girl who'd answered his first enquiry was in reception. Her name, Dora, set in a holder on her desk, struck him as unusual and not in the least representative of its owner, whose smooth honey-coloured fringe, huge earrings and an unmissable portion of bare midriff between her T-shirt and black trousers was the uniform of most Londoners her age.

'Martin Webb for three o'clock,' he reminded her and was rewarded by a flicker of curiosity – no more. Her white-tipped nails tapped almost musically on her keyboard as she asked him to take a seat. 'I told you and Mr Docherty I was Dave Webster,' he explained. 'Sorry.'

'We're all different people. All actors.' She smiled to herself. 'Don't worry about it. Anyway, Mr Pryor won't be long. Monday's his busiest day.'

But Martin, still puzzled by this insouciance, preferred to stand and study the clip-framed series of architects' drawings and watercolours arranged around the walls. Their skill in execution and the vision of twenty-first-century life they seemed to promise the young upwardly mobile left him open-mouthed and unaware that the HR manager was fast approaching from a door near the desk.

Within these pristine painted worlds there was clearly no crime, no stepping out of line or even anything as messy or inconvenient as being ill or dying. The figures portrayed were like Dora. Young, smooth-skinned, well fed, with clear life goals. Deeply alluring in every way.

'That's our Hill Springs development at Malvern,' said a man's voice behind him, making him spin round. 'Due to complete by Christmas. Smart pads, aren't they?'

'Amazing.'

A short dapper figure in a navy-blue suit offered his hand. Where Ed's had been cold and had lingered for too long, this was warm yet perfunctory. Meaning business.

'Nick Pryor,' he said. 'And you're Dave Webster. That right? Rio Docherty just phoned in.'

The girl was looking their way.

'No, he's Martin,' she raised her voice. 'Martin Webb.'

The man, like her, seemed unfazed by this contradiction. Took his application form from the envelope and skimmed the contents without a

106

comment.

'We've got a crisis, Mr Webb,' he began, walking towards the far end of the plate glass front window. 'Confidentially, Monroe are six months behind schedule already, even though good weather's been on our side. The council there have ordered us to complete all work by our promised date, or else.'

'What do you mean, or else?'

'We pay a penalty and it won't come cheap. Apart from that, it's loss of reputation. We need everyone on board we can get.' He focused on Martin the way a fox might size up a full chicken coop. 'So, Mr Webster, when can you start?'

The pause which followed was soon filled as the manager went on.

'We've our own rent-free accommodation on site plus canteen, catering for halal and chechita needs. As much as you can eat. There's also free protective clothing and – the icing on the cake – a month after starting work, you'll have a hundred free shares in our company included in your first wage packet.'

'Which is what, exactly?' Rio's boast now top priority.

'Two hundred a day. Cash in hand. That suit you?'

Martin could see Dora leaning forwards, listening. Docherty had been right about that one.

'What's the catch?'

Pryor looked offended. Checked his watch as if there wasn't a minute to lose.

'You won't be insured by us. That's up to you.'

'Now I get it. I break my back and that's me done for?'

'Three days' training'll do the trick.'

Like some old photograph left too long in the damp, the edges of this particular dream were beginning to darken and curl. Then he suddenly thought of Ed Thom and Den. If Charlene was right and they were on the run, he'd be with Monroe, in the safety of a group. 'Done,' he said.

He saw Dora smile.

'Tomorrow it is, then,' said Pryor, looking relieved. 'Follow me. Just some formalities such as your NI number, and then you'll be on your way,' he said. 'I'll make a call to get you picked up.'

He winked at the girl as Martin followed him into his office and, within ten minutes, with the afternoon sun hitting the blinds and making the already bright walls even brighter, Martin felt that after all the wrong turnings and cul-de-sacs, that life-sized tick-box was looking far more promising.

He waited outside the building for the surge of traffic to ease, then mounted his bike to return briefly to the hotel. Ahead lay an old guy on a tricycle, pedalling leisurely at nil miles per hour. Martin swore under his breath and slowed up behind him rather than swerve out and risk ending up a mess in the road. As he braked, he became aware of something much closer, boxing him into the kerb and causing his bike to grind to a halt with his legs still pedalling.

He saw a black saloon, its tinted windows

reflecting others beyond the pavement and then his own face. A mouth opened in surprise. Car horns now, as his heart froze and the car – a Merc – almost reluctantly left him and overtook the tricycle. Martin logged what he could of its mud-smeared number plate to memory then began to move again. The saloon he'd recognized went through the next set of lights on red and vanished round a left-hand bend.

Twelve

The grey morning did nothing to encourage Evelyn from the warmth of her bed now in the front lounge at the Gables, and once she'd struggled to the front door mat, she wished she'd not made the effort.

MONROE DEVELOPMENTS UK.
14th June 2002

Dear Mrs Scott,
   On behalf of the Managing Director of Monroe Developments UK, I'd like to thank you for your letter of the 1st June concerning our Spring Hills Development. He would like to reassure you that the few caveats from the County Council, relating to our planning application, have already

been fully addressed and he hopes that this
will allay any concerns you might have.
Yours sincerely,
Dora Tebbitt
pp Denzil Turner FRICS. M.D.

'Arrogant idiots!' Evelyn tore the letter up in
disgust. 'Don't they know how much influence I
have in this area?'

Then she saw her reflection as if for the first
time and realized with a hollow ache that as
she'd not attended any Scott's Rifles meetings or
any black-tie functions since early spring, this
so-called 'influence' had vanished. And when
had she last visited the hairdresser, the mani-
curist, the chiropodist? Questions too painful to
answer, because the truth was, these outings put
too much strain upon her degenerating joints.
Although Sean Brownlow never referred to her
appearance, she'd often seen a canny look in his
eyes when he'd not realized she was observing
him. And as for the balance owing from the sale
of her Jaguar, she'd still not had a sou. He was
also becoming a regular visitor to Teme House.
Was this altruism or something less noble?

As she binned the pieces of the letter, all her
anger transferred to this lavish development
aimed solely for the young. Brownlow had
brought her a copy of the plans showing one-
and two-bedroom apartments arranged with
restaurants and bars around an Olympic-sized
swimming pool. Why should the young have it
all? They were spoilt enough as it was.

Evelyn reached for her Zimmer frame, her

thoughts full of the injustices of life and how much longer she could continue living alone without the aid of a full-time live-in carer like Merle. As well as the chandeliers festooned with cobwebs and the curtains full of moth holes, the once-pristine skirting boards were also coated in a thick layer of grey dust.

At least according to her sister, Teme House was getting some attention and she herself seemed to have acclimatized to Kylie Watts' brusque ways. Perhaps for the time being it was best to let sleeping dogs lie, however coarse and lacking in manners they were. Thankfully, there'd been no more mention of Jenny, but that didn't mean the problem had entirely gone away, for the *Manchester Evening News* had recently printed a small paragraph about John Arthur Holt's suicide. She'd cut it out and added it to her small collection, wondering about the possible fallout from two deaths on the rest of that faraway family. But, like the 20th of February 1980, it was water under the bridge. Water equally unsuitable for bathing or drinking.

She returned to the lounge and was just about to settle herself in her tip-and-tilt chair when the hall telephone rang.

'Damnation.'

Her steps towards it seemed slower than ever, her ankles, despite her weight loss, creaking as if they might break at any moment.

Only three people ever called her now, Dr Khan, Sean Brownlow and the young Australian, and, as she progressed across the Persian carpet, she tried guessing which of these three it might be. However, the caller was Merle.

'Help,' murmured her sister. 'I'm so frightened.'

'No yer not,' interrupted the girl's voice. Sharp and angry. 'Stop giving me so much fuckin' grief.'

With only one hand gripping her frame, Evelyn felt unsteady. She also felt sick.

'How *dare* you use language like that in my sister's house, young woman. How dare you.'

'You want to try it here,' the girl protested. 'I'm doin' my best.'

Suddenly, Merle broke in again. Even more distressed.

'Help me please, Jenny. It's hell!'

Jenny again...

The emergency services weren't the answer. Nor was the doctor. And what could she do? There was only one solution, and she'd just have to bite the bullet. However, keeping sarcasm out of her voice was another matter.

'Surely you've called Sean?'

'There's no reply.'

'Wait there while I see what I can do. Promise me you'll do that?'

'I promise.'

Evelyn had no choice. And knowing that made it worse.

Sean Brownlow had just returned to his office to approve the latest engraving design for the firm's most expensive gun, and he promised her he'd go to Teme House immediately.

Why so eager? she wondered. What was his

112

ulterior motive?

An hour later, with still no answers, he was pacing around her lounge with a worried expression on his weather-beaten face. He'd arrived at Merle's to find Kylie Watts gone and he'd taken the initiative to find an alternative solution. It wasn't what Evelyn would have chosen, but then he had all the advantages – including deciding when she should see the company's accounts; when he delivered her shopping – and was making full use of them.

'Sunrise Court have agreed to take her in tonight,' he said. 'She can't be left unattended. She'll have a big en-suite room, three hot meals a day. They're coming to collect her at seven.'

Evelyn felt a chill invade her normally warm dressing gown. It was time to reassert herself.

'No. I want her at home.' She stood, with difficulty, to face him. 'Try Homely Helpers, anything. Please see what you can do.'

Brownlow moved towards the phone and after three calls, gave her the thumbs-up sign.

'Magic. They say they have the perfect placement, and –' he checked his watch – 'I'll be picking her up from the station in two hours' time.'

Thirteen

Frankie's immediate plans for Scotland had been derailed because of a lack of funds, and each day that passed without paid work increased her frustration. A gap of any kind was bad news for her CV, but going on the streets wasn't an option. Since John Arthur's secret visits to her bedroom, cocks had never been high on her agenda, and the risk of being up the duff even lower.

She'd left Briarfield at the end of April after Vera Lloyd suffered a migraine then a projectile-vomiting attack, with nurse Carly Wilde conveniently getting the blame. Her priority had been to take driving lessons – a late birthday present to herself – and buy a car capable of a return journey to Scotland. She'd finally settled for a white Fiesta costing just £220. Despite the rust round its sills and dents to the offside wheel arches, it was a good runner. Although both Homely Helpers and Amiable Aunts had enlisted her on their books, promising a placement as soon as possible, they'd nothing to offer her straight away, so she'd covered an auxiliary's maternity leave at Manchester Royal Infirmary for a month. Sluice-room work mostly, but the money was OK.

In the meantime she had to pray that Gary Cope's tongue hadn't started wagging and that her ongoing search on the parent front would soon deliver the jackpot.

Traces of John Arthur still seemed to linger in Dartmoor Road's airless box room, but Frankie wasn't deterred. She closed its door behind her and locked it, making sure the key's *click* didn't alert Beryl to the fact she was snooping.

She'd done this before – like the pigs – but never for long enough and had been lucky not to have been caught because the wino was one for suddenly leaving her bed without a by-your-leave. One minute she'd be propped up watching TV with a bottle to hand, the next, she'd be on the landing, an unsteady blue shadow keeping tabs on her. At least with the box-room door locked, she'd have a few moments to think up an excuse for being there.

Frankie made for the men's shirts crowded on to two iron coat hangers in the tacky open wardrobe at the end of John Arthur's bare camp bed. The white and blue ones on the far left labelled St Michael originated in Fallowfield for his accountancy job, when she'd first come on the scene as a second daughter. Some had a breast pocket, others not, but it was pockets she was interested in.

Then on to the cheaper sort in khaki, lumber-jack checks or short-sleeved polyester for week-ends in the garden. Her fingers frisked each one with a single goal in mind, to find any clue, however small, as to her origins. The jackets disappointed her, guarding only the odd betting slip or nicked beer mat, brown-ringed, floppy in her hand. Next came the shell suits in a rumpled heap on the wardrobe floor. Her eyes went straight to the navy-blue one he'd always worn on trips to her room. The pants were missing, just like his underwear. Most likely taken by the pigs. She could hear Beryl in the next room and immediately tensed up. If she was to find her rummaging among his things, then God knew what would happen.

She looked around the small room in that dull afternoon light, kept that way by a 1970s patterned blind covering the only window. She thought files, paperwork. He must have stuff like that *some*where and when she'd exhausted all his other pockets, she lay down on the fag-burned carpet and reached under the bed.

Polythene, she could tell. Warm, stretched tight over something she couldn't quite determine. She pulled once, then again, until the bulky package began to move her way.

Her pulse tripped in her neck, her mouth suddenly dry as the object moved closer. Like the eager kid she'd always been on Christmas Day, watching Shannon unwrap the biggest and best presents, yet always hoping she'd get the same. Frankie finally hauled the black bundle free and let out a gasp. For on the top lay a label marked J.A.H. PRIVATE in red felt-tip.

Her thumbnail made the incision and soon she realized that in this higgledy-piggledy mess lay the evidence of his life. Birth certificate, school reports, visitors' passports for those Channel booze trips – his face grizzled even at thirty-eight. The year she'd arrived. There was also, unexpectedly, a will he'd made in better days, which left everything to Beryl unless she predeceased both daughters. Frankie frowned to herself, wondering when and how to ask the old bat what her plans were. And then she noticed another envelope. Tatty around its edges, the postmark long gone, it almost seemed to force itself into her hand. Its faintly typed front – PRIVATE AND CONFIDENTIAL, MR & MRS J A HOLT – made her catch her breath. She sensed something important within its flimsy paper walls.

'Need some more fags, you,' said Beryl sitting up in bed as Frankie rifled through her purse for cash, aware of that envelope burning a hole in her pocket. 'And a pack of Andrex. Extra-soft, mind. And a birthday card.'

Frankie stalled, clipped the purse shut and returned it to her mother's bag.

'Who for?' she asked, stuffing the tenner she'd found in with the envelope.

'You forgotten tomorrow?'

Shit.

'No. Course not.' She went over and stroked the mottled arm which protruded from the night-dress. 'There's not a day goes by that I don't think of her. She was beautiful, your Shannon. Twenty-seven she'd be.'

Beryl shook a fag out of her now empty packet, lit up and eyed Frankie through the first haze of smoke.

'Why I can't go in her bedroom ever again. I

117

mean, it makes sense that the air she breathed is still in there. I'll never forgive that man of mine for what he did to her. I should have seen the warning signs. Couldn't keep his hands off her, could he? "My darling this, my darling that..." '

Her nose wrinkled up, her greying eyebrows met in an unbroken line. Blobs of dried egg yolk embellished the buttons down the front of her nightdress, which hadn't been changed for weeks.

That was a revelation. Frankie had never noticed anything untoward between them. 'Look what he did to *me*, then,' she added, smoothing the duvet's top edge down as she'd done so automatically at Briarfield. No way would she repeat that Shannon had called *her* a slut. That could be seen as a motive. 'Am I supposed to forget that?'

But any sympathy Beryl had was for herself alone.

'I remember once when we went to Southport that time,' she prattled on. 'You were making a right pest of yourself, hitting Shannon with your spade. He was the one who kissed her better, carried her on his shoulders and changed her out of her swimming costume when she got sunburn. The dirty bastard. Now I don't know where she is. If she's even alive or dead. There's no grave to look after. No bloody nothing!'

She repositioned herself against the pillow, running her tongue over her lips as Frankie edged away to close the curtains, do the errand and check out that envelope. Come the morning she'd be on the M61 with a single room booked

118

in Inverary for the night.

'Right then, need anything else?' she asked.

But the drunk didn't reply. Too far gone.

As Frankie slung her bag over her arm, poised to leave the house, the hall telephone began to ring. Why she jumped, she didn't know. These days it was usually social services quibbling over invalidity payments.

This time it was neither. Instead, a brisk female voice she should have remembered.

'Yes? Who is it?'

'Frankie?'

'Yup.'

'WPC Avril Pilkington here. Just making a routine call to see if all's well. I've left a message on your mobile.'

The police liaison officer. Too fucking keen as usual. Still, she knew how to play it. Miss Charm School herself. Nevertheless, it seemed to her that the Saturday traffic outside had suddenly vanished, leaving a silent chill.

'It's really cool of you to bother,' she smiled to affect her voice. 'Mum and I are really grateful and yes, things are pretty much the same here. We get our bad days, mind. But that's to be expected, I suppose.'

'I'd heard you left Briarfield at the end of April,' the officer cut in as if Frankie hadn't said anything. 'Everyone was surprised at that. Being so sudden, I mean.'

Frankie steadied herself against the banisters. If this fat frizzy-haired bitch was hoping for a life story, she would be disappointed.

'I suppose I just made a snap decision, going

in on the bus that last morning. I had done a few years there...'

'I know that, Frankie. But old people don't like change. It frightens them. They feel vulnerable, insecure.'

'OK, I get the drift.' She nearly added, what about *me?*

Up to now none of the pigs knew she was bothered who her real mother was. It was bad enough having to explain away Ellie. That she'd been bathing her in the washing-up bowl when the cops had arrived. All her baby things out for everyone to see. Zinc and castor-oil cream. Nappies, the works.

'I should never have left, is that it?' she challenged sweetly. 'I mean, even you kept going for jobs. I remember you telling me.'

A little laugh, which didn't quite work.

'Of course not. But Mr Patel...'

'What about him?' She was too sharp, too jumpy; she knew. 'What's he been saying?'

'That you could have said goodbye.'

As dusk fell outside, Frankie finished her packing, then realized she'd forgotten Ellie. No way could she abandon her, especially after what Beryl had done to Lila. That behaviour was for the Scotts of this world. Nor could she stuff her into her shoulder bag. She'd be sure to suffocate on such a long journey. And then inspiration struck. She remembered seeing an old car seat at the back of the coal hole, heaped on top of a broken chair, stained striplights and the rest. Within ten minutes, it was at least clean, even though rust had corroded the fittings underneath. Ellie fitted it perfectly.

Before closing the smart tartan suitcase bought specially from Woolies, she made a final check that everything was in order. First, at the very bottom of it lay a kitchen knife with a five-inch blade from Briarfield. Next, her *Guide to Argyll* together with a small dictionary of Scottish dialect, then three changes of clothing plus a dark green anorak she wouldn't be seen dead in around Openshaw. She'd also added Walter's war medals, wrapped in value kitchen towel and tucked away amongst her briefs. So far, these mementos seemed to have brought her the luck she needed. She zipped up the case and returned with it to the crowded coal hole, before helping Beryl downstairs with whatever tea she could rustle up.

She'd conveniently swallowed her lie about having to go to Maidenhead for more training in the care of the elderly. She reassured her she'd be back on Tuesday.

'You've got a spring in your step,' slurred Beryl over her cheese on toast.

'It's not a crime.'

Beryl squinted at her. A blob of cheese lodged in the corner of her mouth.

'You got yourself a man? That it?'

Frankie blushed. In her dreams...

'Give over, Mum. Round here?'

'Our Shannon won't ever get married now. Nor have kids.'

'You don't know. She may have taken a plane to Australia. She was always going on about the

121

Great Barrier Reef. People escape all the time.'

Beryl shook her head, unconvinced.

'Why didn't she ever collect her bag, then?'

'Perhaps she wanted a clean break. Perhaps leaving it behind was a symbolic gesture.'

Frankie's eyes roamed from the full cork board by the fridge to the array of other photos stuck to the half-tiled walls. Shannon might not be walking down any aisle, but here, she was everywhere. The other rooms were the same. Avril Pilkington had taken Frankie to one side and said, 'That's what grief does. It drives you over the edge. Not for ever maybe, but a while at least.'

'Just think what her kids would have looked like. Blonde with big grey eyes,' said Beryl.

'I'll have them for her,' Frankie blurted out, then hated herself. 'You know what I mean...'

Beryl appraised her, from her blonde cropped head to her fluffy slippers. Then shook her head.

'Like you said, my Shannon was beautiful.'

'So what am I? Go on, you've never said. All these years I've stopped here, helping you out.'

She waited, ever hopeful, while Beryl drained the last of her vodka and lime in one gulp. Aware that if the right words came out, she might even forgive her killing Lila and stay put. Go back to caring. Find a guy in town, maybe. Save for a deposit on a two-bed terrace in Westmoreland Road. Frankie saw those wet lips in close up as they began to move. Then a hint of lizard tongue behind yellowed teeth. She waited for the all-important verdict and when it came, was like a chainsaw to a spindly pine tree. A bitter, final

122

blow which drove her from the kitchen, up the stairs two at a time and into the front bedroom which was still hers, to tear up the contents of that envelope and flush them down the toilet. Manchester social services confirming Mr and Mrs Holt as suitable adoptive parents.

'Never one of us, that's for sure' drummed in her brain as she left Openshaw and headed towards the M61 which, the road map promised, would link up with the M6 south of Preston.

'Fuck you,' she muttered, slotting a Beach Boys tape into the dashboard.

She felt secure in her hatchback, cocooned from the world which had hurt her so much, yet all the same, fired up to tackle the last but one obstacle to the kind of lifestyle she'd dreamed of. A glass-topped dining table, an American fridge, a steel-and-chrome kitchen with metallic blinds to match.

At Stafford Services, she filled the tank and, ignoring the Father's Day cards which Beryl always made her buy for John Arthur, paid for a Princess on Board sticker. Then, having left Ellie in the car seat, she treated herself to a Coke and fries, watching all the low-life troop in and out. The grossest people she'd ever seen. John Arthur and Beryl multiplied to infinity. After her snack, she returned to her car, kissed Ellie on her forehead and set off once more into the darkness.

'What's your wee bairn's name, then?' asked the middle-aged woman with bags under both eyes as Frankie let her gear slide from her grasp by the Crachan Hotel's reception desk.

'Beth,' she lied. Glad she'd remembered to remove her wristband.

'She's a braw bonny lass, that's for sure.'

Frankie wished the stranger would mind her own business, all too aware of her beady eyes on her signing in as Denise Shaw from Willow Way, Darlington. The other names were mostly Scottish. McTavish, MacCulloch. From places with names she'd never heard of.

'Just the one night or what's left of it?' asked the woman as if Frankie hadn't already said.

She nodded then followed the wobbly hips out of the hall and along a red-carpeted corridor where sounds of snoring rose and fell like the water just a few metres away from the front entrance. The woman inserted the key to room four and pushed the door open into darkness.

'There we are. Nice and cosy with your own facilities. Breakfast's from eight until nine thirty.'

Frankie was left alone to find the nearest light switch and any kind of heater to take away the room's damp chill. At least 358 Dartmoor Road was warm. She didn't remember much after that: when the seagulls' shrieks outside the window woke her up five hours later, she realized she'd crashed out fully dressed.

'Where are you heading, then?' asked the woman's husband the next morning, as he added her payment to the till.

'Bencarrick.'

'Weather's been bad there. Best to fill up at the

garage next door before you go.'

'I will, thanks,' she said. 'But I don't care if it pours. It's so beautiful here.'

'So they say.'

Puzzling over his last remark, she made her way outside into the blinding brightness of that mid-June morning and, having stuffed the hotel's freebie soap and shampoo into her bag, stood for a moment, eyes shut, listening to the rhythms of that wide sheet of water, feeling the fresh air on her face. It was spoilt by her knowledge it was Shannon's birthday, and the guy who filled her tank being too nosy by half. He kept staring at Ellie. Maybe he was a pamper-sniffer. Whatever, she was glad to get away.

Within half an hour she'd entered yet another world of ox-blood mountains halved or quartered by slabs of forestry the same colour as her cagoule, down whose sides ran cascades of foaming water which drained away under the road.

She glanced at Ellie, knowing she was enjoying herself, and just then, in that split second before the clouds began to fill the sky, she felt a surge of pure happiness. A fierce energy for the last stage of her mission.

Kilfargan ten miles. It sounded so easy from where she was, on a properly made-up road with a reassuring white line down the middle. Her adrenalin rose as the Fiesta took her north. Despite the darkening day and the sudden rain hitting the windscreen, this was still better than home. However, once she'd glimpsed what lay beyond the smaller Kilfargan sign, she began to wonder.

With wipers on full, she'd just stopped to consult the map again when she spotted a shambling figure in a fluorescent cagoule emerge from the broken hedgerow on the left. The likeness to John Arthur made her heart slow. It wasn't possible, surely? She must be going mad. Yet there were those same small-mammal eyes, that mouth which had been where no one else had been before. Even the tilt of that square greying head and the way his hands were curled into fists, just like whenever she'd threatened to tell.

She revved up, feeling an acid attack in her throat. It was him. Him. She was sure of it. But how could that be? Beryl had tipped his ashes into the first wheelie bin she'd found on the way back from the crematorium. The empty plastic screw-top jar into the second.

As she lurched forward, his shape loomed large and yellow in front of the car.

'You fucking idiot!' she shrieked and braked, expecting a massive impact. But there was none. Ellie and her car seat toppled to the floor as the human obstruction vanished.

'Oh my God!'

Frankie checked her mirrors but that vivid presence was nowhere to be seen. If he'd dodged the car, she thought, then where the fuck was he? Then she noticed Ellie lying upside down on the floor.

'Poor baby.' She repositioned her daughter on the passenger seat and, having kissed her better and checked for any signs of bruising, moved off warily, keeping a nervous lookout.

Still unsettled, she struggled along the track, whose bare verges on the right revealed the biggest expanse of water she'd ever seen. Frankie shivered, still chilled from the previous night. She moved into top gear not caring that the car was rocked from side to side by the potholes. Then she checked her watch. Only 10 a.m. But already it seemed more like dusk. Sky, land and water all a grey blur, broken only by the odd block of white bungalows and hand-painted signs for B&Bs. Pine trunks, severed from their roots, lay heaped into vast piles along the track. She realized there was no room for anything oncoming to pass or for her to turn round if need be. She was trapped.

Despite her rising panic, she pressed on, encouraged by Ellie's little smile. Kilfargan was surely close by now, yet her milometer told quite a different story. She'd covered just three miles, and for the first time since crossing the border into Scotland she hesitated, letting the car slow right down. Was this all really worth it?

'Ellie?' she asked her tiny companion. 'What do we do?'

'Think about me,' the baby seemed to whisper and visions of a spacious nursery adorned with coloured mobiles came to mind. The kind of place she'd never had. Where money could buy the best of everything. After all, wasn't her mother on the best agencies' lists? So, she reasoned, feeling calmer now, why should this moment of doubt put it all at risk?

However, just as she'd moved off and changed

up a gear, the car bumped to a stop against something far more solid than the last interruption. This time she really was stuck as the wipers' frenzy cleared away enough rain to reveal a pair of huge black eyes staring in at her.

Fuck.

Then she spotted the stag's antlers reaching out from each side of its head as far as she could see. A quick press on the horn to shift the thing brought a clash of bone on glass and a hoarse cry from her lips. She'd planned to be back in Openshaw that night. Now look. She thought of that hotel owner's odd remark. Perhaps he'd been right, and if she'd been travelling any faster she and Ellie would have been toast.

Five long minutes later, the beast leapt away up the bank and into a plantation of moss-covered trees. Beech, oak and hazel. She'd more than done her homework. Luckily, the windscreen was still intact and Ellie was safe, but she wondered what else could possibly be in store.

Loch Cottage seemed at first no more than a grey rock half embedded in a shingle bank at the loch's side, and from her position in the woods behind it Frankie spotted a thin line of smoke leaving the one chimney and a few limp items hanging from a makeshift washing line. Pants or briefs she couldn't tell, and T-shirts were unisex anyway. She crouched behind a low moss-covered wall which presumably marked out where the so-called garden ended and the wilderness around it began.

She'd left Ellie sleeping in the Fiesta, having

parked out of sight in a dense copse. Now she waited and listened for the slightest clue as to who might be around. She heard the irregular clank of church bells and realized it was Sunday. A day of rest for some, but not her.

Then she noticed that neither electricity nor phone seemed to be connected to this bothy – a word she'd seen in her little dialect book, meaning dwelling. So, how did Daphne Cope's grandson get by here in 2002? How?

Rustling noises drew her attention. She stiffened in fear, her right hand already on alert in her cagoule pocket, as a small mongrel the colour of cream-of-chicken soup appeared and began sniffing around her crotch, then her fingers as if they promised a titbit. She'd be done for if he barked. She slipped on a pair of her latex gloves; their brand name, Performance, always made her smile.

'Dumb boy,' she coaxed as her left hand seized a clump of fur between his shoulder blades and her right delivered her weapon to a soft, yielding home.

'Donny?' called a young man's voice from the loch side of the cottage. 'C'm 'ere. Rabbits, you idiot. Go get 'em.'

No more rabbits for Donny, thought Frankie, much closer now, her woollen-hatted head pressed against the rear wall's wet stones. Her pulse felt oddly slow, as if this weird place, with its sea of silent water which seemed to stretch to the edge of the world, was somehow dulling her metabolism.

Suddenly, the voice's owner, wearing jeans and a baggy black sweater, appeared walking unsteadily to the wall and back. Could this be Gary? All she knew was he resembled his father, whoever *he* was. She recalled those other clubbers shuffling alone on Gee's raised decking and guessed her instinct was right. If this *was* him, then judging by his walk he was probably still a space cadet and liable to say things unaware of their importance. At least here, in all this isolation, who else could he have blabbed to?

She'd worked out how best to approach him, but right now, her certainties ebbed away like the apparition and the stag, and she knew then there was more to Loch Cottage than those who simply ate, shagged and slept there.

Another hesitation, longer than the first in which to remind herself of that call back from Homely Helpers quoting her earnings. Twice she'd asked the caller to repeat it because seven hundred pounds a week was a tenth more than Mrs Beavis's estimate. Mrs Beavis and her beads. The shared cup of tea. She had died of breast cancer less than a month ago and Frankie had gone to her funeral and cried.

She slipped her latex-covered fingers into her normal grey knitted gloves and fixed a smile on her face.

'Hi. I'm Mary Campbell,' she announced to the guy at the cottage door. Her accent deliberately more Dumfries than Argyll. 'Sorry to bother you, but I've got to get to Strachbrae by tonight or else.'

'Oh, yeah?' His deep-set brown eyes checked her out before he stepped back a few paces into the gloomy hallway. She couldn't tell if his pupils were dilated or not. 'Why that place? It's up a bloody bare mountain.' His Lancashire accent as pronounced as hers had once been.

'I'm part of a Glasgow University field trip, but the directions they gave me were crap.' She'd learnt all about field trips from Shannon. Sex being the main activity. Besides, he wouldn't be doing any checking up on her story. 'I'd have bought a map if I'd known.'

He scratched that gelled head which his granny had said was wavy like his dad's. And then she noticed the silver ring on his left thumb. He wasn't bad looking, but now she could see his pupils giving him away.

'Could take a butcher's if you like.'

'Brilliant. Thanks.'

'I'm Gary, by the way. Gary Cope.'

Great. Now she knew.

'You don't sound Scottish.'

'My partner has gone to see her old girl over in Glasgow for the day.'

'Partner?'

'Yeah. Wouldn't live here on me own, would I?'

Stupid Daphne Cope hadn't mentioned anything about a fucking partner. What did the slag know? She hesitated before following his lurching progress to a poky back room. At least if she was out for the day, time wasn't a problem.

She noticed his butt crack showing under his jumper's hem; viewed his pale bare feet as he

131

rummaged in a cardboard box under the tiny window. Still no sign of any mobile phone.

'You didn't see my dog anywhere, did you?' he asked without looking up. 'Donny, he's called. Half Westie, half Cairn.'

'No, sorry, but I'll keep an eye out on my way back.'

He finally pulled out a badly folded Ordnance Survey map from the box and spread it out over the back of the nearest armchair. She noticed his fingers juddering as they smoothed out the creases.

'You got wheels?'

'No. Got dropped off by a sawmills lorry.'

'Take a pew.' He indicated the bottom stair where a dog's blue rubber bone lay in the corner, and within seconds she was seated next to him on the bare wood, thigh to thigh, smelling his scent, part fish, part wood smoke. Waiting her chance.

'I've got a better idea,' she said. 'Let's go outside where there's more light.'

'Good thinking. Need to get a new bulb sorted before Maddy gets back.'

'That her name?'

'Yeah. Short for Madeleine.'

'Nice.' But Ellie was better.

Outside he glanced around for somewhere to park himself.

'How about that.' She pointed at the nearby rock which bore the cottage's name in white-painted letters. There was also room for her to sit alongside him and, like the real gentleman he was, he wiped its surface dry with his sweater's sleeve.

'Right. Now then, Strachbrae.' He rested a trembling index finger upon a fine brown contour line which surrounded Kilfargan and followed it round and round until the peak of over three thousand feet was reached. She found this action strangely arousing but tried to stay focused. 'See that,' he said. 'You'll definitely need a four-by-four. Ever thought of hiring one?'

'I could, I suppose, but just show me the easiest way up to it. Then I'll be gone.'

'Best turn off there. See the track off that B-road?' He looked up at her expectantly.

She nodded, letting him lose himself in that complex of paths and byways where the rural dead lie in unmarked graves and buzzards spin slow circles in the sky, until the moment was right. Her still-gloved hand slipped sweetly into her pocket to shed its woollen skin and finally touched cold hard steel.

Fourteen

Martin wished with every aching bone in his body that he'd ignored that sad git on the Paddington train. Wished he could stop being so gullible. His job was knackering, the food shite.

'Hey, is that you?' A bright female voice made him spin round and drop the book on the floor. 'Martin Webb, isn't it?' She gave him a wicked grin. 'Or do you prefer Dave Webster?'

He bent to pick up the paperback under the secondhand bookshop manageress's watchful eye, but when he straightened, saw someone else looking at him. Dora Tebbitt, not dressed as he remembered, but in oddly old-fashioned clothes. Was she here as part of her job with Monroe or just keeping tabs on him?

'Martin Webb, OK? Anyway, how you doing?'

'Fine.' She indicated beyond the shop where the theatre's white walls dazzled in the sunlight. 'I'd just nipped out of a dress rehearsal there, and when I glanced in this shop window, I knew it was you.'

'And you look like something out of Chekhov.'

'Clever you.' She smiled. 'I'm playing Nina, from *The Seagull*, here at the local theatre. She's a woman driven to act. To be the best. However, in this business – ' she smiled self-deprecatingly – 'some are more equal than others.'

Martin frowned. This wasn't making sense.

'But what about Monroe? I thought you were full-time?'

'I was, but I'd had enough. Couldn't even bear to work out my notice. Seeing you make that new start was the shove I needed. Made me realize that if I didn't try and fulfil my dream, I'd grow to be a ratty old woman.'

'You old? Never.' His words slipped out before he could stop them. But it was true. He could never imagine her wrinkling up like his own mother, or her eyes ever losing their lustre.

She blushed under her pale make-up. 'It was

134

hard, juggling work and the stage. You see, I've been doing amateur dramatics for ages, then this chance came up. We're a touring company, which should be cool.'

'I guess it will be.' But he wasn't sure for whom.

She faced him with her clear grey-green eyes, then unexpectedly brushed brick dust from his donkey-jacket shoulders. 'How's *your* job going? Or daren't I ask?'

'No, don't.'

'Bad as that, is it?'

'Worse, if you must know.'

'Hell, I'm sorry. Look, how about we meet up – say eight tonight at the Red Pheasant, Belle Vue Terrace. Can catch up properly then.'

'You sure?'

'Course.'

'Good luck with your rehearsal.'

Dora bustled from the shop, a grey blur as she dodged the traffic then vanished out of sight. Feeling strangely bereft, Martin paid for the book, unlocked his bike and headed off along the terrace of shops. The pub she'd mentioned seemed a good bet, like all the other pristine premises including Rizio's Italian Restaurant, a framing gallery promoting Edward Elgar prints and Bean Feast, a health-food shop.

He was sweating under his working clothes, his uneven pedalling taking him past the busy sunlit pavements, as if torn between the next dreaded shift with his tricky co-workers and thoughts of being with Dora in six and a half hours. He picked up speed not because he'd made a decision, but because he'd suddenly remembered how vulnerable he was, should his London associates sniff his scent.

He glanced round for any sign of that C-class Merc, but a massive chrome-decked Hummer with a Californian plate was in the way, travelling too fast, taking his meagre space on the tarmac. He swerved into the kerbstone and let it pass, smothering him in a plume of blue smoke.

'You all right, sir?' asked a nearby news vendor pouring out a mug of tea from his flask.

'Fine, thanks.'

The man slurped his tea while Martin checked his front tyre. Then something else caught his eye. Newspaper headline impossible to ignore: REMAINS OF YOUNG MAN FOUND IN SCOTTISH LOCH.

He realized that whoever the poor sod had been, *he* was still alive and, as he moved away, resolved to do everything in his power to stay that way.

In the gloom of an ancient holloway, where specks of sunlight lay like gold coins on the ground, Martin checked his speedometer – one more mile to go – then flicked to a higher gear. Just then, and whether it was a trick of the light, he was never to know, a grey-haired woman seemed to be standing stock-still on the narrow kerbside as if waiting for him to slow down and stop for her. There was something familiar about the bone structure; the way she fixed on him with that intensely searching look, which made him waver.

'Mum...?'

But then a car's horn, a squeal of brakes blasted his brain, followed by the driver's jerking V sign as a Passat just like hers had sped by. Martin blinked, righted himself and, when he looked again, this person so uncannily like his mother had gone. Still shaken and confused by this incident, he turned into the site and waited for the automatic barrier to creak open and allow him in.

'You're fuckin' late,' accused the yellow-hatted foreman once he'd skidded to a halt by the office Portakabin. 'Next time, I'll dock your pay.'

'OK. Keep your hair on.' Then Martin remembered that the man was bald.

'Flash git,' his boss muttered, moving away to where a clutch of Turkish brickies were arguing with three Ugandans. It had taken him two days to work out the peculiar dynamics of the place. Tension had built the night of the England v. Brazil match and had denied him the sleep he'd craved. In the morning, it hadn't been just the verbal wounds that smouldered. A Ukrainian lad had flung a scaffolding plank at a guy from Karachi, accusing him and his kind of plotting WWIII. The foreman had pulled him away, screaming. Kept him in isolation until the lunch break. He should have called the cops, but Martin knew that was wishing for the moon. So much for security.

He opened his locker, pressed his hard hat down on his head, replaced his trainers with boots and slipped on his gloves, still warm from forty minutes ago. As he stepped out into the sunshine, he felt an overpowering feeling of entrapment. Directly in front of him, beyond the cranes, loomed the mighty Midsummer Hill, bearing an intaglio of tracks through wooded plantations and rocky bracken banks almost up to the sky. Perhaps this was another reason for the unrest at Hill Springs. Like him, the workmen were used to the open-plan of level streets, the reassuring permanence of concrete, while here, nature seemed to dominate.

He promised himself that one day soon he'd take his bike and explore what so far he'd only seen on maps, breathe the clean sharp air blowing in from the west. But right now, he had to count out the exact number of roof tiles needed for Phase One, the leisure centre, and just as he was telling one of the crane drivers where to position them, his mobile rang. Without guessing who it might be, he clamped it to his ear.

'Yes?'

'Martin Webb?' The surname represented London. This was now. 'Just to say we know where you are. Don't think this pretty countryside will hide you.'

'Who the fuck are you?' But did he really need to ask? He'd know that voice anywhere ... He felt fear and anger boil up inside his head. Saw the foreman make a move his way.

He turned to yell into his phone. 'Leave me alone, Ed Thom. OK?'

'Wish we could, my friend. Just a warning, eh?

In case you think of trotting to the fuzz.'

The foreman was closer now as Martin ended the call, his throat caked with dust. His tongue not working. No time to check the number.

'You deaf, squire?' demanded his boss. 'We're not a fuckin' charity here. You'll be twenty quid down on Friday if you're not up and at it in ten seconds.'

An hour later the breeze delivered a fresh bolus of debris dust which not only hit his eyes but lodged in his ears, making him deaf to the hum of distant voices growing louder.

A moment's vertigo, ending with the foreman's shrill whistle and his bellowed order. 'Everyone, get down. Over here, now!'

Martin looked in the direction of the command and saw how the site barrier was down as a horde of people swarmed on to the rutted earth twenty feet below him, waving an array of placards as their shouts filled the air like random gunfire.

'Hill Springs out! Build homes for the elderly and the local poor!' Then he heard something else. The dull thud of missiles connecting with the leisure centre's newly built walls; the intermittent crack of breaking glass. If he went down now, he'd be a target too. Shaming cowardice kept him in place. What little training he'd had that Monday morning told him how to crouch in a ball and keep his head covered in the event of a link failure in the scaffolding. Now he did just that, and prayed things would soon cool down.

However, the hubbub increased and the mix of panic and hate rose to meet even his protected ears. Just one sneaked glimpse was enough to see his fellow workers legging it over a wire fence into an overgrown graveyard next door. When he looked again, they'd disappeared altogether amongst the yews and the stone population of angels and Virgin Marys.

It was then he spotted a small group of black-clad figures in hot pursuit, their swastikas and KEEP BRITAIN BRITISH signs bristling above their heads.

'Illegals out! Keep the jobs for *our* boys!' rang the chants as the ambush continued as the protest was taken over. A flung stone just missed his legs. Above the din, came the wail of police cars and the main body of protestors, including an elderly woman in a wheelchair, was fanning away from the development like ants in the face of boiling water. The way his mother used to keep the paths and patio clear during the summer months.

Why would he stay here? Apart from Dora, who'd probably got a boyfriend anyway, there was little reason. He uncurled himself and looked down once more at the scene below. The police cars' blue lights twirled in opposite directions beyond the high wall which bordered the main road. Stopping, starting, the cops were obviously trying to find names to fill their notebooks. Is that what he'd be doing now if his father hadn't had one too many?

What would *he* do once this job and its accommodation came to an end? With a bankrupt for a father and no assets apart from his precious bike, how would he be able to rent, let alone buy anything in this area? He'd been a dickhead to come here at all.

'Don't turn round, Mr Webb. Just do as I say.'

The smell of aftershave reached his clogged-up nose. Boss, he knew that much. Uncool, but appropriate. Now it was more than that. It signified the end of his life.

A blow landed in his lower back and a sick pain tore around his body. He fell sideways against the wall, half of him stopping up the gap between it and the sagging plank. In that moment he raised himself and turned to face his tormentor, but the grey pinched face wasn't Ed's but Den's. The 'mate' who'd helped find his room in Vauxhall. Who had loaned him fifty quid till his first wage packet. But Den was a user. He'd known that all along. Now someone was using *him*.

'Ed chickened out, then?' Martin taunted, feeling nauseous from that kick.

'He's waiting. So move.'

'After you.' And with that he lashed out with his right foot. Heard the crack of bone as his steel-capped boot connected with his assailant's shin. He saw him topple from the plank and dangle above the deserted site.

'Help, you bastard!' Den moaned.

'Where's Ed?' He was tempted to stamp on those black-gloved hands as well. Make them loosen their grip on the linking bolts and watch him drop to his death. But something stopped him. The sight of a diminutive female figure in a grey coat running through the site entrance, then weaving her way between the giant machinery.

Dora. What the hell was she doing here? She came to a stop below him and looked up. Her hand instantly covered her mouth.

'Get some of those cops here!' he yelled at her. 'Quick!'

Her office training had made her do just that and while he knelt down to prevent Den Tanner from falling to his death, a blue-and-yellow-chequered car swerved into the dustbowl and screamed to a halt.

'So, they caught him, then?' Dora looked at Martin over the edge of her wineglass later on in the Red Pheasant's busy bar.

'Yep. And his minder.'

Dora raised her glass to meet his half-full tankard of Fosters.

'Here's to peace at last.'

'To peace.' But any reciprocal smile was missing, for the afternoon's events had left him shaken, with the prospect of yet another trip to the cop shop tomorrow for an ID parade and a further statement. But who was to say his pursuers wouldn't try to silence him again? They'd done it once, hadn't they? 'You were brilliant back there,' he told her.

'What's the matter, Martin?' she said, frowning.

'Nothing. How did rehearsals go?'

'Never mind that.' She leaned forwards, her hair shining under the overhead light. 'Look, what's eating you? What is it you *really* want to do? I guessed something was wrong the minute I set eyes on you.'

Her frankness surprised him. He wasn't used to anyone – let alone a girl – express any concern about him. Ria had been the only one, and he'd almost forgotten what she looked like.

'D'you *really* want to know?'

'Of course. Being happy and doing something you enjoy isn't a sin. Lord knows I had enough of that from my lot. Dad expected me to join the business he'd started – hire cars, if you please – while Mum...' She pulled a battered pack of Churchills from her dungarees pocket, offered him one, then when he declined, lit up.

'Go on.' He watched the first smoke veil her face, making her blink.

'She booked me on this course for organizing conferences. Just before my A-levels. Big incentive, right? No wonder I funked it all, and then I left home to make my own way.'

'Do you see much of them now?'

Dora nodded then took another long drag on her cigarette.

'No way am I a hard nut. Dad's not too well and Mum's got her work cut out to keep things going. So, I try and call in to see them once a week. The thing is –' her eyes suddenly seemed to glisten – 'they're both coming to see my first performance in three weeks' time. Then, after ten days' run here, we're off to York.'

'Fantastic. How long for?'

'A month. Mind you,' she went on, 'I've never forgiven them for naming me Dora. And what about Tebbitt, eh?'

He shrugged, thinking a month was a long time.

'Easy enough to change them.'

'Really?'

'Lots of people do, for one reason or another.'
She shook her head.

'I couldn't. Dora's my grandmother's name and she was sweet. And Tebbitt, well, if anything happened to my dad, I'd still have that bit of him. Anyway' – she focused on Martin again – 'what about you? You never answered my question.'

He saw the crush of office workers around the bar, the full tables of fellow drinkers having a laugh, letting off steam without, it seemed, a care in the world. It was this contrast with what lay deep in his heart, that made him also begin to retrace his steps, starting with his mother's name until he reached those two indelible dates which had encompassed her life.

'Do you have a photo of her?' asked Dora when he'd finished.

'No. It was chaos after she died, but that was the one thing I wanted. I've still got the little marker from her grave under my pillow, but the weird thing is, I don't even dream of her.'

'Seems to me that you're not going to move on until you've seen your mum again.'

Martin gulped, then realized she was serious, giving him the courage to speak out.

'But I did. Today. I'm sure of it. She was standing by the road near the site, as if she wanted to stop me to tell me something.'

'There we go. So you need to ask her why she did what she did.'

'What d'you mean, *ask*?'

Dora brought her chair closer, checking no one at the nearest table could overhear.

'Our wardrobe mistress. She's a medium. It's what she does on the side.'

Martin stared at her. He'd seen them on TV, read supposedly real-life stories in magazines and newspapers. But surely they just played on people's vulnerability and made a quick buck?

'I know she's helped to find missing dogs,' Dora went on.

'My mother's not a dog.'

Dora ignored him and the rowdy upheaval of drinkers leaving other nearby tables.

'There was a case last March, of a little boy from Ham Green who just vanished after a cubs' meeting...'

'And?'

'Well, Carol – that's her name – used a pendulum held over a map.'

Despite his scepticism, Martin found himself hooked on her every word. Deep in his troubled psyche he sensed a flame begin to grow and cast a small but steadfast light.

'Was he ever found?' he asked.

'Yes. In exactly the spot the pendulum showed. Alive and well in some fairground or other.'

'My God. Spooky or what?'

'She wouldn't think so. Oh, and there's someone in the cast who with Carol's help had a message from her dead brother. That's why I mentioned her to you.'

Dora finished her glass of wine and glanced at her watch. For some reason, the prospect of her leaving, triggered in him a sense of panic.

'What's the deal with this medium, then?'

'OK. Every fortnight she holds a séance at her flat. It's free, but any donations go to charity. I'm not sure if she's full up but I can always ask. I'm curious.'

'Join the club.' He dug in his wallet for something to write on and found an old betting slip representing a loss on the Grand National. She smiled as he jotted down his mobile number on the back.

'I'll be seeing her tomorrow and will let you know.'

'Great. Thanks.'

A slightly awkward pause hung between them in which more than anything, he wanted to ask if she was in any kind of relationship because her wedding finger was free. 'And thanks for listening,' he added instead.

'You too.' She slung her bag over her shoulder and added, 'See you again,' then picked her way through the bar towards the open front door. For a moment she stood silhouetted against the evening light as if uncertain which way to turn. When she'd gone, Martin pulled a discarded *Mirror* from a neighbouring empty chair and absently flicked through the news, from endless football to the growing opposition to the Hill Springs site. A photo and story about twenty-five-year-old Gary Cope caught his attention. He'd quit Manchester's slums and its dealers to return to nature, only to end his life in some remote Scottish loch. Until the results of DNA testing were known, he'd been identified by old dental records and a silver thumb ring found nearby.

Martin read of partner Maddy McKay's shock and horror at finding what the loch's seven-foot pike had done to 'the best mate a woman could ever have'. How his grandmother, his sole surviving relative, had been rushed to hospital last night after a serious stroke.

Martin shuddered, despite the pub's heady warmth, then read on how the couple's pet terrier, whom they'd doted on, was still missing. He stared at the man's black-and-white photo, which showed him in front of a block of trees, laughing at what, he couldn't tell. But what he *did* know, with an overpowering certainty, was he never walked voluntarily into that cold infested water. He had a steady job, Maddy seemed a decent sort and their cottage the kind of place dreamt of by most inner-city sufferers.

He surreptitiously tore out the half-page story and folded it neatly into his wallet. He could think of nothing else but that wrong conclusion. He'd go to the cop shop in the morning and voice his concerns. That's all they were at this stage, and doubtless open to ridicule, but there was something in Gary Cope's expression which would make him stand firm.

There was no food whatsoever in the canteen when he returned to the site. The protest had seen to that and if he'd not had his work contract to wave at the new security guards by the repaired barrier he'd have had to kip in some shop doorway till morning.

'You got a woman, I can tell,' observed one of

the workers as they stood together by the one vending machine outside the deserted canteen. Martin inserted his coins and selected a packet of salt-and-vinegar crisps.

'No, I haven't.'

The machine was taking too long and the guy pressed himself closer. He stank of sweat and beer.

'I know where to get woman.'

'Not interested.'

At last the crisps fell into the lower drawer and once he'd retrieved them, he strode off to his Portakabin of six beds and a shared shower and loo.

'Why wank when you can have the real thing?' the guy called after him, but the clunk of his Coke can landing was his only answer. The window of Cabin 4 had been smashed and CAPITALIST SHIT had been scrawled above it. Martin wondered yet again what the hell he was doing here.

He glanced up at the incomplete leisure centre where Den Tanner had opted for life. Clung on with surprising ferocity, given the mess he was in. So why had Gary Cope, happy and free at last, offered himself as fish food so that only his bones remained, washed up on the shingle beach after a storm-filled night? It didn't make sense and, like the loch's tide itself, certain questions returned. What was it he'd known? And who might have wanted him dead?

Aware of a hollow, hungry ache in his stomach, Martin kept an eye on the door, It was the lull before the inevitable storm. His five room-mates were still out but just before lock-up at midnight would all pile in through this door in a crazy wave. Pent-up. Pissed out of their skulls probably after today's events. And who could blame them? Wasn't he after a new start, too? And hadn't that also been threatened?

The room was a tip of discarded gear, the floor clotted with clumps of dried cement and pools of sand and brick dust broken up by footprints. Despite the shattered window, the smell was toxic, leading from the one chemical WC housed with the unreliable shower at the farthest end. He perched on his bed, chewing on the crisps, which tasted more of sawdust than anything else, and opened up the newspaper cutting he'd brought back with him from the pub.

He stared once more at the photos of Gary Cope and Kilfargan's pebbly lochside where a huge buoy lay beached, also a victim of the tide. Whoever had dumped the body in the water obviously didn't understand about the sudden weather changes up there. How a millpond can become a tsunami. How what goes in must at some stage come out, unless of course there are weights involved and a boat to convey the killer and victim to the loch's deepest, most unfathomable parts.

The report said the police were still questioning Maddy McKay, known to possess a fiery temper. However, suicide was still the most likely motive, but her mother's quote that 'Gary was the sunniest lad she'd ever met' did nothing to support it. His grandmother and sole surviving relative was still seriously ill in Manchester Royal Infirmary's stroke unit.

Still thinking of the stricken woman, he looked out of the broken window to see the full moon slipping from behind the hump of Midsummer Hill, growing it seemed all the while as if just for him, adding its acidic glow to the security lights' strobing brightness. The building site resembled a set for some WWII movie, except that out there, instead of Nazis, lurked others equally depraved. He made a phone call to Manchester and penned his first letter to his father.

It wasn't to check on his welfare at the Verne nor dwell on his September 1st release, but to ask two important questions. Which type of handgun would be best for his self-protection, and could he help him get hold of one?

Fifteen

False promises. Life is full of them. Not least Dr Khan telling me that if only I had the willpower, I could carry on almost as normal. Visiting the office, chairing meetings ... What a madman he is! Doesn't he realize the pain I have, just to breathe in and out? I'm afraid he and I will shortly be parting company. It was bad enough making the effort for the Hill Springs protest last Tuesday, but I had to be there. Someone has to speak up for what this town is losing. But my shame at being tarred with the same racist brush as Sean Brownlow still hurts me deeply. Here is a man I can do without. But it won't be easy and I shall seek my solicitor's advice first. I often wonder what happened to that nice looking young lad I saw crouched among the scaffolding on that hideous so-called leisure centre. Was he a protester, like me, holding out for his principles? If so, he should be proud of himself...

Evelyn raised her head from her writing and stared out at the sodden landscape beyond her lounge window. A scene which had hardly changed since the days when Rose and Will Scott had first laid the foundations of their prosperity with Scott's Rifles.

Yes, she'd often walked by the cottages where Rose's father had been born, and marvelled at how his only child had succeeded in her ambitions when women then were rarely more than the servers of meals and bearers of children. The Gables had been bought by her son Thomas after his parents' sudden deaths. Will Scott died instantly in an accident on an icy road, while Rose, who'd given their son her surname, had been mysteriously attacked at home and left to die under trees on the common.

Evelyn shivered as if her forebear's fate somehow presaged her own. She looked over to where her gun room lay, installed by Thomas to protect himself and his own family from further tragedy. She was beginning to feel this unique privacy, this spaciousness not as a haven but a mausoleum. The lofty coved ceilings suddenly seemed too high. The corridors upstairs too secretive. Even the land, once a welcome plateau amongst the encroachment of bracken and ever-growing trees, wasn't really hers any more, but Brownlow's. And was it fear rather than the usual fire which she glimpsed in her eyes as she bumped her Zimmer frame past the big gilt mirror on her way to the kitchen? Fear of decay and death or something far less tangible?

Her stomach reminded her that she'd not eaten since yesterday lunchtime, and a sudden light-headedness made her slump on to the chaise-longue. Her watch showed three o'clock. Two hours past her normal daily snack of crispbread topped by game pâté, but when she finally reached the fridge its glass shelves were bare, save for a pack of bacon turning purple in its sealed plastic coffin.

'How very strange...' she muttered to herself, sure that there'd been more when she'd checked last night. Where was the rest of the pâté? The cottage cheese she also liked, the bumper pack of smoked salmon?

She resolved to ask Brownlow as soon as possible. He should have brought the main weekly shopping by now. She knew he'd not been to Waitrose for three days, but perhaps her request for him to take her to Hill Springs was her ration for that week. Perhaps he was busy, or had simply forgotten. Hardly, she thought. The one thing she knew about Sean Brownlow was that he *never* forgot.

So, what could she do? And in that instant felt

more than a touch of envy for Merle who, needing the aid of only one walking stick, didn't have to rely on a man who was never at the other end of the phone when she called. Who hadn't acknowledged her most recent messages left on his answering machine and who, when he now came on to her land to practise shooting, ignored her. In the past, he'd at least glanced at the house and certainly never left without checking she was all right. So what on earth was going on?

Other irksome problems also kept her awake at night. She'd still not received the firm's half-yearly trading figures he'd promised her. Nor the minutes from the last shareholders' meeting. And then she suddenly realized why. Hadn't she, last month, hinted he'd become too overbearing, too intrusive? Of course. How could she have forgotten that unguarded flash of anger which had so utterly changed his face? A reaction of such intensity it had shocked her.

It was time to act, she decided, to regain control. Just as she'd shut the fridge door she heard his Jeep's diesel engine approaching up the drive, followed by the slam of its boot. Determination drove her outside, to fill her weary lungs with air. Then she noticed he'd parked where her beloved Jaguar used to be. Her special place.

'I'd like a word, please, Sean. I won't keep you a moment.'

But his back stayed turned to her as he stepped up on to the wet grass which stretched away below the treeline. A heady dampness hung in the air, making each bone in her body feel as if they might suddenly crumble to chalk. Pain made her shout more loudly than she might otherwise have done. 'Who is it paid your mortgage when you were laid up six years ago? Who lent you money for that car?'

He stopped, turned to face her, his cap's peak casting his eyes in shadow. Then he lowered the rifle crooked under his arm. She stepped forwards and as she did so, heard the crack of a snail shell under her velvet slipper, then saw its glistening innards attach themselves to her toe. If she stood on one leg for just a second to rub it away, she could fall all over again.

'Who helped you out with Merle, then?' he replied.

At first, she was confused. Then realized he was referring to finding carers.

'That woman you brought in last Tuesday was hopeless. You built everyone's hopes up. You said she was perfect.'

'And so she is.'

'I don't understand.' Another dizzy spell brought on by hunger made her grip weaken on the Zimmer frame.

'The one who started yesterday really *is* perfect.'

He'd always been clever with words and now she was even more confused.

'What day was that?'

His laugh was the strangest she'd ever heard and she wanted it to stop right there.

'Thursday the twentieth. Don't you remember? And the good news is – ' he smiled as he slotted the rifle beneath his armpit – 'she's more than happy to come and help *you* out when the time comes.'

He was playing games. Nasty games; and this particular one was more open than the others.

Evelyn looked down at the slimy mess on her best slipper, stepped out of it and hobbled back to the open front door, suddenly aware that if yesterday was Thursday, then today was Friday the 21st. Midsummer Day, when the Solstice Society, of which he was a founder member, would be holding their celebrations. All the more reason for her to be safe indoors with the alarm set. Why? Because the man who was neglecting her still possessed a key.

Sixteen

Scott. One of three hundred and sixty-five in the area phone book not including those with no phones or who might be ex-directory. But to Frankie, odds of three hundred and sixty-five to one were better than a million to one, so how could she have turned this job down with *that* name attached to it when she'd specifically asked the agency for Worcestershire? The attraction had been a fictitious Auntie Joan in Droitwich. Someone fondly remembered, but not seen since she'd left school. It would be nice to live not too far away to keep an eye on her, she'd added. Homely Helpers had said Malvern was their nearest placement and once they'd described their elderly client's big house in a nice village, with plenty of money floating about, Frankie realized she'd be a world away from the maze of Openshaw's grimy streets and that unlucky little semi in Dartmoor Road.

So, now here she was, deep in the lush Worcestershire countryside, under clouds which suddenly and unnervingly changed everything from dark to light and back again. Where Teme House was one of the most humungous private dens she'd ever seen. Even her car looked like a Dinky toy – no, a *shabby* Dinky toy – next to it. But it wasn't until the tall wax-coated guy who'd introduced himself as Sean Brownlow was showing her round all its nooks and crannies, while Miss Merle Scott was refusing to budge from her commode in the cloakroom, that she realized how much the place must have cost, not only to build but to maintain.

In fact, 358 Dartmoor Road would have fitted into the lounge alone, while the tall arched windows wouldn't have looked out of place in a church. The smell was high too. A mix of perfume and poo, heightened by the central heating which had already made her sweat under her new zip-up cardie. When she'd reminded Sean Brownlow it was the middle of June and maybe too hot for her charge, he'd fixed her with the kind of look which was Mr Patel's trademark.

'On no account must she get cold,' he'd said, with the slightest trace of Irish in his voice. 'I'm here to ensure she gets the best.' Then, once he'd sped away in his flash wheels having promised to return the next morning, she stripped to her T-shirt and added the impressive plastic apron nicked from her last job at Manchester Royal Infirmary.

While she waited for Miss Scott to perform, she wondered how come this guy was so involved. He wasn't even a Scott. If she didn't have enough on her plate worrying about the drip-drip of news from Kilfargan she could have easily let him get to her. But some men were like that. Needing to be boss. Top dog. She'd seen it in his eyes straight away, and how his hand had rested on her shoulder while showing her the view from the study window.

Suddenly, the door bell chimed and before Frankie could check on Miss Scott's progress it chimed again. Someone in a hurry, she thought, opening the door to a ruddy-faced man in a white coat who she guessed must be in his early seventies. The most striking thing about him were his hands encased in latex gloves. The kind she'd used at Gee's that Christmas Eve. Items she still possessed. Just in case.

His van engine was running, drowning the sounds of merrymaking she'd noticed earlier coming from the black hump of land which reared up beyond the equally strange rear garden.

'Will you be needing any fish today?' he asked. 'Miss Scott likes it on a Friday.'

Frankie hesitated and glanced back at the cloakroom.

'What kind of fish?' She thought of pike, with

pink gaping jaws...

'Haddock, usually.'

'OK. That'll do.'

He led the way over to his van printed with the words PETER MADDOX. FRESH FISH. EST. 1965 and slid open its side door to reveal a morgue of grey and silver corpses whose open mouths bore sharp little teeth. Whose dead eyes seemed oddly moist. She shivered as he pulled out a lower drawer containing bright yellow fillets laid out in size order and picked up two of the larger ones.

'They look nice,' she lied while he weighed them and dropped them into a plastic bag. He plucked a sprig of parsley from a nearby hook and added it to the haddock.

'Oily fish means oily skin.' He grinned false teeth as he handed over the smelly package which felt too heavy in her hands. 'Six pounds twenty to you, miss.'

She paid with her own money, but would enter it in the carer's book along with any other expenses, so Miss Scott could repay her.

'Who's *that* looker?' The man eyed the colour photo dominating her opened wallet.

'My sister.'

'You must think the world of her.'

'Yeah, I do.'

'And you are, if I might ask?'

'Frankie Holt.'

She could have lied, but what was the point? Besides, if her surname rang any bells or he'd heard of that problem family from the papers, he didn't show it.

'From up north, are you?'

She nodded, wondering if her voice needed more work.

'Night, Miss Holt.' He finally got into his driver's seat and indicated the top of the hill. 'By the way, you going up there later?'

'What for?'

'Summer Solstice shenanigans. Bit of a tradition in these parts. Mind you, England losing to Brazil will be a bit of a downer. Did you watch the match?'

'No. Anyway, I can't leave Miss Scott on her own.'

'At least you sound a better bet than the last girl she 'ad.' The fishmonger revved his engine. 'And the one before.'

'Thanks.' She smiled.

'Enjoy your meal, then. And,' he added, 'watch out for bones.'

'We will.' Just like the pikes with Gary Cope, she thought. 'See you next week.'

She carried the heavy bag well away from her body, wondering how best to make the kind of meal her client clearly expected. The only fish eaten in Dartmoor Road had come covered in crispy batter and wrapped in the *Manchester Evening News*, while any cooking at Briarfield was restricted to its trained kitchen staff.

She would just have to use her initiative.

'Is that you, Frances?' Miss Scott's voice surprised her, coming as it did from the top of the stairs. At least she'd seen to herself in the cloakroom. Things were looking up. 'What's that smell?'

'Your tea.'

Merle Scott was sitting in the chairlift near the landing, her fat white legs dangling in midair as the green light set into the newel post began to flash on and off.

'Wagons roll,' she chuckled as the chair began to grumble its way downwards and Frankie deposited the fish in the kitchen. She'd only been at Teme House for twenty-four hours, but as she'd told the agency, she was a quick learner, getting to know the ropes.

'I must say, dear, you've got such pretty eyes,' Merle said unexpectedly, allowing Frankie to escort her into the vast beamed lounge and switch on the TV.

'Do you mind me asking if you've any brothers or sisters?' Frankie said. She placed a rug over those lardy knees, thinking it a good time to broach the question. After all, the name Scott had made her gulp audibly when Homely Helpers had first offered her this permanent placement. Was this a big or a small coincidence? That harmless enough surname had lodged in her brain like a disease ever since Beryl had let it slip out, and her next move would be to fill in those dead hours in the afternoon when Merle liked to lie on her bed and listen to Radio 4, by digging where she could to discover if, on February 20th 1980, either she or any female relatives had given birth to a baby and been heartless enough to give her away...

She was just about to ask again when Merle piped up.

'I'm starving.'

'Twenty minutes, promise.' Nevertheless she still hung around for an answer until the silence grew too awkward. Then she took the carer's book into the kitchen to update it while the fish simmered in an old saucepan on the stove.

'A sister,' shouted Merle all of a sudden. Frankie tried not to overreact.

'Cool. What's her name?'

A pause while the yellowy foam bubbled out beneath the saucepan lid.

'Jenny. She's very nice.'

'I'm sure she is.' Frankie watched as the fishy water suddenly overflowed. The gas went off then came on again with a sharp pop, making her jump.

'But I've not seen her for a long while now.'

Frankie frowned to herself as she wiped up the stubborn mess on the cooker and wrung out her cloth in the sink. The agency hadn't mentioned any sister and she wondered why. Perhaps the old girl wasn't thinking straight. That was the most likely explanation.

The TV seemed louder now and, using the ballpoint connected by string to the red exercise book, she began filling in the day's events, including pills taken, toilet visits and ending with the cost of the haddock. Then, just as she was about to drain the haddock and place it in a Pyrex dish, the hall telephone began to ring.

'I'll get it,' she shouted. 'No probs.'

'It might be Sean,' said Merle. 'He's good at checking up on me.'

'I know that.' But it wasn't Sean. Not by a long chalk. Despite the heat from a nearby radiator,

161

Frankie froze as Avril Pilkington's voice reached her ears.

'Frankie? How's things with you?' Her cheery tone seemed wafer-thin.

'Fine, just fine, thanks.'

'Nice part of the world, Malvern.'

Bitch.

'How did you know I was here?'

'It's my job, Frankie. And, despite what you might think, I do actually care about how you're getting on.'

Then came that annoying laugh like the last time she'd called her. The 'I've got you taped' tone.

'I'm doing really well with Miss Scott here, and she's so grateful for every tiny thing I do for her,' Frankie crowed. 'It's brilliant.'

'I'm sure your mum'll be pleased.'

Shit.

'I had to let her know where you were, Frankie. Don't forget, she's already lost one daughter. She rang me an hour ago – worried sick.'

Liar.

'It's been that hectic, I clean forgot. I'll get back to her straight away.'

'She'll appreciate that. So, I'll get off the line...'

'Cheers.'

'Oh, by the way,' added the DC in that same irritating voice. 'Do you remember a Mrs Daphne Cope, one of the residents at Briar-field?'

That name sent another shot of ice through her

162

body right down to her legs. She felt more than numb. Paralysed.

'Course. She's lovely. Is she all right?'

'I'm afraid not, Frankie.' The police officer's voice then changed down a gear. 'She's suffered a major stroke and is on a life-support machine. Prognosis is very poor. I thought you ought to know, considering you worked at her home all those years and were very close to her...'

Suddenly Frankie's throat dried up. Her eyes brimming.

'But she was fine when I last saw her. Ate all her meals, did the crossword with that Mr Smithson, liked a joke, you know the kind of thing.'

'It's now been proved that people can actually suffer and die from a broken heart. Did you know that, Frankie?'

'Course, but...'

A faint click, followed by silence left her feeling dizzy.

'Who was calling?' asked Merle.

'No one important, honestly.'

'I'll have to believe you, then.'

From then on, the day was spoilt, as if one of those great lolloping clouds outside had landed permanently overhead.

'Thanks, you,' Frankie muttered to her absent tormentor, wondering how the hell she knew about Teme House and its ex-directory phone number. Why had she told her about old Mrs Cope?

'I'm ravenous!' Merle interrupted, trying to tip herself out of her mechanized chair. Frankie got

163

there before she fell.

'It's ready.' She forced a smile. 'And I'm peckish too.' An expression which John Arthur used, and like the rest of him, hard to shift.

'What have you made?'

A fucking pig's ear, if you must know.

'A surprise.'

'Good. I like surprises. Don't you?'

'Not much.'

As she walked behind Merle to the dining room, which conveniently led off the kitchen, Frankie observed how her thinning hair sprung in coils from her skull. Grey at the roots, red at the ends; she wondered what colour she'd been originally. Frankie scrutinized the woman's hips, her puckered thighs revealed by the too-short ra-ra skirt she'd insisted on wearing that morning. Was it possible *that's* where she'd come from? Anything was possible.

Once Ellie was tucked up for the night in one of the attic rooms where the other carers had slept, she'd give Homely Helpers a ring. They were on call from 8 a.m. until 2 a.m. and her excuse would be that in order to give Miss Scott the dignity she deserved, she had to know as much about her client as possible.

'Have you heard the news?' asked Merle once she was seated at the far end of the dining room's oval mahogany table.

'What news?' Frankie had had enough to last her into next year. She set Merle's plate down in front of her and passed her the Pyrex dish where the yellow fish lay under a topping of melted cheese.

'I heard it on my radio. A big protest in town at some new building site or other.'

'Right.' Frankie heaped some minted peas alongside Merle's haddock, then helped herself, aware that any appetite she'd had, had vanished.

Frankie pulled a small bone from between her lips, thinking it had taken so little time for an adult human body to be devoured at Kilfargan. Those pike she'd researched beforehand must have been hovering much closer to shore than usual, waiting to pounce. It was a wonder her own ankles hadn't been nibbled as she'd dragged a naked and barefoot Gary Cope across the short expanse of shingle as the rain thinned his blood until it vanished altogether. Then she'd flung the knife as far out into the water as possible.

'A splendid meal, dear,' Merle said afterwards, vanilla ice cream edging her lips. 'Now, you must promise me, you'll not abandon me like the dreadful Kylie Watts did.'

'Course I won't. Don't be daft.' Frankie helped her from her seat in expert fashion and led her to the chairlift. 'This is the most brilliant place. Just think, you can step out of the back door and be up those hills in no time.'

But Merle seemed less than ecstatic. 'Are those odd people still up there with their bonfires?'

'Dunno. Why?'

Merle turned her floury face towards her. It reminded Frankie of those baps Beryl always

165

made her buy whenever she did any shopping. Soft, lightly dusted, but prone to cracking when touched.

'I feel so much safer having you around. That's all.'

Frankie remembered what the fishmonger had said about the revellers. He'd not been unduly worried.

'I'm sure they're harmless. Like Morris dancers, that sort of thing.'

Merle shook her head and, having pressed the start button, trundled away up the stairs, her bare feet dangling with their long toenails and cheese-rind soles in the air.

Once Merle had been topped and tailed then tucked into bed with a battered copy of something called *Mallory Towers*, Frankie climbed the stairs to her attic room where Ellie was waiting. The air was even warmer than downstairs, reminding her of a school physics lesson on heat rising. Of warnings at tech on the dangers of the very young and the elderly succumbing to heart failure.

She released the small sash window's catch, pushed down the lower portion and took in a deep gulp of air. Then she spotted the layer of dead flies trapped on its uppermost frame edge; caught the smell of bonfires from somewhere behind the house. In Openshaw they turned the sky orange every Guy Fawkes' Night, but John Arthur had never allowed one in the garden. Couldn't be bothered, was what he'd said. Merle had mentioned bonfires too, but she'd seemed edgy as if she knew more than she was letting on.

'Come here, my little babe.' She turned to Ellie and held her close, before showing her the dusky view from the window. 'This is better, isn't it? Just think, one day your mum'll be able to get you a proper nursery with nice white cupboards and wallpaper with bunnies on.'

Ellie seemed to gurgle her appreciation and then, with the gentlest tipping of her body, let out a small cry.

'Hey, I know. It's tea time and you're hungry. Got it all ready.'

She reached over for the five-ounce bottle on the dressing table, but for some reason, Ellie was slower than usual. Slower to burp too, so after two ounces had gone, Frankie peeled off the bottom portion of her all-in-one suit and changed her nappy. Just wet this time, which made life easier, and then she cradled her in her arms to brush her soft new hair until it shone.

As she hummed a nice lullaby Mrs Beavis had once sung to the group about wanting the moon to play with, she placed Ellie in her bed, making sure her head was slightly turned to the right. Cot death was every mum's worst fear, and no way would Ellie ever be at risk.

Then, once she'd closed her eyes, Frankie dug out her mobile and Homely Helpers file from her rucksack and dialled their freephone number in Tonbridge.

'We may not have made ourselves clear to you about Miss Scott,' explained a mildly irritated Linda Toye, 'but your client does rather live in

167

her own world. She makes things up. What do her other carers' notes say?'

The question caught Frankie by surprise, but she wasn't stupid.

'Nothing like that. Just that she's forgetful with the cooker and water taps.'

A pause in which Frankie could pick out another office phone ringing. 'But surely these records should be truthful, shouldn't they? After all, they are confidential.'

'Not always, that's the trouble. We've had a spate of complaints from clients who've seen them, so it's best to keep the more tricky assessments as strictly verbal. *Entre nous* as they say. Between ourselves.'

'But this Mr Brownlow seems to know loads,' Frankie challenged. 'I mean, who *is* he?'

An impatient sigh which didn't deter her.

'He works for her sister. Very protective and very helpful, I have to say. I don't know what they'd do without him.'

'You mean Merle and Jenny?'

'No. Merle and Evelyn.'

'Are you sure?'

'Yes, of course.' Linda checked her computer. 'She lives at the Gables, West Malvern Road. Surely that information's in your notes? And her telephone number?'

'Not a dicky bird.'

'I'll sort it straightaway. If we weren't so understaffed, these omissions wouldn't be occurring. At least it seems we can rely on you.'

'Thanks. By the way, I know it's late and this might seem a naff question, but did either sister ever have a kid at any time?'

'Why do you need to know that?'

A warning voice inside Frankie's head made her pause before replying.

'Curiosity, I suppose. Just trying to get the full picture. After all, I'm new here. I don't want to be building up hopes of any son or daughter, or niece or nephew, coming to visit, if there aren't any.'

'I take your point, but there's nothing on file here. Now I really must be getting on and don't forget to keep that record book updated. And private.'

'OK. I'll do it now. Oh, just one more thing...' The question she shouldn't be asking. 'Has anyone been quizzing you about where I'm working at the moment?'

'Who exactly?'

Frankie bit her lip. The word police would be like poison to her plans. She thought of Mrs Beavis's sound advice.

'Doesn't matter, OK? Another dumb question, sorry.'

With that, the line went dead and in the silence which followed, Frankie detected a small noise outside her attic bedroom door. One leap and a quick pull of the handle, told her all she needed to know. She was someone not to be trusted.

At twenty past eleven, with a large quarter moon bossing the whole sky about, Frankie slipped outside with both front and back door keys safe in her pocket. She wouldn't be leaving Merle all on her own on just her second night at Teme

House, but when she'd seen the back of her hobbling down the attic stairs, something inside her had snapped.

However hard she tried for people nothing was ever good enough, and so, if this was going to be the case here – pretty eyes or not – then she was going to start pleasing herself. And by this time next week her bank balance would be seven hundred quid better off.

The back garden smelt not just of damp foliage, but something which made her fish supper turn in her stomach. She sniffed. The earlier bonfire smell had changed. Something was cooking. But surely it was too wet for any kind of barbecue?

The whiff of singed flesh now mingled with those same voices she'd heard earlier. Her torch picked out the steps leading from the patio and then the soft uncut grass studded by what at first had resembled stones. Now she realized that these lumps of granite were in fact graves. Dog graves. One next to the other in rows. Like war cemeteries in northern France. She read the carved-out names and dates of death, Teme House Bridesmaid 1982, Teme House Best Man 1983, and so on, wondering why they weren't known simply as Ben or even Donny, like the dog from Kilfargan.

Her torch beam roamed from one to the other, from the earliest memorial to the latest until suddenly she stopped at another already familiar name. Teme House Jenny.

Jenny?

She searched for the accompanying date, but

lichen had embedded itself where the carving should have been, and it wasn't until she'd scraped the worst of it away with her thumbnail that four numbers became clear. 1980. The year she was born.

The moon, now clear of a dark fleeting cloud, lit her way along a stony path which led upwards from the small wooden gate set in the garden's boundary hedge. There was a different noise coming from the nearest hilltop. A kind of chanting in a language she didn't recognize and when it abruptly stopped the silence felt like that by the loch. A deep deathly pool of the possible.
'Shit...'
Her trainers slid on a muddy patch and if she'd not grabbed at a bunch of bracken she would have fallen flat on her face. The chanting had started up again, in English this time. Something about Rosea's month being the door of the year and then these same raised voices asked Juno Moneta to turn her face away from dark Janus and bring them money and wealth...
Frankie switched off her torch so she wouldn't be seen. Money and wealth. Exactly.
'We've cut the hawthorn now the oak. And Duir comes blackened with her cloak...'
Frankie moved closer, picking her way forward until a plume of pungent smoke reached her nose. As well as the brittle sounds of burning wood, she detected flames more green and blue than yellow or red as they seemed to lick the quarter moon's lower rim. Another bonfire had been lit on the Worcestershire Beacon, closer to

the circle of cloaked figures swaying in anti-clockwise motion as the fire threw up fierce little sparks. Then, as if synchronized, the participants bent down and lifted up their poles crowned with something she couldn't quite make out, except that the earlier burnt-flesh smell intensified. She'd read *Lord of the Rings* as a kid, and to her just then this scene above her could have come straight from its pages. She was tempted to get the hell out, but once the words grew clearer, she stayed rooted to the spot.

'Epona, come and join us here. To swell our luck in this new year. To gold and treasure evermore...'

Suddenly she sneezed and the chain of people now riding their poles broke up in surprise.

'Who the fuck's that?' asked a male Irish voice.

'I'll go and see. Wait there,' volunteered a woman in the same rustic accent as the fish-monger, and within seconds, before Frankie could backtrack to Teme House, her conical form obliterated any view of the hill.

'Yes?' she challenged, upon seeing her.

'I was only looking. Sorry.'

'Where you from, then?'

Frankie guessed she too was local, so it was best to play safe and tell the truth. She was aware of a crown of eyes on her. Waiting.

'I work for Miss Scott at Teme House down there.'

A hostile murmur rose up from the spectators.

'Then may I suggest you go back. This is a private event.'

'Private? But I thought the top of North Hill was public land.'

'I said our *event* was private. Anyhow, what's your name?'

'Frankie Holt. And you?' Nothing to lose, she thought, aware of the woman's companions growing more restless. She also realized what exactly lay at the end of their poles. Skulls, bigger and longer than human ones, some with antlers, others not. Closer inspection showed bone partly covered by black scorched skin, flapping in the night breeze.

'Juno Moneta's slave,' replied the woman.

'I'm a slave, an' all.' Frankie followed this with a dry laugh to hide her unease at what was going on. She shivered. June it might be, but the day's wetness still clung to her clothes, reaching her bones.

'I thought the actual solstice was at twenty-four minutes past one.' She'd spotted a New-Age type poster at the local garage.

'You're absolutely right. But as most of us have day jobs, this is the best we can do. So you're interested in our ancient traditions, are you?'

The question threw her. She'd not come prepared.

'Yeah, suppose I am. Just read some Walter Scott ghost stories. Talk about weird.'

'Nothing's weird when you loosen the shackles of conventional thought, Miss Holt.'

'Carol? You coming?' called out that same man's voice as before. 'We need to finish this thing off.'

'OK, Sean. OK.' Then she lowered her voice. 'Why not bring yourself along to my next séance in a fortnight's time? My place, 6 Quarry Terrace, Malvern. Eight o'clock.'

'Séance?' She'd seen those on TV as well and not been impressed.

'I guarantee that afterwards you'll see the world differently. For the better...' The woman clambered back up the slope. 'Be there.'

That sounded pretty damned chesty coming from a total stranger, yet all the same this might lead to her making the one friend she'd never had.

'By the way, Frankie,' Carol Piper's voice reached her from on high, 'I bet Juno Moneta'll be smiling at you from now on.'

'Why's that, then?' She had to get back to Merle, but at the same time, needed her to spell it out. She felt her pulse quicken.

'Miss Scott and her sister. They're the richest people in Malvern. Didn't you know?'

'I'd no idea.'

'Scott's Rifles, it is. Bang, bang. Not very nice, but I can't complain.'

'Can't complain? I don't get it.' Wondering if the Sean that Carol had spoken to was Brown-low. She dare not ask. At least, not out here in the creepy moonlight.

'Evelyn's been a brilliant benefactor to our theatre here. Without her we'd have shut up shop years ago.'

'I see.' Evelyn again. The second person to confirm it.

* * *

Frankie emptied Merle's commode of stale pee, disinfected it then filled the washing machine. She then attended to Ellie, prepared Merle's breakfast and made a shopping list ending with her own necessities. A new phone card, cheese-topped baps, ciggies and the *Gladiator* video for when she was alone in her room. Then, still preoccupied by last night's events, and the fact that Avril Pilkington was hell-bent on winding her up, she cleared away Merle's breakfast mess and joined her in the lounge, where she was reading the local paper.

Its banner headline still referred to the Hill Springs protest and was accompanied by a further half-page photo of the fracas. Milking the event for all it was worth. 'LOCAL RACISTS REAR THEIR UGLY HEADS!' While underneath in a smaller font, 'Local Businesswoman Lends Her Support'.

'Why, that's Jenny!' exclaimed Merle, point-ing a chipped orange-varnished nail at the black circle containing a diminutive wheelchaired woman and her tall companion. Frankie peered over her shoulder thinking, *Target*. Lately she'd dreamt of nothing but guns. The speed of them. Their silence. The damage they cause...

'And look, Sean's with her too.' Merle brought the page closer to her nose, then looked up at Frankie, bewilderment in her eyes. 'What on *earth* were they doing there?'

'God knows.'

Damn.

She'd broken her new rule never to swear or blaspheme in front of a client. Just in case. All

175

the same, she was puzzled at how Merle could recall Sean Brownlow's name but not that of her own sister. How this mystery man who'd prattled on about Malvern's history to her seemed to have his feet well and truly under the carpet of not one but two camps.

'I mean, what's the deal with him?' she muttered to herself. 'And anyway, who's Jenny?' Merle overheard. She was definitely not as dim or ga-ga as she liked people to think.

'You ask too many questions, my girl. I may be seventy-three, but I *do* have all my faculties.' And before she could elaborate further on this, the shadow of a vehicle outside glided across the room and she saw Sean Brownlow ease himself from his Jeep, green Wellington boots first, then one corduroyed leg after another, topped by a cable-knit sweater and a face darkened by stubble. He could have stepped from the pages of a Land's End catalogue, she thought, although easily old enough to be her father. No wonder he was indispensable to these two old ducks. And now here he was, brown-leather briefcase in hand, checking up on things, his fox-coloured eyes missing nothing. Including her. Like the first time, not a very nice experience.

He kicked off his boots on the hall mat. A smear of white ash on each heel reminded her of last night. Was he into all that kind of stuff? It seemed unlikely. He kissed Merle on both cheeks and sat down on the settee to open his case. He must have been a handsome guy in days gone by, Frankie thought. Today, Merle was making a will, and she was to be one of the witnesses.

'Everything's ready,' she heard Brownlow say. 'Won't take long. Easy as pie, in fact.'

The formalities took six minutes exactly, and most of that was taken up with Merle's neighbour, old Mr Crowe, having trouble writing his name. Normally, she'd have been able to decipher who Merle had favoured, but Brownlow had been shielding the crucial 'I bequeath...' statement.

The smile on his face only lasted until Mr Crowe hobbled back to the house next door and the will safely signed was in that smart leather briefcase. After that, it was let's-keep-Frankie-on-the-go time.

'This needs a polish,' he said, opening the top drawer of Merle's mahogany desk and extracting a block of Teme House headed notepaper and matching envelopes, all decorated by bright-eyed spaniels. The kind of dog she'd never seen in Openshaw. 'Is there somewhere we can chat?'

She suppressed a sigh of irritation. She had jobs to do. And jobs not done meant no pay.

'How about the kitchen?' She'd just cleaned up there, after all.

'Let's go.' He led the way, touching the back of Merle's chair in the process. She looked up gratefully.

'Tell me, Sean,' Merle suddenly called after him. 'Why were you at Hill Springs with Jenny on Tuesday?'

'It's *Evelyn*,' he reminded her sternly. 'She's a very persuasive woman.'

Third time lucky with that name, thought

177

Frankie, still puzzled. She followed him out of the lounge, and, as she went, glanced at the paper. There, in a column labelled 'Around the UK' and slotted in between a Doncaster park rape and a chip-shop fire in Hatfield, was a name which made her legs seize up. Daphne Cope...

'Everything all right?' he said, looking at her intensely.

'Fine, thanks.'

But it wasn't. Gary Cope's grieving grandmother had died in the early hours of the morning. DNA tests on the bones found in the loch matched a remnant of dried blood found beneath a pebble.

Frankie urged herself to stay calm or she could blow everything. She pulled out two oak stools from under the breakfast bar and settled herself opposite Sean Brownlow. Years of working for picky male bosses had taught her that the best method of deflection was to ask a question. Those less focused always lost track. It would be interesting to see how he responded. She spread both hands out on the bar's smooth cool wood and looked her adversary in the eye.

'Who's Jenny?' she asked. 'Is there another sister I don't know about? Or is that the name of one of Miss Scott's spaniels?'

If he was surprised by her question, he didn't show it.

'What's given you that idea? Anyway, they're *King Charles* spaniels. Monarchs of the canine world.'

She tried not to let this put-down get to her. Instead, she pointed out of the kitchen window where the rows of memorial stones dominated the garden.

'There's a dog's grave out there with that same name on.'

'Really?' He seemed genuinely surprised. 'I've never noticed that.'

She kept up her stare. Then he coughed – the nervy kind – while two fingers pulled the chunky neck of his jumper as though he needed more air.

'I've heard Miss Scott call her sister by various names and could count on both hands those she's ascribed to me.'

'What names exactly?'

'Oh, Robert, Ralph, Raymond, that sort of thing.'

'But they all begin with r. Jenny's quite different from Evelyn in every way.'

Another little cough as he placed the headed paper in front of him and withdrew a red ballpoint from his trouser pocket. It was then she noticed the state of his right thumb and index finger. Both badly calloused and in sharp contrast to their smoother neighbours. His nails, too, seemed to be lined not by dirt exactly, but something tomato-coloured, almost black near the sides. Then she realized with a shiver, she was looking at dried blood.

'Are you implying I'm a liar, Frances?'

He wrote *DUTIES* at the top of the notepaper before she could answer.

'Now then, down to business. We need to clarify your role here, Frances, so there's no confusion.'

179

'I'm not confused.'

She spotted a blackbird beyond the window, splashing in the bird bath. A deep envy for its freedom touched her heart.

'I'd like you to start polishing all the wood and silver. And let me know if you spot any wood-worm, other corrosive pests or excessive tarnishing.'

'Certainly.' Although she'd not liked the way he'd said pests.

'And when you next take Miss Scott in a taxi for shopping or chiropody or whatever, you must pay, *then* ask for a receipt.'

'I spent six pounds twenty on fish for last night's tea.'

'Tea?'

'Supper, whatever. Anyway, I thought Homely Helpers would settle it.'

He shook his head.

'This is what I mean, Frances. There *is* confusion. *I'm* the one who'll be paying you your wage every month and reimbursing you for any expenses.'

'*Month*? I thought I'd be paid every week.'

He held out his hand instead. 'Do you have a receipt for the fish?'

'I wrote it down in the record book.'

'Not the same, I'm sorry. So remember next time, receipt, receipt, receipt.'

She felt queasy. He was a total shit and there was nothing she could do.

'If we don't clarify things they get out of hand. As they did with our last two incompetents,' he went on.

'Our? You related to Miss Scott, then?'

He blinked. Shifted a little uncomfortably on his stool.

'Absolutely not. I'm her sister's production manager.'

'Rifles?'

'Stalking rifles. The aristocrats of the game world. How did you know?'

'Just guessing,' She said shrugging. 'Anyway, why bother stalking? Why not just shoot?'

'Ah.' He glanced at his watch as if judging how long it might take to explain. 'Stalking is the overture, the prelude to a symphony, if you like. Cunning versus fear.'

The wet blackbird winged its way over the back garden and up the hill out of sight. She imagined it being hit, flopping, falling and dying in agony. She stared at the sheet of notepaper and his small spiky writing, which looked like a load of dead birds' legs all mixed up together.

'But there are tactics which take years to perfect. Yes, years...'

'What tactics?'

'You keep out of sight. You don't break the skyline and walk close as you can to the target. Close as you can until the moment...'

Despite the warm kitchen, Frankie suddenly felt cold as his trigger finger tapped the breakfast bar.

'Now then, when I've gone, please make sure those instructions of mine are copied into your carer's record book. By the way.' His eyes met hers. 'May I take a look?'

Was this intimidation or what? She hesitated,

thinking about guns again, and that he might not be the best person to cross.

'Very thorough,' he murmured once the red exercise book was open in front of him and his gaze had roamed over her latest notes. 'I wish we'd discovered you before either Miss Watts or Mrs Huggett had crossed the threshold.'

'I like doing it. Writing, I mean. I like getting things exactly right. Every last detail, you know. It's my training. I had the best...'

'And where was that, then? I'm sure Homely Helpers did tell me.'

'Openshaw.'

'And your place of birth?'

'Fallowfield. Why?'

'Funny how it's always one's early influences which last the longest,' he observed, his head tilting slightly as he studied her.

Bloody cheek. Her background, or lack of it, was nothing to do with him. She felt as if she was in that loch all over again. Its water deepening, darkening around her...

'I'm also curious to know why there's a child's seat in your Fiesta,' he asked, invading her private space even further. 'Do you have a younger sibling?'

'Oh, right. Yeah. She's called Ellie.' But no way was she letting on where she was and she reminded herself to hide her properly whenever she left the house.

'Why do people have to shorten names like that?'

'How d'you mean?' Thinking he was such a rude big-head.

'Eleanor was the powerful beautiful Eleanor of Aquitaine. You must have seen the film, *The Lion in Winter.*'

'Yeah. Twice,' she lied, when in fact the only films she liked were romance. Girl meets boy, girl gets boy. So different from her own life.

He slipped off his stool and like that other time, let his hand rest on her shoulder perhaps a second too long.

'I'd also like to take a proper look at your CV. Perhaps you could drop it off at my office on Monday as I may not be able to call in here.' Before she could react, he'd dug in his trouser pocket and from his wallet extracted a black business card embossed with silver lettering and a motif of crossed rifles. The card felt oddly cold in her hand. 'I'll be working late, until eight o'clock.'

'Would you like tea or coffee, Mr Brownlow?' she asked. It was either that, or making for the drawer where Merle's kitchen knives were kept. He stalled her offer with a raised hand.

'Best be going.' He reached for the exercise book and handed it back to her. 'Keep up the good work, Frances, and if there's anything you need, just ring my number. Oh, by the way, Miss Scott's gardener comes every Wednesday. He's Polish. Called Piotr. Now there's another damned stupid name, if you ask me. His money's in a brown envelope in the second desk drawer on the left. Can't trust him further than we can throw him, mind. Just like that lot who've been working at Hill Springs. At least they've had the decency to bugger off.'

'Who do you mean?' Then she remembered the photo showing swastika placards.

'All the world's scrounging scum, I'm afraid.' With that, he strode back to peck the balding top of Merle's head and was soon outside on the gravel drive, glancing up at the darkly shifting sky. Frankie was by the door, about to close it behind him, when his voice suddenly reached her ears.

'One last thing, Frances.' He fixed her with a warning look as he held his car door open. 'Next time you leave Miss Scott on her own to go prancing about on North Hill, please have the decency to tell me first.'

Seventeen

Monday 24th June. When Martin had phoned Manchester Royal Infirmary last Wednesday morning, posing as an old family friend of Daphne Cope, he'd met resistance. Yes, she was receiving the best care, but no, she wasn't conscious, and for that reason hospital visits would serve no useful purpose.

He had attended two separate ID parades before work, each lasting only five minutes, and was still reeling from Ed Thom and Den Tanner's icy stares while lined up among other makeweight guys. He would be the principal witness at the inevitable trial. Along with Charlene, who unlike him had her own copper for protection.

Those two men's shadows seemed to blight his every move. Their single-finger sign to him as they were led back to the holding cells, as real and powerful as any bullet, and as he cycled away from the premises he wondered yet again if his father had received his begging letter. And about Gary Cope.

Completion Day at the site had got to be a fairy tale. This project was now badly understaffed and unlikely to be finished by next spring and Monroe was being investigated for using illegal workers. Martin had even been quizzed about his roommates but retorted that he'd kept himself to himself and knew nothing.

He stared up at the sky. Summer was still a dream somewhere beyond the leaden clouds which seemed magnetically attached to that bare range of hills. Dora and he had spent Saturday evening exploring Hangman's Gate high on the Worcestershire Beacon. They'd found not only the sodden remains of solstice fires still harbouring unidentifiable bits of bone in their outer ashes, but also charred clumps of black wiry hair. Despite Dora's reassurances that the revellers used only parts of animals, he'd felt a strong urge to run downhill.

But then she'd pulled him close and they'd kissed for the first time, their faces wet from the driving rain, and he felt all his demons had grown wings and flown high, out of his mind and, finally, out of his life.

* * *

Having finished work and shifted the day's debris from his scalp, from everywhere, under the shower's erratic flow, Martin cycled to the library, where late-night opening meant he could access one of their computers.

Gary's funeral together with that of his beloved grandmother would take place on Wednesday. He'd phone HQ in Worcester and tell them he had to go to Blackheath on cemetery business and would be back the next day. It wouldn't be easy as he was one of only three roofers left, but death wasn't backache or a hangover. It was untouchable.

As he walked past the photocopier he noticed a young woman in a denim jacket struggling to find the right money in the unzipped portion of her purse. She seemed tense, nervy and in a hurry.

'Here, let me help,' he said, bringing out his own small change and searching for silver amongst the dross. 'What d'you need?'

'Just fifty pence. I've almost got it.'

Martin handed her his sole remaining one but she hesitated, and only when she looked at him did he realize how striking her eyes were. Not just brown, contrasting with her cropped blonde hair, but flecked by a lighter tone. The kind he'd seen in nature books when he was a kid. Half animal, half human.

'You're really kind. This is such a drag,' she said.

'Forget it. And good luck.'

'You too.'

Then he passed through the exit turnstile and

186

braved yet more rain to reach the Taj Mahal takeaway where a small queue of people was waiting. As he collected his order of chicken tikka and a nan bread he realized he had left the train timetable by the computer.

He returned to the library ten minutes before closing time. There was no sign anywhere of the striking-looking girl and, on a hunch, having made sure no one was looking, he lifted the copier's lid. There lay an A4 sheet covered on both sides with neatly typed details of someone's CV. Someone called Frances Ann Holt, born in Manchester on 20th February 1980, who was now a full-time carer. Was this related to the girl he'd just met, or was she doing someone else a favour? Hard to tell, although the age and accent seemed good matches.

His conscience told him to return the CV to the copier, but curiosity won. The name was familiar. The library's warmth along with the aroma from his takeaway tormented him. He wondered what the hell he was thinking of. He must be barking. Was his life so lacking in adventure that he had to go all that way to the middle of bloody nowhere and possibly place himself in danger? Even under suspicion? All for someone he'd only heard about on the news?

c/o Spring Hills Development,
  Ross Road, Malvern. Worcs.
  1/7/02

Dear Ms McKay,
  You don't know me but I'm near enough

your Gary's age to be able to sympathize with you over your tragedy up in Kilfargan and I'd like to help, because I do believe – and it's more than just a gut feeling – that your Gary never would have killed himself. It's not as if I'm one of those psychic types. I'm not, but I do feel this one strongly. If you want to give me a call on the mobile number included before next Wednesday, please don't hesitate. It will be treated in strictest confidence.

Yours,

Martin D. Webb

He wasn't expecting any response. Why should she at this time of grief be bothered about what he thought? Most likely he'd be branded a nutter. One of those ghouls who hang around road accidents or make hoax 999 calls.

As he slipped the letter into the nearest postbox in time for the last collection, he wished he'd had the balls to make the journey north. He could have been on that Glasgow plane by now and Loch Cottage by lunchtime. So why had he changed his mind? Fear of losing his job? No. Being there so soon in the middle of someone else's grief was too insensitive. Too intrusive.

More rain, more shit. Tuesday morning was worse than yesterday and, having feasted too long ago on three pieces of cold toast and lemon curd, he was just about to heave his heavy waterproof on to his shoulders for the start of the afternoon shift when suddenly his mobile rang from deep in its pocket.

Dora. He smiled in anticipation of her voice. But not for long. The female stranger trying to override the bad line was tense and tearful. Also, strongly Scottish.

'Mr Webb?'

'Yes.'

'It's me. Maddy McKay. I just got your letter. D'you mind me ringing?'

'Christ, no. I'm glad you felt you could.'

Beyond his Portakabin window a familiar figure seated on a bike was chatting to the guards, his hair stuck flat against his skull. Was Rio Docherty here as a trouble-shooter? Whatever, he didn't need this distraction right now.

'Like I said in my letter,' he went on, 'something's not quite right about what I saw on TV and read in the papers. Especially your partner's photo.'

'What d'you mean?' A sob more than a question and he knew he had to tread carefully if she wasn't to slip away altogether.

'When was it taken?'

''Bout a week before ... you know...' Her voice faltered again before she continued. 'We'd been to this brilliant pub for a meal. My birthday it was. And afterwards, we were just fooling around outside. I've never felt so happy in all my life. Gary too. I know because he said so. And that's God's truth.'

'I can tell *he* was happy too. That's why I got in touch.'

'Anyway,' she sniffed, 'the big thing was, he wanted to borrow my car to go to Oban this week on his half-day off, to buy me a ring.'

Hardly the agenda of a man intent on killing himself, thought Martin, feeling his own eyes begin to sting.

'Sorry about this. Just wait a mo,' he said to his caller, as he saw Docherty walk towards his billet. He locked himself in, then crouched low. He heard Docherty calling out his name.

'What's going on?' came Maddy McKay's panicky voice.

'Nothing. Everything's fine. I'm on a building site, that's all. Bit busy. Look, there's just a few more things I need to know ... I don't like asking this, but what was he wearing when you last saw him?'

'Why?'

'Because as far as I know, there's been no media mention of him wearing any clothes or footwear.'

'Jeans and a hooded fleece. I found them on a rock. Neatly folded with his trainers on top. Even the thumb ring I'd bought him for Christmas. That's why the cops thought it was suicide. In preparation for some kind of purification thing, this psychology guy said. As if Gary knew he'd done something bad and had to atone for it. He's the crazy, not my Gary.'

'Was he getting letters or calls from anyone he was afraid of? He'd been mixed up with some pushers in Manchester, hadn't he?'

'That was ages ago. Before he met me. Before going straight with a proper job an' all. But he'd never talk about it. Used to go ape if I so much as mentioned the D word.'

'Drugs? Were there any former girlfriends that you knew of?'

'The cops asked me that, but no. At least, he never said. And I never heard him call out anyone else's name in his sleep either, like some guys do. But when he'd had a bit to drink, he *did* talk about me and him going back to Manchester. The dark nights here used to get to him, see. Me, I'm used to it. He missed his gran too. Now she's gone as well...'

Her words seemed to disintegrate into the fresh squall of rain slapping against the window. Docherty had given up knocking and jogged back to base, weaving his way between the earthmovers locked into the yellow mud.

'So I'll never know what she meant on that last little card she sent. The police reckoned it was an old woman rambling on.'

Charming, he thought, aware of a change in his pulse rate. Another reason why the Met would never have been the seat of his dreams. His father had probably been right. Not that he'd ever admit it.

'What did this card say, exactly?'

'That he should tell them what he'd told her about what he'd seen at some disco in Manchester. I mean, the handwriting was all over the place but it did seem important to her. I honestly don't know what this is all about...'

'When did he tell her?'

'I've no idea.'

'So, where's this card now?'

'In my bag, where it's always been.'

An idea was forming in his mind. OK, this was

pushing it, but nothing ventured...

'Can you trust me?' he asked her.

A pause followed, dominated by the weather's din.

'Yes.'

'If you can get a copy made and sent to me,' he pressed on, 'it could be really useful.'

'I could give it you personally. The funeral's tomorrow. It's not private, you know. I'd like people to show that wherever he and his gran are now, they're still loved. It'll be at three o'clock at St Mark's, Ashton Road, Openshaw.'

'Openshaw?'

'Yes. Near Manchester.'

Just then the line crackled and died, giving him no chance to reply and leaving that particular place name clinging limpet-like to his brain. He withdrew the CV from his jeans pocket and studied it once again. Whoever it belonged to had lived there. Someone whose baggage was bulging with coincidences.

He was right. Death was the best excuse he could have had for time off work and when he'd asked Docherty – now the new foreman – he'd simply nodded. However, if Monroe hadn't been promised another forty workers from a completed development in Hounslow, then the answer could have been different.

Manchester drew him into its crowded heart. Here at last was the summer he'd been missing. The sky clearer than any he'd seen so far in Malvern. The sense of life lived on the streets. Of a welcome anonymity. The sky multiplied by

192

reflections in the high-rise windows of office blocks and department stores, but once he was ensconced in the grubby sprinter train to Ashton under Lyne, that buzz, that colour seemed to fade.

He arrived at St Mark's Church fifteen minutes early, far too warm for comfort under his black-leather jacket. Too reticent to join the small group of people hovering outside the vestry door, their shadows reaching the nearest, oldest graves but not the pair lying newly dug, covered by green cloths, alongside the church's dark eastern wall. Clearly this wasn't the expected turnout – his mother's had been the same – and he felt a rush of pity for Maddy McKay.

He was trying to identify her and her mother when suddenly two gleaming hearses followed by a black saloon, reminding him of Ed Thom's Merc, pulled into the lay-by immediately in front of the open wrought-iron gates. With military precision, both coffins were unloaded and carried by the funeral staff up the uneven pathway, through the vestry and into the gloomy nave.

Martin tensed as a petite young woman wearing a black wide-brimmed hat emerged from the saloon and teetered on her high heels next to an older woman who tried to support her by holding her hand.

'I'm fine, Mam,' she insisted, then unexpectedly glanced back at him.

He sat in the pew by the door where an elderly verger, having finished handing out prayer books and the order of service, joined him and

193

promptly began to blow his nose into a large clean handkerchief.

'Percy Smithson, I am,' he announced when he'd finished. 'And I paid for all this, you know. Least I could do so these poor buggers had summat decent at the end.' He sniffed, then wiped his eyes. 'I knew Daphne well, by God, yes. Here one minute, gone the next. Makes no sense. No sense at all. I last saw her the day before she had her stroke. Bright as a button, she was. We used to do the Telegraph crossword together every Saturday. She was on top form till the end. Mind you, in hospital she couldn't say owt. Just looked at me in an odd way. And, see that Indian gentleman over there –' he pointed to a half-filled pew further down the aisle – 'that's Mr Patel, who runs the home she was in. He's shocked about the way she went. And as for that poor lad lying there...'

The organ music grew more sonorous, drowning the intermittent sobbing which echoed eerily into all the highest places. Martin forced himself to look at the coffins facing the altar. Identical in every way, including the spray of white lilies on each.

'She doted on her Gary, did Daphne,' his neighbour went on. 'Worshipped him, you could say, which isn't surprising, given one thing and another.'

But before Martin could ask him if he'd ever met Gary himself, the vicar emerged from the sacristy and the organ music faded.

Martin wondered what his 'one thing and another' might have meant.

Percy Smithson vanished straight after the service, not even staying for the two interments. Martin was about to seek out Maddy McKay when he spotted her breaking away from the other mourners.

'I guessed it was you,' she said, catching up with him, and he saw how the pale face beneath her veil was wet with tears which she made no effort to wipe away.

'I'm sorry,' was all he could say, while he noticed from the corner of his eye the plain white van, which until then had lurked in the background, was now approaching the occupied graves. Two men got out, pulled shovels from the back and began to set to as she withdrew a blue envelope from her black shiny bag and passed it over.

'Here's that card, remember? You can keep it and by the way, my mobile number's on the other side, just in case.'

'Thanks.' He registered the date and postmark. 7th May 2002. He slotted it carefully in his jacket pocket. 'Is your dog still missing?'

'Donny? Yes. And he never strayed far from our cottage. Never. And he made a real racket whenever anyone called. People were surprised such a din could come from such a wee beastie.'

Fresh tears flowed and Martin told himself to choose his next words with care.

'Look,' he began, aware Mrs McKay was approaching with a strained expression on her face, 'it's important you find him. I'll come up there myself if I have to. I don't want to upset you, but

195

someone may have wanted him out of the way. It seems a coincidence that both he and your partner disappeared at the same time.'

The older woman, who'd already placed her bag on the car's rear seat, turned to face him. Touched his arm.

'Maddy and I do appreciate your coming here, and there is something you can do to help. Find out about that disco in Manchester that Gary went to.'

'Mam, *don't* say his name. Not today. I can't bear it.'

'I know, my love, but we want to know why his gran was so bothered about it that she went to the trouble of writing to him.'

Martin said, 'I'll do my best, I promise.'

Two weak but grateful smiles and then, seconds later, their car pulled away from the kerb, soon to be lost among other traffic moving into town. He watched it go. Heard the regular plop of earth against wood coming from the graves and ran along the pavement to where the original group of mourners were dispersing.

Mr Patel was about to cross a busy road with those same two plump care assistants Martin had noticed in church. Their overalls showing beneath their coats. Sadness in their eyes. He tapped him on the shoulder.

'Excuse me, Mr Patel, but can I have a quick word?'

The man spun round, his moist eyes looking him up and down.

'Who are you? Not a reporter, I hope.'

'No way. Do me a favour.'

'Good. My staff have had enough of those parasites recently, disrupting their routine, asking personal questions. They even came here before the service. I asked them to leave in no uncertain terms.'

'I'm one of Gary's mates. I believe you run the home where Mrs Cope was being looked after.'

The man and his entourage stepped back from the kerb doused in dust from a passing bus. He brushed himself down, clearly annoyed at being detained any further, but the girls seemed glad of a few extra minutes off work.

'I've not got much to go on, but I think she may have known something which had a bearing on Gary's death.'

'Young man, in this country we have the best police force in the world. Believe me, I know. *They* are the people you should be telling this to. Not me.'

'Have they paid you a visit yet?'

'Get off,' said one of the girls. 'If it's old people, they don't give a monkey's.'

'So who was her main carer, then?'

'Frankie was,' she said before her boss could restrain her. 'In fact, I'm amazed she never showed up today. She was the one who chatted to Daphne all the time and when she left Briarfield it was like, "Where's my Frankie gone? Where's my best girl?"'

'Briarfield, you say?' Martin tried to recall the CV in his pocket.

Mr Patel made a renewed effort to cross the road.

'Was Holt her carer's surname?'

'I don't think that's any of your business, sir.'

'Frankie nicked a book from your office, though,' volunteered the other girl with fatter, pinker cheeks and greasy hair tied back in a ponytail. 'Mrs Lloyd said so. You know, before she had that vomiting attack.'

'Mrs Lloyd was changing medicines at the time. They were causing her some confusion.' He strode towards the traffic island as if to forestall any more revelations about life at Briarfield. 'We want no more intrusions, Mr Webb. We have work to do for those still in our care.'

Martin decided to follow the trio, ensuring he stayed out of sight whenever one of the girls looked round. Once at the home, he'd pose as a visitor for this Mrs Lloyd and find Daphne Cope's room, because, despite Mr Patel's agenda for him, the day wasn't yet over.

'Mrs Lloyd, please,' he smiled at the girl at the desk, who tapped in the necessary code. She ushered him towards the visitors' book on a table further down the corridor, where he saw immediately that Percy Smithson had been Mrs Cope's only caller since the book started in August 2000.

'Vera's in her room. Number thirty it is. This your first time here?'

'Yes. Our neighbours who know her thought she'd appreciate a visit as they are away.'

'That's very nice,' she stood over him as he resurrected the name Webster, preceded by James. He also noticed, from the nearby residents' list, that Mrs Cope's room was currently number thirty-six.

'Just go up the stairs and turn left,' said the girl. 'You can't miss it. She's flower mad.'

It wasn't flowers he could smell in the corridor but a mix of kitchen and toilets, which seemed to coalesce in the stairwell as he reached the first floor. With his pulse on overdrive, he scanned the corridor, reasoning that without CCTV surveillance and all the bedroom doors open he could have nicked anything. Not that he'd want to. Every room seemed the same, personalized only by different-colour dressing gowns and different framed photos of toddlers who, judging by their clothes, had long grown up and gone away. Bowls of pot-pourri and faded artificial flowers stood amongst half-finished packets of Rich Tea biscuits and other detritus of lives on the wane.

The stale air filled his throat as finally he reached room thirty and saw as promised an elderly woman standing with her back to him, fiddling with a vase of red flowers on her windowsill. Her white hair was unbrushed, her legs like a pair of Twiglets protruding below her pleated skirt. But at least she was busy. Too busy to notice him moving to the room at the corridor's end whose door still bore the label of its dead occupant and a poster announcing that Frankie Holt was her lead carer. Having checked the coast was clear he went in and frisked the wardrobe, the chest of drawers and bedside table for anything, however small, that might tangibly connect her to her grandson.

First, the top drawer, full of crossword puzzles completed by two different styles of writing. One bold, the other lighter, less confident. The same as on the card and its envelope. The second drawer was almost empty, save for a photograph showing a handsome young woman standing next to a small boy in short grey trousers. The boy's face seemed to bear a resemblance to the one in the *Mirror*. Judging by the slightly faded paper and the date on the reverse, this could well be Gary's father.

Next, something which made him catch his breath. A newspaper cutting dated 20 June 2000, of a car having crashed into a goods train in rural Suffolk. A Mr and Mrs Kenneth Cope, both aged forty-nine, had been killed outright. Their son, a recent arts graduate at Manchester University, was being comforted by his grandmother.

Martin stared at the grainy crash scene – a saloon car mangled under the front of a goods train, while in the distance, on that terrible summer's day, cows were grazing without a care. So, Gary wasn't a dropout, then. Not by a long chalk. He'd finished his degree at one of the top provincial universities. But this image of death possibly represented the beginning of the end.

He could hear Mrs Lloyd running her tap. Her basin was near her door. He mustn't be caught, but there was still one more drawer to go. Different stuff in here. A postcard from Gary. And a letter for Mrs Daphne Cope dated 22 April 2002 with a smudged Argyll postmark. He was just about to open it when a shrill voice behind him made him jump.

'What are you doing in here, young man?'

Vera Lloyd limped towards what he assumed was a panic button. With the letter in his grip, he pushed past her and down the stairs where a delivery door lay conveniently open.

Eighteen

Wednesday 3rd July 2002. Who can I talk to? Confide my deepest fears? My only sister, whom I have attempted to protect for many years has betrayed not just me and herself, but everyone in our family who has gone before. I would prefer not to believe her, but she was emphatic and coherent on the phone, in a way I've not heard for a long time.

On Saturday morning she made her will solely in favour of – I can barely write his name – Sean Brownlow. As if he's not had enough. Apparently, at her insistence – but I don't believe this for one minute, unless she's acted out of spite towards me. All I can do is speak to Regis Fleming and ask his advice. Doubtless he will agree that my delay in making my own will out to Merle is a blessing. Yes, to think that all my hard work, plus the proceeds of Samuel's consultancies and investments, could have one day slipped into that man's pocket.

Evelyn paused, listening to the grandfather clock

strike five. She was helpless, but still too proud to ask any of her workers' wives to help. Too fearful of losing her status. Besides, her proximity to Sean Brownlow at the protest had left a bad taste in everyone's mouths. Or so the town's civic society had informed her in a letter. Something she could well do without.

She heard an unfamiliar car approaching up the drive and before she could move away from her desk to improve her appearance, noticed a tall young woman with very short bright blonde hair bob up and down as she placed a number of Waitrose bags by the porch. What on *earth* was going on? Evelyn wondered, and then with a sudden shot of fear realized this might be the start of a distraction burglary.

'Miss Scott?' called out the visitor. 'I'm Frankie. Your sister's carer. Got some shopping for you. Thought you might need a few things, just in case.'

Frankie? The first time she'd heard that name. She'd been too weary to check, and Brownlow hadn't volunteered any more information. She blinked in surprise. So how on earth had this stranger guessed what she'd wanted? Her neglect was a very private matter. Even Merle didn't know. With a grateful smile she unlocked the outer door, struck immediately by this carer's sheer energy, her responsiveness compared to the previous ones.

'Sorry it's not the usual kind of car you see on your driveway,' the young woman went on. 'All I could afford at the time.' She smiled disarmingly. 'Anyway, let's get this lot in before the rain picks up.'

'The worst summer I can remember.' Evelyn stood aside with her Zimmer frame while the girl transferred the bags into the hallway. 'They've even forecast flooding.'

'Not surprised,' said the girl, handing over the till receipt and waiting without the slightest sign of impatience while Evelyn rummaged in her handbag secured to the top of her frame with a giant bulldog clip, and withdrew twenty pounds in notes. 'And as for your car, if it gets you from A to B, that's all that matters.'

'Thanks for the cash. Mr Brownlow says I've got to wait till the end of each month before he'll settle up. But what do I do in the meantime? That's the problem.'

'I can see I'll have to have words with him.'

'Thanks.'

'Is Frankie short for Frances?'

'Yeah. Why?'

'I'd prefer to call you that, if you didn't mind.'

'Fine by me. Makes no difference.'

Evelyn gestured towards the kitchen, and the girl picked up the shopping and heaped it on the table in there. Muesli and a carton of full-fat milk. Eggs, a fresh pack of bacon, a box of six mini apple pies, a bag of white rolls. Cherry tomatoes, a slab of mild Cheddar and a large pale broiler chicken.

'Your sister's being very kind to me, by the way.' The helper opened the fridge door and, having found a cleaning cloth in the sink, began wiping down the empty shelves.

'I'm glad to hear it.' But something made the

girl stop what she was doing and turn to her instead.

'It's that Mr Brownlow, innit? You don't need to tell me, Miss Scott. To be quite honest –' her strong capable hands closed round the chicken, dimpling its thighs as she pushed it on to the empty glass shelf – 'he's interfering in everything. My job included. He'd probably go ape if he knew I'd come here.'

It wasn't simply the chill from the fridge which made Evelyn shudder despite her warm dressing gown.

'By the way,' the girl added, now twisting the bird's leg stumps to fit the too-small space, 'I heard some tasty gossip in town just now.'

'What kind of gossip?'

'The cops – I mean police – have pulled Mr B in.'

'Whatever for?'

'To do with Friday's solstice thing. Talk is it wasn't an animal he'd been burning. Now then – ' she faced Evelyn over the box of mini apple pies – 'where d'you want these?'

'In that cupboard over the wine rack.' Her voice sounded feeble. Could this girl prove to be a godsend? An informant to keep her in the picture?

'Tell me, Miss Scott, and you can say it's nothing to do with me, but I *am* a bit confused. Your sister calls you Jenny, but everyone else says Evelyn.'

Evelyn tried to compose herself for her coup de grâce. The worst thing she could ever utter and she hoped God would forgive her.

'I shouldn't be saying this, least of all to you, a stranger,' she began. 'But Merle is mad. Quite mad. Please remember this and the fact that her illness can only get worse.'

Nineteen

'Stupid cow, you,' Frankie admonished herself as she drove away from the Gables, thinking of her fruitless trip to the library for her CV. 'Have you not got enough to think about?' None of the dozy staff in Sleepy Hollow had had a clue as to its whereabouts, so now her personal stuff was up for grabs. Great. She'd even written her client's ex-directory phone number beneath the address. She wondered if that tasty guy in the black-leather jacket who'd helped her out had seen anyone use the machine after she'd gone, but the chances of finding him again were remote.

The visit to town hadn't been a total waste of time. Before shopping at Waitrose for Evelyn Scott, she'd calmed herself down by buying a natty pink suede rucksack and also used the library's PC to search for any information on Scott's Rifles and the family's history. In the late sixties, she'd found, Evelyn had taken over the business from her parents after completing an engineering degree at Brunel University. She'd married Samuel Colby in 1974, who'd died from a stroke in November 1996. However, apart from details of various rifle-design developments and the factory's expansion, there was precious little of real interest. Certainly nothing about a child. Nothing about any Jenny either. As for the company's website, it was a dreary affair of end-of-year statistics and global outlets. It showed that Evelyn Scott must own millions. And she'd still been ever so grateful for that little favour with the shopping.

Yes, she'd made a hit with her, all right. She had even given her a five-pound tip. Stood outside her porch as she'd driven away; a small hunched figure waving after her for longer than necessary. And then as her car had reached the main road, who should have been swerving on to the drive and nearly colliding with her? Evil Eyes himself, wrenching his wheel to avoid a collision. Fixing her with a look of pure fury.

As she drove back at speed, with Ellie's empty car seat rocking backwards and forwards, she realized she'd have some explaining to do at her next inevitable interrogation. Fresh anger made her speed even faster along narrowing roads.

After a late tea of scones and jam watching the six o'clock news with Merle squeezed into a childhood ballerina's outfit, Frankie made the call to Tonbridge.

'What if he docks my pay, or doesn't hand it over?'

'Mr Brownlow would never do that. He'd have to give us a very good reason why.'

And then a question that had been bugging her since leaving Briarfield.

'By the way, do I *have* to use the word "client"?'

'Yes. It's one of our most important rules.'

'Where did you go to just now?' Merle whined when Frankie reappeared to turn the volume down.

'Just up to my room.'

'No, I mean before that. You were gone for over an hour.'

Frankie gave the V sign to the back of her head. At least she'd had an answer ready.

'I had to get some stuff for myself from the corner shop.'

'You can't simply leave me on my own. What would Mr Brownlow say?'

She knew only too well.

'I'm sorry, right?' Then she pointed to Merle's pale pink ballet pumps. 'D'you want me to do up those ribbons for you?'

'Thank you, dear. That's most kind.' She stuck out one plump foot after another until Frankie had tied both ribbon ends into neat bows, making their owner's pale trapped flesh bulge out between the criss-crossed weave. Reminding her to put the turkey in the oven or supper would be too late.

A news item on Scotland suddenly appeared on the TV. Frankie stared as Kilfargan's wooded lochside filled the too-large screen. During Gary Cope's funeral in Manchester, fellow workers from the fish farm had organized a search for the couple's pet terrier and found him near Loch Cottage with a fatal knife wound to his neck. A tearful-looking scrubber now faced the camera. Her eyes the same colour as Shannon's. However, Frankie noticed with satisfaction that her skin was all blotchy and unhealthy looking.

'Whoever did this to Donny is sick, sick, sick,' she burbled.

'My goodness, Frances, what a world.' Merle clicked the remote to increase the volume as some plainclothed pig at a press conference expressed doubts about the suicide verdict in such a strong Scottish accent Frankie barely understood him. But when the word 'exhumation' came over loud and clear, she gripped the back of Merle's chair. Frankie wished Kilfargan would disappear for ever. She'd had enough of those gloomy trees, that endless sheet of grey water.

'Best get cooking.' She smiled at Merle before slipping one of her many pairs of membranous rubber gloves over her hands in advance of stuffing the turkey. Then she heard a familiar name on the regional news bulletin.

'Sean Brownlow, a fifty-two-year-old bachelor from Upton, has been released after questioning by Worcester CID over the alleged disappearance of Mohammed Shalah, a former Algerian hod-carrier at the town's Hill Springs development. All but one of the illegal workforce have been traced and police are appealing to any witnesses who might have seen him in the area after the afternoon of Tuesday 18th June.' A description of the missing man followed, but it was Brownlow's which lodged in her mind.

Those eyes, piercing, hypnotic. The way he jerked his head to one side when he stared at you. The sudden restless movements of his limbs. A man so fit, so toned, despite his age, that he could barely contain himself. What had *he* been up to, she wondered. Mr Fucking Perfect.

'We also urge anyone else who either attended the North Hill solstice event or happened to be nearby to contact us immediately.'

Nearby?

She'd been that all right. Close enough to smell the singed flesh, hear those weird blood-curdling cries. But no way would she put herself forward and she hoped that mouthy Carol Piper whom she'd met there would also keep her gob shut. She was tempted to accept the woman's invitation for tomorrow night so she could find out what else she knew about Brownlow.

Frankie suddenly wished that she lived some-where big and busy where she'd be just one among many. Anonymous, carefree. And best of all, her secrets intact. At least she'd used those gloves at Gee's and Kilfargan. Something to be proud of...

The bird was already spitting noisily in the oven's heat and Frankie loaded up the gold-plated hostess trolley with two of everything to set the dining table. Merle muddled her way into the hall.

'Why do you keep that doll upstairs?' she ask-ed, checking her appearance in the brass-framed mirror positioned over the telephone table.

That doll? How dare you...?

'I mean, most girls grow out of them by the time they reach their teens. At least I did.'

'Bully for you,' Frankie muttered then bit her lip. She laid down the cheese knife she was holding, reminding herself to stay calm and rational the way Mrs Beavis had demonstrated during that first year at the tech. It was five years ago tomorrow since she'd walked through those front doors.

'She's not a doll.'

'Really? So I'm blind, am I?' That pasty face topped by a cheap tiara suddenly didn't seem harmless any more. A too-bright slab of sunshine which beamed between the curtains hit the woman's cheek. Fell on the sharpened blade of the black-handled carving knife lying on the white cloth alongside its matching two-pronged fork. She'd been poking around in her room. Her one precious space. Unless, of course, Brownlow had snitched on her.

'She's called Ellie Scott, is that right? I saw it on her wrist band.'

'Yes. So? I made it up yonks ago. Coincidence, that's all.' Just hearing her say that surname brought a sudden flush to Frankie's cheeks as Merle manoeuvred herself into her chair at the table's head and tucked her linen napkin into the scooped neck of her bodice.

'I'm going to be blunt here, Frances.' She looked up at her, the fake diamonds in her tiara winking in the sunlight. 'I don't want her in the house any longer. You've been taking dried milk up to the attic. It will encourage mice.'

Frankie gulped and eyed the carving knife again.

'I find her presence upsetting.'

Frankie's stomach seemed to contract. The turkey smell from the kitchen bringing a rush of nausea. What the *fuck* was she saying?

'Upsetting? Why?'

'Please try and understand. That's all.'

Frankie felt her head begin to heat up.

'You can leave her out with the rubbish. The bin men come on Monday.'

'Bin men?' Frankie could barely repeat it. 'You can't be serious. She needs looking after. The way I look after you.'

'I want her out of my house *now*.' Merle indicated the front door with a wave of her hand. 'Before I have my supper.'

Furious tears blinded Frankie's eyes as she ran up the three flights of stairs and reached the attic room where Ellie was sleeping peacefully. The blur of light from the window and the dark corners under the eaves merged with the memory of Dartmoor Road. She saw the murderous Beryl all over again snatching Lila from her grasp. The one person she'd really loved...

Soon her baby daughter was in her arms, wrapped up in the threadbare hand towel which the last helper had left hanging under the washbasin. Only when she'd reached the last set of stairs did she notice the stains on it. Blood and cum.

'I don't want her in your car either, if that's what you're thinking...' Frankie stopped and gripped Ellie closer.

One step at a time, Frankie told herself, feeling dizzy and slightly sick again, aware of the turkey stumps beginning to burn. She was very close to Merle now and it was time to sort this issue out once and for all. Like any other mother would do where her child's well-being was at stake. She had the right to look after Ellie in the best way possible. Her daughter was hers. For keeps.

'*Look* at her.' Frankie peeled away the towel and placed it over the back of the nearest dining chair. 'She's beautiful. What's your problem? Is it the nappies? The bottles? The way she stares at you?' She eyed the stick. 'Tell me, Miss Scott, or I'll forever be wondering.'

Merle glanced sideways out of the window which, like its counterpart in the lounge, over-looked the drive.

'I'll call Mr Brownlow...'

'Him again? He'll be far too busy to bother with you.' She came closer still and tapped the pale flaccid flesh of Merle's forearm. 'Now he's got your money.'

She enjoyed watching that face change to a scowl as she tried to stand. The stick fell to the floor and Frankie picked it up, aware of its solid weight.

'How dare you remark upon my affairs, you cheeky madam.'

'I'd rather be cheeky than old like you, you waste of skin.'

With one hand she swiftly moved any cutlery and glasses out of her tormentor's reach, just in case. With the other, she held out her daughter.

'Now then, Ellie wants you to kiss her and say

212

sorry for what you said about her. She wants to be loved, you see.'

Merle shut her eyes, pursing that obstinate lip-sticked mouth.

'I said, kiss her and say sorry.'

The way John Arthur had said 'kiss it' and she'd obeyed. This, however, was different.

The ballerina swallowed hard. Her fat hands curled around the arms of her captain's chair. She broke wind. Tried to get up. Frankie wasn't finished yet. She placed the newborn into the frilly lap, her head leaning between both breasts visible under the taffeta bodice.

'I'm waiting.'

Merle flinched, her hands leaving the chair as if to pick Ellie up. Then she dropped them back again.

'Can't even do that, can you?' Frankie snarled.

'Help!'

'Can't think of anyone but your stupid fat self.'

The stick's handle now nestled in the palm of her right hand. Such a perfect fit, she thought, that once the first blow had dislodged Merle's tiara and sent her false teeth flying from her mouth, she found she couldn't stop. Just like her client, now screaming out her long-buried secrets...

The Mulberry handbag could wait. Besides, tempting though it was, if she nicked the matching purse inside which contained precious little cash but a Barclays Visa card and its PIN number, that would be too obvious. Everything must be made to seem as if its owner had

213

wandered off.

Frankie's mind was like the fast spin on a wash cycle and when she inwardly clicked stop, the solution to her dilemma appeared. It was a risk, but like Scotland, one worth taking.

While Ellie sat snug in her car seat, looking calm and contented despite the lapse in her routine, and Merle's overstuffed body filled the Fiesta's boot with not a centimetre to spare, she drove through to her chosen destination.

With her shades on her nose and the visor down, Frankie weaved in and out of the double-parked vehicles until the lines of terraced houses gave way to trees and North Hill's steep fern-covered sides loomed up on her left. She passed the drive to the Gables; one glance told her that *he* was there. Maybe with another homemade will.

As the road climbed upwards, her mind lurched from one image to another. With each bend she could feel Merle's dead weight shift from side to side, sending the steering momentarily out of control. She gritted her teeth, thinking about the cold meat in the boot. There'd been no blood. Not like the fish-farm worker. No extensive bruising either. Just the one deep depression above the left painted eyebrow, beginning to turn a funny colour as she'd pulled her over the gravel to the car. A colour which reminded her of John Arthur's cock.

Why hadn't the stupid old bag told her in the first place the real reason she'd not been able to hack a newborn in Teme House? That it brought back too many memories of a birth in a private clinic in Surrey and what her younger sister had done despite Merle's offer to bring up the baby for her so she could keep working. She'd even named her Jenny – after the midwife who'd delivered her, because Evelyn couldn't be bothered.

'When was this Jenny born? When?' Frankie had shaken her, tried to squeeze that mouth open and instead got orange lipstick all over her fingers.

But too late. That was her lot. A bubble of spit had billowed and shrunk in the corner of Merle's mouth. And, like her car now, Frankie's mind had slipped into overdrive. She knew that cryptic grave in the back garden was nothing to do with any dog. It was Merle reminding her sister of her past. And the reason Sean Brownlow had benefited from her will. She wondered whether Evelyn Scott had left all her wealth to sister Merle, whether Brownlow now had everything...

Christ, the woman was heavy. Nothing at Briarfield had prepared her for this. Frankie cursed as she prised both bare legs out of the boot and began dragging the body to the closest clump of high ferns. Then something caught her eye. A blue-and-white police cordon surrounded the spot where that bonfire had been; where she'd met Carol Piper. It quickened her movements. Made her forget to breathe. She should have realized this wasn't the best place to hide something so substantial, and yet...

If only she'd listened to Mrs Beavis and kept control of herself. And then it occurred to her that if and when the aged ballerina was ever

215

found, it would look as if the man due to inherit her estate was taunting the pigs with another crime. Pushing his luck.

By now, the corpse was already attracting flies.

She scoured the wild grazed hilltops stretching away for as far as the eye could see. There wasn't another soul around. She must get back and burn the walking stick to make it look like her client had wandered off, and then carry on as normal.

Using her handy latex gloves, she crammed Merle's tiara back on her head and those dentures back into her mouth. Then she pulled her white knickers down to her knees. She slithered back to the Fiesta, relieved to notice that its tyre tracks were merged amongst many and her footprints blurred with those who'd come up for the bonfires last Friday. However, her satisfaction was short-lived. Ellie looked too passive. Too detached from everything that she, her caring mother, had just gone through.

'You could have stopped me fucking killing her,' she snapped. 'But you just lay there. I mean, if you'd made a noise, or said something, I'd still have a nice roof over my head.' She reversed into a muddy lay-by and rejoined the track leading from the road. 'You just bloody lay there, Ellie. You let me hit her all those times. You *must* have heard what she was yelling at me. Now look!' She nudged her, then noticed a posse of mountain-bikers approaching around an oncoming bend. She slowed up, lowering her shaded eyes as they passed, missing their waves of acknowledgement, scared they might get a good look at her. Be unwanted witnesses.

Frankie passed the Gables yet again and saw Brownlow's Jeep had gone. She swore she could see a thin tense face at the lower bay window. She stepped on the gas, not caring that Ellie had tipped out of her seat and was lying on the floor with both her legs in the air.

'You stop there till you've said sorry an' all,' she muttered. 'You're the reason we'll be poor all over again. D'you know that?'

Black clouds had congregated over the top of North Hill, obliterating the last small scraps of blue, so that by the time she turned in through Teme House's double gates, letting out a gasp of relief that the production manager's car wasn't there, a sly rain had begun to fall.

She wiped the stick thoroughly with a cloth from the cloakroom. Best to leave it in the umbrella stand, she decided. That way it would seem as if Merle had gone out and forgotten it.

She returned to the kitchen and was just about to take the roast bird from the now cool oven when a slight sound from the room overhead made her freeze. Holding her breath, she deposited the full, heavy baking tray on the nearest worktop and crept into the hall. There it was again, but more frequent now. Footsteps, bringing a man downstairs and into the hall. Despite his black woollen hat pulled low over his eyebrows, she recognized him all too clearly. His top lip was bleeding, his left eye bruised and swollen.

Piotr.

'Miss, him after me,' he breathed before she could ask what the hell he was doing and how he'd got in. 'I had to hide somewhere...'

'*Who's* after you?'

'Man with gun. Like so.' He imitated a hunter, rifle cocked, ready for the kill. 'I hate him. He told me to go back to fucking Poland. England for the English, he said.'

'Mr Brownlow?'

He nodded. She could smell his sweat, his fear.

'Is this the truth?'

'He's hated me from the first day he see me here.'

Piotr was a problem for her. He'd wonder where his elderly employer was. She had to lose him somehow.

'Look, I'll pay you,' she said. 'Then you'd better shift. I'm sorry but I don't want trouble here.'

His eyes lit up. He came down the rest of the stairs, squeezing past the chairlift and glanced around, a deep frown embedded in his forehead.

'Where's Miss Merle, then?'

'I've been out looking for her. She's taken herself off again. One of her usual walkabouts, I reckon.'

'She never go out of the garden. I no understand.'

Frankie willed herself to keep cool.

'She'll be back, you'll see. I'm honestly not that worried. At least, not yet.' She opened the desk drawer and withdrew a brown envelope bulging with cash. 'Best if you don't say anything until we know for sure. OK?'

She handed it over, thinking there was always the newly sharpened carving knife if he made things difficult.

'Thank you, Miss Carer.' He counted out the notes, his damaged lip even worse close up. 'I can go back to Cracow now.'

Should she stay or go herself? That was the big question, which only she could answer. And then, gritting her teeth and thinking about what Piotr had just said, she pulled out a handful of hair from behind her left ear, and deliberately let it fall to the floor.

Still smarting from her self-inflicted injury, Frankie called round to the nearest neighbours in Wye House with a worried look on her face, and having asked them to look out for Merle, copied up her version of the day so far in her carer's record book. She then phoned a startled Evelyn Scott to ask if she knew anything about her sister's will signing.

'May I ask, is it any of your business?'

Where was that friendly voice from Wednesday? she wondered.

'I was a witness.'

'Really? Why didn't you mention this when we met this morning?'

'It's been preying on my mind, that's why. I wasn't sure that was the best time to say anything.'

'Say what, exactly?'

'I wasn't happy with the way Mr Brownlow behaved towards your sister. He set it all up, didn't he? That was obvious. Then made her sign for him to be sole beneficiary. Practically held her pen, he did. I saw it all.'

A pause you could have cut with a knife.

'Where's Merle now?'

'On the toilet. She's a bit constipated. Why I'm able to call you.'

'Tell her to ring me the minute she's finished.'

No thanks, no gratitude. But that didn't really matter. The net around Mr Bossy Corduroys was tightening. She phoned Malvern police station and told them that Merle had wandered off from the toilet and she was now very concerned for her safety. She'd added that the fleeing gardener seeking refuge in the house said Sean Brownlow was hanging around and armed. And by the way, did they know that he'd twisted her client's arm and now stood to inherit all her worldly goods?

'We'll get DC Pilkington to call you,' said the desk sergeant flatly.

Frankie gulped. The last person she needed to hear from.

'How d'you know *her*?' she asked.

'She's been promoted. Now a detective constable with the West Mercia Constabulary. Reassigned to your case.'

Frankie's blood seemed to slow to a stop in her veins. She was aware of a draught from somewhere upstairs.

'My *case*? What case?'

A pause. The guy was looking stuff up on his PC, she could tell. Technology had made her unique history common knowledge.

'Since your sister disappeared and your father died, DC Pilkington has kept an eye on you. You've had a lot to contend with, Miss Holt.

We'll get a car round there ASAP.'

Frankie wasn't waiting.

She locked and bolted the scullery door, because Brownlow had keys. Feeling that same draught, stronger now, and realizing a bedroom window must still be open somewhere, she ran upstairs on aching calf muscles, past painted portraits of spaniels with sorrowful eyes, happy eyes; every expression under the sun.

Big dirty footprints led along the landing which in turn reached the Blue Room where Evelyn Scott used to stay. The moment she stepped through the open doorway, she saw the tall sash window half-opened, its curtains dancing in the wind. The matching pelmet askew.

She hurtled down the stairs and out of the front door. If Brownlow was after the gardener, she might well be next. Teme House wasn't safe any more. She wasn't safe. She had no option but to get out.

Twenty

Martin stepped off the bus in Manchester's Piccadilly and joined commuters freed from their desks. He felt it was better to strike while the iron – or rather, his curiosity – was still hot.

The city centre's air seemed warm and stale in his mouth as he nudged along, shoulder to shoulder with the suits thronging the pavements. His next port of call was a place Gary had anguished about in that last letter to his gran.

2/5/02Loch Cottage, Kilfargan

Dear Gran,
I hope you liked the flowers we sent you for your birthday. Thought they'd brighten up your room a bit. I'm writing rather than phoning because no one ever answers who could bring the phone to you. I reckon your carer needs to sort it out.

Anyway, it's about my girl from uni. The one with the white hair you once said looked like a film star. I know you said it was odd she never asked me home but I tried not to let it bother me. If she didn't want me to meet her family, that was her business. But it did become an issue. It started to get me down and when all my mates were getting jobs or gapping just like her until their post-grads or research degrees I couldn't get my act together. Then, out of the blue, just before Christmas, she dumps me. No reason given. I tried phoning, texting, the works, but no reply. In the end, I found out where she lived and went round.

Gran, you'd never have put her with that hole. Never. No wonder she kept quiet about it. But it wouldn't have mattered to me. I started doing stuff with Mum and Dad's money which was meant to help me

buy my own place. I knew where to get it. (Pegasus, he's called. 37 Mitcham Road Moss Side. If anything happens to me. I still owe him money.) Don't tell a *soul* and tear this up when you've read it. Then I saw her again. Xmas Eve before last at Gee's. I was stoned, mind, and she must have had a few as she didn't recognize me at all and I didn't have the courage to go over to her. The more I've thought about it, the more I know there's *no way* she'd become a dyke – excuse the expression – or that she'd topped herself. She had dreams to go to Australia. That other girl she was with wasn't all over her because of love. But hate. If I go to the cops I'm done for. Pegasus is still out there, waiting.
Your loving Gary xxx

What had happened to his ex, and what had the cops got to do with it? Had there been a crime? Martin frowned as that account spun round and round in his head. Why hadn't Maddy known this ex who'd obviously been special to him? Maybe Gary had kept quiet about her. He wouldn't tell Dora about Ria, would he? Who *had* that mysterious other girl been? The one associated with the word 'hate'?

There was only one Gee's in the Manchester metropolitan area and it wasn't far. The reinforced front door lay half open and beyond it he could see a Japanese girl hoovering the dark green carpet. Her tiny skirt barely covered her butt, so that when she bent down to untangle the flex he turned away, embarrassed. He bypassed her to reach the Reception desk where a shadowy figure lurked by an open drawer in the far corner.

'Excuse me,' he yelled over the hoover's whine. 'Can you help me?'

'We're closed,' replied a female voice in a strong Birmingham accent. 'Can't you read the sign outside?'

'Yeah, but that's not what I'm after. I need information. Were you working here Christmas Eve 2000 by any chance?'

The girl came closer. Green hair, green-felt two-piece and eyeshadow to match. Clearly the Gee's uniform.

He extracted his Monroe employment card complete with photo and the site address. 'I'm a roofer. But my mate's in hospital here. Asking about a white-haired girl he used to go out with...'

'You mean Shannon?'

'Had she been at uni with him?'

'Yeah. She was me mate an' all, mind,' the other said, watching the young cleaner move away down the lobby. 'Bloody good laugh we were having, until the adopted sister came along.'

'Sister?'

The girl nodded.

'Bitch Face. Jealous was her middle name. I don't know how Shannon stuck it with the miserable cow. I bloody wouldn't have. Who's this mate of yours?'

224

'Gary.'

'Yeah. She said she'd outgrown him. He was clingy, you know the sort. I'd swear he was here an' all that night. Can't be sure though. You can guess how heaving it gets...' She fixed him with a strange look as the hoover faded to silence and the cleaner disappeared around the corner. 'Doesn't he know about her, then?'

'Know what?' Martin felt a chill seep through his clothes.

'Oh, hell.'

'Please...'

'She fuckin' vanished, didn't she? Dancing the one minute, gone the next.' She leaned forwards. 'I reckon she'd had enough. She'd said to me before she was going to Oz to do bar work, whatever. Even though she'd done this degree. Just shows how pissed off she was with every-thing.'

'I heard there was this other girl with her. That theirs wasn't a friendly encounter.'

The cloakroom girl shrugged.

'Don't know nothing about that. Shannon had her own agenda. She wanted out. Told me loads of times...'

'Did anyone see her or the sister leave?'

A laugh followed.

'You must be joking. We get thousands in on that night. But, like I said, Bitch Face was here. On the pull, I reckon. Looked a right freak with that brown cardie, them cropped jeans.'

'What was her name, d'you remember?'

'Don't think Shannon ever said. Mind you, one thing I do remember...'

Martin waited as she marshalled her thoughts.

'She did mention something about her having a doll. Yeah. That's right. She thought it was right weird.'

'A doll?'

'Yeah. One that looked like an hour old...'

He wasn't sure if this wasn't just to divert him. Minutes were ticking by.

'Look, is there anyone else I can speak to about Shannon or any of the pushers?'

Her face instantly changed. An angry blush hit her cheeks.

'There's *no* pushers here. Never have been. If Mr Gee even *hears* that word, then – ' she drew an imaginary line across her throat – 'that's me off the planet.'

He stepped back from the curved mahogany desk and headed for the door.

Something wasn't right. She was just an employee of a lucrative set-up and if he had to go and see a criminal to find out more then so be it. As Martin retraced his steps over the bridge and struggled against the flow of humanity until he spotted an empty cab for hire, he wondered who this despised sister might be. He also couldn't get the girl called Shannon out of his mind. Although Gary Cope was now represented by a rough mound of soil and turf, both he and Maddy McKay deserved justice.

'Thirty-seven Mitcham Road, Moss Side,' he said to the driver. 'And hurry.'

'You sure?' The guy seemed slow off the mark. 'Why?'

'You tooled up?'

Not yet.

Martin didn't reply. The cab itself was stifling, its window jammed, but he kept his jacket on simply to prevent anything falling from its pockets. And while Rusholme became Moss Side and the houses smaller, jammed side by side with not a tree in sight, he began to wonder if this wasn't all a waste of time and money.

'Know someone there, then?' quizzed the driver above the murmur of some local radio station.

'Just looking.'

'Want me to wait? Mitcham Road throws up a stiff pretty well every Saturday night...'

That idea hadn't occurred to him. But what he wanted to find out, wouldn't take long.

'Cheers.'

They turned into a cul-de-sac ending in a high brick wall supporting a railway line festooned with wires and other paraphernalia.

Martin got out by number 37, and as he walked over to the battered looking front door, he heard the taxi making a three-point turn to reposition itself behind him.

No bell or knocker, not even a letter box, so he used his knuckles three times and waited. The place didn't seem lived in, nor were there any blinds or curtains in any of the old sash windows whose sills were covered in bird shit and weeds almost obscuring what was clearly a reinforced cellar window. It was here that he saw a faint light being switched off, then a minute later, picked out footsteps echoing towards him.

He rapped on the wood again only to have the

door pulled wide open, leaving his fist foolishly in midair.

'Are you Pegasus?' he asked, feeling dumb.

'I might be. Who the fuck are you?' asked the albino, eyeing first Martin then the taxi in the road.

'Martin Webb.' And out came the Monroe card again to confirm it. The man snatched it from his grasp and let it drop to the ground where it settled among a clump of dandelions. Martin didn't respond, instead pulled his wallet from inside his jacket, extracted two twenty-pound notes and the *Mirror* cutting, which he unfolded. 'I need to know anything you can tell me about Gary Cope. This is all I can afford, OK? And it's my last chance...'

The man glanced at the article, then the waiting taxi.

'Tell your fuckin' nanny to go, first.'

'I've got a nine thirty train to catch. Last one today. No can do, sorry.'

The albino leaned forwards and took the money. Held both notes up to the light then stuffed them in the pocket of his camouflage fatigues as if they were bits of litter.

'Poor bastard. Not my usual punter, I must say. I told him, this is not going to make stuff happen for you. It's not the fuckin' Holy Grail, but did he want to know?'

A dealer reading him the small print? Hardly the response of a wronged man, thought Martin.

'Can you think back to Christmas Eve 2000 at Gee's disco?' Martin asked.

'Not too hard to do that, man. Why? What's up?'

'So you were there?'

'Along with most of my associates, yeah. Gee's welcome mat's always there for the likes of us bringing in business. Not for the pigs, mind, sniffing round after Gary's ex got tipped in the fuckin' river.'

River?

'You mean Shannon?'

'Shannon Holt, yeah. Never found her body...'

Holt...

Martin picked up his Monroe card, aware of an oddly sweet smell coming from inside the house. Despite the sun sinking between distant silhouetted factory blocks still warm on his skin, he felt cold. Next he dug out the folded CV from his jeans pocket. Opened it out as the other man's strange pink eyes alighted on the first upside-down line. 'Good job I learnt to read, given all this paper you're shoving at me.' He peered closer. 'Frankie Holt. Where d'you get this from? Let's take a butcher's.'

Martin's empty stomach churned around to match his brain. Somehow the right questions weren't coming out.

'Didn't know they lived there,' the guy observed, handing him back the sheet. 'But it's true about the old people's homes. Shannon told me that's what she did. We'd got talking round the back by the store room. She wasn't buying nothing off me, mind. Preferred to get pissed. But hey, I didn't hold it against her. She was ace, fancied her myself.'

'Gary claimed he saw her with another girl. Getting up close and personal.'

'Only her dad ever did that.'

'*What?*'

'I see your pram's getting impatient.'

Martin glanced round at the waiting taxi. One more question left to ask. The rest he could dig out from old newspapers.

'What did she look like, this Frankie?' he asked. 'Did you actually see her that night?'

'Course. But I know a scorpion when I see one. Tall, skinny, dark auburn hair in spikes. Should carry a fuckin' health warning, her...' He fixed Martin with a suddenly hard stare. 'Confidential, all this, yeah?'

'Sure. Thanks. Look – ' he handed him a Monroe card with his contact details – 'if you hear of anything else, just buzz me. OK?' The guy took it without speaking, then the front door began to close.

'I'd talk to that sister if I was you,' he said from the hallway. 'Then you can tell her about Gary.'

The Birmingham train was twenty minutes late, giving him ample time to buy a paper, a coffee and a cheese baguette for the journey back. The taxi had cost £23, but he reckoned it had been worth it. If he'd had the time, he'd have liked to have gone to that Dartmoor Road address listed on the CV.

As the train roared through Stockport he opened up his *Manchester Evening News*. His weary eyes skimmed the day's news with little interest, his mind elsewhere – on that brief sordid detail of Shannon Holt's life and the rest of what Pegasus had revealed. What he needed now was an accurate description of the woman last seen with Shannon Holt that night, and it now seemed that the only ones who could oblige were either the owner of that CV or the two deceased both six feet under.

Martin skimmed the newspaper a second time, sensing that maybe there was something he'd missed, when, with a gulp, he noticed a small paragraph nestling between news of a mugging in Nottingham and a sea rescue off the Scilly Isles. *Pet Dog Found Dead.*

After that all he could see was Gary Cope's laughing face and hear the clods of earth hitting his coffin.

Twenty-One

By Thursday mid-morning, the summer mist which concealed the sheep-strewn fields beyond the road hadn't lifted, instead it had merged with the unbroken grey sky. Evelyn knew this kind of weather, where moisture hung undispersed by even the smallest breeze, was the worst for her bones. Despite the Gables' sturdy walls, this still, silent enemy managed to creep in and finally drive her to her bed.

Rest gave her too much opportunity to think.

Not about Scott's Rifles' latest sales convention at the NEC in Birmingham, but other matters far more injurious to her fragile health. Since Frances had phoned after Piotr's visit, the telephone at Teme House had remained unanswered. The police had phoned, singing Frances's praises. She'd done everything by the book, not only telling them Merle was missing, but also reassuring them she was doing everything to find her.

Evelyn finished her cup of tea and gingerly moved her legs from under the blanket. Despite her worries about Merle, she must make sure that by three o'clock that afternoon she was up and looking lively, for her GP, Dr Woolley, and a Susan Chance from social services were coming to assess her future care needs.

Needs? Evelyn sighed at that euphemism as she made herself comfortable in the sitting position against the bed's walnut headboard. All she needed was for her bones to stop testing her to the limit and for Sean Brownlow to stop harassing her for an alibi for that summer solstice evening on North Hill. The arrogance of the man knew no bounds. Yes, he'd admitted being on the summit with his dead animal heads, so how could she say she'd been playing cards with him all evening? She couldn't and she'd told him so.

No wonder his face had turned purple and his Jeep screeched away down her drive leaving a pall of nasty blue smoke hanging in the air. But her conscience was clear. Besides, with what else was going on, she'd nothing to lose. She'd

232

heard his hatred for those foreign workers at the Hill Springs site. She'd tried to propel her wheelchair away from him but the ground had been too churned up. She'd felt shame and anger, mostly at herself for her feebleness.

No wonder he'd offered to take her there. It certainly wasn't in deference to her arguments. The whole local community must think she endorsed his views. That wouldn't do Scott's Rifles any good at all.

She stared out at the thickening mist which had even devoured the triple rows of firs below the fields, realizing that her fax to the Board demanding his dismissal would be there by now. Even in his hand. She would just have to wait for the inevitable and knew it wouldn't be long before he'd be storming up to her door with his threats. And then with a jolt she thought of guns. Her hand hovered over the desk phone. How easy to ring him and agree to his demands, just like before. But this was one too many.

She was on the point of calling Teme House instead, to remind her foolish sister what kind of man would be benefiting from her misplaced largesse, when the front-door bell chimed. She started, letting the handset fall from her grasp and skitter across the floor.

'Damnation.' She struggled from her bed and, having launched herself at her Zimmer frame, reached the inner porch to find Merle's carer Frankie, standing there with tears streaming down her pale frightened face.

Twenty-Two

Frankie wiped her face with her fleece sleeve leaving traces of brown mascara on the fabric. Hungry and tearful, she waited until Evelyn Scott had opened the front door. The first thing she noticed was the stains down the front of her dressing gown while her hair, well, if you could call it hair, was too long, too grey, too greasy. No different from Beryl in Dartmoor Road, thought Frankie. Except what lay in her bank account.

'I don't mean to bother you,' she began, 'I've just tried calling but no one answered.'

'I've been in the utility room. It's a long way from the telephone. And anyhow, young lady, I've been trying to phone *you*. The police told me you were worried Merle had wandered off somewhere ... Is she back yet?'

'If you'd just let me in, I'll explain.' Frankie coughed twice then shivered. 'This mist's getting to my chest. I don't need pneumonia, least not now.'

The woman indicated the oak bench next to the hall phone and Frankie duly sat down, clutching her pink rucksack, suddenly desperate for a fag.

'So, you've left Merle on her own?' she quizzed. Her tone more than frosty, and Frankie tried to guess why.

'You're not to worry, OK. But ... but ... she's still missing.'

'Missing? Whatever do you mean?' Those watery blue eyes widened in shock.

'I don't know. I've been looking everywhere.'

She saw Evelyn frown as if this didn't seem right at all.

'Since when?'

Frankie's tear ducts obeyed her again. More wet cheeks followed. There was to be no comforting, no concern about herself. After all, hadn't she once had a kid and couldn't even be bothered to name it? And what had she done with her that had upset Merle so much?

'Yesterday. Around seven in the evening. After I'd phoned you. I'd just got her roast dinner ready. Turkey it was, with all the trimmings. I've kept a record here.' She opened her rucksack and pulled out the red exercise book, thinking, if this doesn't impress her, nothing will. 'Anyway, as I was saying, I'd just nipped upstairs to have a quick wash, tidy myself up kind of thing, while she was in the toilet, but when I came downstairs –' she spread out both hands in a gesture of despair – 'she'd vanished.'

'Just like that?' Evelyn Scott continued to scrutinize the exercise book's most recent pages.

'Yeah. Not the first time she's done that, neither. She went off the same way last Monday night but I never said nothing. Didn't want to worry you, see? I found her up the hill at the back.'

'Merle?' The old woman frowned.

Frankie nodded, ashamed that when she got

tense, her language suffered.

'She was going great guns. No stick no nothing. Not like you, if you get my meaning.'

Bad move. She scolded herself, but sometimes things just came out. Evelyn Scott slapped the carer's book shut and flung it down.

'So, she's been deceiving us all along.'

'Can't say, can I? You know her better than I do.'

Frankie retrieved the book without further comment while those old hands clenched and unclenched on her frame as an aura of more than anger seemed to surround her. Frankie edged further away on her bench.

'But there's something else,' she sniffed, wiping her eyes again. 'It was so scary. When I'd come back from looking for her, I was attacked.'

'Attacked? Please explain.'

The lie came easily. She was enjoying herself.

'By Mr Brownlow. He must have come in through the Blue Room window before I'd had a chance to close it.'

'You mean it was open?'

'Yeah. Look.' She cocked her head sideways to reveal her bruised neck. The bare patch of scalp still hurt when she touched it.

'Nice, innit? Plus a gun in my back. Prodded me downstairs with it until I managed to escape. I'd been waiting for the police to arrive, but they didn't. And when I called them again they said I was to just lock myself in and try them again this morning.'

'And did you?'

Frankie shook her head. She'd done everything necessary to cover her back. To place Brownlow under suspicion. She noticed the old woman's face had grown paler, like some old skull popping out from her dressing-gown collar. She looked at that shrunken chest, wondering how many heartbeats were still left inside it.

'Can't I get you something to eat?' she asked hopefully, suddenly realizing she was starving. 'Or d'you fancy a hot chocolate?'

'No thank you. I have some calls to make.'

She heard her stomach rumble as Evelyn Scott moved her frame nearer the phone and began to dial a number she clearly knew well. Frankie took the opportunity to slip the leather-bound address book into her hand and quickly scan its pages.

It was empty. All the entries obliterated by a thick coat of Tippex. She returned it to its place aware now of an even greater danger looming. Not just for Evelyn Scott, but possibly herself. She listened as the widow barked a short message on Brownlow's answer phone. By doing this, her plan could backfire big time. He was to report back by midday about Frances's serious accusations and his part in the signing of Merle's will or she'd be querying its validity with her solicitor that very afternoon. She then called the police station. As Frankie was her sister's carer, she'd see she was at Teme House within half an hour to meet them.

Frankie felt her insides tighten. She'd spent the whole night in her freezing car to be safe, for fuck's sake. This wasn't happening. Piotr had been frightened. So was she. She'd had long hours overnight to think about that man with the weird eyes, and now she realized why. Within days, thanks to her, he'd be at least a millionaire. Teme House and all its trappings would be his. Supposing he picked up that answerphone message? Even heard from the pigs she was stitching him up? He had as much to lose as her.

'I'm a mum. I've a kid to look after,' she pleaded. 'You can't make me do this.'

Pale-blue eyes registered more than surprise.

'You have a child?

'Yeah. Little girl. People do, you know. Even if I don't look the yummy mummy sort, I love her to bits.'

'What's her name?'

'Ellie. Short for Eleanor. After Eleanor of Aquitaine.' She almost added Scott but said Holt instead.

Had there been a tiny flicker of those eyelids at that surname? An imperceptible tick of the lips? Frankie wondered if Evelyn was impressed at her historical knowledge or whether Brownlow had also given her a copy of her CV. Whatever, she stayed silent.

'Look, Miss Scott,' she began, her lie about the assault too far gone to alter, 'there's no way I can go back to Teme House. Sean Brownlow's up to something. I know it.'

'Where is your daughter now?'

It was as if she'd not said a word but Frankie was not risking her daughter's life again.

'Up near Manchester. My mate looks after her while I'm away. She's dead nice. And I trust her, no problem.'

'And how old is this Ellie of yours?'

'She's new. 'Bout a month now. I hate being away from her, but...' More tears arrived on cue. 'I have to earn a living too.'

'Exactly. And as for this Brownlow business, you've been watching too much crime on television. His concern for my sister is sometimes extreme, I admit, but it's nothing more. Why should he attack you?'

Frankie bit her lip. That same hot reckless colour rising in her neck. Merle's fat body was probably being picked over by foxes as she spoke. It was too soon to lose her wits all over again. She saw Mrs Beavis as clear as anything in her mind. Her encouraging smile, her sound advice.

'Maybe he's jealous of you and me getting on so well.'

Evelyn Scott didn't comment on that.

'On your way now, Frances,' she said, proding her arm. 'Just remember, you're our employee. Please, I beg you, comport yourself in the correct manner at all times. And don't forget to let me know the moment Merle returns home.'

'Police? It's me, Frances Holt, again,' she panted. 'I called you yesterday evening but no one was free. I'm in Colwall, just by the pub I think. I'm too scared to go back into Teme House like Miss Evelyn Scott told me to do. Mr Brownlow's after me. Please come—'

She broke off, sensing a vehicle behind her. Without waiting to find out, she stuffed the carer's book into her pink rucksack, alarmed the car and ran towards the bleary lights of the pub. Sounds of laughter from inside the Doe and Deer grew louder as she hurtled towards its one open door. A row of figures, silhouetted against the bar's lights, turned to stare as she found the only empty seat with a view out to the murky gloom.

Her pulse leapt in her neck, her wrists, everywhere, while her mangled brain tried to exclude the penetrating din of Sinead O'Connor from a nearby speaker. She needed a shower and change of clothes. Could smell her own underarm sweat as she checked her purse for cash and found Evelyn Scott's five-pound note still intact.

Her mother? Was it possible?

She shook her head. No, that had to be sick joke of the year. There was no way that cripple at the Gables with those almost colourless eyes could be her. She was too short, for a start. Too unlike anything she'd ever imagined for all those years. Tall, active, a perfectionist like herself. And had she come across anything at that mansion to confirm what Merle had said was true? No. But to be fair, she'd hardly had the chance. 'Stuck-up bitch' was the only match so far. Well at least the crone had seemed interested in *her* having a kid. When the moment was right she'd show her Ellie in the flesh. But could Beryl's opinion be trusted? She needed to find out.

'Can I be bringing you something over?' called a friendly Irish voice from behind the bar. It belonged to a smiling guy who looked like a grey Jesus, with eyes she found vaguely familiar. There followed a pause in the banter for her reply.

'Bacardi Breezer – grapefruit, please,' she said, 'and some pork scratchings.'

All she could afford till she next went to the bank, and another thing Shannon used to slag her off about while she was on her veggie trip.

Frankie made her way towards the bar, aware now of more than the whiff of drink hovering in the stuffy air. Of eyes roaming up and down her body. Ganja, that was it. Musky-sweet, making her headache worse. The guy pulled a packet of scratchings off the display unit behind him and handed it over. The cellophane wrapper felt hot, slightly moist from his hand. The crispy rind the same colour as John Arthur's eyebrows.

'I know. You're at Teme House, aren't you?' he asked.

Frankie froze.

'Who told you?'

'Carol.'

'Carol Piper? That New-Ager I met last Friday?'

He laughed showing yellow teeth.

'Hey, she'd take that as a compliment, would Carol.' He stared at her head. 'Miss Scott bin nibbling at your hair an' all?'

She'd forgotten about that bare patch of scalp behind her left ear. She froze, then seized her moment.

'Have you seen her, then?' she called out. 'She's been gone since yesterday evening. Why I came here. To ask.'

'No, we haven't. Least not recently. Bit of a recluse of late.' But Frankie was now by the door, pulling it open.

She grew aware of someone else standing on the other side. Someone reluctant to give way. Avril Pilkington in full police uniform, her hat giving her extra height, was now gripping her arm and escorting her outside to her unmarked Mondeo. In Openshaw she'd had a white Fiesta. Just like her. She'd also put on more weight and for that reason would now be known as the Sow.

'I've been trying to get back to you after your call to us last night,' she said. 'But you seem to be very evasive these days.'

'I want a solicitor,' Frankie said straightaway, just like she'd seen on TV dramas.

'For goodness' sake, this isn't an interrogation. I'm here to help.'

That's a new one, thought Frankie. She looked more like one of the screws from *Cell Block H* than a helpful pig.

'Look, I still need to find Merle Scott,' she said. 'Why I went in this pub in the first place. Supposing something's happened to her? *I'm* responsible...' Her voice had the right kind of end-of-tether tremble. In contrast to that busy saloon bar, the stillness in the car park seemed to isolate every word she said. Avril Pilkington then turned to blame her for not staying at Teme House last night and not contacting them that morning as promised.

'I couldn't stay there! I was scared out of my wits. Mr Brownlow was lying in wait for me. Look what he did to my fucking hair!'

The Sow peered closer but took care not to touch. However, something about her body odour was eerily familiar. Even the way her eyes kind of narrowed as she homed in on her scalp.

'I had to kip in a bloody lay-by. Any pervert could have been hanging around.'

'We'll look into this, of course, but at the same time, as you've just said yourself, you do have a duty of care towards your client.'

'Even if I'd had Brownlow's gun in my back?'

'I'm afraid it's your word against his, Frankie. He claims he was working late in his office.'

Frankie wasn't listening. The recent sounds of gunshot still in her ears.

Bang ... bang ... bang...

'I thought there was a law about firearms.'

'Why do you say that?'

'Because he goes shooting at the Gables for a start...'

'He's held a Section One Firearm Permit for years. And the shooting range there is part of his job. Has it occurred to you that Mr Brownlow might have had some concerns about your being in Teme House? That he may have felt uneasy?'

'About *me*?'

'Yes, Frankie. You.'

She moved towards her white Fiesta, which lay shrouded in condensation. She had to collect stuff before it was too late. Never mind Ellie's things, she'd just remembered the cagoule she'd worn to Kilfargan, her tartan suitcase and the shower gel from the Crachan Hotel. Thank God again that Merle's keys and Gary Cope's note giving his Scottish address were safe in her pink rucksack, while those used latex gloves could stay in her pants until she could find a public toilet to flush them away.

243

The Sow's voice followed her.

'I have to say, Frankie, things do seem to follow you around.'

'What things?' Wishing she'd taken a mega swig from that Bacardi bottle for more courage.

The Sow moved round to her driver's side door and peered at her over the top of the car.

'First, there was your sister, then your father, not forgetting some incidents at that home you worked in.'

'I can't believe you're saying this. *Nothing's* been my fault.'

'Some people are unlucky, Frankie. Fact of life.'

Unlucky. Was she, Frances Ann Holt, indivisible from that dump on Dartmoor Road?

'And since Mr Brownlow had your CV, he asked us to run a check on you. The kind which Homely Helpers must have done too. In fact I was the one they came to for the details.'

Frankie squeezed her eyes tight shut. This wasn't happening. Her precious dream of betterment crumbling by the second.

'But my references ... Surely he'd seen those?'

'Oh, yes, according to him they were excellent. But he had to satisfy himself.'

'So I'm not fucking good enough. That it?' She challenged, her cheeks burning. 'Here, look.' And, for the second time that day, pulled out the carer's book from her rucksack and opened it at the sections she'd written. The Sow didn't even glance at it.

'What about that missing immigrant, then?'

'The police are still working on it. They admit

they were too quick to point the finger at Mr Brownlow. No, the problem for him at the moment is you taking time off for this and that, and shopping for Miss Evelyn Scott. It's not your remit, Frankie. She never asked you to.'

'I was only being helpful. The poor woman had nothing in her fridge because he'd forgotten.' Her voice faded as that damned two-way began crackling again. The Sow informed whoever was calling that Mr Brownlow had offered to give the police his set of keys to Teme House to help them in their search.

Frankie swallowed hard. The last thing she wanted was company. Then DC Pilkington changed her tone as if they were both best mates, which was even more annoying.

'I'd like you to think really hard of anything, Frankie, however small, which may help us find Miss Scott. I mean *anything*...'

'I'll try.' Sensing the worst was over, hoping her frown looked sincere. There'd been no mention of her being questioned at the cop shop like in *The Bill*. Just the fear of Brownlow sussing out her strategy. 'One thing, mind,' she began. 'Why doesn't he just fire me? Get someone better to see to the old girl?'

'He's enough to deal with right now, as you can imagine. It's not been easy for him.'

The only one who'd not had it easy was *her*.

'Easier now he's got her dough under his belt, I'd have thought,' she quipped then added, 'He bullied her into it. I was there. Maybe I saw too much.'

'You've made that serious allegation twice

now, Frankie. Mr Brownlow could seek legal advice.'

'I don't care. If he is at Teme House and I've not been protected, then I'll kick up the biggest stink ever.'

The Sow threw her a look of undisguised scorn.

'He's just informed my colleague DI Manson that he'll be off to Upper Wych in the next five minutes to help with the search.'

'Merle can't have gone *that* far. She left her walking stick behind. Like on Monday.'

'People sometimes do the oddest things. Maybe she didn't need her stick as much as you thought. You said as much to her sister this morning.'

She's been busy, thought Frankie, as a group of people left the pub and, upon spotting the pig, scuttled away into the gloom. Suddenly, from somewhere came a scream, then distant voices. Colwall was suddenly a busy place, she thought, shivering hard.

'What was that?'

'Oh, just your usual country nightlife, and by the way, Frankie.' She lowered her voice. 'From my viewpoint, you could spend more time looking inwards, not outwards at other people. Get my meaning?'

Before she could retaliate, the Sow had squeezed herself into her Mondeo and ordered her to follow as best she could.

What she wanted to know was why Brownlow was suddenly the blue-eyed boy, incapable it seemed of doing any wrong. Did she have a thing for him? And this imagined scenario made her slow up and swing to the right into Allotment Way where she knew its earth track led directly to Teme House.

However, any advantage gained by this short cut was soon cancelled out by her having to drop to ten mph or risk scraping the iron fencing ranged along either side. She'd only been this way once before on foot, on her second day at Teme House, and knew there was no room for anything else to pass, let alone a pedestrian.

She wound down her window, letting the cold mist into her space so she could listen as she crept along. Just in case. Then she heard a sound. A whirring noise, followed by a single dull light, veering from side to side, coming closer.

Instinctively, she sounded the horn and braked hard, aware of naughty Ellie rolling around in the boot.

Christ...

A cyclist, some crazy geek, dismounted and tried to negotiate his way past her nearside wing mirror. She then recognized the guy who'd lent her fifty pence at the library. Her annoyance at meeting someone she vaguely knew here of all places, when she was in such a rush, was matched by a sensation not felt since Justin Rosser had nibbled her ear and brushed his hand over her tits at that churchyard barbie. This guy had nice eyes, kind of greeny-grey.

'Good job I wasn't going any faster,' she said, revving up so he'd realize she wasn't just here to enjoy the foggy night. 'Or you'd have been toast.'

'Bloody daft me riding around here, but I was on trains all day yesterday and at work today. Had to get out. It was doing my head in.'

Then he seemed to hesitate, as if there was still something he wanted to say, but she stepped in, thinking of Avril Pilkington and her attic room at Teme House. How seconds were ticking by.

'Got to go. Sorry. Thanks again for your help at the library.' Then she remembered her CV. This was as good a time as any to check him out. But she had to be careful. 'By the way, did you happen to find anything in that copier after I'd gone?'

'Didn't go near it. Why?'

'My mate left something personal behind, that's all. No worries.'

'Yeah. OK.' He looked at her, frowning. 'This isn't a good road, especially now. There's a place to turn round further up. You might just be lucky.'

'I've never been that,' she muttered under her breath, glad when he finally waved then disappeared. No time to wonder who he was or where he lived. That Sow would already be at Teme House poking around with her fat ringless fingers.

With a final surge she soon reached Teme Rise and saw the white hulk of its biggest house looming up through the mist. But why was she on her own? Where had that Mondeo gone? Frankie parked on the drive and listened hard through her half-open window. Perhaps the Sow had been involved in an accident. Perhaps something more urgent had come up. She thought of Merle; half imagined her dressed in her ballerina's gear coming through the milky mist, calling out her name with those orange lips. 'Jenny ... Jenny...'

Was it possible she'd been found?

She blinked. Not for the first time did she think she was losing it, but fear of what lay beyond the front door made her stick to her seat. Even though she'd had to pee outside her car door, it had been the safest option until morning. Despite what the Sow had said, Brownlow could still be inside Teme House. Her belongings all nicked. Her heart his next target.

Frankie was aware of a biting hunger hitting her stomach. She remained cocooned in the car by something more solid than the fog thinning now around Teme House, exposing its whiteness like Merle's skin beneath the fern fronds up on the hill. She felt a wall being systematically built around her, brick by brick, leaving only the smallest gap for any escape. Her breath came in wheezy gasps, each one more forced than the last.

Her phone started ringing inside her rucksack and the caller wasn't giving up.

'Yes? Who is it?' Then she immediately recognized the urgent voice at the other end.

'Avril Pilkington here, Frankie. I took an emergency call while you were trying to follow me. Where are you now?'

'Teme House. Waiting for you. Waiting for Merle.'

'I wouldn't. Get out and quickly. Take yourself

249

over to the Gables. That's the best. We've told Miss Scott to expect you.'

'But what about her sister? I need to stick around for her, surely?'

A pause in which she felt her heart slow up. What she really meant was she had to reach her bedroom.

'Don't worry about that for now. Please do as I say. Get going.'

Twenty-Three

Martin had gone to sleep thinking about the blonde in the Fiesta he'd met last night, wondering what she was doing on such a bad road in fog. His own reckless ride and a stop at the pub had helped him unwind and he'd slept like a dog

Despite it being pay day, news that a Sean Patrick Brownlow, production manager with the local Scott's Rifles, had been found in Upper Wych last night, shot in his right eye with his right hand blown off altogether, made breakfast in the site canteen a more sombre affair than usual. Rio Docherty knew he'd been at the Hill Springs protest, shouting slogans and even chasing one of the Muslim hod-carriers out of the development.

'Look no further,' he'd said, transporting his mug of tea and two slabs of toast out of the building. 'It's a tit-for-tat job. Someone's had enough. Trouble is, the guy's not dead.'

Martin shivered. Put down his mug.

'But why shoot him like that?'

Docherty shrugged.

Martin was sitting next to a subdued Danesh Mahtoum, a former chemistry teacher from Baghdad and now prolific brickie, as he picked at his toast, skimming the *Malvern Gazette*'s front page with Scotland still on his mind. Then he pushed his plate away and began to read aloud.

'According to other workers at the firm's head-quarters in Priory Road, the fifty-two-year-old bachelor had always been something of a loner, but to certain members of the hunting-and-shooting fraternity in the area he certainly never merited the recent label of racist thug.'

'All you people say that,' interrupted Danesh, finishing his mug of coffee. 'I know what Mohammed had to put up with here. I should have warned him not to run off like that when we hit trouble last week. He should have stayed with us. Ridden out the storm. But he'd got fear in his legs and fear is the springboard which propels us into dangerous waters.'

'Sad business.' Martin checked his watch. In four and a half hours he'd be meeting up with Dora, and meanwhile the blighted morning seemed to stretch away for ever.

'I have the profoundest feeling,' his companion began, 'that however much this man might have been despised, no one here would have committed such an act. I spent two thousand pounds to get to Britain. Less than most, but think of the shame of prison, or worse. Of not providing for your family. No –' he pushed his chair back from the table and slipped on his working gloves – 'I would say this man had tired of life.'

Martin too stood up. The world of the dead and dying seemed to be crowding into his head; his own mother jostling for position amongst the rest.

He stuffed the newspaper inside his donkey jacket and went to collect his gear from his locker, blinking in the rare brightness, imagining being suddenly blind, the pain that Sean Brownlow must have suffered. As Martin negotiated his way to the breezeblock shell which was to be the stores, where two older guys were unwrapping the stock of roof tiles and loading the hoist, his mobile's familiar ring made him stop in his tracks. He immediately recognized the number and the Scottish voice which followed.

'Is that Martin Webb?' Maddy McKay seemed in a hurry. Even more tense than when he'd last called with an update. Last time he'd left her more confused than ever. Not knowing whom to believe.

'It is. Any more news?'

'You won't bloody believe this,' she began. He'd never heard her swear before. Something was up.

'The police called me last night. They say Donny wasn't the only dog who'd been found stabbed...'

'What?'

'There've been at least three more in the

village itself...'

He felt his efforts at making connections slipping away. Whoever had murdered Gary Cope surely wouldn't have hung around in a small community like that and risked being seen committing more crimes, however deranged they were.

'Just hang on in there,' he said as the first batch of tiles was laid at his feet. A hint for him to get moving. 'I'm not giving up on this, OK?'

'Maybe. I'm leaving, anyhow. Mam will have me till I can sort something out. Gary and me were only renting Loch Cottage, so it's no big deal. I'll never go back there again.'

Martin ended the call with a promise. The kind he'd made his own mother. So, that made two he intended to keep.

Just then he spotted a yellow van stopping at the security barrier. After the obligatory check, it moved off to stop again, this time outside the site office. The driver leapt out, opened its rear doors and handed a brown package to Docherty. It wasn't until the man began walking towards his section of scaffolding that he realized the parcel was for him.

'From Weymouth, eh?' The foreman watched as he signed for it then nimbly clambered down to return the form to the driver. 'Bit heavy for a tuck box, that,' he quipped on his way.

'Cheers, mate,' Martin called out after him, feeling the dead weight between his now gloved hands, realizing what it might contain. Had his old man delivered the goods? Was this going to be the start of a decent relationship with him? In his deepest heart, he hoped so.

The rogue cloud moved away, and once again the breast-shaped hill seemed to beckon as a tremor of empowerment rushed through his body. He thought of Ed Thom and Den Tanner and anyone else who might think of putting him through more of the same. With the early sun on his cheek, he thought again of his mother. She'd not even let him play with a water pistol, for God's sake.

'We're not some fucking holiday camp,' Docherty bawled at six pipe-layers playing rugby with a hard hat. 'Play or pay, lads. Your choice.'

Martin laid the package down in the middle of the plank and got to work.

During the first tea break he managed to dodge his fellow workers heading for the canteen, and with the package concealed under his donkey jacket, took it to the relative privacy of the empty dormitory. Here he unwrapped the layers of cheap brown paper until he reached a battered shoe box which, according to the words on the side, had once contained a pair of ladies' suede court shoes, size five. The style, Sahara.

He hesitated, aware of a powerful sense of déjà vu. Hadn't those shoes once belonged to Louisa Webb? He even remembered shopping with her for them in Blackheath and thinking how exotic that name had sounded for a mere pair of shoes. Had this been sent deliberately?

However, as his fingers tussled with the string and Sellotape which sealed its two halves together, he sensed a need for caution. He felt sweat erupt under his hair, his clothes. This

254

imagined 'gift' could be anything. More carefully now he carried the box outside and slunk round to the rear windowless wall. Here in the intermittent shade he finally prised off the lid to discover not only a nest of black tissue paper but a truly nauseating smell.

He ran back inside for the length of cane used to clear the gunge from the bathroom's one sink, most of its length darkened by frequent probing. Now it probed something quite different and once he'd nudged the protective paper to one side, and seen what lay beneath, his tea and cereal welled up his throat and soon covered the steel toecaps of his boots.

'It was some old sheep skull, for God's sake. Riddled with maggots.'

'Ugh, pleease!' Dora toyed with her prawn-cocktail salad in the Doe and Deer. He could be more detached about it four hours later, having used up that tea break to chuck the thing into the woods next door and bury his mother's shoebox. No way could he tell Dora about the warning note which had accompanied it. That his dad would be next if he asked him for anything again. Nor let on he was in prison.

They were only in this particular pub before their walk instead of after because she'd said she was starving. And now she sat opposite him, her hair and skin radiant in the window's light. No bra either, he noticed, under her T-shirt, and despite the horrors of the day, found himself wondering about panties.

'You should tell the police,' she said, seemingly unaware where his thoughts were leading. 'It's obviously one of Ed Thom's contacts. And what might he dream up next?'

'Christ knows.' He'd so far left his cheese roll untouched, with more than a niggling worry that his father might be having a rough time, all because of him. 'But I guess you're right. Best to wait till we're outside again.'

That seemed to satisfy her and she resumed eating, glancing up to return the barman's smile as he busied himself cleaning glasses. Martin noticed a deepening colour where her neck met her T-shirt. He'd noticed this same guy also eyeing up those few women in there last night. Went with the territory, he reckoned, but if he kept it up with Dora, he'd soon sort him out.

'Back again then, are we?' enquired the pony-tailed man, holding a glass tankard up to the light and giving it an extra wipe. 'Nice to know we've got satisfied customers.'

'You've a great location,' Martin humoured him, aware of Dora casting him a curious glance. He wasn't in the mood. He wanted to be out on the hill with her. 'I mean, look at it.' He indicated through the open door.

'Yeah, a good job too. It's my bloody pension.' A more wry smile this time before he disappeared through a doorway marked KITCHEN, leaving the young lad who'd served them to deal with new punters who'd wandered up to the bar.

'So when were you here?' asked Dora, folding her paper napkin into a tight square. 'Or shouldn't I ask?'

'Last night, actually. I'd just gone for a mad

256

spin on the bike to clear my head.'

'But it was foggy. You could have been run over.'

'I'm here, aren't I?' He smiled.

The Doe and Deer was totally different now, in the daylight. In fact, worse. Its cobwebbed corners, the peeling posters for this and that gig featuring artists he'd never heard of were all highlighted by the sunlight. Even the collection of sex dolls heaped up in the corner behind the plasma screen, their limbs pinkly shining in varying stages of deflation, their open mouths part of some weird silent chorus.

He'd been in too many pubs to count, but this place had an atmosphere he couldn't put his finger on. For a start, it seemed to be even colder inside than out. All at once, strains of REM came on via the ceiling speakers. He'd played the track non-stop when Ria had gone. Was it an omen...?

'Are you all right?' Dora asked him.

'Yep, fine.'

'You don't look it.' Her eyes still probed his face. He'd missed her on Wednesday and would miss her again once she started touring with the play. That looming loss was too much to bear. He glanced behind him at the open door, wanting to be out of the pub, away from those painful memories. Up on that massive hill with the breeze on his face and her hand in his. It didn't matter that the greedy clouds had just devoured the sun. He needed to create some distance between himself and the evils of the world.

'You off, then?' The grey-haired barman was

now back in action, screwing a new gin bottle in place upside down amongst the row of spirits.

'Up the hill there.'

'Hope the weather holds for you. Oh, and by the way,' he added, now fixing himself a beer, 'watch out for this old biddy who's gone AWOL. Short, bit on the plump side, funny hair. You know, orange and grey. Miss Scott, she is. First name's Merle.'

Martin frowned at hearing that name. It was somehow familiar. He dug in his jeans back pocket then produced the folded, now slightly crumpled CV.

'What's that you got?' asked the man, while Dora slung her bag over her shoulder and pushed her chair in against the table. Martin wondered if he was normally so nosy.

'It's odd, that's all.'

'What is?'

'There's a Miss Scott mentioned here. And her full-time carer's called Frances Ann Holt.'

'Correct. Calls herself Frankie. I met her yesterday evening. She was up half last night looking for her. Came in here to check if any of us had seen the old lady.'

'What does this Frances look like?'

'Now you've got me.' He paused, wiped up some spillage on the bar with a tea towel and scratched his head. 'I know you'd think that in my job I'd remember everyone clear as daylight, but Hell's teeth, I don't.'

'But she was in here last night, you said,' Dora interrupted and the man's smile faded.

''S right. Blonde, like it's not her real colour...'

'In spikes?'

'Get off. Smooth as butter. Not an inch of fat on her either, mind. Skin-tight jeans and a blue fleece top. Looks like she could do with a good meal. Yeah, that just about sums her up.'

'Did you notice any car?'

He laughed.

'You mean a crate? Sure. White Fiesta. Scrapyard job, I reckon. Mind you, I don't get involved with how my punters get here. Just so long as they pay up.'

Martin tried to ignore a chill permeating every pore of his body as he escorted Dora outside, aware also of the man's eyes on his back.

'Why's this Frances so important to you all of a sudden?' Dora had her car keys ready.

'I can't say. At least, not until I'm sure...'

He climbed into her car, more than preoccupied by what was unfolding around him. He'd stood close enough to her last Monday to smell her scent, then meeting her again last night and being hooked for a second time into those hungry animal eyes.

'If you want North Hill, we need to find the sign for ve-hicular access.' Dora suddenly butted into his thoughts. 'And I know it's none of my business, but you should call the police about that revolting sheep's head.'

A helicopter, hidden by clouds, grumbled overhead as he spotted a blue-and-yellow-chequered police car heading the way they'd just come.

'Wonder what they're up to,' she began, changing up into top gear.

259

Martin did not answer as they turned right up a single lane road which led to an empty car park marked out by a circle of granite rocks. He was slowly, inexorably entering a web from which there might be no escape.

He peered out of the car window while Dora began muttering some lines from *The Seagull*, as if to remind him of her ordeal to come. He'd never understood how actors could memorize so much, and not just their own parts. Perhaps the craft was something he too should take up, because his roofing job needed little more than muscle and by the time the development was finished he'd be brain-dead.

From where he sat, he could see the top of the Doe and Deer's thatched roof and further east those of the mansions in Teme Rise. Last night they'd seemed so forbidding in the mist. So impersonal. And just then, those connections he'd been fearful of losing began to make sense. That headway he'd made in Manchester had been on Wednesday. Now it was Friday. He had to move fast...

'What time do you have to be back at the theatre?'

She checked her watch.

'Seven fifteen.'

'Right. Let's go. Teme House first, then.'

Disappointment lengthened her features, and for a split second he wavered.

'What about our walk?'

'We'll do that afterwards, OK?'

'My mum and dad always did that.'

'Did what?'

'Promised me stuff.' For a brief moment she was no longer the confident girl-about-town, but a kid all over again...

'You know the kind of thing. Once you've passed your this your that. Once you've got your A-levels. Hey, you know something?' She turned to him, her eyes glistening. 'I never did get that pony they promised me, even though they had a whacking great paddock at the back of their house. I actually reminded them and guess what dad said?'

'Sorry, I can't.'

Seconds were ticking away. His impatience hard to keep in check.

' "When you're the next Helen Mirren, my girl, you'll be able to buy yourself a bloody race-horse." '

Her bitter laugh hung in the air as she circled around the car park and back the way they'd come. Five minutes later the car was bumping along Teme Rise to the vast white house beckoning them closer.

'Hey, look at those!' Dora pointed at the white-and-tan painted spaniels who graced each pillar beside the slightly open wrought-iron gates. 'Aren't they cute.'

About all that is, he thought, observing the deeply rutted gravel drive which led to the front of the empty-looking Teme House. He suggested Dora park on the roadside past the gate, and keep the engine running just in case. Before she could protest yet again, he squeezed himself between the gates and ran along the curving length of gravel as lightly as he could. He checked that the front door was locked, then moved to the rear of the house. Here he drew breath and took his bearings.

The lower sash windows were all secured. Likewise a plain door set into a small archway. The garden here seemed well cared for, with lawn edges recently trimmed and the kind of flowers his mother had grown nestling in the borders. However, round the back was a different story and it wasn't just the population of weird stones jutting from a raised plateau. Someone had been careless, for in the house's shadow lay an old wooden ladder almost concealed by weeds. Most of its rungs were missing, and those remaining were almost split in two. Martin's eye travelled up the less well-painted wall until it reached a small sash window – one of four – at the second-floor level. Why was it partially open and who might still be inside?

He set the ladder against the pebble-dashed wall. That was the easy bit. The climb proved treacherous and for every step up, with his trainers wedged as close to the ladder's sides as possible, he dropped back two gaps.

'Damn it.'

A couple of dog-walkers were in full view halfway up the hill, and for a breathless moment he pressed himself close to the creaking ladder, glad at least he was still in shadow. Once they'd moved away, he negotiated the last few steps and with all his strength heaved up the lower part of the window and squeezed himself through the gap. No way could he have entered through the top section. Not with such a rotten windowsill beneath.

The floral curtain trapped his left arm, causing him to twist awkwardly on landing inside the room. He held his breath, wishing he'd used Dora as a lookout at the foot of the ladder, but too late now. He scanned the sparsely furnished bedroom with its mid-blue walls, matching carpet and bedspread. Clearly no one had slept in it for a very long time.

Once on the landing, he listened hard for the slightest clue that he had company and once satisfied, pushed open a half-glazed door to his right which led to a flight of narrow wooden stairs. He was looking for one room only. Frankie Holt's. The wooden stairs seemed to beckon strongly, and he was soon on another much smaller landing with two doors. The first was an empty airing cupboard which smelt of damp. The other had a Scooby-Doo ID card stuck to it at eye level. The kind he'd used as a kid. Earlier names were obscured by FRANKIE written in black felt-tip. The door was stiff and he shoved his shoulder against it, stumbling down a step into a room, more a cell than a bedroom. His pulse was on edge. Aware of Dora waiting and the possibility of cops catching him red-handed. Being banged up like his dad.

Whoever these books belonged to was quite a reader, he thought, judging by the number of titles crammed on the two sagging shelves. Titles he should have got round to reading himself. Most originating from book sales at Openshaw library and costing no more than ten pence each. Given her home address on that CV, he assumed they must be Frankie's.

Next he focused on an open-fronted wardrobe, home to a tartan suitcase half hidden by a dark-green cagoule, a range of jeans and tops mostly with Primark and Matalan labels. All size ten. Touching these clothes felt wrong. Worse was looking at her unmade bed and imagining her lying in it.

He slipped the cagoule off its metal hanger and, aware of a slight weight on the left side, checked its pocket. He pulled out a small vinyl-coated dictionary on the Scottish dialect, and inside it discovered several words ringed in red. Warmer and warmer, surely? He rolled up the garment and slotted it with the booklet inside his jacket. Then he moved to the dressing table, opened its top drawer and stepped back in sur-prise. For there, neatly folded amongst a collec-tion of war medals, Milton sterilizer tablets, packs of latex gloves and Pampers nappies, lay a number of babies' pink knitted cardigans and sleep suits for newborn to one month old, plus, intriguingly, a pink plastic wristband.

Ellie Scott. D.o.b. 10.11.2000

Was it possible she'd brought a child with her to Teme House? But how come that surname, Scott? The CV hadn't mentioned one. Perhaps these baby clothes were part of someone's past, but if so, why did a trail of milk powder on the dressing table still smell fresh?

Odder and odder.

After placing the plastic wristband in his pocket, he closed the drawer and scanned the other items laid out by the triple mirror. An array of girlie stuff in plastic bottles, including fake-tanning lotion, moisturizers and hair gel. However, it wasn't these which held his attention, but green-blue toiletries all labelled Your Gift from the Crachan Hotel, Inverary.

He stuffed each item into his jacket pocket and scrambled down the stairs the way he'd come, wondering if he should look round some more while he had the chance. Or get the hell out.

The landing seemed longer the second time around and now he noticed a set of man-sized dried-mud footprints leading from that strange Blue Room. Could it be that their owner was still around somewhere?

He began to run and once he'd thrown the cagoule out of that same rear window followed it down the ladder, splintering his palms in the process. He walked down the drive, careful not to attract any possible attention. But once he'd passed through the gates he noticed Dora's familiar car had gone.

Instinct made him move. Running half a mile to the village, where to his relief he spotted her car in the doctors' surgery car park. He gestured for her to come out of the waiting room but she turned her head away. He had no choice but to go in himself.

'I wasn't that long,' he said first. 'Look, I'm sorry.'

'I didn't feel safe outside that house. I had to move on. I saw this car come by,' she said, 'and for a moment I thought it wanted to turn into Teme House. But it stalled right next to me and the bottle-blonde bitch inside gave me such a death stare. If looks could kill...'

'Anything else about her?' Martin said, trying to bury his unease.

'I couldn't really see, and anyway, I didn't want to meet her eyes. But I remember the car. A rust-bucket white Fiesta.'

'Come on,' he said as the only other occupant in the room was summoned for her appointment, 'let's have our walk, eh? You can read out some of your Nina lines. I never did pay much attention to Chekhov in school. I'll make it up to you, Dora. Breaking promises and all that.'

'I don't like you being so secretive.'

'Neither do I, but right now, I have to be.'

That circular car park they'd visited earlier was no longer empty. A decrepit VW camper van was parked near the litter bin, its dirty curtains drawn together.

Soon he and Dora were following a well-worn track towards the bare summit. It was signed as Donkey Way and punctuated by red bins for dog waste, but instead of admiring the view and the subtle blurring of green to more distant blue, all he could think of was the car that Dora had just seen. And why hadn't its driver actually gone into Teme House where she worked?

Martin held out his hand for her and she took it. 'My mum was always hot on knowing what was where and which rivers were nearby. She'd memorize the heights of hills and mountains. She was...'

'Go on.'

'She was cleverer than either me or my dad.

266

She got an MA from the LSE. She could have been anything.'

'She was your mum.'

'Not enough for her, though, was it? She'd have admired you for doing what you did. Dad wanted her to stay in the kitchen and that was that.'

They resumed walking in silence while the grass at either side of the track grew coarser, rugged clumps of rock giving way to bracken – mostly brown, damaged by dogs and other marauders. He remembered being shown a reproduction of Max Ernst's *The Forest* in an art lesson. He felt if he followed Dora, who was now crashing through the brittle fronds, he'd be just the same. A prisoner, like his father.

At least this little trip was doing her good, he thought. She was getting stuck into her character's part now, reciting a gloomy piece about men and beasts, great and small, all extinguished, having accomplished the sad cycle of their lives.

He turned from her earnest performance to get his bearings, saw the roofs of those large houses in Teme Rise and with a jolt to his heart suddenly sensed that Merle Scott wasn't merely missing. This wild yet accessible place harboured too much history, too many echoes of past lives. It made him shiver.

Dora smiled as he pulled her to him, her cheek warm against his, her eyes closing as his lips found hers. She smelt of the bracken and some of it lay in her hair, matching its colour exactly as she urged him on, ignoring the sudden invasion of flies which buzzed around their bodies. He pulled her down into that russet world, where nothing mattered except the ache below his belt, but just as his hand pushed up her T-shirt to reach her breasts and explore her firm brown nipples, she let out a scream. Then another which made him rear up off balance and keel over.

He landed on something both hard and soft. Something which explained the frenzied flies and the strange sweet and sour smell of decay, turning his stomach to ice.

Twenty-Four

Friday 5th July. 2.30 p.m. The police have just left after questioning me for too long, but I fear they'll soon return, unlike my sister, who hasn't been home for two whole nights now. I am so weary after their interrogation – yes, that is the only way to describe it, and still feel demolished. Although the new Detective Constable Avril Pilkington who called me yesterday has been most solicitous, DI Manson in contrast seemed to forget who I was and what I've achieved here for my community. Who is he to address me in that manner, almost blaming me for what's happened to Sean and Merle? I am neither his nor my sister's keeper.

However, his implications still hurt. He feels

268

the motive for Sean's self-harm is strengthening. After all, I'd just sacked him, refused to give him an alibi, and lastly, I'd already instructed Regis Fleming to challenge Merle's will. Then, as her only sister, her estate will pass to me. The girl is adamant he actually held the pen for Merle to sign, that he coerced her into the whole business, and I must say I'm inclined to believe her. The police say they're waiting for the patient to come out of his coma and speak for himself. I fear that is no more than a pipe-dream. Some of my staff have been to Worcester Royal Hospital to see him and then reported back. 'Stable' is the word they use to describe him. Language can be so inadequate. I should know.

Meanwhile, that nice DC Pilkington insisted I stay here with the girl and be vigilant. I wish now I'd not been so honest in giving them my version of events but, as I've said earlier, I cannot lie. Frances is back from shopping now and moving around, vacuuming, dusting, cleaning windows. Although I draw the line at her escorting me to the lavatory. She seems genuinely upset about my sister but constant talking about her isn't going to help. Besides, I feel she talks too much and in doing so, lacks sincerity.

Now what's she doing upstairs? It makes me uneasy, hearing the floorboards like that. Ah. Heavens, here she is, Frances Ann Holt, silent as a ghost, asking me what she should order when the fish man comes to call. That she would like a change from haddock...

269

Twenty-Five

Frankie was in a strop. She'd neither showered for three days nor eaten enough to stop her stomach rumbling, and on top of all that, Evelyn Scott was hardly putting out the welcome mat. She wondered who or what might have caused this change of attitude.

And what had the Sow meant last night by telling her to avoid Teme House? What the hell was going on? And why had that pig at the police station been so abrupt when she'd asked if there'd been any news of Merle?

By the time she'd sorted the rest of the shopping – mostly cleaning stuff – her blood felt as if it had gone beyond boiling point. And then there was Ellie, still in her boot. She stepped out of the warm Fiesta, making sure she wasn't being spied on.

The day was filled with such stale heavy sunshine that she had to make an extra effort to be sharp, on the ball. From where she stood in the drive, the ranks of full-blown trees behind the Gables seemed to have swallowed up North Hill. These weren't normal-sized oaks and chestnuts. They were giants, shutting out the daylight, adding to her growing sense of entrapment.

Best if Ellie was still kept out of view, she

decided, but the car boot was too dark, too oppressive for her, and might cause problems later on. She had a better idea.

'Thanks, you,' she muttered to her daughter, carrying her round the back of the house to the boiler room. Here was warm and not too light, with a tiny window she could look out from.

'I'm sorry, Mum,' Ellie seemed to say, blinking her eyes as Frankie tied her pink bonnet under her chin.

'OK. Tomorrow, if you're good, you can come up to my room.' For now, however, this was a halfway house and still part of her daughter's punishment. 'I'll see you later with your tea.'

Her plan to collect more clothes for her and all the other stuff from Teme House had been scuppered. At least there'd been no sign of Brownlow near the place, and Gary Cope's note with his Scottish address was safe in her pink rucksack. But those Inverary items were there for all to see. Why she'd not dumped them in the first place she didn't know, but collecting stuff from those few trips as a kid had always been a kind of anchor for when 358 Dartmoor Road had done her head in.

The moment to retrieve them was lost. A posh social worker called Susan Chance had just phoned and informed her that Miss Scott now needed full-time attention and wasn't to be left alone for one instant. If she needed a break she'd have to get cover. When Frankie had asked why there'd been this sudden change to her commitments, and why she couldn't be back at Teme House to wait for Merle, the social worker hadn't said. Making her nervy. And Christ knew how she was going to get to that séance tonight. Her one bit of promised fun.

She kicked her car wheel in frustration and marched to the front door with her excuse for her fifteen-minute absence already on her lips. But that wasn't necessary, for once she was inside, she saw that Evelyn Scott, who protested that she didn't need a live-in carer, was fast asleep in her bed in the airless lounge. Her dry lips apart, allowing small grating breaths to escape.

The Gables had been open house to her or anyone else. So much for Miss Scott's usual security. She could nick whatever she liked and make a run for it, but that was too easy. She'd not come all this way to let her *real* vocation slip through her fingers...

Having peeked at the sympathy cards ranged around the room, her eye travelled to a lifelike oil portrait of a family in their best clothes. The eyes and hair colour of the woman and boy bore more than a resemblance to the two Scott sisters. When the crone woke up, she must ask her who they were, gawping at her like they owned the world. And she wasn't welcome in it.

She examined the sleeping woman more closely and realized then how much more neglected she was than Merle. How much more she'd have to do here to keep things ticking over. But at least the fancy dresser had brushed her hair and kept her nail varnish matching her mouth. At least she changed her weird clothes whenever they got whiffy. And had the teeniest weeniest sense of humour.

She'd better phone Homely Helpers to explain that Merle was still missing and how the police and a senior social worker had advised her to stay at the Gables. When she'd asked Evelyn Scott if Mr Brownlow would still be paying her, those weak old eyes had glazed over as if she'd forgotten his name already. Was her new client's short-term memory failing? Or, like her sister, was she pretending?

Frankie knelt down to touch the claw-like hand which hung over the edge of the bed. Where Beryl's had been fat and stubby, ending in bitten nicotine-stained nails, this was slim and delicate with raised blue veins and bones no bigger than those of a rat she'd had to dissect during a biology lesson. This practical subject was always her favourite. She'd never forgotten the little surge of power when her scalpel pierced the creature's fur. No English composition on 'My Summer Holiday' could match that.

She stroked Miss Scott's head, fixated by the pink scalp beneath the mess of hair. Yes, Miss Scott it would be, until she could be sure. Until she'd had some more questions answered. Even then, she reckoned the word Mum would sound weird. She scoured her face for any similarities however small which might exist between them, but saw none. Maybe Merle had made a mistake.

Suddenly she noticed a small oblong shape jutting through the velvet dressing gown between the old girl's tits, what was left of them. Careful not to touch any skin, she lifted the fabric and saw beneath the nightdress neckline a black leather-bound book. Her curiosity was aroused, but just as she was about to remove it the woman's hand flew up defensively and another snore escaped her lips.

Frankie stood up and silently padded out of the lounge, calculating when she could safely try calling at Teme House. Time was running out. Time to save her skin.

She'd never believed in God, even after Beryl had made her attend Sunday school with Shannon, but God, whoever, wherever he was, seemed to be on her side right now. In Evelyn's bedroom she found a nondescript Boots carrier bag sandwiched between a stack of nightdresses in a posh chest of drawers and, like during her visit to 358 Dartmoor Road's box room, anticipation made her fingers shake.

She couldn't help forcing the bag open and spilling the contents. Even though both velvet curtains were wide open, the light from the window was poor as she raked through various photographs of Scott's newest factory plus invitations to posh dinners and cocktail parties – all the bits and bobs of a wealthy, busy life – until she found a small pile of newspaper cuttings, constrained by a new-looking elastic band.

She forgot to breathe once she realized these were all items of news related to the Holts, some including her own name and age at the time. The first began with her swimming achievements whilst still at primary school. Next, John Arthur's sacking from work; the Tech's town-hall diploma ceremony, then Shannon's degree photograph and speculation on her disappearance, while the last, concerning Vera Lloyd's illness and Daphne Cope's death in hospital, lay on top.

Frankie slumped into another chair feeling more than sick at the thought that the old woman sleeping so innocently downstairs *must* know who she was. Questions whipped round and round in her mind. Had Evelyn herself left the cuttings there? If so, did this prove she was her mother? Could Merle have lied about her having had a baby girl?

Having returned the cuttings to their bag in the right order, something else in the drawer made her catch her breath: a congratulations card showing a pink pram surrounded by balloons. Frankie peered closer and saw how a tiny portion of photograph had been cut out and stuck on the pram where a baby's head would be. It showed a newborn's face, just like Ellie's, topped by a crown of dark hair. Her pulse thumped as she opened the card.

To Dearest Little Jenny.
   Welcome to the world, from your loving Aunt Merle. Xxxx
   D.o.b. 20/2/1980

Frankie rubbed her fleece sleeve across her eyes and looked again. That birth date matched hers! A deep yearning vied with hatred as yet more questions flooded her thoughts. Merle had written 'Aunt', hadn't she? What more proof did she need? But why no envelope with Evelyn Scott's name on it or at least some reference to her in the message? There was only one way

275

forward. She must contact the clinic and find out what Evelyn Scott had done with her baby.

She was returning the Boots bag to the top drawer, between the lilac silk nightdress and one in caramel lace, when she spotted a plain cotton garment jutting from the pile. Curiosity drove her to pull it free and as she did so, noticed the scooped neckline, and row of poppers down to the waist. It was a maternity nightdress designed for easy breast-feeding and yes, there were even dried yellowish stains.

She sniffed them only to gag on the sour-cream smell still impregnating the fabric. And, there was more. Near the hem at the back lay the embroidered initials FC. Could the C mean Clinic? It was possible.

'Frances?' called out that all-too familiar voice from the hallway. 'What are you up to now? I don't like the way you creep around my house. Come down here at once.'

She moved more quickly than she'd ever done in her life and once outside the door sneaked further along the landing and leaned over the banisters.

'Been hunting for my hairbrush. Have you seen it anywhere?'

'No I haven't and I'd never have associated one with you in the first place.'

Frankie bit her lip as she rejoined her in the hall, aware of that strange book still in place. Then, unable to shift that rancid smell from her nose, made for the kitchen.

'Would you like a nice cup of tea?' she enquired in her most polite voice. 'There are still some

Jaffa cakes left.' Why not remind the bitch what she'd done for her?

'Just tea will do.'

'Please yourself, because I am,' she muttered to herself, filling the kettle.

'There we go.' She smiled, picking up both full coronation mugs and taking them to the wooden kitchen table under that watchful – no – suspicious gaze. 'This'll do you good, and when we've finished, I'd like to make some calls to see if there's any news on your sister.'

Instead of showing gratitude, Evelyn Scott lifted her Zimmer frame and crashed it down on the tiled floor.

Christ, she's got some strength, thought Frankie, grabbing her mug and retreating to a safe distance by the fridge.

'I *can't* have you interfering, Frances. Is that clear? You're here solely at my discretion. Remember that.'

'The police fixed it. Not me. Mind you, Miss Scott, I do think you need proper looking after.'

'I'm not listening. Now, if you'd kindly occupy yourself with something useful and leave me in peace. Tomorrow, we'll have a serious talk.'

The tone stung like the time she'd poked her stick into a wasps' nest in John Arthur's garden. It made her glance at the drawer below the main worktop which housed a set of barbecue prongs. Twenty per cent wooden handle, eighty per cent pure steel.

No, she told herself. Not yet. One stupid mistake with Merle was one too many.

'Can't be keeping up with all this,' the fish-monger said, weighing out two pounds of dark blue mussels and tipping them into the same kind of bag he'd used for Merle's haddock. 'First you're down Teme House, now you're here. Is it 'cos of what's happened?'

'What d'you mean, happened?'

The fishy smell brought on a fresh wave of nausea. She gripped the bag too tightly.

'Haven't you heard? Two walkers found your old lady's body this afternoon. Up on North Hill. Half-eaten, mind. Terrible business.'

Frankie leant against the van for support. Then shut her eyes.

'Oh God, no. That can't be true. Got her a roast tea ready, everything.'

'What a shame. Apparently she was dressed in some fancy ballet dress and dancer's shoes with ribbons. Not much left of them, mind. Nor her feet. Mrs Crowe next door had often seen her wearing that outfit, so she guessed immediately from the police description who it was.'

The bag of mussels fell from Frankie's grasp, hitting the ground with a dull tinkle of cracking shells. Peter Maddox bent to pick it up and, having handed it back to her without any offer of replacing them, resumed his account. 'Mind you, she'd been clobbered on the head good and proper, poor soul.'

'Who could have done a wicked thing like that? I can't believe it. Unless Sean Brownlow wanted her out of the way.'

The man turned to her. A frown changing

his face.

'What d'you mean?'

'He forced her to sign a will in his favour last Saturday.'

'I see.' He turned to face the big house. 'How d'you know that?'

'I was a witness. Nothing I could do.'

'Mark my words, there'll be a load of secrets seeing the light.'

'Secrets?' She was aware of Evelyn Scott staring at them both from the lounge window.

He nodded. 'I've not been driving from house to house round here for thirty-seven years for nothing. I've seen stuff, heard stuff.' He re-adjusted his hat and moved towards the driver's door. 'Best be off, Miss Holt. Still a few calls to make before I can put my feet up.' He looked towards the Gables and gave the owner a small, respectful wave which she didn't reciprocate.

'To be honest, I've never had much time for this Miss Scott. Only reason I call here is 'cos I got a living to make. Haven't the cops been round to tell her?'

'Not so far. Looks like I'll have to do it.'

She then used her most appealing expression, practised in front of her mirror in Dartmoor Road.

'Look, Mr Maddox, I've a huge favour to ask you.'

'What's that, then?

'Could you possibly take me to Teme House and back here again? I need to, you know, say goodbye to the place. After all, I loved it there. And Merle ... It won't take long. I'll pay you.'

279

'Why, when you've got a car?' He looked over to her Fiesta, wet and forlorn in the deepening gloom.

'I feel safer with you.'

'Why's that, then?'

'D'you know this Sean Brownlow? Well, I'm scared of him. He gives me death stares for a start. And yesterday he was shooting non-stop over there and I'd swear he was aiming for me.' She pointed to the nearby field.

'That's bad. Mind you, may not have been him. Lots of odds and sods have been caught on that land of hers.' He indicated towards a large green barn. 'I bet you don't know what goes on in there.'

'I don't really want to, thanks.'

'No harm in showing you. So you're in the picture, so to speak. Where Mr Brownlow tests the latest rifles. It will take two ticks. That's a promise.'

As they crossed the wet field, he told her in between wheezy breaths how much time Sean Brownlow had spent honing the minutest technical detail of the latest stalking rifle. How obsessed he'd become, and how, despite Miss Scott's suggestions, no apprentice, however capable and keen, was allowed to impinge on his job.

As they neared the barn she stopped behind the fishmonger, aware her pulse was too fast. Supposing Evelyn Scott could see them both. As she drew closer, she saw something which made her heart turn over. Four huge stags stood in a row, all in different positions. One faced her, another was turned sideways while the other two had their heads angled away to the left and right.

Christ Almighty...

They were as real as those stuffed heads in the hallway, reminding her of the paintings at the Crachan Hotel except that when she looked more closely she saw the damage had been done by more than one high-powered weapon. How the creatures' skin in and around the black circles over where their hearts would be was pocked by various bullet holes. Some were as neat as full stops, but others had left the skin and stuffing hanging free.

'Nice, eh?' said Mr Maddox going over to a digital display box set halfway up the rear wall. 'No wonder I'm into bloody fish.'

She thought about that bossy well-spoken man whose temple this clearly was, and wondered how anyone sane could spend more than a minute here. She was on the point of asking if they could leave this weird scene when all at once came a grating noise. Without warning, the beasts began to rotate in slow motion as if they belonged in some freaky funfair.

'Better be going, or the wife'll be fretting if I'm late back.'

With that grating sound fading now in competition with the rain, as they reached the driveway, she couldn't miss her chance. Teme House was priority.

'Can't you please just tell Miss Scott that you'll bring me straight back in ten minutes?'

He relieved her of the mussel bag and took it to the porch. Then he called out Frankie's message and suggested the old woman lock up after him.

'My good man, let me be quite honest...' A shrill voice rang out in the damp air. 'I never wanted *anyone* here. Tomorrow, believe me, I'll be making things quite clear to her.'

Frankie guessed what she meant. But Miss Scott wouldn't be the only one making decisions.

'And may I please remind you, that field you've just trampled over is private property.'

With that, the door was closed on him and by the time he'd rejoined his van Frankie was in the passenger seat, her rucksack in her lap.

'I couldn't say nothing about her sister, mind,' he said, setting off. 'She'll find out soon enough.'

His van stank and his overall had acquired fresh stains. But none of this mattered. What did was his word 'secrets'. She'd have to try and open the can of worms somehow.

'Merle told me her sister had a daughter once,' she began when he'd turned out of the drive. 'Is that true, d'you know? She's not just making things up?'

'She's *dead*,' he reminded her. 'And no. I've never heard anything like that. Mind you, nothing wrong with Merle Scott's marbles, whatever folk might say. She used to play daft to punish her sister. Her way of getting back at her. She told me that once.'

'Punish her for what?'

The man shrugged.

'Please try and think, Mr Maddox. Does February 20th 1980 ring any bells?

'Some time ago, that ... Hang on, though...' He peered straight ahead through the intermittent wipers then flicked on his side lights. The road, the houses adjoining it and the huge hill to the left were all indistinguishable in the murky light.

'You were saying?'

'My daughter was the registrar for births and deaths in Malvern at the time. Clever-clogs she was, our Dawn, just like her brother, but she had to leave her job.'

'Why?' Frankie was sensing her search grow warmer.

'Hassles, anonymous phone calls.'

'Man or a woman?'

'Dawn never said. She didn't like me asking. But my guess is it was Samuel Colby, Miss Scott's husband. He was much older than her, see.' The fishmonger glanced her way as if unsure whether to proceed or not. 'Couldn't hack the fact she'd been with another man.'

So, here it was. At last, and from an outsider too. Her blood seemed to run hot then cold as he paused to let a truck out from a side road. She recalled that framed photo in the lounge showing a benign-looking man more like Father Christmas than an angry freak.

'So there was a baby?' At the risk of sounding thick, she had to ask.

He nodded.

'So who *was* its father?'

Maddox took his left hand off the wheel and scythed it from side to side under his chin. Frankie shuddered.

'Go on. Tell me,' she goaded, remembering

283

similar scenes in Dartmoor Road.

'Why you so interested in all this?'

'I'm not. OK? Just curious to know what happened to it.'

Jenny.

'God knows.'

By now they'd reached Teme Rise and immediately she spotted a blue-and-white police cordon across the white house's wrought-iron gates.

Fuck.

At least there were no cop cars anywhere to be seen. That was something.

He glanced at her with a puzzled expression on his face, then slowed up, checking his mirrors. A woman passing by on a bike gave him an odd stare then moved on.

'I'd have thought you'd be first the police told about the old girl. I mean, you lived with her. Looked after her.'

Frankie did some quick thinking.

'No, nothing so far. They just said that I was in danger if I stopped here any longer.'

'Danger? Why's that?'

And then, eagerly, she embellished some more about Brownlow.

'You be quick, Miss Holt. Got a key?'

She nodded, then having sprinted along the surrounding privet hedge to where she knew it was thin enough for her to squeeze through, found herself by the front door.

Tension, which made her key take too long to turn in the lock, turned to fear. Three minutes later she realized that not only had Merle's purse containing her Visa card and clearly printed PIN number disappeared, but also someone had paid a visit to her attic bedroom.

The drive back seemed to take for ever. The van was extra-sluggish, ploughing through the wet unlit roads; the fishmonger far too chatty, crowding her thoughts with local business gossip, when all she wanted was to find out who'd got to Teme House first. Who the fuck was on her case? And what sicko had taken Ellie's little wristband?

The only answer was Sean Brownlow. But how could she challenge him now? It would make her seem too much on the defensive as if she had something to hide.

She sat with her former employer's beige suitcase on her lap. It contained the smaller tartan one plus necessities for a stay at the Gables. As the van neared the house, she felt an invisible net slowly begin to close in. Her nerves quickened. Her throat needed a drink. From the road, the Gables seemed more lit up than usual and the moment they reached the drive she knew why. A cop car was parked by the front door. Her gut feeling had been right after all.

'Hey up. Time to exit,' Maddox said, not even attempting to enter the driveway, as if he too, had something to hide. 'These aren't my favourite people.'

'Wonder what they want,' she said, passing over a fiver for his trouble, trying to sound as casual as possible to disguise the new fear lurking inside her. 'By the way, where does your

Dawn live now?'

'In the Old Post Office, Malvern Link. Why?' He revved the engine and she reached for her door handle.

'No reason. And thanks again.'

'My pleasure. See you next Friday. I hope things get sorted. Miss Merle was a special lady. She had principles. Unlike some.'

Frankie ran up the tarmac slope and locked the beige suitcase in the Fiesta's boot, too distracted to wave her co-conspirator goodbye. Steeling herself for what lay ahead. She had the tartan case hidden inside the bigger one, but who might have clapped eyes on it at Teme House?

She spotted the familiar figure of DC Avril Pilkington, already in the porch to greet her. Her frizzy hair, cut even shorter, made her extra pig-like as she led the way through the airless hallway, which smelt of mussels, into the lounge, where a middle-aged guy in a brown suit introduced himself as Detective Inspector Manson. He then lowered himself on to a green brocade couch next to Evelyn Scott. Clearly in shock. No way was she her mother. No way.

'May we ask where you've been, Frankie?' The Sow gestured her to sit in the desk chair already turned to face the room. 'And if you choose not to cooperate, we can always ask your chauffeur.'

She thought of Merle half gobbled up, deep in the bracken. Of someone probably bleeding her account dry, and scrutinizing her own missing property. Attack was therefore the best defence.

'Had to collect my things from Teme House,

didn't I? Anyway, I also thought Merle might have turned up. I've been saying my prayers for her safe return non-stop.'

'What kind of things?'

Quick. Think...

'My period's due and I needed my Tampax. OK?'

The DI coughed. The Sow's eyes on her making her rabbit on...

'It felt really weird going back in the place and her not being there. I can't understand why she's not been found yet. Surely someone must have seen her.'

Both pigs looked at each other as if to say, which one of us is going to quiz her some more? Finally the guy leaned forwards.

'We'd like to take a look in your rucksack, if you don't mind. Miss Scott here has already kindly allowed us access to your room.'

Fuck.

She wanted to go up there immediately and check for herself nothing had been nicked. Then she remembered TV dramas. 'Did you have a search warrant?'

'Oh, yes,' said Evelyn, demure as Daphne Cope. Except the difference was, she'd got brains. And as if on cue, the suit held it up for her to see. What was going on? What did they know? And had they, not Brownlow, also gone to her bedroom at Teme House?'

'Your rucksack, please, Miss Holt.'

'Why?'

'Procedure, that's all.'

'Do *you* still have Merle's keys?' barked

287

Evelyn Scott, as a bonus.

'Too right I do. I was in charge there, wasn't I?'

Manson held out his hand in anticipation as she peeled the rucksack off her shoulders and handed it over, glad there was nothing incriminating inside. Gary Cope's letter had joined the latex gloves inside her pants. And they were hardly likely to look there, were they?

'Can you think of anyone *else* who might have a key?' he asked, his right hand already probing inside her bag before giving her wallet some air. He then appraised the contents.

'Not Piotr, that's for sure. He used to ask Merle to open the scullery door for him so he could plug the lawnmower in.'

'OK. So who's this?' He angled Shannon's photo towards her. The mortar board cast a shadow over her face.

Frankie willed more tears to come. Tried to blink them away, aware of the Sow eyeing her every breath.

'My sister, Shannon. At her degree ceremony. I miss her so bloody much as well.'

'I'm sorry.' He slotted it back into place. 'Her case is never closed, remember that.'

Frankie sniffed and smiled.

'Thanks.'

The DI then retrieved the spaniel charm key ring and placed it inside a small plastic bag with a self-seal top. Despite his efforts at being nice, her pulse was playing tricks again. She made herself think of Kilfargan. A success story despite that threatened exhumation.

'I hope you left *my* sister's house secure,' Evelyn turned to her, interrupting her thoughts.

'I pride myself on being thorough.'

'By the way, where are those "personal" items you said you needed from Teme House? There's no sign of them.' His eyebrows almost touched his hairline. The bastard.

'Someone had nicked them, hadn't they? Perverts.'

Suddenly the room darkened; the sun overpowered by the biggest, blackest clouds she'd ever seen. The temperature drop reached under her clothes, causing her to shiver again as the suit finally returned her rucksack. If he was disappointed, he didn't show it.

'I'm afraid, Miss Holt, we've some very sad news, which, understandably, we couldn't tell you the moment you walked in the door.'

'What news?' Her hungry stomach shrivelling up to nothing.

'Your client, Miss Merle Scott, has just been found brutally murdered. She'd been badly beaten about the head and appears to have suffered a massive cranial haemorrhage. It's possible she was also sexually assaulted, but we don't yet know for sure.'

Frankie saw six eyes waiting for a response. Someone should turn on a light, she thought. The room was like a pit and she was falling. Falling, unable to speak. She must make her reaction sound fresh, real.

'When did this happen?' she said at last.

'Difficult to say, given the state of decomposition.'

289

'I can't believe this. She was a dear, funny old lady.'

'Indeed she was. Miss Scott will be coming with us to the formally identify the body.'

'Who'd want to kill her?' Frankie gathering momentum after her bad start, switched on the desk lamp. 'Unless Sean Brownlow couldn't wait to pick up...'

She'd already predicted the Sow's death stare. 'Mr Brownlow's already given a statement,' she said sternly. 'We'll also need one from you as to your whereabouts on Wednesday evening from five o'clock onwards.'

Frankie plunged her head into her hands, urging herself to keep cool. Mrs Beavis's face shone into her mind, reminding her to keep her nose clean at all costs.

'You're not suspecting me as well. Are you?'

'At the moment, we're simply making enquiries.'

'I loved her. I thought she was brilliant. I mean, we had a laugh.'

New tears came then. The hot, burning kind, and she was aware of the brown-suited guy coming over and resting a hand on her shoulder.

'We know that. We just need any information we can get.'

'Course you do,' she sniffed, looking up at him in gratitude for his unexpected show of kindness. She then looked Evelyn Scott in the eye. 'I know what you must be thinking. That I was careless, maybe not even around at the time she took herself off, but if that turkey could speak, he'd tell you I'd just got washed and changed

290

upstairs, got him out of the oven to start carving, and when I called out to ask Miss Scott if she wanted stuffing, there was no reply.'

'*Nobody* knows what I'm thinking.'

Frankie felt as if a blob of icy water had landed on the back of her neck. The DI withdrew the promised statement sheet from his briefcase and placed it on the desk.

'Best if you write everything down, Frankie. With exact times if possible. Thank you. Oh, and we're wondering why Miss Scott was found wearing an old tiara.'

'She loved it, that's why. Wore it all day on Wednesday. I even offered to clean it for her but would she take it off? No way.'

That silence resumed while she wrote out her account in handwriting much smaller, tighter than usual, punctuated by nervous glances over her shoulder at the Holy Trinity sitting there, waiting as her lies unfolded.

She signed and dated the statement, then passed it back to the suit, puzzled that neither of them queried her minute-by-minute story. Was Miss Scott in denial or didn't she care?

'Why would anyone want to do that to a helpless old lady?' she demanded. 'I don't get it. Except she was pretty well off.'

For a second, Evelyn's head turned her way as the DI kept talking.

'There's no evidence of robbery on her person, but her house keys are missing and it's odd there was no sign of any purse in her bag which we found in the dining room. Also, the manila envelope labelled "Gardener Cash until 1/9/02", left in Miss Scott's desk, was empty. We'd have to speak to Mr Brownlow again, of course, if and when...' His voice tailed away.

'What d'you mean, if and when?' Frankie looked from one to the other.

She knew something else was up. That same fear made her fists close. Made her nails dig into her own flesh.

'Maybe she took her purse herself. I mean, she might have needed it but didn't fancy carrying a big bag around...'

Evelyn Scott shook her head.

'Merle *never* needed money. I saw to that. Anyhow,' she focused on her, 'it was the carer's task to check it was safe.'

'That's not fair.'

The old woman ignored her, turning to her visitors. 'We must alert the bank now before funds start disappearing from her account. Why didn't you inform me of this straight away?'

The DI got up and, having exchanged whispers with her, moved away into the hall, his phone at the ready. Meanwhile, the Sow fiddled with her tights, obviously not comfortable being in such a posh house.

'All done,' he said reclaiming his seat, his body language now more impatient. 'Back to this crime. We're guessing whoever killed Miss Scott had taken her body by van or car or whatever. Dragged her up the hill, realizing it wouldn't be long before the wildlife up there took its toll. The couple who found her spotted a camper van in the small car park there. Looked like it had been parked a while. We urgently need to contact the owner. They may have seen something too.'

Frankie wiped her eyes again. She'd not noticed any car park, let alone another vehicle.

She was aware it was time for a diversion. 'I saw big muddy footprints leading from the Blue Room at Teme House after she'd gone. Second floor up. I reckon they should be tested ASAP.'

The Sow's lips began to move and Frankie willed herself to be on guard.

'This assailant of yours. Can you describe him more fully?'

'You've asked me that already. I just knew the man behind me was Sean Brownlow. I recognized his aftershave. Brut, it was. Anyhow you said yourself he didn't trust me.'

That got her. She'd spotted a ladder in her tights and was twisting the fabric round her fat calf so its white skin wouldn't show through.

'And why would that be?' asked the suit.

Frankie warned herself to stay on top of the game. To be strong.

'He was really possessive of Merle. But it wasn't just me he thought was crap. He gave the other carers a hard time too. But I witnessed her signing her will for him to pick up, didn't I? He gave her no choice. It's all in the record book.'

'This record book. May we keep it for the time being?'

'Sure.'

Frankie pulled open her rucksack and handed over the red exercise book, where no detail of her lies had been spared. That Merle could manage perfectly well without a stick. She suddenly remembered something else.

She left her seat, hurried into the hall and returned with the blanked-out address book. 'Look at this. All Tippexed out.'

The Sow took it from her while Evelyn's skeletal hands locked tight together. 'I know something's going on, but Sean Brownlow's the one you should be talking to. OK, you said he'd been working late that night, but who can prove that?'

'We've three very reliable witnesses. From his office.'

Frankie felt a tremor of fear. Her lie was like a boomerang, winging its way back to hit her where it hurt most. 'I'm *telling* you, that trigger-happy guy I saw by the barn was Sean Brown-low. Same as at Teme House.'

The DI closed the carer's book and passed it to Evelyn Scott. Her fixed expression gave nothing away as she turned the pages.

'You ought to know that as we speak, Miss Holt, this same man is fighting for his life. He may not make it to the morning.'

Her empty stomach was as leaden as a rock. Evelyn Scott was following her every move. The old woman must have known about this all along. Or else she was a fucking robot. Her next statement proved it.

'Mr Brownlow had keys for both our houses, which I'd like returned as soon as possible.'

The two pigs exchanged an awkward glance.

'Of course, ma'am,' said the Sow. 'We'll make that a priority.'

Frankie noticed her hands trembling in her lap.

'What happened?' she asked. 'This is awful, what with Miss Scott and everything...'

'Sean Brownlow was found near his Jeep by a dog-walker in Upper Wych at four o'clock yesterday afternoon. There seem to be two possibilities. Either he was lured there by someone he knew or,' he glanced at the old woman sitting corpselike next to him, 'it may have been attempted suicide. At the moment, there's little evidence of a confrontation so this seems the most likely cause, although we are checking his office emails and his mobile phone. However, if either of you can add anything which might help us, we'd be grateful.'

Frankie knew what 'help' meant. Gripped the sides of her chair. Her carefully constructed vendetta crumbling to dust.

'He seemed to hate Miss Scott's gardener,' she said as evenly as possible. 'Made fun of his name for a start. Piotr, it was. Said bloody foreigners should go home. Bad stuff like that.'

'Please describe this Piotr if you can.'

Frankie was about to deny she'd ever met him, but Evelyn Scott beat her to it.

'I saw him many times at Teme House, though not to speak to. He was well built and always wore a black woollen hat almost over his eyebrows. He's a fine worker and despite my former employee's tragic condition, I'm appalled at his racism. Without so-called "foreign" workers, Scott's Rifles wouldn't be where they are today and my greatest humiliation ever was to be seen alongside him at that protest. I'm afraid after that his job with us was no longer tenable.'

295

'He shocked many others in the community, too. By the way, any idea where this Piotr lives?'

Frankie seemed to shrink back even further in her chair, but no way was she helping them to find him. Not with Merle's pay prematurely in his pocket. She held her breath.

'I'm ashamed to say we never had an address. He seemed to exist on the fringes of society here.'

The Sow nodded as Evelyn Scott stood up and pushed her Zimmer frame over to a large oil painting which took up most of the wall between two side bay windows.

'I'm still very concerned about Teme House, Detective Inspector.'

'Let me reassure you, ma'am, that the open rear window is now boarded up. The old ladder lying nearby has been destroyed and the gates cordoned off.'

'Is the house alarmed?' Evelyn addressed the man.

The policeman crossed the carpet towards her so she could whisper the code to him.

'Right,' he said afterwards. 'We'll get that seen to the minute we leave. DC Pilkington feels that in the interim it's best if Miss Holt remains here with you.'

He ignored the drop of her jaw. The mouth tightening in protest. 'Not just because your doctor and Mrs Chance have advised it, but Miss Holt is, after all, a connection between you and your late sister.'

'One whom I was never permitted to vet.'

'Well, you seemed happy enough for her to do

296

your shopping.'

Evelyn Scott turned her face away as Frankie smiled at him gratefully, thinking that steel not blood must run in the old woman's veins.

Frankie's grip loosened on her seat's arms as she watched Evelyn Scott move even closer to the painting which had bothered her since she'd first clapped eyes on it.

'My forebears in 1857,' its owner began, as if she was a guide in the National Gallery, except that her voice betrayed a quiver of emotion. 'Rose Swithins and her husband Will Scott.'

'Who's the young guy?' asked Frankie, thinking that these possible ancestors could provide another welcome distraction.

'Thomas, their son, just before he sailed for New Zealand, and when he eventually returned, he moved into this house with his young family and helped run the successful company his parents had begun. He took it over when his mother died and the name has continued until now. And that name, my good people, is sacrosanct. Unless a miracle occurs, it will end with me.'

Those last two sentences hit Frankie like hailstones.

'And one final matter, just for the record.' The businesswoman's breaths seemed strained as if there weren't many of them left. 'I'm already contesting my late sister's recent will. It's true Sean Brownlow forced her hand. Frances here told me so in no uncertain terms. That deed will collapse in court like straw in a tempest, and her estate will pass to me.'

'Surely that'll take ages.' A relieved Frankie had already worked out the implications.

'My lawyer says one month at most.'

Frankie watched in the dusty silence as she made her way back to her chair, but didn't sit down. The DI followed, urging her to contact them at any time if she recalled anything else, however small or inconsequential, about her late sister or Brownlow. Frankie liked the word inconsequential. Knew all too well how it was the little things which mattered.

'You must also be on your guard, Miss Scott,' added the suit.

'I've been on my guard all my life,' she retorted. 'And where's it got me? By the way, what about arranging a funeral?'

'We'll let you know immediately after the post-mortem. Now then, perhaps Frances can help you get dressed. We need to get the identification over and done with as soon as possible.'

'Can't I just wear a mackintosh over this?' asked Evelyn indicating her dressing gown.

'Of course.'

Frankie chose a smart beige raincoat with a tartan lining, reminding her of her special souvenir suitcase.

'Hasn't Fanny told you?' began Evelyn, slipping one thin arm after the other into the sleeves, grimacing with the effort of it and keeping her secret book in place. 'She's a young unmarried mother with a baby daughter up in Manchester.'

Frankie stopped breathing as both visitors stalled in the hallway. Mrs Beavis's caution came to mind.

'Who's Fanny?' Manson turned round.

'The girl here. It's the diminutive form of Frances, didn't you know?'

'Please don't call me that. OK?'

'I never knew you had a daughter,' said the Sow, all of a sudden, as she scribbled her notes. 'When was she born?'

'Tenth of November 2000. Why?'

Frankie stared up at the stag's head directly above her, whose outspread antlers cast a weird network of shadows over the wall. Its mouth lay open revealing a large bristly tongue, just like the ones John Arthur bought from the local butcher's for her to slice for his sandwiches. Watch yours, it seemed to be saying. And she did.

'Your baby...' the Sow butted in, her tone altogether more encouraging.

'She's beautiful. Perfect, in fact. And I'm so proud of her.'

'Any father?' asked Evelyn Scott.

'He died on manoeuvres in Germany. We were going to get married once he returned.'

'Oh dear, dear. What a shame.'

Was that a tiny grimace on the Sow's lips, wondered Frankie.

The detective, however, seemed more human now. Maybe even fancied her.

The grandfather clock struck seven, making her jump. With the two pigs walking on ahead, the bereaved sister locked up the house then Frankie helped her to the police car, despite the woman flinching at her every touch. Once she'd been shoehorned into the front seat, Frankie realized she'd no umbrella or a key for later. She also had to check her room.

Suddenly Evelyn Scott lowered her window.

'Tell me,' she said. 'Do you recall Merle's last words to you before she left?'

Frankie blinked in surprise.

'It's all in my notes, like I've said.'

'I've read your notes. But now I'm looking at your eyes.'

'Yeah, so?'

' "Eyes are the window to men's souls." Who said that?'

'Elizabeth the First. But I'm not a man.'

'When I return from this ordeal, I'll need time to sort things out before our chat tomorrow. Have you somewhere to spend the evening?'

Frankie was unsure how to respond.

'Yeah. But I'll need a key. To get your tea ready.'

Without answering, Evelyn Scott pulled out the Yale from her bag, then, as if something had made her change her mind, put it back again.

'It doesn't matter about dinner, or how late back you are. Just ring the doorbell. Oh, by the way.'

'Yes?'

She knew both pigs were listening. Especially the Sow, while the DI was starting the engine.

'I don't like you touching me when I'm asleep, understand?'

'I was only checking you were OK. Christ!'

'There's something else,' the invalid called out. 'Next time you intend snooping around me and my bedroom, please have the courtesy to ask

300

me first.'

Bitch.

'Honest to God. I don't do stuff like that.'

'Well, if there's one thing that doesn't lie, it's a camera.'

Frankie spun round. Felt blood drain from her face.

'What d'you mean, a camera?'

'I've had CCTV installed in every room here, ever since my husband died.'

Frankie gulped, then ran past them down the drive and along the West Malvern Road. She hid in a dark unlit gateway until her tormentors had gone, feeling the cool night rain touch her skin.

Twenty-Six

Martin still felt worse than sick. He felt defiled, unable to eat or drink anything after finding that half-eaten corpse. Once he'd dialled 999 from his mobile and endured the operator's seemingly endless questions, he and Dora had waited as instructed for the police team to arrive. He'd asked DC Pilkington if the victim was Merle Scott and took her tearful silence for a yes. The rest was a blur of activity as yet more personnel arrived and the area cordoned off. Once both his and Dora's statements had been taken inside DI Manson's warm Mondeo, Dora had reassured him she was fit to drive, so they'd set off in convoy for the police station, where tea, sandwiches and the services of a counsellor were on offer. Having declined all this, they'd been interviewed separately in adjoining rooms. No, he'd no idea who might have wanted to kill the missing former spaniel-breeder, and no, there'd been no one else around on North Hill apart from that camper van with its Cymru sticker.

He could have handed over Frances Ann Holt's CV, Gary's letter and those few items he'd taken from Teme House – now in the boot of Dora's car – but he didn't. Not yet. This was for him to deal with. He'd promised Maddy McKay. If he needed police help, he'd ask for it. Meanwhile the cagoule and the toiletries would be safely locked up at the building site.

Once he and Dora had left the police station, drained and miserable, he checked his watch. An hour to go to the séance – the last thing he felt like, especially since the sky was like night and a thin rain had begun to fall. However, while Dora drove him to her ground-floor bedsit so they could have a fag and share a bottle of Pepsi, he began to have a change of heart. With a gnawing certainty he knew it wouldn't simply be his mother he'd be trying to reach tonight, but that once laughing, happy Gary Cope and the woman, now a corpse, dressed in a tattered ballerina's outfit, whose chewed-off tongue had been left sticking to her neck. Her one eye staring up at the sky, the other a pool of dried blood. Her pants too had been gnawed at and were just a scrap of cotton. Her feet, he'd noticed, had no toes.

He hoped that the elusive Frankie Ann Holt, linked by rather more than his intuition to the other bizarre event hundreds of miles away, was still around. He hoped that the police hadn't driven her away. He had to see her again. Draw her out about what that CV *didn't* show.

'Shall we leave the séance?' Dora asked him as they passed a lit-up Waitrose on foot, having decided to leave her car in favour of drizzly fresh air. The supermarket seemed almost obscenely cheerful in stark contrast to what had lain due north up the hill. 'You don't look too good,' she added. Her hair lay damp against her head and her skin smelt of the soap she'd used. Magnolia Ice. He suddenly wanted to kiss her again and feel her breasts under his hands as if doing so might expunge that grotesque violation only a few hours ago.

'I'm fine,' he took her hand and squeezed it instead. 'Should be interesting.'

'The whole point was that it should *help* you. Not just be interesting...'

'I've met Merle Scott's carer, you know,' he said, suddenly changing the subject.

'You never said.' She turned, her eyes narrowing as if sensing a possible rival. 'And?'

'Each time I've had this feeling she looks kind of hunted. Vulnerable.'

Dora snorted, unimpressed.

'Hunted by what? By whom?'

Martin shrugged.

'And then, in a split second, it's as if *she's*

303

become the hunter.'

'You mean she's a schizo? That she's dangerous?'

'I don't know. I can't explain it, except that when she stared at me that time in the library. I felt like a mouse facing some ravenous predator.'

Dora shivered. Withdrew her hand.

'Do you really think she could have clubbed that poor woman to death?'

Martin shrugged, watching shoppers leave the store with their bulging green-and-white carrier bags. Normal people doing normal things. But surely any one of them could be pushed to the limit? Be compelled to do something inhuman in a moment of madness? Or simply to defend themselves.

'But surely if she was her carer, I mean, that's not the sort of job nutters go for, is it? I thought there were lots of checks on them.'

'So did I. But people are easily fooled. Look at me and those wankers I worked with in London. I thought my boss and Den Tanner were great guys until things turned bad.'

At that moment a half-familiar figure jogged by. He noticed the bright hair, the pink rucksack, the neat butt in those skintight jeans. That same sweet scent lingering in her wake.

'Eye-candy, huh?' Dora said sourly.

'It's her. C'mon. Let's follow.'

They kept her in sight until she disappeared down a damp side street to the right. Solid windowless walls reared up blocking out the last of the daylight. Suddenly Dora lurched against him, crying out in pain.

'I've twisted my ankle. Damn these pavements!'

The other girl looked round briefly, then continued her effortless pace until she'd disappeared from view down yet another narrow street.

'Someone's in a hurry,' Martin observed, helping Dora regain her balance then bending down to rub the sore ankle. 'By the way, where the hell are we now?'

'Crook Street. Very appropriate, don't you think? It's a wonder the poor old folk here aren't falling about all over the place.'

'They're doing worse than that,' he said darkly, thinking again of Merle Scott.

He paused while he took out his mobile and called directory enquiries.

'We're going to be late,' Dora mouthed. 'Hurry up!'

Martin turned away to dial the number he'd been given. He had to concentrate as the line was bad and the woman's voice which reached him was so heavily accented as to be almost unintelligible.

'I'm Nigel Barnes,' he began, aware of Dora's growing impatience. 'I believe my sister may have stayed at your hotel recently. My mum and I are really worried as we've not heard from her for three weeks.'

'What's the name?'

'Her married name's Frances Holt. She's twenty-three.'

'Let me check.'

Too many seconds later came her reply.

'Can't help you, sorry.'

'She was in a bit of bother at the time. May have used a different name. She'd have been on her own, I'm sure of that. Early twenties. Very slim...'

'There is *someone* I remember. Saturday June fifteenth. Here it is. Denise Shaw, from Darlington. Yes, that's right. And she had this doll with her. Ever so realistic, it was. I was quite taken in by it at first.'

'Doll?' His stomach had already shrunk to a hard sick ball. Gary Cope had gone missing the following day.

'Forgotten what she called it, but treated it like a proper living baby. My husband and I thought that a bit odd, if you must know.'

'Did she have a car?'

He swore to himself he'd chase Frances Holt to the end of the earth and find her. Before she found anybody else...

'Right. My husband thinks it was an old white Fiesta. He's good on cars, is Hamish. There was a child's car seat in the front.'

White Fiesta...

The reception faded.

'Bloody hell!' he shouted.

Dora pointed down the road to a small terrace of stone-built houses almost entombed by a crescent of matching dark grey granite. Forbidding was an understatement and, like those stones, matched his mood entirely. At least Dora wasn't plaguing him with questions. At least she'd picked up on his mood.

'Hey, there it is,' she announced, lengthening

306

her stride. 'Flat two, number six.'

Suddenly a plump dark-haired woman appeared at the window and pulled down a black blind, immediately darkening the road in front. The other two windows followed suit and for some reason he felt uneasy.

'That's Carol,' said Dora. 'She's cool.'

He was torn between a possible spiritual link-up with those he loved and wanted to help, and placing his hands around that jogger's neck while she spat out the deadly truth. He was regretting now that he'd even considered Dora's crazy idea. Louisa Webb or no Louisa Webb. Weren't there enough problems in the real world, he asked himself, without dabbling in the next?

The dark-haired woman emerged from the front door, bearing a wide smile. She embraced Dora then stepped back to appraise first her, then him.

'This is Martin Webb,' said Dora.

'The one you've been talking about non-stop.' She winked at him then grew serious. 'Glad you could both still make it especially. It must have been truly a shock to find Miss Scott like that.'

Her warm earthy voice was the kind to encourage confidences. No wonder she was a medium, he thought.

'It was. And I'm glad I wasn't on my own.'

'I won't rub it in, but we really missed you this afternoon,' Carol said, looking at Dora. 'The rehearsal wasn't the same without you.'

'I hated letting everyone down. Did Polly manage all right?' Dora asked, blushing.

'She did. But no way is she Nina.'

Just then he wanted to hold Dora, tell her he too thought her short performance on North Hill had been amazing, but Carol Piper was already in the hallway and up the stairs. Her ample hips were emphasized by a colourful dirndl skirt, her feet encased in green velvet slippers. She stopped at the end of the landing by a doorway beyond which lay a small room almost filled by a round oak table and five unmatching chairs. The faint sound of Celtic music came from somewhere else together with the flush of a nearby lavatory. He wondered idly who else would appear. Then he realized why he felt so claustrophobic. Why a headache seemed to be in the offing. The room had no windows, no fireplace, no nothing. Dora too, seemed hesitant and hovered near the door.

'As you can see, we're five tonight,' the woman announced, placing a white candle in the centre of the table and lighting it using a box of matches from her skirt pocket. She waited to see if the tiny flame would survive.

'There's me, of course, and you two, plus Edward Hollis from the college – he's the head of art there and has just lost his dear father. And then – ' she glanced back at the still-open door – 'there's Frankie.'

Frankie...

Martin clutched the back of the nearest chair. It wasn't that common a name. Footsteps along the floor outside. The luminous blonde hair and eyes he'd not forgotten since last night. Light and darkness all in one.

'Hi.' She smiled, looking around and lifting that pink rucksack up over her head. Her movements graceful, hypnotic. He forgot to shut his mouth then saw Dora looking his way.

'Do you prefer to be called Frankie or Frances?' asked Carol Piper, fiddling with the chairs, so the spaces in between were equal.

'I'm not fussy. And hey – ' she looked over at Martin and grinned – 'I still owe you fifty pence.'

He felt her gaze rest on him for a second too long, and felt that same heat increase to attack his whole body. Any clever reply stayed locked in his throat.

'But I just want to say straight off that this isn't my usual thing, if you get my meaning. Carol here twisted my arm to give it a go.'

'I did indeed, Frankie, because – and I'm sure you won't mind Martin and Dora here knowing it – when I met you, you seemed stressed out.'

'Really?' Suddenly defensive, eyeing everyone in turn. Especially Dora.

Carol nodded, checking her watch.

But, he thought, the woman was wrong. Unless, like Dora, this stranger was a bloody good actress. He watched her move around the table, touching each chair in turn until she stood next to him, looking him up and down. The heat under his clothes was becoming unbearable. And so was something else. Something quite unplanned.

That desire for Dora which had died in the bracken had returned. But it wasn't for her.

'We'll give Edward another minute,' Carol

Piper said, before turning up the music in the room next door so that the rhythmic chanting made the girl in the blue fleece begin to sway and, in one swift, electric moment her butt brushed his thigh.

'This is to bring joy to the spirits who are waiting,' the hostess added, spreading her arms wide. 'So, think love. Prepare yourselves for a great and abiding union.'

The only union Martin could think of was with this person now letting her left hand deliberately and openly brush against his fly...

He felt dizzy. Saw Dora move towards the door, mouthing her excuses to her friend. And, before he could stop her, she'd gone, followed by Carol Piper, who returned with a frown on her face.

'I'd better see what's up.' Martin made a move, but the woman raised her hand to stop him before ushering in a man in his mid-fifties wearing a lived-in tweed jacket.

'Dora's fine,' explained the woman rather too brightly. 'Just needs an early night, which, given her experiences today, is understandable. Right, this is Edward Hollis, who's taught at Malvern College for more years than he cares to remember. His father passed on last month and I know things have been difficult for him. I hope, Edward, we can help you find some peace.'

'Thank you,' the man murmured, his eyes fixed on the candle.

'And now it's time for more introductions. Firstly –' she indicated the lithe blonde girl – 'this is Frankie Holt. For Edward's benefit, I'll just explain that she's just endured a tremendous blow today with the tragic loss of her employer, Miss Merle Scott. Like the rest of you, she'll need all the support we can give.'

So, thought Martin, Frances Ann Holt. No time to dwell on the significance of this, however, because the woman in charge was steaming ahead with her own agenda.

'Dora brought her new friend Martin along so he can communicate with Louisa, his late mother.' She pointed at him with a flourish. 'They were also the ones who found poor Miss Scott this afternoon.'

He saw Frankie's face pale even further. Her hands clamped over her mouth.

'And now, before we start the proceedings, I have some items of news to share with you.' The New-Ager turned down the music. 'Firstly, you may or may not have heard the ghastly report about one of our long-standing Solstice members, Sean Brownlow. He was found brutally attacked last night at Upper Wych. Apparently he'd been helping in the search for Merle Scott, his employer's missing sister, and now he's in a coma at Worcester Royal Hospital. Prognosis is poor.'

The blonde too had something to say. Her thigh now against Martin's. His erection on the rise again as Dora's image faded.

'No, I reckon he tried to top himself. Evelyn Scott had just given him the sack because he'd inherited all Merle's money.'

Carol Piper soon regained her composure. The candle's glow turning her skin the colour of

311

custard.

'As an upright citizen of Malvern, I *should* say, let's hope our police get to the bottom of it all soon.' She moved nearer the table and spread out both hands as if to support her weight during the next pronouncement. Her solemn expression changed to one of barely concealed excitement. 'Secondly, some truly wonderful news. Our theatre director phoned me earlier. I can hardly believe it. Miss Evelyn Scott called him to say that having to identify the body of her late sister made her rethink her priorities. She therefore intends to leave two million pounds to help sustain that excellent institution for years to come.'

Martin sensed the girl next to him stiffen.

'What about the rest of her stuff?' asked Frankie.

'I believe it's to be ploughed back into her stalking-rifle business, with trust funds set up for the employees and their children. Anyway, that's what Nick Dawes said.'

'Stalking rifles?' Martin had no idea about the nature of the business, thinking it unusual a woman of that age should be in charge.

'Was she ever an actress herself?' he asked, thinking guiltily of Dora, wondering if he should phone her. He hoped she'd forgive him.

'No, but she often sponsors our productions. She never missed a first night if she could help it. However, as you probably know, she suffers terribly with osteoporosis. I caught a glimpse of her an hour ago in a police car. She looked stricken.'

'Well, I'm her carer now,' announced Frankie,

moving away from him. Each action as ever, neat and precise. Missing his frown, his clear unease. 'She's been badly malnourished for too long and you should have seen the state of her fridge, apart from everything else...'

'So you'll be busy, then,' Martin said, his desire, like all his unasked questions, slipping away. He found himself observing the smooth hair on the crown of her head, wondering how easy would it be to darken and turn into spikes. And then he noticed an irregular bald patch behind her left ear and puzzled how it had got there. Had she been in a fight? Was she into self-harm? Whatever the cause, it looked odd.

Just then, Carol Piper switched off the light and removed a carrier bag from under the table. He sneezed as a stale herby smell filled the room.

'Bless you,' Carol Piper said, passing round four leather beaked masks and slipping one over her head. 'As you probably know,' she continued, her voice seeming to come from far away, 'these are plague masks. In the old days these beaks would have been filled with herbs to keep noxious smells at bay. I've already cleansed them spiritually for our purpose tonight.'

Martin stared at these primitive yet powerful devices which, in the candlelight seemed more likely to encourage evil than repel it. He also saw Frankie sniff hers and wrinkle her nose. But hadn't her whole demeanour changed since news of Miss Scott's generous will? Or was he imagining things? Then he thought of the pink plastic hospital strip bearing that baby's name and birth date. Now there was no means of tracing who had issued it or, unless he asked Frankie directly, finding out who the mother was. Perhaps there'd been a tragedy and the infant referred to had died. Or perhaps Ellie Scott, wherever she was, was alive and kicking ... A child with the surname Scott ... And then he remembered what the Inverary hotelier had said about a strange doll and child's car seat.

He saw the carer watch him as he finally pulled his own mask over his head trying now to focus on why he was here. To reach Louisa Webb, of course. The woman who'd used one of his blunt razor blades and sawn at her flesh as if trying to detach her hand.

Through tiny pinprick holes, he saw Carol Piper kill the music, letting silence drop like a heavy cloak, keeping the whole town, the whole world outside at bay.

He heard Frankie sniff again under her mask. The girl with too many secrets, too many co-incidences attached to her like that rucksack to her body. And it wasn't until she was quiet that Carol Piper asked for each participant to think hard about who they were trying to reach.

'The stronger your thought projection, the clearer will be their response through me. I'm only the mouthpiece, remember. The conduit.'

Martin thought of Gary Cope and, in a reckless moment, wondered if he shouldn't produce that photo of his laughing face which had propelled him all the way to Manchester for clues. And if it really was that startlingly attractive bird now sitting on his right who'd killed both Gary and his pet dog, her reaction might be very useful. He took a deep breath and dropped his right hand into his jacket pocket.

'Is it OK to have an image to look at?' he asked.

'If you must.' The medium sounded faintly irritated. 'However, you mustn't finger it, nor must anyone here make physical contact with anything other than the table. In turn, I will enable you to fulfil your own predestined lives in the world. I am part of your individual life plan, already sensing your unique presences, personalities and energies essential for your spiritual growth. Now,' she whispered, 'I am ready to ask each of you who is in your thoughts. Who do you want to reach?' She turned to the man by the door. 'Edward?'

'Alfred George Hollis. My father.'

'Martin?'

'My mate, Gary Cope.'

He heard his neighbour draw in her breath.

'Are you sure it's not your mother who's waiting for you?' asked the medium.

'Quite sure.' He laid the photograph in front of him and immediately heard a chair scrape against the wooden floorboards. Saw through his twin eyelets how Frankie Holt now stared at him and then the picture with intense interest.

'Frankie?' Piper jogged her firmly.

'I'd like to know who nicked my stuff from Teme House.'

Now Martin held his breath. So why that sudden reaction to his statement about Gary? Was his hunch right?

Despite the warm room he felt cold, and in that gloomy light the whites of the dead man's eyes and both rows of vivid teeth seemed to detach themselves from the photograph and float up towards him. Other questions for his neighbour swelled and died in his throat as rain slapped against the front wall of that terraced house, but then grew louder, sharper, more insistent. His head seemed about to explode. The smell inside his mask changed to a sour sappy tang, reminding him of his mother pruning the old sycamore trees in the garden.

Louisa Harriet Webb, are you there?

'I sense a coming,' murmured the medium's disembodied voice. 'Yes, I see a woman in a shroud with her feet bound together by a cord. She's crying to be freed, crying for the future.'

'What about my father?' complained Hollis.

'And my *real* mum and dad?' Frankie added with sudden feeling. Martin didn't dare break the silence which followed but was puzzled by her surprise outburst.

'Hush. Listen...' The medium's voice changed to a higher key, disembodied and charged with an even stronger local accent. 'I am Rose Scott of Stocking Farm, Malvern.'

Scott? Martin pricked up his ears; strained to listen as the woman told her story of hardship and struggle; how her end had been the cruellest ever devised. Paddy Brownlow, who'd eventually found work in a local undertaker's, had done his worst by burying her alive. But the worst wasn't yet over...

'A warning, then,' the woman continued, 'that

316

where there is one death, another will swiftly follow. This is my torment, my greatest torment.' Her breathing became deeper, more throaty. The atmosphere was electric. Martin felt sweat erupt all over his body. He wanted to leave. He wanted to stay. If this was a con, it was pretty convincing. 'Merle is with me,' the medium added. 'She forgives her younger sister but cannot protect her from her own kin's hand.'

'Own kin's hand? What the hell d'you mean?' Frankie challenged.

'Now that Sean Brownlow's scheming soul has crossed the river between life and Hell, there will be another to take his place. And the one who will prevent it is here among you.'

Soul? Martin glanced around the room. Had no one picked up on the fact he might be dead?

'Beware the cunning Irish and any woman who wants what she cannot have...' the voice went on. 'That is all I have to say for now.'

But there was no time to dwell on the possible significance of these strange warnings because that urgent rain outside eased and in its place came water – yes, no doubt about it – filling the room with a haunting echo. He glimpsed a monochrome panorama of a loch with its shore of pebbles and detritus, the only colour being a trail of blood leading to the water. His hands covered the photo of the laughing face.

A Mancunian voice this time.

'Tell Maddy I still love her. Tell her to stay away from one called Mary Campbell. I never topped myself. Can't you see? Can't you see? Please don't give up on me. Please...'

317

Martin was jolted from this apparently spectral pleading by a noise to his right. Frankie again. This time standing up and pulling the plague mask over her head, leaving her hair more in disorder than definite spikes; her face thin and gaunt.

The carer barged her way past a startled Edward Hollis to the door.

'Sit down!' ordered Carol Piper. 'Or you'll destroy everything.'

'So what? It's destroying my *head*, that's what,' she retorted, blocked off by the art teacher refusing to budge. 'I've not found out anything of use to me here. Who's got my things, who my real mum and dad are and all that. And before you ask me, no, I don't know their fucking names, so there.'

Martin's empty stomach began churning, half of him magnetized by what he'd heard via the medium, the other half aware that he couldn't afford to let Frankie Holt out of his sight. He stuffed Gary Cope's photo back in his wallet.

'Let me go!' she yelled. 'Or I'll call the pigs. This is illegal. I need to be back looking after Miss Scott, not stuck here.'

Before Carol Piper could stop her, Frankie had slipped through the door and was bolting down the stairs. Martin excused himself and followed, jettisoning his mask on the way.

'I'll try and reason with her,' he shouted back. 'Calm her down.'

That seemed to do the trick and now with the powerful spell broken behind him, he gave chase along the path. When his target glanced round as

318

if to check she wasn't being tailed, he dived back into the porch. What had she meant by wanting to find her real parents? Had she been fostered, adopted or what? But any pity he might normally have felt for her wouldn't come. Those long fit legs were quickening the pace. The pat-pat-pat of her trainers on the wet pavements filled his ears to the repeating rhythm of those extraordinary words. *'The one who can stop her is here among you...'*

Yesterday's mist had reappeared by stealth, so that each time Frankie Holt turned and cast around with those hunted eyes, he managed to stay invisible. They were on the main road now, between enormous Edwardian houses whose lit windows suggested comfortable, carefree lives beyond. The opposite of his. He thought of Dora and wondered what she was doing now. How that one crazy moment in Quarry Terrace had driven her away, and not only that but the Teme House collection was still in her boot.

Damn.

To his horror the girl, darkened by trees, turned his way. He decided it was now or never. There was nothing to lose. Or was there?

'Mary Campbell, eh?' he crossed the road and called out after her. 'Or is it Denise Shaw? I'm really confused, Frankie.'

He tensed, every last part of him wired up as she turned and began to walk towards him with a puzzled smile on her face. He stood his ground as she stopped a few paces away ostensibly to adjust the pink rucksack on her back.

'I don't get it,' she challenged. 'You *know* who

I am.'

Do I? Do I really?

He had to think on his feet. Keep her talking. The street light overhead cast her face the colour of the moon. Her tongue oddly pink in her mouth. In a sick, wilful moment, he imagined it in his mouth. He scrutinized her every movement, both her hands stroking her yellow hair, then slipping into her jeans pockets. Only the eyes stayed the same.

'What have those names got to do with me?'

He had to be cleverer than this. What the hell had he expected? An admission that she'd chosen them to suit her purpose, followed by the confessions of a serial killer? Softly, softly, he told himself.

'Look, I thought about changing mine from Webb to Webster when I moved here from London. It's no big deal. I wanted a fresh start. See how I'd get on. Maybe like you ... I didn't realize about your parents,' he said, aware of the faintest drizzle on his forehead.

'Why should you? Anyway, it's not very interesting.'

'I don't agree. Besides, you sounded pretty wound up back there. I can't imagine what not knowing must be like.'

At that her whole demeanour seemed to soften. As if he'd touched the most vulnerable part of her.

'It's shit, if you want the truth. But I've had long enough to get used to things.' She focused her awesome eyes on his, still keeping her distance. 'You got a mum and dad, then?'

320

'Yeah. Did have. Mum's dead and Dad...' He hesitated, trusting his instinct yet again. 'He's banged up.'

She laughed an explosion of amusement and victory. Her open mouth like one of those sex dolls at the Doe and Deer.

'You're kidding. What for?'

'Drunk in charge of a passenger jet, that's what. One false move in twenty-six years. He's lost everything because of a damages claim. No house, no nothing to come home for...'

'Except you.' She smiled and his planned attack began to evaporate even further.

'One way of looking at it, I suppose. But it meant my one big dream of joining the Met was a non-starter.'

As soon as the words had left his mouth, he realized what a dickhead he must seem. However, she showed no reaction at all.

'And your mum. What was up with her? If it's not too painful.'

Martin switched his gaze to the trees above. Ash and oak, overblown and acidic in the muffled artificial light, discharging larger drops of water on to him now, forcing him to close the gap between himself and her, enough for him to see the furrow on her forehead deepening.

'No, it's OK. She killed herself.' He drew his right hand across the other's wrist.

'Oh, poor Martin.' She came closer, touched his arm, her eyes now glistening with tears. 'And then there's that mate of yours you mentioned back there. Gary, wasn't it? Hey, seems like you've had more than a basinful.'

321

'True, but...' He had to quiz her about her reaction to his photo. But his resolve was melting.

'Look, me needing to find my mum and dad is zilch to what you and some of those old folk I've cared for have had to put up with,' she went on. 'Sometimes I wonder how people manage to keep going. I mean, take Miss Evelyn Scott here...' She checked her watch and glanced up the road. 'I'd better shift myself or she'll be wondering where I am.'

She leant forwards and planted a warm moist kiss on his cheek. For a split second he was tempted to pull her close, to feel that firm lithe body next to his. To experience again that aching shot of desire which, despite everything, hadn't completely left him.

But she was already on her way. Supple yet strong, like coiled wire he thought. Yes, that was it. Coiled wire...

He stared after her as she ran, that brief kiss still burning his cheek, feeling as if suddenly stripped of all his instincts which had spurred him on so far. She'd expressed so much concern. Hadn't her eyes seemed to melt in pity when he'd mentioned his dad's predicament? And yet, as the misty distance increased between them, why was he the focus of his own interrogation, not her? He realized then with a jolt he'd not asked about her missing sister.

Shit.

He followed her once again from one bleary street lamp to the next, all the while wondering about the haunting hour spent in Quarry Terrace.

Had it all been a set-up? Anything was possible, even Dora slipping out of his life for good.

Having extracted his phone and found her number stored in its memory, he waited for a reply, ready to apologize and denounce Frankie Holt as a hard little tramp. But when an automated voice invited him to leave a message, all he could say was his name.

Too late now to ask when he could collect that important stuff from her car because that rucksack's faint blob of colour had vanished from view. For a moment he was torn between running all the way back to Dora's flat or keeping on the carer's trail, but someone from that so-called séance had lodged in his mind. Rose Scott for a start and her purported warning 'that where there is one death, another will swiftly follow'.

And didn't Frankie Holt now care for Evelyn?

'Beware ... a woman who wants what she cannot have.'

To an outsider, that could also have sounded like a load of old cobblers, but not there, in that room buzzing with atmosphere. So, what did that mean exactly?

Keep going.

He shivered, then quickened. Suddenly, at the end of a long six-foot-high wall, topped by a wooden fence, a plaque depicted two crossed rifles bearing the name 'THE GABLES'. Most house plaques he'd seen had flowers or bird themes, not these instruments of death, and the more he stared at them the more he knew he needed a weapon. He felt danger prick at his skin, change his heartbeat to one he could hear, as he took in the sloping tarmac drive which led to an even bigger mansion than Teme House, its four brick storeys like a rusty smudge against sombre green vegetation, yet dominating the hill beyond.

The earlier glow from a semi-curtained lower window vanished when a light came on in the hall. As he walked towards the porch, he picked up an impatient knocking sound, the hum of two voices from within before the front door slammed shut, and then with a jolt he spotted that same white Fiesta's boot with the Manchester plate jutting out from the far corner of the house. He crouched down between its nearside and the field's rocky bank to check the mileage. 83,000. Enough for a Scottish trip five times a year, he thought, but it was the empty child's car seat that made him start. He'd not noticed that last night. Nor the fag-burnt upholstery. Who was that child's seat for? The traffic noise in the road below suddenly grew quiet as he remembered that Scottish hotelier's remarks.

For a moment he stood in the porch, unsure what to do next. If he rang the bell then Frankie might come to the door. If he left some kind of note for Miss Scott she might get that too. No, he'd make a phone call the moment he got back to the site and warn her she could be in mortal danger.

Twenty-Seven

Friday 5th July 9.30 p.m. Too much is hurting now. Even my poor mind after what I have just seen and heard at the hospital, and knowing what I must endure for tonight at least. My biphosphonate tablets have run out and my ribcage presses so hard against my lungs that when she arrived back, banging on the door as if she owned the place, I could scarcely move to admit her. Not that I want her here, you understand, but the police insisted that I should not be left alone. It seems every agency I have tried is on holiday or has no spare staff. I cannot write about my terror nor what this evening revealed without my pen faltering. Seeing my own flesh and blood so ravaged in death. Hearing too that Brownlow died less than an hour ago in intensive care without ever regaining consciousness. But I cannot weep for him and feel that at last a brutish chapter of my life has closed. His greed left my defences down and now the seas of my past will swell up to snatch me from what feeble moorings I have.

I must stop now. She is taking a shower and soon no doubt will be in to check on me. To stare at my face, no doubt comparing her features to mine, calculating how much she is owed ... The phone is ringing. I must go...

'Is that Miss Evelyn Scott?'

'It is. Who, may I ask, is calling?'

'Martin Webb. I work on the Hill Springs site.'

'I'm sorry, but I'm not prepared to speak to anyone from that hideous place. Who do you think you are to call me, when everyone knows how much I oppose it?'

'Is Miss Holt with you now?'

Evelyn frowned and glanced upwards.

'Yes, why?'

'Please be careful, that's all. We found your sister's body today. You may be next.'

Evelyn felt her knee bones begin to give way beneath their bandages.

'I beg your pardon? What are you talking about?'

'Please. Here's my number if you need to call any time.'

'Have you told the police what you've told me?'

'I'm just about to.'

After the unsettling call ended, Evelyn locked her diary and tucked it inside the bodice of her nightdress. She knew the girl had seen it there, but where else was safe and accessible for her to write when she had to? She listened hard to the house around her, suppressing that huge longing carried for so many years in the recesses of her heart. That one final piece of the complex jigsaw which had been her life now in place. For courage, she focused on the portrait of Rose Scott and her family. Upstairs the stranger's footsteps were leaving the bathroom. Instinctively, she reached down into her dressing-gown pocket and felt the one small key which only she possessed. She gripped it tight, holding her breath as her eager Homely Helper made her way downstairs.

Twenty-Eight

The next morning Frankie wished now she'd not left that séance in such a hurry, on impulse just like she'd touched that Webb guy's fly. If she was honest with herself, everything she did was on impulse. That was the trouble. She'd have to learn to think things through. Or else...

Her client was still fast asleep in the gloomy lounge as she removed the two suitcases from her boot and took them to her room. The old crust was probably getting her strength up for that promised 'chat' she thought afterwards, sniffing inside the fridge where yesterday's uneaten mussels were beginning to stink. She binned them and made a combined shopping and 'to-do' list for the coming weekend, beginning with phoning the Ferndene Clinic.

She glanced out of the kitchen window which overlooked the over-run vegetable garden beyond. If the mean old cow hadn't decided to leave all her money to a stupid theatre and her business, she'd have been happy to go and sort out the dump. But not now. Oh, no. Everything had changed. With Merle's assets taking a likely month to be added to her sister's wealth, and if she really was her mother, then things could be in place sooner than expected.

With a plan already formed in her mind, she pushed the fridge door shut. From that moment on she'd resolved to do the bare minimum to keep Homely Helpers off her back. She also wondered how long it would be till she was bollocked again for snooping in the old girl's bedroom.

As she jotted down what *she* would like to eat, she rewound last night's events in her mind. News of the will had almost derailed things, but what about that Martin Webb? He seemed to be on her case big time. Yet who *was* he? A poshy, working on a building site, seeing how the other half live. She could tell types like them a mile off. So why had she felt the need to soften – or rather, stiffen – him up? How come he'd known Gary Cope? Maybe it was a wind-up. Anyone could have read the papers and got hold of that photo. She'd seen it too. Thought it flattered him. But she'd been a cretin to draw attention to herself like that. She should have shown no emotion at all.

And then she remembered what he'd said about his one big dream. Darker, more obstinate questions surfaced. As the pigs hadn't mention-ed anything about her souvenirs, could *he* have taken them from Teme House? After all, Tits-and-Ass was conveniently waiting in her car outside. And the dumb New-Ager had said someone in the room was the only one able to save Evelyn Scott? Hardly that comatose art teacher, Hollis.

Shit, she was getting paranoid. Heard her client stirring in the lounge, the thud as her alarm clock hit the floor. Time for a cup of tea. Just a quick in-and-out job and then off to town.

'Nice cuppa for you,' she said, placing the silver tray on the bedside table and parting the moth-eaten curtains. There was nothing cool about the weather outside nor her client, who stubbornly refused to look her in the eye. 'I'm just popping into town for some bits. Sooner I go, sooner I can be back. OK? And can I borrow one of your raincoats? It's pissing down out there and,' she lied, 'mine's still at Teme House.'

Evelyn Scott struggled to sit up to reach her teacup and, having waved her away, began to speak. 'I need a repeat prescription for my biphosphonates – there's an earlier one in the top right-hand desk drawer. And while you're there, get me a length of surgical bandage. Three metres minimum.'

'Do I pay for these up front like the other times?' She eyed a chequebook lying temptingly within reach.

'Bring me the receipts and I'll settle up once you're back. That was Mr Brownlow's arrangement, wasn't it? When you get back we'll sort it out and have our little chat.'

She'd not lost her memory, then.

'Oh, and another thing...'

Frankie moved towards the raincoats in the hall and chose a beige Burberry one.

'About your vehicle. When you return, be so

good as to leave it right round the back well out of sight, will you? This is the Gables, you know. Not some junk yard.'

Frankie bit her tongue as she plucked an umbrella from the stand. She repositioned her rucksack on her back and without further ado stepped out into the wet morning. Her pathetic car stood on the drive, which, like the old crock herself, wouldn't be shifted. Not until she'd sorted a few things.

She opened the driver's door and got in. She was about to pull her seat belt over when she realized with a sickening jolt her fuel gauge was almost on empty.

Fuck. In this weather too.

Having duly moved the embarrassment round the back, she slammed the door in frustration and ran down the drive, relieved to see the red front of an approaching bus. She flagged it down, paid her fare and gratefully sank into the nearest seat. Her posh mac was soaking, the umbrella too. Rainy days in Openshaw were nothing like this.

'You from the Gables, then?' the fat driver called back to her. Thankfully there were only two other passengers, a man who she guessed was in his sixties, engrossed in his newspaper, and a schoolgirl wearing a shiny purple cagoule.

'I work for Miss Scott,' she panted.

'So you know, then?' He swerved around a parked van, causing the old man to complain.

'Know what?'

'Her factotum's just kicked the bucket. Last night it was. Eight o'clock, so they say.'

'You mean Sean Brownlow?'

''Sright.'

'Could be suicide,' said Frankie.

'Get away. Him? No, murder's the name of the game here. You wait.'

She pressed her nose to the dirty window, imagining that same glass all around her like some weird prison for the rest of her life.

The gorilla seemed to be enjoying himself while her mind raced on, still trying not to lose sight of the rainbow's end. OK, everything had its downside. Especially now. With the production manager off the scene, she, despite her best efforts to incriminate him, would be suspect number one. However, if she played her cards right while waiting for Evelyn to annul Merle's will, she could be seriously quids in. She rubbed away the condensation on the glass to reveal the roof of the barn. She thought again how its weirdly real inhabitants had started to rotate like that. To be alone in there for just five minutes would send her barking.

'Trouble for Monroe's as well, I'm telling you,' opined the driver, breaking into her thoughts. 'I'm proud I went to that protest. Proud Miss Scott was by his side. So there.'

The old man lowered his newspaper and Frankie realized he wasn't your usual old git but had probably been a headmaster or similar professional.

'I'd say enough *local* people wanted to see him maimed or worse,' he said meaningfully. 'I used to work for Scott's until the stress of it all got to me.'

331

The driver glanced round, clearly interested. The bus was halfway down West Malvern Road and Frankie hoped her stop wouldn't come too soon.

'Miss Scott saw to it personally that my pension were such that I now have no money worries, but she had to fight him all the way. He'd forget he was merely production manager, lording it over everyone, even the rest of the Board, whenever he had the chance. Even our pagan events, which he muscled in on...'

'Can't imagine you doing stuff like that, if you don't mind me saying so, sir.'

'All part of my research for a book I'm writing on ancient Worcestershire. I've always been a history buff. Started it years ago when Mr Terminator started making my life hell.'

'That what you called him, eh?' chortled the driver, pulling in to a crowded bus stop.

'Everyone did. Says it all, really.'

'So you're saying it could be a pissed-off worker there?'

'I believe the forensic team are testing the ballistics. Then they'll have a better idea who's responsible. At the moment, it's pointing to someone who was an excellent shot. Maybe even trained in firearms.'

'An army type, perhaps?' suggested the driver. The bus began to smell of wet coats and BO. Frankie wished she still wore her plague mask. Protection against a world of people closing in on her.

'Who knows?' He turned her way before rolling up his newspaper and leaving his seat.

'Do please give Miss Scott my sincere condolences when you next see her. I'm Gerald Purser, by the way. Was a good friend of Samuel, her late husband, and my goodness, in those unenlightened times he needed every friend he could get.'

As he struggled to reach the exit, Frankie wondered what he meant, and once he was on the pavement outside the charity shop, pulling up his raincoat collar, he glanced up at her, a deep frown adding to his already lined forehead. She too barged her way off the bus.

'I'm sorry to bother you,' she began, smiling her best smile, 'but you mentioned Mr Brownlow also worked at Scott's.'

'Yes, he did.'

'And you said there were tensions?' she prodded.

'Too right there were. Especially with a guy there called Maddox. Keith Maddox...'

'Any relation to the fishmonger?'

'Yes. His son. Nice chap. He designed a prototype pointed bullet which would have been even more penetrative than a waisted one ... Now this, combined with other work he'd done, would have taken the company into the stratosphere. However, Sean wasn't having any of that. Oh no.'

'And?'

'Edged Maddox out pretty damned quickly to take all the glory. Of course, Miss Scott should have intervened there and then, but like I said, he seemed to exert this influence over her from day one back in '79. Even her late husband couldn't understand it, but he had his own business interests to deal with. Besides –' he lowered his voice to stop his words reaching the wrong ears – 'he'd come out. Gay, you understand. So you see, with one thing and another, Miss Scott had enough to deal with.'

'What happened to Keith Maddox?'

'The poor bugger left the company claiming he'd been victimized. By God, I know how he felt.'

Frankie remembered the fish man mentioning his son as clever. Maybe Keith Maddox still bore Brownlow a big grudge. And who could blame him?

'I shouldn't speak ill of the dead, but Brownlow had bad blood in his veins.'

'Bad blood?' Frankie shook water off her mac collar. Why just then did she feel her own turn cold?

'His great-great-grandfather Paddy Brownlow had buried Rose Scott alive back in 1872. He was forty-seven at the time, and she was a fifty-eight-year-old widow. It was a heinous act which was left unpunished because of cover-ups.' He turned to look at her. 'Perhaps if Miss Scott had known, early on, she'd never have taken *any* Brownlow on to her books or into her bed.'

'You mean, they had an affair?'

But the former accountant seemed suddenly distracted by one of the shop assistants leaning into the window bay and altering the display. Frankie realized time was slipping away.

'Look, Mr Purser, I know you might think this is cheeky of me, but Merle Scott let on that her

334

sister once had a baby. Born on 20th February 1980...'

The old man edged away along the charity shop's window. It was hard to gauge his reaction to this news.

'I'm afraid I can't help you,' he said finally. 'However, all I know is my boss and her husband took a break around that time. Busman's holiday, she'd said to us, but it was odd because she'd never once had a holiday. Never.'

'What does busman's holiday mean?'

'Business with pleasure.'

'I've learnt loads of new stuff today.' She touched his damp arm. 'Thanks for sparing the time. I must dash now. Don't like leaving Miss Scott for too long.'

'Of course not. You strike me as a very sensible young lady. But,' he looked at her oddly, 'she should be able to take care of herself, you know.'

'Why's that, then?'

'She's got this gun room. Didn't you know? It's where all the prototype stalking rifles are stored. Must be into treble figures by now and worth a bloody fortune.'

Frankie watched him nudge his way past the line of shops until he'd disappeared into one. It was bad enough the Gables had CCTV, but, if he was to be believed, an armoury as well? That thought had spooked her badly at first, just like her imagining Evelyn Scott and Brownlow at it like rabbits, but she realized that particular facility might be to her advantage. Once she'd had the answers she was looking for.

She hurried on to Boots where, having bought the required bandage, a pack of notelets and more night-time-sized Tampax for herself, queued up with what seemed like half of Malvern's population. After ten long minutes she waved Evelyn Scott's repeat prescription at the guy in a white coat who was now free. He looked her up and down as if she was something nasty stuck under his shoe, and finally, after a load of daft questions, handed over the pills.

'They're not the crown bloody jewels,' she muttered, snatching them from him.

'But Miss Scott's the closest we have to royalty here.' He handed her the change and moved away to another wet customer.

'Blotted her copybook at that Hill Springs protest, mind,' came a familiar voice from behind her. The publican from the Doe and Deer, his face redder than she remembered it. 'Full of surprises, is our Miss Scott.'

'What do you mean?'

'Nothing you need to fret about.'

'She's a great lady, OK? Just like her late sister.'

'You must be the only one who thinks so.'

Waitrose next, costing thirteen quid cash. At the checkout she rammed the shopping into both carrier bags, smarting at the injustice of it all. She'd had precious little since starting at Teme House.

Now, two bags the heavier, she stood outside and wondered what to do next.

'Prioritize, Frankie,' Mrs Beavis had always advised during her one-to-one tutorials on

336

Thursday afternoons. 'First things first.' She could hear her voice so clearly, even now. The one woman who'd seen her potential and given her a chance. And yet she knew she'd let her down three times. Shannon, Gary and Merle, and here she was, keeping on, ignoring the weather, following signs to Hill Springs Development.

She could have caught a bus, but what was half a mile? Besides, the fewer witnesses the better. Martin Webb would be taught a lesson he wouldn't forget. If her and Ellie's pot of gold wasn't to be just some mirage, he had to be warned off. It was a pity she'd chucked the Briarfield knife away, she thought. It could have been perfect. However, Evelyn's one would do. She had liked the feel of it in her hand when she'd cut bread for toast earlier. How its blade had run so smoothly through the loaf.

At the site gates a dozy-looking guard stood by a red barrier and took her details. He seemed impressed with her double-barrelled name, the fact that she worked for a leading City bank and had brought her friend some shopping. He soon directed her to the canteen where right now Mr Webb should be on his first tea break. Either that or in Portakabin B.

The dormitory was empty. It stank of sweat, pee and worse. How could he even step inside this scabby dump, she wondered, searching for anything recognizable of his. Plenty of baseball caps. Plenty of trackies, reminding her of John Arthur, but on the bed nearest the far wall lay a cycle cape. Identical to the one she'd seen lying next to him in the library.

In three strides she was looking under his pillow, under the bed, in every pocket of every garment she could find until she reached the Holy Grail. A pair of jeans half hidden under the thin duvet. Stuff in the right-hand pocket. Serious stuff, she could tell.

Shit.

She pulled out two slightly crumpled sheets of paper, one white, one blue, which sent blood rushing to her head. Her CV and a letter to Daphne Cope from her fucking grandson. She stared at the cramped writing, mesmerized, reading only a few words as her mouth became dry. Shannon had been his girlfriend. Jesus Christ. How the fuck did *this* get here? And the realization that the liar had also nicked her CV made her other hand feel for her knife.

Suddenly there came the sound of approaching footsteps, a squeak from the only door. She swiftly stuffed the sheets inside the front of her mac and whipped round to see a short dark guy with a beard and glasses.

'May I enquire as to your name? And also ask what you are doing here?'

'I'm Dora Tebbitt. Martin's girlfriend. I was just dropping off some shopping for him.' She pulled a pack of cheese-topped baps from the bag, and left them on the bed. 'Where's he now, d'you know?'

'Having tea in C1. Shall I let him know you're here?'

His mobile was already out of his pocket. Panic crept into her voice.

'Don't worry, thanks.' She smiled again, this time more stiffly. 'He likes surprises.'

With that, she said goodbye and retraced her steps. Having made sure no one was on her tail, she found herself back at the gates. As she ducked under the barrier she froze, forgetting to breathe, as a guy wearing a black woollen hat moved away from the cop shop. As he turned towards her she was certain it was Piotr. But why was he coming out of there? What had he been up to? She'd assumed he'd gone back to Poland.

Frankie quickened her pace along the street above Quarry Terrace, where canopied trees seemed to bend so low under their weight of water they almost touched the top of her umbrella. Still an orphan. Still trying to find her moorings, she told herself.

'D'you know where the Old Post Office is?' she asked the first person she met on an otherwise deserted stretch of green.

'Straight on, then left at the end of the Common,' replied the woman pushing a buggy covered over by a plastic hood. Normally, Frankie would have peered in and babbled some baby talk to it, but not now. There were important things to do. 'You can't miss it. The sign's still up outside.'

The small parade of shops which straggled away from the main road was as far removed from anything in Openshaw. The Old Post Office was close, crammed in between a funeral parlour and a florist's whose potted geraniums, ranged along its front, seemed defeated. But not her. The possible lever she needed lay just feet away.

She rang the bell and stared up at the three-storey house where the rain had left its mark on the new cream rendering. After the second ring and a growing frustration that no one was in, the front door was opened by a boy in his late teens with a sandwich jammed between his lips. He looked her up and down, just like the guy in Boots, then once she'd asked if a Dawn Maddox lived there, called upstairs for his mum.

'Yes?' A stout woman in her mid-fifties dressed in a navy jumper and skirt reached the door and evaluated her visitor through thick-rimmed glasses. Frankie noticed she wore no wedding ring. A single mother like herself, perhaps? A promising start, then. 'Well, what is it?'

'I can't really talk on the doorstep. It's confidential.'

'You're not the police, are you? A plainclothes officer?'

'Course not. I'm a carer with Homely Helpers.'

The Maddoxes *are* jumpy, she thought, as the woman elaborated on her fears.

'You see, my Gavin's been in a bit of bother with his friends recently.' Her accent not as local as her dad's, suggesting she'd probably lived away. 'So, who are you?'

'Frances Holt, new to the area, and, having just met your dad, there's something I urgently need to find out before ... Well, before too long, at any rate.' She laid down her shopping bags and umbrella on the strip of plastic carpet protector which led from the front door along the hall.

'Best come through,' she said. 'I haven't got long, mind. Gavin's got a badminton practice at half eleven and as there's no dad I'm the chauffeur.'

'Thanks for seeing me, anyway.' She noticed the former post office counter had been professionally converted to a bar, and on seeing the row of bottles on show was tempted to ask for a Breezer. Her proven formula for courage.

'All Gavin's idea, this.' The woman gestured for Frankie to take a bar stool while she defied her tight skirt by taking another. 'At least it stops him and his friends being a nuisance round the town. Now then. How can I help you?'

Frankie was aware of the lad lurking by the door but once she'd eyeballed him he disappeared.

'Your dad mentioned that you used to be the registrar here, back in the early 1980s.'

The woman smiled and pushed her glasses further up her nose.

'He's far too chatty for his own good, you know. I keep telling him he's like a talking newspaper.'

However, he'd clearly not mentioned *her*, which was something. The less this woman knew the better.

'Well, I'm glad he chatted to me because ever since I was eighteen, I've been desperately trying to find out who my *real* mum and dad are. Or were. I can't move on till I know for sure. And yes, I have searched in the library and on the Internet, but – ' she shrugged – 'apart from one small clue, nothing doing.'

Dawn Maddox studied her driving licence.

'Your name does seem familiar, now why can't I place it?' She gave a short laugh. 'Do you know, ever since I gave up my job, I've been hopeless at remembering things.'

'It is important,' Frankie reminded her.

'I understand your need, Frances, but why are you here, in Malvern? Why me?'

Frankie leaned forwards, lowering her voice.

'That one clue I found led me to believe it's possible that Evelyn Scott of the Gables, West Malvern Road is my mum. And stuff that your dad said yesterday made me think I was getting warmer. I just thought you could put some flesh on the bone, so to speak.'

The woman seemed to blink at that expression, while outside, the downpour pummelled the room's sash window, increasing Frankie's resolve not to leave empty-handed.

'Have you heard about her sister?' asked the former registrar.

'Merle? Yes. Shocking news.'

'It's dreadful. Especially in Malvern of all places. And her, she had the kindest heart. I even bought a King Charles spaniel puppy off her just after I'd started my new job here. To help her cope with the disappointment it was...'

'Disappointment?'

'She accompanied her sister to my office the day before the statutory deadline of forty-two days to register a birth. Then of course, I had to send the completed form off to Surrey.'

Frankie felt the flutter of anticipation spread through her whole body.

'Surrey?'

The woman nodded.

'That's where the birth occurred.'

'Do you mean the Ferndene Clinic?'

Dawn Maddox twisted on her stool in surprise.

'My, you have done your homework, Frances. Yes, that's the place. I don't know why the baby girl wasn't registered down there, but I seem to remember Miss Scott discharged herself the next day. A risky thing to do straight after a Caesarean. Anyway, as I was about to say, Merle begged Evelyn in front of me to let her keep the child.'

Not surprising her mother was too posh to push. Frankie tried to stay focused. Imagining herself like Ellie as a newborn...

'Where was the baby while they were with you?'

The other woman paused, a fleeting look of distress in her eyes.

'Merle was carrying an Oxfam bag. The baby was asleep at the bottom, all wrapped up as it was a cold day, but also I suspected so no one would see her. In the end, although Evelyn Scott was adamant about giving her away for adoption, she did let Merle name her.'

Frankie took a risk. Her mouth feeling numb. 'Jenny?'

'Correct. But that wasn't the end of it. Oh no. There was still the matter of a surname.'

Frankie's pulse quickened. The period pain deepened. That image of the Oxfam bag all too clear, all too symbolic of her life so far.

'She, I mean Evelyn, refused to let either her

married surname or her own be used. Again Merle protested, and I remember this as if it was yesterday, because I always strived to create a calm atmosphere in my office.'

Frankie waited, her bellyache almost unbearable.

'The baby woke up and began to cry so hard I thought her little lungs would burst. I urged them to decide as soon as possible. Merle suggested Brownlow, but her sister looked as if she was about to kill her.'

Frankie gulped, aware of the woman's eyes on her.

'You mean Sean?'

Bad blood Brownlow and there is another to take his place...

She tried to shake those horrible words from her mind as the woman answered.

'Yes. How come you know his name?'

'Your dad again. And someone else I met today.'

'Have you heard the news about him as well?'

Frankie nodded. Biting back tears.

'I'm so sorry.' But somehow, she didn't look it, even though she leant over and patted her arm, talking some more. Almost too quickly, Frankie thought.

'No wonder it's all stayed in my mind. All the fuss. The disagreements. The phone calls which I now know were made by Merle. *She* wanted to be registered as the mother, you see. But it's against the law.'

So the nuisance calls hadn't been Samuel Colby, then. Frankie felt hot tears begin to cloud her vision.

'In the end I had to give up my job. It was too much, waiting for that next call or encounter with her. I'd wanted to live in London anyway. To get away from small-town troublemakers. I think in the end, it changed her completely. Some say it turned her mind.'

Frankie concurred, simply for something to say. When really, she wanted to be proud that at last she had a mum and dad and she'd given them a granddaughter. 'But why did you come back?'

'Missed my family, people I'd gone to school with, I suppose. Ties are so important. In your case, Frances –' the woman shrugged, then looked at her with a steady gaze – 'you may have lost your father, and that's tragic, but you have gained a mother, and she's probably devastated by Mr Brownlow's death. You see,' she went on in a solemn tone, 'your date of birth and that given on the birth certificate tally exactly. Your name is Jenny Merle Scott.'

Frankie was too consumed by Dawn Maddox's revelations to note the crowded pavements, the heavy traffic around the former post office. Her dream was dying.

'Mum and Dad,' she repeated to herself even though the photocopied certificate only bore Evelyn Scott's name and that Dad word had a bittersweet taste. Compared to him, Evelyn Scott, for all her secrets, her ice-box manner, came up smelling of roses. All the more reason to try and make her accept her. Her agenda had changed. Love, not revenge and money, was now top of her list.

Did Sean Brownlow ever realize her mum had given birth and that he was the father? Unlikely. However, Merle *must* have known as she'd suggested his surname for her, but had she ever told him? Why else did she happily make her will out to him? Because then, once he knew about his Jenny, she would have been next in line.

These questions gnawed at her the way Beryl used to eat corn on the cob until every last little speck of yellow had gone and her chin glistened under a layer of melted margarine. And being the next of kin, shouldn't she go and see him at the hospital to kiss his shattered forehead and place a flower on his chest before he was stuck in a fridge and then cut up in a post-mortem? No way.

So vivid was her image of him with a gaping socket and a handless right arm that she failed to notice a silver Mondeo glide along and halt just in front of her. As she passed its nearside on her way to the bus stop, a female voice suddenly made her pull up short.

'Frankie, have you got a moment?' Avril Pilkington's unmade-up face pressed against her barely open window.

Fuck...

That knife was in her pocket. She prayed it wouldn't show through the wet fabric.

'Sure. Sorry I look such a heap.'

'Hop in, why not? We can get you back to the Gables. Save you getting any wetter.'

Frankie stalled. Saw DI Manson in the driver's seat staring straight ahead. Something was up. Panic swamped her mind like the water which seemed to have turned the rest of her to pulp. She wanted to run, but her legs disobeyed.

The rear passenger door unclicked in readiness. She now had no choice.

Manson turned to his colleague. 'If July the first be rainy weather, it will rain four more weeks together.'

'Someone got it right, then,' said the Sow, glancing back as Frankie placed the shopping bags and brolly by her feet. Alongside her lay a black briefcase together with an Ordnance Survey map of the county and a roll of blue-and-white police tape. The kind she'd seen on North Hill and on the gates at Teme House. She was busy with mental arithmetic. Her mum must have had that fling with the young Sean Brownlow when she was forty-four. It was unreal. Unimaginable. The Mondeo was already climbing up the drive which still spewed surplus water into the road below, giving her no chance to wonder further, and once DI Manson had pulled up the handbrake, he finally addressed her.

'We'd like to take a quick look at your car, Miss Holt, if you don't mind. Shouldn't take long in this weather.'

'My car? Why? You saw it only last night.'

The pig retrieved the briefcase and waited, presumably for the keys, as he drummed his fingers on the steering wheel. He then opened his door for the rain to drive in.

'I'd like to see your search warrant, if that's

OK,' said Frankie.

'Voilà.'

Too quick by half. Just like yesterday. Checkmate. She watched with rising panic as he opened her boot, began probing like a heron in a pond, then dropped tufts of the grey-fibre lining into three plastic bags. He snapped them shut and labelled each with a black marker pen.

She wanted to snatch the bloody things from his hands. But perhaps if she stayed cool this would all blow over.

Fat chance.

Afterwards, having locked the car, the Sow approached her while Manson fetched the roll of tape from the Mondeo. Their waxed coats shone with water.

'We'll need these keys for the next day or so,' she said. 'Then it's all yours again.'

'But I'll need it for Miss Scott's shopping. And she's got a clinic appointment.'

The man paused while winding the tape around the car. They exchanged a glance and the Sow's smirk returned like one of Merle's persistent turds in the pan.

'I'm afraid it mustn't be touched. At least not until the experts have taken a look.'

'Experts? Why?' She noticed her Mum watching from the lounge window. 'What are you implying?'

The Sow spoke first, shaking her sleeves free of rain.

'Nothing. We're examining other vehicles as well because some fibres have just been discovered in your late client's hair. And, as I'm sure you understand, we have to explore all possibilities.'

She was loving it, Frankie could tell. Sinking her sharp little fangs deeper into her flesh. She'd once seen a pig's head on display at the butchers in Ashton Road. It had mean teeth just like her. And why no mention of fingerprints? Surely they were priority if you were a suspect?

Perhaps, after all, she was paranoid.

'By the way, I've arranged for a Mrs Susan Chance to come over and join you and Miss Scott at two p.m. Extra security, you understand, just until certain matters are cleared up.'

'What matters? Why d'you keep talking in riddles?' She nearly added how, despite his supposed bad blood, her real dad had been clever and successful. Water dripped like a veil from the Sow's hat rim, but it didn't hide her knowing smile.

'A few items which we believe were taken from Teme House.'

Frankie felt as if the rain had suddenly turned to ice. That the black sky stealing North Hill and its neighbours' distinctive profiles, had also reached her mind.

'You mean someone went into my bedroom there as well?'

The Sow looked at her senior colleague.

'Did we say that's where they came from?'

Shit.

'So, what was in your bedroom there that you didn't want anyone to see?' he asked, cutting the tape and stuffing the rest of the roll in his coat pocket.

349

She remembered fishing trips with John Arthur and Shannon up by Swineshaw reservoir. He'd offered them the floundering perch to feel before removing the hook and chucking it into his keep net. Now it was her turn, and there was only one way out.

'Girl stuff. You know.' She eyed him as if he was a pervert. 'Bras, pants, panty-liners. D'you want me to go on?'

Why was the Sow still smiling?

'No we don't,' said Manson. 'But I think we should explain to Miss Scott here why your car is being left in this way until it can be collected.'

'Collected?'

'Of course, neither DC Pilkington nor myself are forensic experts. It should be back here by Wednesday at the latest.'

No good mentioning Evelyn Scott again, she thought. No good arguing either.

11.15 a.m. Two hours forty-five minutes to go until the social worker's visit. Frankie ran upstairs to check out her room and hide the items from Martin Webb's jeans. Her trip to Hill Springs would certainly send out the right signals and if the two-faced thief had half a brain cell, he'd back off right now.

To her relief, a quick search showed nothing was missing, but the thought of those two pigs poking around her stuff made her wipe everything with her cleaning cloth.

She then shed her wet clothes and changed into her new electric-blue jogging gear and white trainers. Comfort and practicality, given what the rest of the day might hold. She would tell the businesswoman that she was her birth mother. Bring it all into the open at last. But unlike those happy-ending books she'd read, she'd hold back from flinging her arms around her neck; shrinking the past twenty-three years into a moment's joyful reunion. The fact her mum didn't want her was all too real. From now on she'd just have to try harder to please her.

She retrieved the knife, hung her mum's mac on the drying rack in the kitchen and strategically placed a line of paper towels underneath. The drips from its hem were the only sound as she used the roller towel to rub her rucksack dry before repositioning it on her back. Next, she filled the kettle, sorted the shopping and made two mugs of decaf coffee. She knew exactly how her mum liked it, weak with just half a sweetener, but as her special knife blade severed the tablet, both halves pinged out of sight.

Frankie swore under her breath. Not an auspicious start, snapping another with her teeth, tasting the bitter residue in her mouth. A taste of things to come perhaps? Whatever, she was ready. Up for it, in fact.

'I've got your pills as well,' she said brightly, hoping to break the funereal atmosphere. 'Where d'you want me to put them?'

Having glared at her colourful outfit, her mum indicated towards the place mats on the desk. All at once, the phone began to ring. Frankie jumped, aware of coffee tilting from the mugs. She set them down near the fax machine, now buzzing into life, delivering a sheet of official headed paper: *REGIS FLEMING BA. MA. LLB. Solicitor for Oaths.*

From her years at Briarfield, she was used to rapidly reading upside down when Mr Patel completed his weekly staff-assessment forms. It seemed her mother had a very strong case for the annulment of her late sister's recent will.

'Come away at once!' Evelyn snapped, advancing with the aid of her frame. 'That's confidential.'

'Sorry.'

'I should think so too.'

'Look, I know what you're thinking.' Frankie blocked off access to the fax. 'But I never harmed a single hair of your sister's head. And do you know why? Do you?'

Her mum pushed past her and snatched at the slightly smudged sheet.

'I have no idea. Now, please excuse me.'

'Because she told me things I'll never forget as long as I live. Beautiful things, actually. What everyone needs to hear, especially someone like me who's had such a shit time with a shit family, trying to do my best, all the time wondering who my real mum and dad were. She was no more mad than you or me.'

With an impatient expression on her dry old face, her mum checked her Cartier watch. At least two grand's worth, thought Frankie, noting its loose strap on that twig-thin wrist. Her mum folded the faxed sheet and placed it in her left-hand dressing-gown pocket.

'Besides, I was only there seventeen days,' Frankie went on. 'Why would I want to risk losing my job in such a brilliant house with a really nice client?'

Finally her mum spoke, but her voice, instead of showing comfort and reassurance, was ice.

'I have received some very upsetting news about Mr Brownlow. He passed away in hospital last night. I and the company owe him a huge debt. Therefore I would ask you to respect my feelings.'

Anger burned within Frankie, her whole body underneath the tight-fitting Lycra.

'Feelings?' she challenged. 'Well, I'm sorry, but I've got them too. And what I'd like to know is what nasty little secrets you're keeping in that little black book under your nightdress? Why you hoarded all those cuttings on me and my crap family? You've been keeping track of me, haven't you? Why? If you were so bothered about me, why not get in touch? Tell me I had a real mum, not Beryl who always favoured Shannon, nor a dad who did the most disgusting things to me.'

Suddenly, the grandfather clock stopped her flow by chiming out half-past eleven. Then, without warning, Evelyn leant forwards on her Zimmer frame, snatched up the framed photograph of Samuel Colby and flung it across the room, where it fell, shattering against one of the wall-to-wall bookshelves.

'But that's your *husband*.' Frankie stared open-mouthed at this violent outburst. She went over to the wreckage and bent down to pick up what she could. Her jogging gear adding to her sense of suppleness. Total mobility.

'Really? I *don't* think so. But when did I find out who *he* really was?' Her mum's voice like barbed wire. 'Too late of course.' She angled her gaze towards her. 'Just like with you, Jenny.'

Frankie felt as if that same barbed wire was piercing every small part of her. Also, that future she'd dreamt of for so long, a life with someone she could call Mum, was slipping away like the summer rain down that Tarmac drive. Ellie wasn't the only important person to have let her down. This woman, who was now struggling over to the bookshelves and fiddling with some encyclopedias, also didn't want to know. How much more fucking obvious did she have to make it?

She stood up to face the woman, a triangle of picture glass glinting in her right hand.

'Put that down, right this minute.'

'Only if you say eight really important words.'

'What are those?'

'I love you, my daughter, Jenny Merle Scott.'

She waited for that frozen mouth to move but, if anything, it firmed up even more.

'I'll count to ten. One ... two ... three...'

With surprising speed, her mother pulled a small key from her pocket, inserted it between the first and second volumes of the *Britannica*, making that loaded section of bookcase swing round, catching Jenny off balance. Bringing a musty chill into the room as her mum and her Zimmer frame disappeared once the cleverly disguised door had swung back into place once more. But not quite. A small gap remained through which she could see racks of rifles and her mum trying to lift one from the wall. She inched the door wider and, forgetting about any possible CCTV surveillance, followed her into a dark world of wood and steel hung four deep around each wall. The smell of oil, polish and age filled her nostrils.

So this was the gun room, and her adversary was now armed. She had that same proud look as Rose Scott in the painting. Proud and fearless. She eyed the piece of glass in Jenny's hand.

'What kind of mother behaves like this, Frances?'

'You've got a bloody cheek. Anyway, I'm not Frances. I'm Jenny Merle Scott.'

'Don't be ridiculous. Put that glass down at once.'

She knew how to hold a rifle all right. Trouble was, it meant letting go of her frame.

'No. I've been a much better mum than you and that's why I'm here. To find out how you can live with yourself after what you did...'

'What I did? I don't understand.'

'You will.'

With her right hand, Jenny unzipped her jogging top by a few inches and withdrew the folded copy of her birth certificate, warm from being next to her skin.

'Take a look. Ring any bells?'

The still-open door cast a thread of white light down the old woman's body as she gripped her rifle even harder and peered at proof of her betrayal.

'You and Sean Patrick Brownlow, eh?' Jenny taunted. 'That's a fucking joke. Whoever'd have thought it? You and him bumping and grinding. Was it the corduroys you went for or his charming smile?'

'Stop it! Stop it!'

Jenny kicked the rifle from those old hands and caught it. Trained the barrel on that heartless heart. Saw the name Accura inlaid into the gleaming mahogany. She more than liked it. It had class.

'D'you know something?' she began. 'Ever since I could think for myself I've wanted to find out who my real mum and dad were.'

'You were a mistake. That's all there is to it.'

'A mistake?' Jenny gulped. That word just then, the worst in the world. 'Charming, that is. As if I was some ant you crush, then wash down the plughole. So why go the whole nine months?'

'Eight months it was, and Merle persuaded me all along. She said abortion was a sin and if I did that everything else would suffer. My business, my health...' She steadied herself on her frame. 'Hindsight is a wonderful thing, Frances, and casting judgements the easiest thing in the world.'

'It's *Jenny*, OK?'

She then thought of Mr Patel and the word 'sorry'. Easy indeed, but no way would she be saying it. Nor referring to her as Mum ever again.

'So my dad never knew about me?'

'No, but he blackmailed me about the affair all the same. Three thousand a month since my husband died, once I'd rejected him. He said it

356

was also revenge for what his ancestor Paddy Brownlow had suffered at the hands of the Scotts. All lies, of course. I should have paid more attention to our history, then I'd never have let any Brownlow near Scott's Rifles. Or me. He destroyed my address book and started taking food from the fridge to weaken me. He was a truly evil man. And, you know what they say round here? Bad blood never dies.'

Jenny shivered, the gun wavering for a second as the grandfather clock in the lounge banged out midday. One more question needed an answer.

'I found a nursing nightdress in your bedroom. Why, after all these years?'

'I was waiting, wasn't I? They were my only mementos.'

'Of me?'

The old woman nodded. Wobbled against her frame.

'How could I guess I'd given birth to a murderess? You had such a lovely face. Such a peaceful look about you.'

Jenny jabbed the Zimmer frame away from the old woman's grip. She toppled and fell. Tried to sit upright while her companion, no longer a daughter, stood watching.

'Calling me a murderess is quite an accusation. Please explain.'

'You tell me.'

Even now the bitch couldn't give. Jenny kicked her shins but even then no cry of pain followed. Just a puzzled, pitying look.

'I said, *explain.*'

357

'Your father never consulted with me when he hired you from the agency. But when, after Merle had vanished, you told me your daughter's surname was Holt, I realized you had to be Frances Ann Holt from 358 Dartmoor Road, Openshaw, with a missing sister and her former boyfriend recovered from a Scottish loch. Oh, yes, I knew all about that from someone at their university who didn't want it leaked to the media. And you thought she was dead, didn't you?' A tiny sick smile played on her lips. 'Well, at least Beryl knows now.'

Jenny blinked. This wasn't happening.

'Where's Shannon, then, tell me?'

The bitch was ignoring her. That hurtful mouth on the move again.

'No wonder when DC Pilkington suggested you stay on here I had to voice my anxiety. I also have young Martin Webb to thank. He telephoned me again just after you'd left for town and said he'd call in to check on me. So before you do anything foolish just go into the lounge and call the police.'

Evelyn Scott faced her now, her features white and taut like an origami face she'd once made during an art lesson. It had come to life. No longer belonging to a weary sixty-six year old, but a woman challenging her to destroy what she'd come all this way south to do.

'Fuck off. If you'd let Merle keep me in the first place, none of anything would have happened. I'd have been happy with her and her dogs there. So happy. Just think, no dirty old man making me do stuff. No Beryl buying Shannon nice gear from M and S while I made do with dead people's cast-offs. You even put me in a fucking Oxfam bag to see the registrar.' The chink of door light was widening. Seconds ticking away. 'And have you ever had to do night shifts in a factory or sort fucking potatoes till the skin comes off your hands? Have you?'

'When I arranged for the Holts to take you, they were a decent hard-working family. I even visited them.'

'Well, you should have stayed a bit longer. And now you can make it up to me. I can't have your love but Ellie and me are going to have your dough. I want you to call your solicitor and tell him the daughter you've been waiting for has at last come home and will be your new beneficiary.'

'He won't be there. It's Saturday.'

'Leave a message, then. Or send a fax.'

She stepped forward. The skinny old arm firmly in her grip. The desk phone getting closer, while the smell of frightened pee grew more pungent, Jenny hunted around for that fax she'd seen earlier.

'What's the number?'

'I don't remember.'

Without warning, the old woman suddenly lifted up her frame with such speed it caught her unawares. First she struck her on the head and then the fax machine, causing its plastic casing to split and a frantic bleeping sound to fill the room.

'Ouch! You bitch.' She pressed the rifle barrel into her bony back, aware of blood trickling down her cheek. 'That fucking hurt.'

'Now you know how poor Merle must have felt.'

'There's a phone in the hall. Move. It's your last chance.'

Quarter past twelve now, and her charge falling to the floor, refusing to budge.

'Damn you. *Move!*' She kicked her again and again, this time all over.

Her cry the first honest sound she'd made for years, thought Jenny. That just like herself, her *real* life had been wrapped in one long lie.

'I'll count to five again. Or else. One ... Two ... Three...' She kicked the prone figure over on to her back.

'You're wasting your time. Go, Jenny, while you've got the chance.'

'Bothered about me at last, eh?'

'I've always been bothered about you, but my will is solely for those who deserve it. The theatre and my business...' Her final words were delivered in a clipped defiance as the rifle pointed at her right breast beneath the dressing gown. Jenny could see her blue carotids pumping away. Her hands now over that stupid little book, her mouth sealed.

Somehow the gloomy afternoon billowed into the room like an unfurling sail, wrapping her whole bruised head in its darkness. She felt trapped again. Doomed, unless she freed herself. The single shot was all it took. The vibration seemed to draw fresh blood from her head as a different, thinner version sprayed her face and her spotless new jogging suit.

'*I've always been bothered about you...*' pealed in her ears as she stared at the broken corpse lying face down in a map of blood. What to do now? The pigs would think *she* was the guilty one and finger her straight away. Weren't they already sniffing round her and her car, for God's sake? She'd no option but to hide the body. But where? She bent down and tested the dead pulse, trying not to glimpse those still-open eyes.

She rifled the kitchen drawer near the sink for that special knife, then returned to the body. Only the *smell* of blood bothered her, but it wasn't until she spotted her mother's Caesarean scar – puckered like her own efforts in the after-school sewing class – stretched between those two bony hips that she paused in her work and felt suddenly sick.

Ten minutes later, with both new knee bandages unravelled and the clock marking out half-past midday, the tartan suitcase fetched from her room was crammed so full she had to stamp on the bulging lid to make everything fit.

No need to wash, she decided. The rain would sort all that. Her problem was going to be other people. However, this end of West Malvern Road was much less busy than nearer town and she'd just have to pick her moment to sprint across to where those sheltering woods were waiting.

She glanced at her cordoned-off car as she went over to the boiler room. Even her Christmas and birthday presents hadn't been that well wrapped up.

Her baby daughter as usual, half turned her way. It was time to forgive and forget. Life, as Mrs Beavis had said on more than one occasion, was too short to bear grudges...

'I'll be back,' she whispered. 'Then we'll go far away and live somewhere nice like I always promised you.'

'No, Mummy. Take me, please. Don't leave me.'

Jenny stalled. God knew she'd got enough to carry. But how could she resist that plea? Ellie was now all she'd got. Then, gripping the laden suitcase handle even more tightly with her right hand and Ellie in the other, she took a deep breath, prayed no one else was around, and when the road was clear, splashed her way downhill into a wet, green and concealing world.

Twenty-Nine

'Red moon tonight, so I've been told.' Rio Docherty brought Martin's tea over to where he sat in the works canteen. He was a sociable guy, but now wasn't the time for a chat. Besides, the noise of the rain on the roof overhead made conversation almost impossible.

'Yeah, right,' he said.

'So, more weird goings-on up the hills tonight unless this rain keeps up. Cops never did find what happened to Mohammed. Poor fucker.'

Martin stared out glumly at the grey blur beyond the window, barely listening. North Hill was invisible now.

'Summat wrong?' asked the foreman. 'Is it me wanting you in today?'

'No. Money's useful. Had a few expenses recently.'

'Your flat in Barnfield, eh?'

'Where?'

Docherty smiled as Martin recalled his pathetic boast to him on the train.

'Look, I was just trying to impress you. Dumb of me really.' His voice tailed away, reflecting his disappointment with not only himself but Dora's sneaky act last night when she'd kindly informed the cops that items he'd found at Teme House were in her car.

'I know,' the man leant forwards even more. 'It's wimmin trouble, innit? Has the tasty Miss Tebbitt been mucking you about?'

'You could say that, yeah,' Martin said. He stared at his own untouched tea without interest. He'd only come down from the stores roof to get out of the rain, not for the company. Now the canteen was filling up and the reek of wet clothes and sweat attacked his nostrils. Since the protest's fallout, which had hit the firm hard, Docherty had read the riot act to the troops old and new. Monroe's had already been fined, got a bad press, and work was behind.

'Family's loaded, mind. But her joining us was out of spite. Now they're subbing her big time with her new career. Nice, eh? My folks just left

363

me two piles of ash.'

Martin scraped his chair away from the table, made his apologies and headed for the door. Normally he'd have wanted to know more about the guy's history, but not today. He needed his lunch break; during that hour he'd see that every second counted. His top priority being a call to the Gables to check the whereabouts of Miss Scott's carer and that the old girl was OK.

There was no reply from the Gables when he called again at the start of his lunch break. Something wasn't right, but no way could he move off site without shifting the mud and sweat which clung to every part of him. A shower might make all the difference to success or failure.

As he approached his bed to peel off his stinking work gear, he noticed a pack of cheese-topped rolls perched on his pillow. Waitrose too. Odd that, he thought, examining them. Maybe Docherty was thinking he looked underfed. If so, why'd he not said? Having salved his conscience by thinking they were too good to waste, he tore open the cellophane and stuffed one in his mouth. Then he headed for the shower.

However, the process took too long and his change of clothes clung to the wrong, damp places as he dressed. He cursed his slowness, aware of precious time being wasted, so that when Mahmout appeared and greeted him warmly with a pat on the shoulder, telling him that Dora had called in earlier, he'd already brushed past him and was running towards his bike.

Thanks to Dora, the cops were on his case and likely to charge him with breaking and entering. That would mean the end of his current job, his fresh start. Like Evelyn Scott, she wasn't answering her bloody phone, and despite his mood, that hurt the worst. She had betrayed his trust, and as he pedalled his Raleigh Tourer like a madman towards the town's police station he hoped he wouldn't catch sight of her near the theatre.

Suddenly his phone rang. He slowed up to take the call.

'Yo. That you, Webb?' Someone in a traffic jam. Or else a bad line.

'Who's this?'

Martin immediately thought Ed Thom and was about to end the call when the voice went on. 'Pegasus here, man. Moving house and found this note from Gary. Wasn't into emails, him. Was about to chuck it out.'

'And?' Another drenching by a passing coach. Swiss number plate, he noticed.

'Dated sixteenth of May. Came with his final payment. It's about Shannon's disappearance. Says he now remembers what this girl with her was wearing. Cropped jeans and a brown cardigan. It's all here. Should have remembered when you came over. Too much crap in my head, that's the trouble.'

Fuck...

'Oh, and get this. Another mate of his reckons Shannon Holt survived. Mind you, I'd take it with a pinch of salt.'

365

Martin was soaked to the skin. The streets swirled water and debris, slowing him up, and once he'd used the cashpoint and reached the police station in Victoria Road, he was so busy thinking about the mysterious Shannon Holt, he almost forgot to lock his precious bike.

Sergeant Ruffin, who'd phoned as he'd trekked back from the Gables last night and suggested he call into the station as soon as possible, wasn't on duty. So he spent fifteen dripping minutes relaying everything he'd gathered on the blonde carer to a DC Avril Pilkington, busy at her PC. She'd been reserved and noncommittal throughout, but admitted that she was glad of any information he had.

'I've got plenty,' he said, digging in his jeans pocket, then realized the right-hand one was empty. Shit. Where was the CV and Gary Cope's letter?

'I don't get it,' he muttered, searching again while the copper waited. Then told her exactly what was missing, followed by a detailed description of the young woman who'd left her CV behind in the library. Also that no one had answered his latest call to the Gables.

Then he remembered the cheesy rolls. Someone had been in the dormitory. Someone who knew he was on the case.

'I need to call work. Quick. Something's up.'

His mobile caught in his jacket lining and wouldn't pull free.

Damn...

DC Pilkington passed him her phone. Rio

Docherty told him Dora had called by with some shopping during his morning tea break. Mahmout had said what a looker she was, tall, blonde, super-slim, which he'd thought odd.

'It wasn't Dora, for fuck's sake.' He ended the call and turned to Pilkington who excused herself and hastened through a door marked private.

'If you think of anything else, call me. And be careful,' was all she said when she returned, handing over a small card bearing her contact details. No mention of the imagined charge of trespass. But puzzlement not relief was on his agenda.

Then Pegasus's parting shot came to mind.

'Someone I met on my Manchester travels reckons Frankie Holt's sister's still around. If so, d'you reckon she'll be safe?'

DC Pilkington's answer was to turn pale, grab a waxed coat from a nearby hook as all hell was breaking loose beyond the entrance, with two armed-response-unit officers leaping into a chequered car, plus two more outriders revving up their machines. To Martin it was like a scene from some action movie, but instead of being in the warmth and security of a room or cinema, this was for real. In Malvern, for God's sake. Almost in slow motion now, the scene continued, excluding him, leaving him feeling foolishly redundant. Therefore, on the spur of the moment, as DC Pilkington, now accompanied by a guy in a brown suit, joined the convoy, he ran outside, unlocked his bike and, careful to keep out of sight, followed behind.

Never had a journey seemed so long, Martin

thought, duelling with the weather and losing yet again. Just like his need to prove to himself and Maddy McKay that despite all the obstacles of a grindingly knackering job, of bent London bookies treading in his shadow, he could still have hacked it as a cop. Could have proved it to his dad as well.

His dad...

That overdue letter to him still unwritten, but no way would he phone the Verne, although to hear his voice again would at least be one constant in an ever-shifting, ever-dangerous world.

As he followed the diminishing tail lights, he thought again of Frankie Holt, clearly desperate to get her hands on what he'd got. Whose strangely plaintive voice at the séance had come as such a surprise. A girl of such contrasts, the word schizophrenic came to mind. There'd been someone like her in the sixth form at his community college, who'd spent weekends collecting for Cancer Research yet just before leaving for university, and for no apparent reason, had stabbed her grandmother to death thirty-five times. He wondered if she'd been released from her psychiatric hospital yet. How the hell do you distinguish the sane from the mad? The obsessive eccentric from someone with a borderline personality disorder?

He suddenly swerved into the gutter, catching his front wheel on the kerb. Once he'd regained control, caught sight not only of spinning blue lights coming from what could only be the Gables, but also something else bobbing along on his right hand side, way below the road.

At first he wondered if that brightness was a trick of the murky light but then, as he slowed up, his heart too seemed to stop altogether. Was it her? And if so, what the fuck was she doing running around on a day like this with the cops so busy?

Torn between pursuing this possible mirage and seeing what might be afoot at the big house, he decided yet again to trust an instinct. All at once, his phone rang again from inside his jacket pocket. The abruptness of it made him wobble perilously close to an overtaking bus.

One o'clock and the afternoon shift about to start. That familiar yellow head almost out of sight and all that mattered.

'Yes?' he panted.

'It's me. Maddy. You sound whacked out, but have you got a minute.'

'For you, yes of course.'

He could tell that caused her a moment's embarrassment before she continued.

'OK, thanks for the compliment, but I'm ringing about Gary. I can say his name again now – just about, anyway – it's all right, but has the very latest news reached you?'

'No.'

The elusive brightness he'd focused on below was a mere pinprick amongst the darkened greens in complete contrast with the hills' scrubbed summits. A moment's panic. If he lost his moving target, what then? More than ever he wished that fucking sheep's head had been a gun instead. But once she started to speak, that regret slid to the back of his mind.

'Two things. Had you heard the Procurator Fiscal has ordered Gary's body to be exhumed?'

'My God. When?'

'Last Wednesday after me and my mum kept on and on about the suicide verdict being wrong. I've just had a call from the police here.'

'Go on.' He was riding along with one hand on the handlebars, swooping down a narrowing lane signed Old Hollow until its tarmac became rubble bumping under his wheels. The rain, now drizzle, blurred the way ahead.

'They found things missed earlier. A knife wound to one of his ribs, for a start.'

'Knife wound?'

Those two words like a sting in his ear as he entered the Heritage Trail and followed the soggy track into a fetid, ever-closing world of vegetation.

'Yes. And big coincidence, they reckon it was made by a kitchen knife with a five-inch blade. The same that killed dear wee Donny.' Her voice wavered for a moment. 'And can you believe this, it turned up on the shingle by the loch? The weird thing is,' she went on, 'the initials BH were engraved under the handle. Now where could *that* have come from?'

'Hang on a minute.' And then he realized. OK, it was a long shot, but nevertheless one worth pursuing. 'Be quick now, Maddy. Call Briarfield Care Home in Openshaw. Better you quizzing them than the cops. Find out if their kitchen equipment was marked in any way and then call this number.' For a few seconds he clamped his mobile to the handlebar as he dug out Avril

370

Pilkington's card and relayed it. 'I've an idea who might have killed Gary.'

'And?' Her impatience was palpable, even from so far away. No time to mention Pegasus's recent call. He could lose too much.

'I can't tell you everything now, but I am tracking her down. Just me and her, OK? Like I always wanted. For you and Gary. I'm on the Heritage Trail below West Malvern Road.'

'*Her*?'

'Yep. And your news just confirms my suspicions. Another nail in her coffin.'

'But why kill Gary?'

'Tell you later.'

He glanced up to North Hill and despite the poor visibility saw blue spinning lights coming from the Gables.

'Promise me you'll back off before anything happens to you. Leave it to them. I couldn't cope if ... You've given me hope, Martin. You really have.'

He stuffed the phone back in his pocket, a fresh surge of purpose driving him on. And then he noticed what appeared to be recent patterned footprints deeply denting the cinder pathway as if they'd led from a weedy track to the left. Size six maximum, he could tell from his days at the pool in Blackheath when he had to put tags on the various trainers left at reception. But did these belong to a male or a female? Hard to say from his height, but there was no time to examine them further. Having skewed the bike around, he followed that weedy gulley thinking how he'd confront her with her past when he caught up with her.

She'd outwitted him last night and could do so again, this time with the help of a knife or something equally deadly. He shivered as he continued through the tallest foxgloves he'd ever seen – the pinky-purple pulse of summer. When he looked again, he noticed a tumbledown shed, whose corrugated sections were held together by ancient, rusted bolts. And, as he advanced towards it holding his breath, he recognized those same footprints as on that cinder track.

He dismounted to take a closer look, but just then something else caught his eye. Pink, yellow, partly hidden by the long grass. Probably some kid's toy, he thought, parting the grass with his trainer's toe, then freezing.

'Jesus.'

Never mind a kid's toy, was this some poor kid, and a dead one at that? Had he stumbled upon yet another murder? He let his bike fall beside him and was about to pull out his mobile from under his cape, when he realized he'd stumbled across a perfect imitation of a baby, lying legs akimbo as if dropped in a hurry.

'Some doll,' he murmured in amazement. He could have sworn its eyes opened of their own accord then swivelled round to look at him. Its skin, like the soft hair curling away from the skull, was so fucking real. He recalled that freak companion mentioned by the Gee's girl and the Scottish woman.

Was it Frankie's? If so, he was on the right trail. A trail now bringing the unmistakeable smell of blood and flowers to his nostrils.

Thirty

There'd not been time to unlock the blood-spattered pain diary she'd found tucked away inside that old nightdress. No time to even pick Ellie up from where she'd dropped her. She must keep on running, and although lighter now without that suitcase, she still had the sodden rucksack on her back, bumping between her shoulder blades. Making her headache worse and her period poised to flow.

Frankie slowed up, her trainers slipping on the wet grass with every stride. She knew someone had picked up her scent, she could tell by the sound of rustling leaves and the crack of dead branches, reminding her of that single shot to Evelyn Scott's heart at close range. Now she was next. She remembered her dad's words: '*You keep out of sight. You don't break the skyline.*'

Fat chance of that. She was as deep down as she could be.

Frankie lurched forwards then righted herself, realizing she'd stepped in some dog shit. Realizing too that the distant whirr of wheels growing ever closer might belong to a cyclist. And who else but Martin Webb? The guy who'd always wanted to be a pig.

Bad news.

Suddenly she took a chance, diving left into a nest of greenery whose wetness soon diluted the worst of her mum's stubborn blood still stuck to her face. She ploughed on, doing her best to close the telltale gaps behind her, until she reached a cinder track which in turn led to a rickety old kissing gate surrounded on each side by sagging pig wire.

The gate was easy. The rest a nightmare. What was going on? Was he waiting for her to return the way she'd come, or was he lifting it over the gate? She tried to run on, but clearly no one had come this way for years and the wilderness now conspired to trap her.

'Ah, Frankie Ann Holt. So we meet again.'

She heard him before she saw him. Heard the push and shove of foliage before the yellow-caped guy finally appeared. Eyes wide as a hawk's when it spots its next meal. He flung down his bike and grabbed its black pump. The only weapon he had. Pathetic, really.

'What the *fuck* have you done to Evelyn Scott?'

'My mum? Nothing, why?'

'Your *mum*? Hey, come on. Pull the other one.'

'It's true. I'm Jenny Merle Scott. Born 20th February 1980 and adopted by the Holts six weeks later.'

He stared at her as if she was mad.

'I've just been in that shack over there. Jesus. Do you want me to spell out what I found there? I've already told the cops. They are on their way.'

Frankie shrugged yet felt her insides turn to

mush. Fear also brought her period surging between her legs. She looked down to see the livid stain spread between her thighs. She was dirty, dizzy with pain and hunger. Nowhere now to hide. The knife she'd recently used and those latex gloves, ditched in the deepest, wildest weeds she could find. Now she had to deflect him. Tears swelled up in her eyes and spilled on to her cheeks. 'She didn't want me near her, even though I tried to be the best carer ever ... All I wanted was love.'

'Liar.'

'I'm not.'

Mrs Beavis's advice was slipping away. It had no place here. Not now. She could see he wasn't listening. It was time to attack.

'Did you nick my stuff from Teme House, and Ellie's birth band? I could get you for theft.'

That stalled him for a moment.

'I had to. Anyway, you helped yourself to my things this morning, didn't you? Pretending to be my girlfriend. You need bloody locking away.'

'Not what you said when I saw you last night,' she teased him with a strange smile, and before she could run, he'd lunged at her. Gripped her shoulders, trying to bring her down, beat her with that pump, but she resisted and spat in his eye.

'You bitch. I know you killed Gary Cope. But you fucked up, didn't you? Thought you'd never be found?'

Frankie didn't answer with words, knowing that she, the Prodigal Daughter, should never have begun her journey to find those imaginary pots of gold. And that's all they were. Imaginary. She'd been had, big time. Neither Sean Brownlow, hated so much someone had killed him, nor her so-called mum had been any better than John Arthur and Beryl. Now, with the sirens' wail drawing closer, she knew escape time was running out.

She cast about to find anything she could use to defend herself. There was nothing apart from her rucksack. His makeshift weapon was following her every move.

Just then, a twig snapped somewhere nearby. She saw him spin round, training his bike pump in an arc on the surrounding undergrowth. A chance to clear him off her pitch.

'Who's there?' he called out.

Frankie swivelled her rucksack round and with all her might hurled it at the back of his head. Dizziness again and another pull of her monthly blood as its buckle brought a yelp and a deep crimson weal. He dropped the pump and went for her again. A rugby tackle to the legs. Too strong for her this time, but someone else was quicker, more cunning. Someone trained to expertly release a single silenced bullet to where it mattered most. Then disappear.

Thirty-One

Martin broke away from the moaning body, his vision blocked by blood. His and hers, plus saliva. His head throbbed like fuck. His mouth rigid with terror, yelled his whereabouts to the police as he tried to guess where that solitary gunshot had come from. The deeper glade of trees to the left or the high weedy bank to the right? And then another crazy, garbled thought. Had *he* been the intended victim, not her? That muffled blast had reminded him of the kitchen in Thom's betting shop and that same rush of fear hit his pulse.

Could it be them again, out of custody and on the run? Where was the law? He crouched low again, knowing whoever had fired that shot must surely have more ammo left. The realization that he was in the wrong place at the wrong time hit him, but if he legged it now, that would be curtains if the cops caught him. He'd have to stay and tell the truth. That he'd been unarmed, wanting only to trap her for the police to deal with. Yes, he'd asked his old man for a gun, and his letter was probably still traceable, but that had been to protect himself from his past. Nothing had come of it anyway. But would that be enough to clear him of being found with a thrown weapon lying somewhere in all that foliage?

He crept back to where Frankie Holt lay spreadeagled among the weeds, her yellow hair drawn back from her face now as white as a pebble, the soles of her size-six trainers matching the footprints near that shack. Bile leached into his throat as he drew closer, her familiar scent still discernible, but this time mingling with something quite different, reminding him of that already familiar tartan suitcase and its contents. How, having unzipped it and pushed the lid open, he'd called DC Pilkington and had broken down.

Those flecked eyes now fixed on his, lips barely moving as blood from a neat hole in Frankie Holt's chest mingled with a different darker kind. If he'd not just thought of those crimson chunks of flesh and bone, that pulped grey-haired head or visualized Gary Cope's happy face, he'd have whispered words of encouragement, tried to stem the bleeding. Instead, he watched her die, as his own mother had done, but that time without him there to prevent it.

'Your Shannon may be alive,' he said, not knowing why.

Another siren wail seemed to be coming closer, as her dry lips began to move. The cops were on their way. At last.

'Snow Queen,' she murmured. 'The Snow Queen ... I saw her.'

'When?'

No reply.

He stepped back, wondering who the hell that strange name might refer to and, more importantly, about Frankie Holt's capabilities even close to death. He'd seen too many films where the bad guy rears up at the very end, poised to kill. He stared at her again, convinced she'd only meagre rations left in her lungs, and for him to remind her how she'd screwed up so many lives would only waste his own. Her lips quivered again.

'Ellie,' she rasped. 'Where's my Ellie? I want her...'

Ellie? *Ellie Scott*? It wasn't *that* common a Christian name.

He dug in his jeans rear pocket for the narrow pink wrist strip he'd taken from Teme House as he remembered the doll in his saddlebag. A hunch the two might be connected. He clasped the soft warm body dressed in a pale yellow sleep-suit complete with embroidered teddy on the chest, and as he lifted her out from amongst his tool kit and Mars Bar wrappers, both eyelids opened to reveal eyes which like before seemed to pierce his very soul. The little cry she made too made him start. So real, so poignant. Within seconds, he'd slipped the wristband over her tiny fist and placed her on the carer's bloodstained chest. Immediately those hunted eyes flickered recognition, even pleasure.

'Thanks,' she breathed, raising her right hand to stroke the creature's matted bloody hair until, like the rest of her, it grew still.

Martin closed her eyes then sensed he wasn't alone. He whipped round and was relieved to see a woman police officer, whom he recognized as DC Avril Pilkington, standing a few metres away. Her whole demeanour was as rigid as the body lying at his feet. He recalled her tears after finding Merle Scott in the bracken, but like him, there were none today for this victim. Instead, a blank sheen glazed her eyes. He also noticed she was unarmed.

'Christ knows who shot her,' he shouted. 'And why? That's what I want to know.'

The DC stepped forwards and bent over Frankie's dead body. As if forgetting he was still there, she reached for the doll, then drew back.

'We've been busy with that suitcase you found, otherwise I'd have got here sooner.' She looked at his head, then the rest of him. 'You all right, Mr Webb? You're bleeding.'

'She flung that bloody rucksack at me in self-defence before whoever it was finished her off.'

'Must have given it all she'd got, judging by the damage.'

'Sod this. Who killed her, because I didn't?'

The doll slid off Frankie's chest and began to cry.

'That's what we're here to find out.'

Then he saw they had company. More coppers. Subdued, ritualized – yes, because they had to be. He knew every step of the next process after an unnatural death from time spent poring over police training manuals. And now, yet again, he wasn't only another witness but a possible suspect. For murder.

DI Manson seemed to think so too and, having exchanged brief whispers with DC Pilkington, cautioned him in a way he'd seen countless times on TV. Martin saw his future slide away. He'd be taking over where his dad was leaving off. Banged up. End of story.

'Have to do it, son.' The DI's voice seemed to come from a long way away. 'DC Pilkington says you were here when the shot was fired.'

'She saw me, then?'

'Yes. Before she had a chance to reach you. Why we'll need to take a full statement from you and get that head looked at.'

Yours needs looking at, not mine, he felt like saying, hoping her conscience would come to his defence.

'So where's my gun?' he challenged them both.

'We'll have to find it, won't we?'

Martin glared at her. Still jotting things in a pad. Refusing to catch his eye or explain why she'd kept shtum.

'Why the fuck would I want to kill Frankie Holt?' He pointed to the bicycle pump at his feet. 'That's all I had on me, for Christ's sake.'

'You were the last person to be with her when she died.'

He couldn't argue with that. But it was what she'd omitted that made him want to thump her. While the other armed officers were searching for the murder weapon, Manson crept around the carnage in front of him, pausing to take in the doll, still expelling those same little cries. Just then, his two-way sparked into life. Forensics were on their way. When the call ended, he turned to Martin.

'By the way, son, you need to know we took a call from a Maddy McKay in Glasgow just now...'

Martin waited for praise, for exoneration, but any ray of hope in that department was soon extinguished.

'She repeated what you'd just told her. That you tailing Frankie Holt was what you always wanted. Something for you and you alone with the police merely as spare parts.'

Damn. Time to fight back.

'So nothing useful about the knife wound or the weapon used having come from Briarfield Care Home?' he argued, feeling his neck and face turn scarlet.

'Indeed. And talking of Briarfield, one of its residents complained you were snooping in Daphne Cope's room on Wednesday. Now, don't think we're not grateful for what you told my colleague earlier today, but...'

'But what? Go on. Say it.'

'You can't go taking the law into your own hands.'

'So where were you lot just now? Someone had to do something. When I saw her running like a bat out of hell down here, what else was I supposed to do? I had to stop her. Keep her for the frigging law to deal with. Can't you see?'

Silence, save for the doll's eerie mewling. Silence in which his anger almost made him blind as DC Pilkington called for a car to collect him. And as he squinted at the ominous yellow-and-blue vehicle waiting between the trees, he felt suddenly overwhelmed by everything that had happened to him since that day his father had fucked up. From now on his life would never be the same. He wondered what he'd do now. If he'd ever see Dora again, and where he'd go. He was forced to admit that he was just as lonely and endlessly searching as Frankie Holt had been.

Word reached DI Manson that a police-issue 9mm automatic had just been found ten metres away from Frankie Holt's body, and the fatal bullet which had lain in her chest perfectly matched the others in the weapon. The heat was now on to test it for prints and discover which of the ARU team had decided to take matters into their own hands. The investigation would take time and involve more than just the local CID.

Meanwhile Martin's statement was still in progress and more questions and answers would follow. He'd missed the start of the afternoon shift at Monroe's, but what the hell. Other news had come through about the now vanished VW camper van on North Hill. It belonged to some guy in Leamington Spa. A lead which Avril Pilkington was delegated to investigate further.

'Who's the Snow Queen?' Martin asked, aware of steam rising from his clothes like a racehorse after a hard run.

'Why do you need to know that?' Pilkington was surprisingly quick off the mark.

'Frankie said it twice after she'd been hit. As if, I don't know...' He shrugged, unable to find the right words. 'She was accusing someone. The one who shot her maybe?'

'Delirium, most likely,' said the DC quickly, screwing up her cup and lobbing it into a nearby waste bin. For some reason, Martin found her presence strangely inhibiting.

'We'll look into that once we've found Miss Holt's killer,' said Manson, filling his mouth with tea and swallowing it. 'As for the poor Scott sisters, I can honestly say, in all my years in the Force these have to be the most heinous crimes I've encountered. Whatever drove the girl to kill we'll never know. I'm normally a believer, but God must have been seriously off duty this past week. And – ' he glanced at the officer next to him, those tension lines deepening round his eyes – 'heads may roll because as far as this last crime's concerned, we didn't reach the Gables in time.'

'Yes, sir. But we were busy picking up her daughter. Or rather,' added DC Pilkington darkly, 'her butcher.'

Martin recalled the carer's boast about her real identity. So, it was true. He looked from one copper to the other for some expansion on this, but a short, dense silence followed until Manson spoke.

'We'll have to shout that fact out loud and clear when we're being grilled. By the way, does Beryl Holt know yet?'

'I've just informed her, sir.'

'So she'll be down to ID the body?'

'Apparently not. There's a new TV arriving any day now. She needs to be around, so she said.'

'Try her again ASAP.'

384

'I will, sir.'

Martin stared at the rest of his tea, letting it grow cold, reminding himself he must phone his dad. The least he could do. Then he added more lines to his statement, trying hard to be accurate.

DI Manson turned to him. A leaf fragment trapped in the hair above his ear.

'Thanks to you, Maddy McKay and Piotr Kopeck, the gardener at Teme House, who informed us only this morning how Frankie had paid him off to keep his mouth shut, we finally realized what we were up against.'

'And Dora Tebbitt,' Martin reminded him. Her name never far from his thoughts.

'Absolutely. And equally, how were we to know Sean Brownlow was blackmailing Evelyn Scott?' said the DC. 'That he had keys to everything, even Teme House after Merle was killed?'

'Blackmail?'

'Sure. After she was widowed, she turned him down. Bang went any chance of him inheriting. Why he neglected her – even took food out of her fridge – and targeted Merle instead. And apart from nicking some nice stuff from Teme House, he made a hefty cash withdrawal using her card.'

'What's the history?' asked Martin, all too aware of taking up precious time. But this was one helluva puzzle and so far he'd only had a few pieces to play with.

'The Brownlows go back a long way in Malvern. He felt he was righting wrongs by getting what he could from the two sisters. But Evelyn Scott innocently employed him, didn't she? Walked into his trap unaware. For someone normally so thorough, it was a serious mistake. So was their affair.'

'Affair?'

'Oh, yes. Went on for some time, did that. She wouldn't have wanted that kind of gossip in the public domain, would she? This is Malvern, not Milton Keynes, don't forget. Anyway, it's all recorded in the top-secret part of her pain diary she'd been keeping since July 1st 1997. Talk about a double life.'

'Why July 1997?'

'That's when she became incapacitated and vulnerable. Writing everything down was the only way others would know the truth.'

'Was he Frankie's father, then?'

Manson nodded, and Martin felt a pang of pity for the girl now sharing the same hospital morgue. Thought again about his own father. All he'd got.

'Of course she was trying to stitch him up over Merle Scott's death, but his alibi was rock solid.'

'So who killed him?'

'Someone with the strength and hatred to have wrenched his weapon from him. That's key.'

Manson picked up his styrofoam cup, drained the last of his tea and slapped it down, crumpling its base in the process. 'Whoever shot Brownlow with such accuracy must also have known how to use a high-powered rifle with a pointed bullet at close range.'

Martin winced.

'It's an important clue,' Manson went on. 'Another former employee at Scott's had only recently developed the prototype, but, as usual, Brownlow was trying to take all the glory. Revenge seems to sprout from the bloody ground here,' he added bleakly.

Then DC Pilkington finally spoke.

'According to his sister in Malvern Link, our man left for London early yesterday morning. I've organized a tail.'

'Good. Fishmonger's son, correct?'

'Yes, sir.'

Martin spotted Pilkington swiftly transfer what could have been a photograph from her outer jacket pocket to an inner one. As he wondered what the crumpled item might have revealed, she patted it as if for good measure before addressing her boss.

'By the way, sir,' she began in that same clipped voice, 'it's been confirmed Frankie was officially registered as Jenny Merle Scott. Nice to carry the name of someone you're going to murder, isn't it? And she even had the gall to phone us on Wednesday evening saying she was worried sick about the poor woman. Trouble was,' she continued, unaware of Manson's slightly raised eyebrows, 'we didn't have any-thing on her when I suggested she go to the Gables on Thursday night, but I had a gut feel-ing. Had to test our caring carer. Kill two birds with one stone, if you like.' A small hard smile nudged her lips. 'Trouble was, it seems no one wanted her after all.'

Martin stared at her. The word iceberg came to mind.

Manson too, shot her a glance. She'd clearly

spoken out of turn.

'Talking about Miss Holt's relationship with her mother, there's something else you should know. It's bizarre in the extreme.' He paused to extract a photocopied sheet before continuing. 'This morning's pain diary entry states – wait for it – that the proceeds of Merle's contested will to Sean Brownlow are in due course to pass to Jenny's own daughter.'

'Daughter?' Martin interrupted, looking from one to the other. 'So she *did* have a kid after all?'

'For God's sake...' DC Pilkington scraped her chair back from the table. Apart from Frankie at the séance, Martin had never seen anyone so tense as she stood up and wavered for a moment before asking for a break.

Manson's smile was replaced by a puzzled frown. 'I'll tell the DS you're taking the rest of the day off. Seems you could use it.'

'Thank you, sir. I'll be a hundred per cent tomorrow.'

'You'll need to be once the shit hits the fan.'

As she passed Martin on her way to the door, she looked at him in a way he couldn't fathom.

When she'd gone, the DI also stood up and turned the heater down. The room was over-warm now, and Martin suddenly felt as if he could sleep for a week. The fag too had calmed him down and he resolved to buy a week's supply on the way back to the site. Having signed the final part of his statement, he handed it over, aware his writing had grown smaller, tighter than ever. The result of a guilty conscience.

'What's this granddaughter called, then?' he asked.

'Eleanor Holt. Like I said, it's a long crazy story,' Manson went on. 'And unless you're a shrink, you'd probably never believe it.' He reached out to shake Martin's hand. 'Thanks again. We could do with keen people like you in the force. Ever thought of it?'

'No. He hasn't.'

Dora.

Martin spun round to see her dressed up as Nina, as delicate as a porcelain doll. Their eyes met for a brief, fiery moment until Manson thanked her for her initiative.

'I only did what I did because I was scared stiff of her. I knew those things from Teme House were probably her property *and* important by the way you were being so secretive.' She faced Martin once more. 'Can't you see that?'

What could he say? She'd had his best interests at heart and he'd badly misjudged her. With the London duo's trial looming, he'd need her more than ever and then, as Manson began to clear the table, he asked himself what the hell could he offer *her*?

'She liked her souvenirs, did our young lady. Always a classic sign of insecurity. Apart from her hotel items, we found a letter from Gary Cope giving his gran his new address, and forensics got their skates on to match blood embedded in one of the cagoule cuffs with his. They also matched fibres from Merle Scott's hair with those from the Fiesta's boot. The wonders of technology. Now then,' he eyed Martin.

'Think seriously about what I've suggested.'

'Over my dead body,' whispered Dora, as he ushered them both out of the room.

'Please don't say that.'

'OK. I'm sorry.'

'Incidentally, you didn't come across a colour photo of Shannon Holt on your travels by any chance?' Manson asked. 'Frankie, I mean Jenny, showed it us today at the Gables. Striking young woman. White-blonde hair, nice teeth. Was in her wallet, which of course, we've got.'

Martin glanced at Dora, but how could she understand his dilemma? Should he mention Avril Pilkington's recent action? Perhaps his future depended on it. A future he'd dreamt of for years.

Even before he'd finished speaking, the DI had disappeared through another doorway. Martin heard one shout then another as he and Dora stepped outside. A faint sun was appearing between the clouds. So why was he shivering? Why did he feel that somehow things weren't over yet?

After *The Seagull's* final dress rehearsal before Monday's opening night, Dora collected Martin from her flat and drove past the now silent building site towards the Malvern Hills Hotel. In the car he told her about her impersonator and as much as he knew of Jenny Scott's fractured life. How he'd been fooled at the wrong time. How he hoped to find the least artificial-looking flowers for his mother's grave and visit his dad in prison.

'Prison? Why?' Her eyes widened in surprise.

Damn. Now he'd blown it. The one secret he'd told Frankie Holt, but not her. Perhaps when the time was right.

'It's no big deal. He'll be out soon.'

'I'll come with you to see him, if you'd let me.'

'Thanks, but he might fancy you.'

She gave him a playful shove, but there was nothing playful about his next question.

'Tell me something,' he asked her. 'Is the name Ellie short for Eleanor?'

She nodded. 'Why d'you want to know?'

'No reason. Except I feel as if I've just stepped out of some really weird, sick world.'

'Come on, Martin,' she squeezed his hand. 'It's all finished now.'

'Is it?' He looked at her impossibly smooth face, the touches of rouge still on her cheeks, and thought of that disturbing little creature he'd seen lying in the grass.

'Do you think Evelyn Scott really believed she had a flesh-and-blood granddaughter?'

Dora sighed.

'I guess people believe what they want to.'

'Great,' he said bleakly as Dora pulled up into the pub's crowded car park, searching for the right metaphor to describe the carer who'd wrecked so many lives in pursuit of her own. 'She was like an orphan tsunami,' he added. 'Yes, that's it.'

'Please explain.'

'First you get the earthquake, miles away from this calm inviting sea which begins to swell until,' he paused, thinking of Shannon, of Gary and Merle, 'it becomes unstoppable.'

'A grim background shouldn't make you a killer, though.'

'I'd say anything's possible. But God knows why that woman copper risked Evelyn Scott's life by insisting Frankie stayed on with her.'

'Incompetence, most likely.'

'I'm not so sure. Supposing she knew all along Evelyn was Frankie's real mother. If Frankie got banged up for killing her, she wouldn't see a penny of her inheritance. An added punishment in her eyes.'

'So why shoot her?'

'Something snapped. If I was her, I'd be planning a new career.'

After an hour in the pub, they walked together from the car park hand in hand and up the steep cobbled track towards the Worcestershire Beacon. The air felt cool on his skin, even though her hand was warm in his, and a breeze had shifted the heavy clouds from the sky leaving the amber-coloured moon reigning supreme. Even though the girl he loved was close by, he felt far too alone with something he knew was beyond this world. Something truly, incomprehensibly evil. He gripped her hand more tightly as they walked along the earthen track. To the left of it, was a sheer drop of some fifty metres to a lake of dark water.

'Manson told me the Gables had CCTV installed,' he said. 'No expense spared. But the new film wasn't added until Friday when

Frankie Holt was shopping in town.'

Dora shivered. 'So?'

'Evelyn Scott must have been scared shitless after I'd phoned her, realized it wasn't working and decided to get someone round pronto to sort it out. She also phoned the cops. Anyhow, Manson said the footage shows her hiding stuff left right and centre, locking her desk et cetera, but the weirdest thing was when the team played back the tape from the final sequence, they heard a noise.'

'What noise?'

His teeth seemed to jam together, trapping what he wanted to say. Dora glanced at him, frowning. Waiting.

'Like nails being banged into wood. Bang, bang, bang...'

'You mean, furniture being assembled?'

'No.' He paused. 'I reckon a coffin.'

'My God. Why?'

'Who knows? Maybe we'll have to go to another séance.'

Dora turned to go back, pulling him with her. That late evening breeze was now several degrees cooler. The layers of distant hills were a uniform spectral grey, matching her coat. 'By the way, the theatre caretaker said that last Thursday, one of the Scott gravestones had been dug up and flung on the ground. He was quite upset as it's near some of his old relatives.'

'Which Scott was that?'

'Rose, I think.'

Could Sean Brownlow have been responsible? wondered Martin. If so, sad bastard. Then he repeated the woman's cryptic warnings from the séance, which had included Frankie Holt herself.

'How strange.' Dora shivered again. 'Brrrr ... I've gone all cold.'

He too sensed a current of icy air snake around his body.

'Manson said once Dad's in the clear and I've joined the Force, I can look through the CCTV film sometime, plus the Scott history and secret stuff on Frankie which Evelyn had kept since 1995. And,' he glanced at her, 'I'm going to, OK?'

His tone surprised even himself. The anger which had festered and gnawed at him like a cancer over his mother's death had become transformed into hope.

Just then, his mobile rang. It seemed oddly out of place among the trees and mysterious hollows.

'You've not seen DC Pilkington on your travels, have you?' Manson sounded tense. 'She's not at her flat and not answering her phone. Now we know why.'

'Go on, sir.'

'I'll have to trust you with this. Be careful. Her thumbprint was on the gun that shot Miss Holt.'

'Jesus.'

'If you get a sighting, don't approach her. Get back to us immediately.'

'Will do. We're coming down from the Beacon. Dora's with me.'

'Get to safety as quickly as possible. My officer was trying to frame you over Frankie Holt's death. She most certainly knew her and had to kill her. You could be next and we simply don't have the manpower to protect you.'

They held hands and ran as if the world was going to end and they had only a few moments left. Ran so fast that all the dusky colours around them fused into a rushing blur of greys and greens and browns.

Once they'd reached her car and drawn breath, Martin repeated what Manson had said.

'*She* must have been the Snow Queen,' he added, fastening his belt. 'But what was she to Frankie, unless ... unless...' What Pegasus had said had sown a preposterous idea, and he quickly shoved it to the back of his mind as Dora silently drove back along the Ross Road into town. Just before they reached the Hill Springs site, where the Portakabin lights seemed a welcome refuge, she looked him in the eye.

'There's something I've not told you,' she began, 'because I didn't want to add to your worries.'

That cold air through his open window, touching his heart as he waited.

'Frankie called me late last night. Yes, I know I'd not been answering you, but I was curious when this new number came up...'

'For fuck's sake, that nutter could have been outside your door. Anything ... What did she want?'

'She just said she hoped we'd be very happy together and,' she stalled, 'I shouldn't say this. For a start, it's not fair and...'

'Go on.' He interrupted as a tiny irreverent smile lifted the corner of her mouth.

'She added ... you'd make a crap pig.'

He paused. No smile.

'In this case, she was right.'

'Detective Constable Webb, that's not true and you know it.'

He turned toward her, enfolding her in his arms. Just then, the huge moon which had until that moment breasted the top of the Beacon, began to slowly, imperceptibly, fall out of sight.

Epilogue

The new detective constable checks her watch yet again, praying that she won't be standing there so vulnerably with her suitcase for too long. Each time a Mondeo of whatever colour passes by she retreats further into the dripping shadows, holding her breath. With her mission accomplished, she'll return to the bargee who pulled her from the icy River Irwell, gave her a home, a new identity and ambition to become who she had to be.

There's been too much rain since she arrived in this eerie, overrun corner of England. Too much in her mind for normal life to proceed to plan. So much hatred, equalling her own, which propelled her hands to bury the infant beneficiary in a secret, muddy place...

The familiar VW van looms out of the opaque afternoon, casting spray on either side, its engine noise a roar of hope. To her, now a fugitive like greedy Jenny, its welcoming lights can't come soon enough.

Her small suitcase has been added to by the only memento she's chosen to keep. Her own photo from the carer's wallet, with the words SNOW QUEEN erased from the reverse. She wills her journey home to start. But she's too keen.

The driver too sleepy to see her, and while Dawn Maddox nervously pours herself a second double gin in her front room across the road, the roar of brakes, the squeal of tyres and a dying woman's scream fill her ears.